Thomas Turner

and the Book of Curses

Caleb S. Lewis

Thomas Turner and the Book of Curses by Caleb S. Lewis

Published by Caleb Samuel Lewis
Spring Branch, TX

www.CalebSLewis.com

For permissions contact:
help@CalebSLewis.com

Cover by Peter Lewis.

Hard Cover ISBN: 978-1-7320034-0-8
Soft Cover ISBN: 978-1-7320034-2-2
eBook ISBN: 978-1-7320034-1-5

In dedication and memory to Keith Dale Sizer
(September 6 1988 – February 25 2012)

I would like to dedicate my book to my best friend Dale. When I first began writing my first Novel I had no idea who I would choose to dedicate it to, but I knew I would want to dedicate it to somebody at some point. Originally when I started this book I had two ideas, 1. I wanted to give people a thrilling tale from my imagination. 2. I wanted it to get turned into a movie one day, so my best friend Dale could have his dream come true of wanting to be an actor. Little did I know that he would die two weeks before I even finished writing it. Regardless why I started my book what mattered was the time I spent with Dale. We knew each other since I was 4 and he was 5. We spent most of our lives together like brothers; I even considered Dale a brother. Like when we used to go to our neighborhood pool and sit at the bottom of the pool, we had tons of fun together. We fought all the time like brothers and argued but in the end, he was one of the only friends I had willing to set me straight if I was acting out in a bad way. He had such high class he would be too embarrassed to admit when he did do immoral things, but he still tried to maintain those views of good morals on how a person should live and he definitely was a wonderful person for that. If somebody needed help he would be there for that person. He was a hard worker when he could get a job. If it weren't for him my whole story plots may not have even existed, he definitely influenced how my story went. We knew each other's darkest secrets but never used them against each other. If you were down about something he would be there to listen to your problems. For a while he even lived with my family. If anything, his parents raised him to be the perfect kind of man he was when he died. All though he won't get to play the part of the character I made for him I am glad I still finished this book and his legacy will live on in literature. I got more years like I wanted with him for I feared he would die when he joined the Marines, but God sent him home before it was too late. When he died a few years later, it was a shock as it was from a mere fall out of a tree and landing on his feet. It seemed so unlikely since he climbed so many trees throughout our life. After he died I knew who I wanted to dedicate my book to. He will always be remembered in my heart as one the best friends I ever had. To anybody who reads this book will think of him in a way he may have once imagined how to live. Now that he rests, and people are waiting to see him once more for his charismatic personality his memory shall live on through great adventures in my stories. In his honor I hereby dedicate this book to the memory of Keith Dale Sizer.

Acknowledgments

Chapter Art Organizers

1. Peter Noah Lewis

2. T.C.N

Editing Suggestions

1. Stephanie the Librarian

2. Deanna McGrew Bleasdell

3. Phyllis Lawrence

4. Terry Allen Lewis

Editors

1. Caleb Samuel Lewis

Illustrators

1. Peter Noah Lewis

2. Rafael Aaron Morel

3. PanaYis Yiasimi

Sources

1. Matthew Kirkwood

2. Caleb Samuel Lewis

Contents

Chapter 1
Just a Normal Teenager

The near future
Monday, March 09th, 4:07 P.M.
Smithsonian Valley High school, Texas

This story is about the life of a teenager who lived a normal life, but whose life was about to change. For he thought he was like any other teenager but truly didn't have any idea what he was or what an ominous force had in store for his future, as well the destiny that lay before him in the days to come.

Near the beginning of spring one sunny afternoon in the near future, at Smithsonian Valley High School in the blazing heat of Texas two boys stood fighting in the courtyard of their school.

The scrawnier boy opened his eyes looking up at the light gleaming through the leaves of the tree above him. He got up brushing the dust off of his pants as he saw another punch coming for his face from the bulky, tall boy in front of him. Quickly he jumped back to avoid being punched.

The bully clinched his fist tight readying another punch out of anger. So, he threw another punch aiming at the other kid's face. Seeing the bully's fist coming right at his face, the smaller boy should have been thinking about how much the punch was going to hurt; however, he was only thinking about a girl, at school, he had not been brave enough to talk to earlier. Anytime in the past, when he had talked to the girl, he would experience an unexplainable feeling that would last for hours after her presence was gone.

Ironically he did have the chance in the hallway a few minutes prior to getting stuck in this scenario. Filled with fear after this next punch he might be too bruised & embarrassed to talk with her.

The scrawny boy's name was Thomas Turner but he liked to be called Tom. Tom being a nerdy kind of teenage boy in the sense he liked video games and obtained lots of knowledge, but different from most nerds in the sense of how he liked to watch all kinds of sports. He even occasionally liked to ride a skateboard; being clever with science, math, and people skills didn't really benefit him much though in the social aspect like skateboarding did.

Tom was unlike like most teens of his time because his parents raised him to be loving & caring towards anybody he met. He didn't want a bruised face, so Tom tried jumping up to avoid the bully's fist. Tom ended up getting knocked back to the ground by the bully. The heat scorched down upon Tom's face as he laid there in agony.

Tom didn't want anybody thinking he might be a wimp, so he quickly got back up thrusting forward tackling the strong one to the ground. But the bully dragged Tom down with him punching him in the ribs as they laid there. Tom groaned at the pain he felt in his side.

Tom got up angrily shouting "This is the end of it! Why, are you always attacking me?!"

"Because, Tom, you've done nothing except bring torment to my life. You know very well what you have done to me in times past Turner!"

"I'm sorry, but I don't have a clue what I did to bring you so much grief in the past, but I never meant to. I am sorry Justin for whatever reasons you have held this grudge with me."

But just saying sorry wouldn't cut it. For something much darker had been brewing in Justin's heart, just as long as he held this hatred against Tom. Justin's past made him into a teen with many regrets & angers built up inside of him that made him treat others very poorly. So even Tom's love & kindness might not be enough to heal the wounds on Justin's heart, or would they?

Tom reached out his hand saying "We don't have to be enemies Justin; you know we could be friends if you wanted?"

Just for one moment Justin considered the possibility of having a friend, somebody who might actually care for him instead of despising his very existence. But only for that one moment did he even consider it possible such things might happen. Then he snapped out of what he considered to be a delusion or something beyond being possible for his life.

As Justin broke down into tears he yelled at Tom "Leave now Turner! Get away from me before I make your life worse! Stay around me long enough you're bound to get hurt!"

Tom, being a caring person sympathetically felt the torment in Justin as he gazed a few feet across the dried grass of their school at the look on his face. He wanted to reach out to console Justin by putting his hand on his shoulder, but felt it might only lead to more fighting or abuse.

"Justin…"

"Leave now! Go before I beat you more!"

Feeling concerned for him, Tom decided to walk off leaving Justin there by himself with nothing except his own broken spirit in despair. Justin never liked emotions of this kind; finally he endured a long overdue emotional breakdown. Clearly, this began a long process that could shape and define Justin's future. But neither of them knew a hint of what things might be coming for them over the course of their lives.

Finally, alone, away from Justin Tom obtained time to think about things more reasonably instead of being rushed by dodging a fist. The pain Justin felt still placed a sting in Tom. Seeing Justin's reaction of how hurt he looked affected Tom greatly. So Tom tried to think why or when did he hurt Justin so much to the point it might have brought him to tears to hold resentment that long.

As long as Tom could remember, Justin seemed to have been mad at him. He recalled a time where Justin talked to him casually in elementary school around the age of 10. Then it dawned on him as he walked thinking about these things what may have occurred as well as when. To Tom there could only be one time in his mind that possibly might be the moment Justin referenced Tom being cruel to him.

While Tom walked through the heat of the courtyard he remembered being ten having lots of fun in the gym during athletics one day with many of his class mates. All the kids threw a rubber ball at each other. One girl tried to dodge the ball quickly; she failed though making her out for the round. The girl who threw it cheered with excitement that she had gotten the other girl.

Tom saw her basking in her own personally applied glory, and then quickly threw the ball at her when she wasn't paying attention. One boy on the opposite team, Tom's best friend, smirked throwing it directly at Tom as a playful act. Tom rolled his little eyes being a little annoyed by his friend. But the ball bounced off of Tom landing right next to Justin.

Justin bent down to pick up the ball hearing a noise making him concerned. Then Tom kiddingly decided to release his anger of his friend by channeling it towards somebody else by making fun of Justin. For the noise Justin heard existed as a perfect opportunity to be ridiculed.

Tom yelled so everyone could hear "Looks like Justin is too big for his shorts. See he ripped them with his big butt."

All the children began to laugh pointing their little fingers at Justin. Stress overcame the obese young boy in that moment. Full of anxiety, holding his face Justin noticed tears running down his face. Quickly he ran off ashamed at what happened, being very angry at Tom getting them to all mock him. Obviously none of the other kids cared, they just enjoyed the embarrassment of his shorts ripping.

Tom gave it some thought. Could that have been the whole reason all these years in middle school, even the past two years of high school why Justin picked on Tom the most as well the other kids that were more scrawny than him? He figured logically that incident could be the reason why he had toned up, becoming so muscular & bulky as he grew out of that fat childhood period.

Surely, because of these thoughts, Tom felt guilty about what happened to Justin taking responsibility for what happened all those years ago. It might be the only reason Justin harbored so much anger in him or could there be more to the story than just what Tom recalled for that one moment; only time would tell?

After dwelling on the memory of Justin for a moment, Tom remembered how he ended up in the courtyard looking for his best friend after the bell had rung earlier. He had run into the girl he had been too shy to talk to. Normally he leaned towards being the most open guy anybody might ever talk to, but for some reason he couldn't even comprehend why he felt a little nervous trying to talk with this likeable girl. He figured that his friend took the bus and that's why he couldn't find him.

Since he needed to wait for his brother to finish with basketball practice, and wait for his sister to pick them up, he decided to go waste some time having fun at the recreational center next to the school like he normally did. This stood as the place to go if anybody ever got stuck at school once it ended. It existed as somewhere to do homework, workout and socialize under adult supervision (clearly the school board didn't want the kids left alone after school to commit illegal activities).

While walking to the rec center from the school grounds Tom began to dwell on how his bruised arms were too obvious. Lately he'd been working up the courage to talk to the girl he liked, telling himself in his mind that he would obtain the courage to talk to her no matter what. Clearly he didn't want to have to tell her about the bruise, or explain how he got it from being beat up by a bully. How could he explain it to his siblings once they came to get him? So he devised a plan to have a skateboarding accident so it might look like he got it accidentally.

Once he got there, Tom went to sit down at the juice bar. His fight with Justin had made him quite thirsty; it was unusually hot for a day in March.

"So what will it be today, Tom?" the Juicer asked him.

"I think I will have the magnetized banana mint protein smoothie," Tom requested with enthusiasm.

Magnetized drinks were all the new rage because of their health benefits recently discovered scientifically. Tom gave the Juicer some money after he made it, and then slurped it down quickly enjoying the refreshing sweet taste. When he was done he hurried to the locker room so he could get his board out to go have some fun at the skate park outside. The time came where Tom needed to actually accomplish his plan to get one more bruise while still having some fun on his board.

Tom walked outside onto the pavement with his board wondering if making a cover story on how he got his bruises in the first place would be the right thing to do. He didn't want anybody to know how he'd been weak against Justin especially the girl that he thought about a lot, but in the end no matter what a cover story would just be a lie to the truth. Skateboarding, being risky as well addicting, gave Tom an adrenaline rush, so if he got a bruise from that he would have to be honest about both bruises logically in his mind. Honesty or not it was time to have some fun.

To Tom, video games, movies or even music could give him thrills, but nothing got him excited as the feel of getting on a board going fast while doing amazing stunts with tricks. Having adrenaline rush through his veins as his heart pumped very fast provided him with a sense of power to accomplish wonders. It made him feel like he could be something more special. But just having a feel for something remained unlike anything compared to actually being more than what he realized.

Tom stepped forward doing a noseslide where the hill slanted pushing down on the board rushing down the hill quickly as he pulled a rad kick flip. It felt to him as if the world had frozen in great awe just to look at him. Quickly as he approached the pipeline, Tom ollied up the quarter pipe to grind rail. The rail came to an end so he axled off onto the hill picking up speed going down the hill approaching the bowl curve, so he did a tailslide to slow himself down as some of the kids watching cheered him on.

Since all the kids cheered Tom on, he felt an obligation to impress them with the next trick (clearly the phrase "don't fall for peer pressure" didn't apply to him in his mind). Tom looked down the giant bowl thinking what his next trick might be that could really impress the others. On a whim of an idea he did a vertical nosedive with his board into the bowl. Picking up speed, Tom accelerated up the other side of the bowl doing a hand stand once he got to the top.

But the rush got him to the point he didn't concern himself on safety measures with his next trick.

As he flipped back down from his hand stand he quickly drew his arms back for aerodynamic balance speeding down the bowl building up his speed again. The adrenaline coursed through his veins as he started to carve curves of the giant cement bowl picking up lots of speed. Tom then tried to get as high as he could then swerved down into the bowl going in a straight line flying up, and out the other end of the bowl.

Tom got some air so he tried to do an air walk, as he brought his board back down. After he completed the trick he thought of adding to it by doing a 360° turndown when he descended. Clearly though Tom was so enamored by the rush he got didn't think clearly about the momentum in the one moment of his trick. While trying to spin, he spun too quickly, then the board hit the ground bumping against him, which sent him flying, and rolling onto his already bruised arms on the cement below him in the giant bowl. Some of the kids gasped in horror as they saw Tom's body hit the cement.

Tom wanted to be a good honest person about his bruise but after this poor decision, with too much quick thinking, would he even have the chance to be honest. Would he ever get the chance to resolve his issues with Justin now that he may have made an error in judgment just trying to impress other kids or talk to the one girl who impressed him with only her presence? Time would tell if Tom or Justin truly might have the greater destiny that neither one of them had known was coming to them. Maybe after all Tom was just a normal teenager. For how could Tom possibly have a great future if his body was just lying there with him not moving at all…

Chapter 2
Roots of a Different Kind

AD 1221
Saturday, April 17th, 8:38 P.M.
On the outskirts of Brichtelmeston, Britannia

It was a somber yet eerie evening as the carriage with the mysterious cloaked maiden rolled down the path of dirt through the elm forest near the southern part of ancient Albion. With extreme tension she sat there staring off out into the fields that were covered with dew & mist as the sun was about to set. Worried of what was to come, she waited as the carriage approached a small cabin made of yew wood.

"Here we go madam; I believe this is the cabin you spoke of." The carriage driver said.

"Yes, thank you very much." The mysterious maiden said with an odd unrecognizable accent as she pulled out a gold bar from under her cloak giving it to the carriage driver.

"You are far too generous ma'am."

"Good evening sir, have a blessed life." She said as she smirked putting up the red hood on her cloak as she walked off.

But as soon as happiness had come from giving the driver so much, it was gone remembering why she was tense in the first place. She stood there waiting for the carriage to be out of sight and out of mind. The sun was almost down, but with every moment of lingering the fear in her heart got deeper.

Now that the carriage was gone, she walked into the field next to the cabin. Raising up her arms with her hands held out she mumbled something under her breath. The wind began to blow as pieces of wood flew into the air. All of them had come together into one big pointy stack in an instant.

The mysterious cloaked maiden whispered under her breath, "Ignis."

Instantly the whole pointed stack of wood was set ablaze turning into a big bon fire. The maiden walked off past the fire staring at the sea nearby and noticed the sun dissipated over the horizon. As soon as the last bit of red light disappeared she stared south again at the sea looking up toward the stars. The mysterious lady watched them closely as though she was anticipating something to happen.

After just a few minutes of lingering and anticipation her patience paid off as she saw a bright light zipping across the sky. It was as if a star had left its spot to move about of its own free will. Quickly the star got closer and closer approaching her cabin near the woods.

The giant ball of light descended from the heavens down onto her field. As it landed it changed from being an orb of light into a human shaped figure of light then the light faded as it formed a normal looking person. Walking out of the settling dust, the human figure gave the maiden a stern scoffing look.

"Do we really need to do this?" the man said to her in a language not known to any man or woman on earth.

"Yes, I need to return home to tell them about this plague running through the land." She responded in their language.

"I'm sure they already know, besides couldn't you have just flown here yourself. You know instead of having to make a bonfire to signal me?"

"If I had done that then they would have noticed me and tried to get me sooner. I could already feel their presence at work in Brichtelmeston. I am almost certain they felt mine as well since our natures are contrary to theirs."

"That is true, but you know they can't really hurt us."

"That is the point, I think they finally have been able to get through to us because of this plague."

The man had a horrible expression of fear on his face. It was as if somebody had just told him a loved one had died. The dreadful feeling filled his body inside and out.

"What is this emotion I am feeling right now? I have never felt it before."

"That is the feeling of fear, being scared or anxiety." The maiden said.

"It's a horrible feeling; I don't like it at all. What if the shadow kingdom is listening to us right now?"

"Then you better pray they don't send any of their followers to get you."

"I don't want to have to worry about things like the humans do. Are you sure this plan will…" Then as soon as he tried finishing his sentence a loud clash of thunder and lightning lit up the sky as strange winds were brewing. The elm trees in the forest near by all began to rustle as fast paced winds came blowing through the woods. Concerned the maiden and the man looked up at the stars vanishing as dark clouds started pouring into their area.

"We need to get out of here quickly, I think they are coming!" the man said.

"No, you need to stay here so you can instruct my heir on what they will need to do. I know their destiny is crucial to the future of this realm."

"How do you know that?"

"We don't have time to debate these things!" The maiden said as she saw body figures with flaming torches emerging off in the distance in the woods.

"Alright, but you better be right about your heir releasing me someday."

"If not, you know what will eventually become of you."

"I know, I just don't want to face death."

"Don't worry you will be protected. My relatives have the deeds to this land that live far to the east of here. But I have to get going to the knights in the east who are taking me north to the gateway." She said fearfully as rain was pouring down on them really hard.

"Just do it!"

"See you soon."

"Goodbye." he said as he reached out his hand with concern.

The cloaked maiden mumbled sad words she didn't want to utter but felt she had to. Instantly her friend started to cringe glowing as he compressed, curling up into a ball which then turned into an oval shaped rock that started to glow in many colors. But no rain was falling on the rock as she stared at it floating there for one quick moment. Then she bent her head down in despair as she mumbled something under her breath again. Instantly, with a bright flash he was gone.

Off in the distance she saw a mob of people approaching her field with pitch forks and flaming torches. The maiden mumbled a few words and then there was a flash as a glowing stone appeared in her garden, which stopped glowing as soon as the mob approached. The crowd was yelling with furry at her. Most of them were angry chanting "Let's kill the witch!" As they approached her she burst off as a ball of light headed east off into the darkness of the night...

Disgruntled, Justin stood there very depressed, head down crying, about how he almost had a chance at a friendship, just as he saw Tom walking off. Life never felt easy for him with all the things that had happened to him over the years. Sure he had followers who would listen to whatever he fearfully requested, but they weren't friends who actually cared for him.

Justin started heading over to his pickup truck thinking about what it would be like to have Tom as a friend. Tightening his fist, not being able to comprehend having somebody there for him in any situation he opened his truck then got in.

"I can't see myself ever having a friend, whether it be a good friend or maybe a girlfriend, it's just impossible for anybody to care for me since all people are just monsters and cruel jerks." He thought to himself.

Once seated in his vehicle, Justin remembered that look on Tom's face like he was genuinely concerned for him as a friend. "But it just couldn't be possible Tom would even care for me as a friend," he thought to himself remembering the time Tom taunted him, bringing their whole class to hate him, molding him mad, once again. While remembering that particular memory, he reminded himself of the reason he always went to the gym to get stronger (So he could prove that nobody could take him on).

For the next hour, Justin sweated, working out hardcore at the gym so he could keep his routine going. People at the gym, though, couldn't help but notice that look of rage and despair on Justin's face. They pondered why he was always in such a foul mood, never showing a sign of happiness. But of course the reason Justin was so unhappy, not thinking well of other people went far deeper than just what Tom had done to him that one time.

Sitting bored there at home after working out, Justin started doing his homework. "This is dumb. Why do they make us do a whole day of this homework then come home to do more." He thought as he pulled out his work from his back pack. "Wish I had something else to do like a video game console, or maybe some things to go play sports with so just maybe I could make a friend; but people can't be trusted. It would be nice to have a friend or a brother instead of feeling like I have nobody to trust in this world. That would be really cool." He thought as he did his homework.

Justin got really curious about how to make friends, or if he should even trust somebody to be a friend considering how much he felt betrayed by certain events in his past. "Tom definitely seems like a really good friend though. But how can I ever trust him as a friend if I can't forgive him for what he did?"

For the first time in a long time Justin was making some progress towards becoming a better person. He figured if Tom was such a nice guy and genuinely sorry, he could accept him as friend. But all this could have been just serious loneliness since he didn't have anybody he felt he could trust in his whole life. So Justin made it his priority to apologize to Tom the next day at school.

Dwelling on all this stuff while doing his homework Justin noticed his hollowatch phone just buzzed. But the next thing he saw in his messages sent a shock through him. The message said

"Hey Justin, you know that Turner kid you're always so mad at wanting dead? Well today might be your lucky day. I heard he had a skateboarding accident and might be dead."

Although he was quite bruised, and hurting from the fall he sustained Tom wasn't dead quite yet. Tom heard the voice of his sister as he lay there in pain. When he opened his eyes he noticed that there were lots of people surrounding him and his sister.

"Tom, are you okay?!" she said with a frantic voice.

"Ugh, yeah Jessica I'm fine just in a lot of pain. What are you doing here already?

"I got off work early today. You know benefits of being married to the shop owner. But geese you really had me scared there for a moment. I came in to the center to pick you up and heard you were out here unconscious from an accident, you're lucky you aren't dead."

"Yeah yeah I get what you mean. But you don't have to get all worked up about it."

"Tom, seriously, you should do this stuff with some pads or protection."

"I know, sorry let's get home."

After getting up, they got in Jessica's minivan heading for Tom's home. Jessica's baby wouldn't stop crying which was very irritating to Tom and Jessica, but they both loved him regardless. While they were driving Tom wondered if maybe he could get some dating advice from his sister (clearly girls were a mystery to him as if they were their own species).

"So Jessica, you think I would need a job to get a girlfriend?"

Jessica laughed, saying, "Really Tom? If she is that kind of girl she isn't worth it. You don't want a gold digger for your first girlfriend."

"Hey for all you know I have had plenty of girlfriends."

"Yeah right, then why ask for girlfriend advice?"

"Okay, you got me there. But no, I don't think there is one selfish thing about her."

"Uh oh, looks like you really have fallen for this girl."

"If you met her or watched her you would understand."

"Watched her? What are you doing stalking her like a creep?"

Tom, a little embarrassed said, "No I just notice her a lot and have this feeling for her I can't begin to describe, even if I tried."

"Well, what is this mystery girl's name?"

"She is so gorgeous and her name is Tara."

"Tara huh...well, if you want to date her, a job might help but shouldn't be necessary. Put it this way, Tom, if her feelings are the same or close to how you feel for her then it might be worthwhile to date to see where things will lead. But then again, it could work out for you if at first she hates you. I think the best thing you can do is stop being too cautious to talk to her and just be her friend."

"How did you know I am too nervous to talk to her?"

"Because you're acting like any typical boy would when he wants something but doesn't want to lose it. Obviously, you have feelings for her rooted in you and she might notice them but that won't really be a bad thing unless you move too fast with her. So just try being her friend for now."

"Thanks Jess, that all has made me feel much better."

"You're welcome Tom."

Once Jessica dropped Tom off he ran up to his room so he could finish his home work for the evening which he loved doing. After working on biological math (a new subject in their time) Tom thought about playing on his Z-Triad, but noticed the sun was setting and decided he wanted to go watch it set so he could look toward the stars. Tom climbed out his window onto his family's roof sitting down on the edge of it staring off at the hills near his neighborhood, just as the sun was setting and the stars were becoming very noticeable.

Tom always felt an attraction to the stars like a desire to explore them or go beyond his subtle simple life in Texas. But as he sat there, Tom thought about Tara as he saw the beauty of the sunset and the stars making him think of how beautiful she was like just them. Then he noticed, as he looked down on his yard, a memory from his younger days.

Tom remembered the same night of the day that Justin had been embarrassed at school, how his mom came out of the house carrying his little brother while he was playing tag with his older brother and Jessica, while their dad was cooking hot dogs on the grill. They were having a great time together.

Tom's mom asked, "So did you have a good day at school?"

"Yes mommy I did. It was so funny, Justin ripped his pants!"

"Tom you shouldn't laugh at other kids despair." His mother said sorrowfully.

"Sorry, didn't mean to be bad."

"It's okay, but you should say you're sorry to him tomorrow."

"I will try to remember to."

Then their father said the hotdogs were ready and they all rushed inside except for Tom. Tom stayed outside because he could hear yelling over his fence in the backyard at Justin's house and was curious what was going on. So Tom stayed to see what was up since he was such a curious child.

While Tom sat there staring into the stars Justin was remembering the same night that Tom was remembering, the very night that made him think all humans were monsters that would do nothing but betray and hate one another.

Little Justin fell hitting the ground hard as his father had shoved him holding a beer in one hand and a cigarette in the other. Justin started crying as it had hurt him quite a bit.

"Oh, stop whining you little brat!" His father yelled at him.

"But daddy all the kids made fun of me today at school laughing at me."

"Listen here you little twerp, you need to learn to take care of yourself. Nobody in this world is ever going to give a crap about you and you need to learn to just accept failure."

"Daddy you care about me don't you?"

"Listen here Justin, you were never meant to exist! You were a mistake that should have never happened."

Justin started to cry more intensely as his father took another sip of his beer and puffed in more of his cigarette.

"You're a worthless piece of crap and so is your mother! All you do is whine like a little baby! I can't take anymore of dealing with y'all, I'm leaving. Tonight will be the last night either of us has to ever deal with each other."

"Why daddy?! Why are you leaving us?!"

Justin's father scoffed walking off leaving little Justin in the dirt of their backyard. Little Justin lay there in despair like somebody had just ripped out his heart, crying, curled up on the ground. Little Tom looked through the hole in his fence witnessing the reason Justin hated humanity and everyone in it with no trust to spare.

On that night many years ago, for the both of them roots of different kinds were sown into their lives. Tom was taught to love and Justin was taught to hate anybody who might come into his life. Tom learned he could count on his parent's for guidance and Justin learned that he couldn't count on anybody for trust or anything. But the question remained, did the maiden's roots spread to make a family of love or a family of hate? Where did her roots come from? Would Tom's root of love be rooted in Tara as well or was he in over his head? Clearly Justin's root of bitterness was more than just Tom getting the class to laugh at him. But would Justin ever learn there were people he could trust? Only time would tell what was to become of all these things taking place.

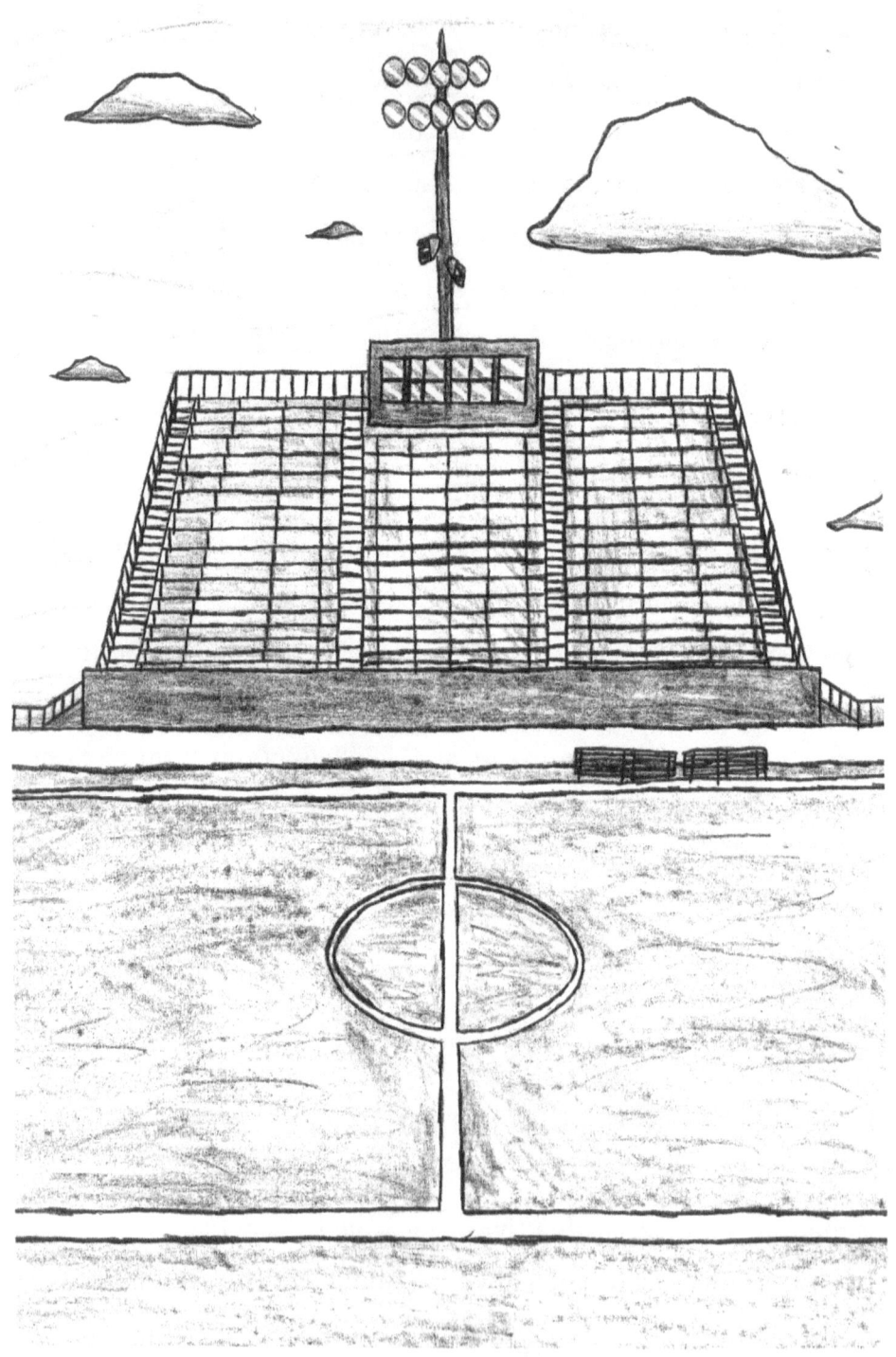

Chapter 3
Wanting More Out of Life

The near future
Friday, March 13ᵗʰ, 6:10 P.M.
Smithsonian Valley Recreational Center, Texas

As Tom waited for his sister to pick him up he was reading about psychology, being reminded of his conversation the other day with Justin. He never had expected what happened to occur though, so it boggled his mind. But it had caused him to look into psychology to figure out what was going on, which in turn had made him remember the events that had occurred two days prior.

Around 12:10 lunch time after Tom had set down his plate on a table outside at the courtyard Justin walked up to him shouting from a distance. Not realizing what Justin was saying, Tom quickly freaked out, but realized it wasn't aggressive yelling.

"Hey, Tom how are you doing today?!"

"What? Mmm…what did you say?"

Justin laughed as he approached Tom, "I said how are you today?"

Tom, somewhat hesitant about Justin's attitude responded "I'm good, but are you okay? You seem to be acting a bit odd for a guy who just beat me up the other day?"

"Oh yeah that's right…sorry about that Tom and sorry for all the times I have gotten mad at you. I really shouldn't be mad at you over that dumb dodge ball scenario; it has to do with other personal problems that's why I held that grudge against you"

"Yeah, I kind of remembered the other night what else happened to you that evening. I figured it might have something to do with your father. But I do accept your apology and sorry about your dad leaving you like that."

"Well, you're spot on with that situation. It truly has been my father's doing that has made me so upset with life and myself, but I figured I shouldn't hold that anger against you since it will do nothing but make me more angry. I figured I wanted more out of life and you said you were willing to be my friend, so I thought I should take you up on your offer to be friends instead of enemies.

"I know it's not easy growing up without a father even though I have always had mine; but since you are trying to overcome your hatred for him it will benefit your life a lot. You know, focus on the good instead of all the bad. Plus, I realized you were in a state of destitution which is why I tried being your friend even though you were mad with me."

"Destitution, what does that mean?"

"It means somebody who doesn't have friends."

"Oh, okay I get it. Well, would you be my friend?"

"Alright, but no more bullying me or anybody else. I will try to help you with your anger issues and resentment. You know, be there for you as a friend."

"Sure thing Tom, I know I should be more kind towards others instead of being mad all the time at everybody. I truly do just want some real happiness for once instead of temporary happiness."

"Temporary happiness, what do you mean?"

"Oh nothing, that's not important now."

Justin clearly had wanted this to work out since he wasn't used to having friends. But as with any friend-ship there is always a point when one friend may be head over heels for a girl. Tara walked up to Tom with a warm smile on her face.

"Hello Tom, sorry to interrupt, but I was going to say I had a great time talking to you yesterday. I also wanted to know if you were going to be at the game Friday?" Tara said very kindly.

"Yeah, you bet I am. I wouldn't miss it for the world."

"Cool, see you there, then." Tara said as she walked off waving goodbye to them.

Justin didn't look too happy though about the situation. But as soon as Tara was gone he tried not to be angry. So he tried to be nice instead of angry. Why was he so angry though? Was it just because Tom had been invited by Tara or was he feeling like she would pull him away from him as friend? Clearly Justin had never had to deal with friends or with girlfriends or females that may be interested in a friend. So since this was new to him he tried to remain calm but underneath he did feel somewhat resentful she had just interrupted their conversation.

"So Tom, you like her?" Justin said with curiosity.

"Yeah, she is so amazing. Whenever I am with her it's a feeling that's indescribable."

"Sounds like you really like her. There have been a few times I liked some girls."

"Yeah, but Justin you don't get it. This isn't like one of those feelings where you just like them at face value, it's something more than just the feeling you might get for multiple girls at once. Trust me when you find the right girl this feeling will come to you and you will know she is the girl of your dreams."

Justin wondered what this feeling could be and said, "Well I will take your word for it. Hope I do find a girl that could make me feel that way. And I hope I feel good enough about myself to be willing to try to get with a girl like that."

"You will be good enough just have some confidence in yourself for once. The other day when you beat me up I was still too shy to talk to her, but after my skateboarding accident I figured I should talk to her regardless of how insecure I was about myself and my sister gave me a bit of a pep talk about it."

"I wouldn't know, I don't have any siblings."

"Speaking of which I was wondering, would you like to come to my brother's final big basketball game Friday night?"

"Sure, I would be glad to, never been into sports that much, but they could be interesting."

While sitting there thinking about all these things that had occurred Wednesday, Tom noticed a basketball fly towards him real fast. So he reached out grabbing it before it hit his magnetized smoothie. Then he heard his friend speak to him.

"Man, Tom, weren't you listening? I called out your name many times but you didn't respond," Said Benny.

"Oh sorry Benny, I just was really busy thinking about Tara, Justin and daddy issues in psychology," Tom said as he held up his book about psychology.

"Tom, I will never grasp how you love science, psychology, and sports all at the same time. You know it's just unusual for a nerd to be into athletic things and science stuff all the time."

"For one, being into athletics doesn't mean I can't be into science and knowledge in general as well. For two, psychological studies don't really have too much to do with science, but more like the cause and effects of our actions. But some might debate about how chemicals can or could affect our psychological states."

Benny just laughed and made a hand signal indicating an airplane flying right over his head while making an airplane sound. Then Tom laughed about it as well.

"Okay, I get it right over your head, you didn't understand it one bit."

"Tom, you know that smart stuff isn't really my strong suit. But still I wanted to ask if you are going to John's game tonight or going to go home and relax?"

"Well considering Tara is going to be there and expecting me I wouldn't miss it for the world."

"Oh hung up on Tara still are we?"

"Of course I am, if only you understood how I felt about her. But first Jessica is taking me to apply at SpotOn then, I will come to the game afterwards."

"I bet it will be an exciting game and if she is expecting you, then, you never know she might be interested in you after all."

Distracted, Benny noticed a hot girl walk by who made an eye brow-raising look towards him. Instantly allured, by her he said "bye" to Tom and ran off pursuing her in all her illustriousness. They had been friends since Tom was four and were the kind of best friends that you would think would always be together. They grew up together, like brothers, always being there for one another if possible.

Scoffing watching Benny run off after a girl, Tom noticed his hollowatch phone buzzed. Seeing it showing Jessica was waiting outside for him. He hurried to get in the car as he and Jessica headed for SpotOn. Tom went inside and went to an application booth trying to hurry but also trying to do it right. After quite a while of exhaustive informative questions about himself and how he would respond to certain situations, Tom was finally done with the long application. On his way back to the school with Jessica he wondered if Tara, Justin or Benny would be there waiting for him.

⎗ ⅃ △ ⋈ △ ⋈ ◇ △ ⎗ △ ▽ ⩜

Justin of course was sitting there in the bleachers at the gym while people were showing up for the game and as he waited for Tom to arrive. While sitting there Justin pondered how he was going to approach his followers about his change of character. He wondered if he should tell them he wanted to stop bullying people or tell them maybe he was sorry for his actions that caused some of them to follow him in the first place. Justin knew that some only followed him out of fear because of the way he would pick on them. But none were like real friends to him. Did that mean that he would stop getting money from some of them to buy drugs to give him some form of happiness?

Because of these thoughts, Justin was growing very anxious waiting while watching as the people poured into the stadium. He figured maybe he could still have some of his followers, maybe only bully people once in a while. But that would be going against his deal with Tom. After thinking about it for perhaps too long he told himself to relax, figure it out later and try to enjoy the game.

Soon Justin saw Tom walk in the gym and waved over to him with enthusiasm. Tom waved back with a look of perplexity on his face. So Tom walked up to Justin trying to figure out why he was acting so happy and odd. Obviously Tom was feeling that being around Justin would be socially awkward because Justin was acting rather odd.

"Hey Justin, excited about the game? Sorry I am late I was busy applying at SpotOn."

"Mmm…yeah I guess so?"

"Well, you are or you aren't."

"Yeah, it will be lots of fun," Justin said trying to sound enthused about the game rather than Tom being there.

Clearly Justin was putting too much value on their friendship making Tom feel uncomfortable. But this was all a result of Justin's upbringing and how he had never had a true friend he could count on. So it made it where even the slightest interest in a friendship or potentially romantic relationship with a girl would cause him to over read the scenario. He was always making the other feel uncomfortable.

A good example of this was Justin's first love interest when he was 11. There was a girl he found cute and interesting but when he tried to admit his feelings to her he really over did it. Justin was so obsessed with her that he pushed her away, always bugging her whenever she would walk in the classroom. Clearly she hurt his feelings because of this, but he was the one being a nuisance to her constantly.

Justin didn't want to make the same kind of mistake with Tom as his first friend. So he reminded himself that he needed to work on these things. Hopefully, Tom would understand the wackiness Justin was going through.

Justin then said after thinking about these things. "Tom, listen I understand I have been acting odd lately, I see it on your face how I look like a penguin with a bunch of seals."

"Not the analogy I would of used, but yeah that's for sure."

"Sorry I am not used to even having a friend I don't mean to be so clingy, but it's like I can't help it."

"Yeah, well Justin, people might get the wrong idea about you if you keep it up. I am certain you don't want that and neither do I."

"That's true, but honestly I'm not sure how to approach just being a friend?"

"Well for one when you see your "friend" whether it be me or somebody else you make as a friend, don't jump for joy like you just beat a level on a video game or just got lots of money," Tom said with a stern look on his face.

"Yeah, I think you're right. Sorry I'm just not a very good social butterfly like most people."

"It's okay I am sure over time you will figure out how to act normal around people. Now let's just sit down and wait for Benny and Tara to get here."

Tom sat there wondering where Benny or Tara were. He was getting kind of bored waiting for his brother John's game to begin, so he told Justin he would be right back. Quickly Tom started pacing down the side of the bleachers as he scanned them looking for any sign of Tara. Sure he wanted to find Benny but he definitely was keeping more of an eye out for the only person who truly mattered to him at that moment.

Soon enough he found Benny sitting at the top of the bleachers and went up there to see if he wanted to go sit with him somewhere else. Benny agreed to it and as they were heading down Tom saw Tara walking in with a friend. Quickly, without any concern about telling Benny where they were going to sit, Tom ran off to greet her.

"Hey Tara, would you like to come sit with me and Benny and Justin?"

"I certainly would," Tara said with a smile. "Oh but let me see if my friend wants to join us."

So after talking to her friend the four of them headed back to join Justin. Benny wasn't too happy about Tom running off so quickly and having to chase him but he could tell how much Tom was crazy for Tara, which made him try not to get too upset over his shenanigans. Once they all got over to Justin's side of the bleachers they greeted him and sat down as the game was about to begin.

As the game started, Tom daydreamed about getting a job. He wondered even with the job he applied for at SpotOn if Tara would actually go on a date with him. He wondered if getting a job was worth all the hassle just so he could get a girlfriend. But then he remembered his pep talk with Jessica and remembered he really had nothing to worry about; just try to be her friend. Lost in his daydream, Tom was startled to reality by the halftime buzzer. He quickly stood up and headed to get some snacks.

While he was waiting in line he looked up at the score board noticing that the Smithsonian Valley Rangers were winning with a score of 21 to 16. He got some popcorn with the money his parents gave him that morning and headed back to the stands.

Once the game started again after halftime, Tom again got lost in his thoughts about something trivial other instead of his own brother's basketball game. He was deep in thought about a video game he had been playing, "Ring of Mystery III", and whether or not he would ever get past this one level of the game. As he was playing the video game in his mind, he was interrupted by the noise of the crowd. Looking up, he saw that the Rattlers were now winning 31 to 29.

The game was now getting so close and exciting, that Tom found himself actually watching the game. As the game came to an end, Tom watched as his brother John brought the ball down the court with only 4 seconds remaining in the game. With the score 48 to 47, the ball was clearly in the court of the Rattlers over the Rangers per chances of winning. John shot the ball with 2 seconds left in the game. The ball went clean through the hoop bringing the Rangers a win and the crowd to a frenzy of yelling and cheering.

Tom sat there thinking "Man, could life get any more clichéd? Why can't there be something new and exciting for once?" Lately, he had felt that life was too predictable and he wanted something new and exciting in his life instead of his same old boring routines.

Now that the game was over lots of people were headed out of the gym ready to go home. But, Tom remembered about how in a week or two there was going to be a soccer game for his little brother and thought he should take advantage of it. So quickly he ran up to Tara as she was about to leave.

"Hey Tara, I was wondering if maybe next Sunday after church if you wanted to come to my little brother's soccer game since you seemed to like this one with my older brother so much?"

"Wow…Yeah that would be amazing, Tom," Tara said with a very ecstatic look on her face.

"I'm sure you will love it. Well see ya later."

"Goodnight Tom."

Tara walked out the door not knowing Tom couldn't stop staring at her. Then Tom invited Benny to spend the night like he normally did on Fridays. But, of course, Justin was there and took notice of these things. He wasn't too thrilled that he didn't get any kind of an invitation from Tom. This annoyed Justin because he knew that Tom had invited everyone else to different events. Then, Tom said goodbye to Justin as his family and Benny headed home to celebrate John's winning score.

Today was a special sentimental day in two ways for Tom, for one he was getting to spend time with Tara and for two he was going to his little brother Martin's game. He took pride in Martin as a little brother since he wasn't too annoying but kind of a clever little kid with artistic skills and athletic skills. So after Church, Tara went with the Turners to Martin's game.

Arriving at the field Tom and Tara ran up to the top of the bleachers together racing each other playfully. Tom's family watched in observance at Tom & Tara's odd behavior as they were certainly having a great time. Once they sat down at the top of the bleachers Tara was curious about some things.

"So Tom, how was your evening after the game last Friday?"

"It was good. Benny spent the night and helped me beat a level on Ring of Mystery III, The one I couldn't figure out on my own."

"That's cool, I guess? So what's all that hanging out with Justin lately about?"

"Well, I remembered an issue of his from our childhood and realized why he is so messed up and has trouble dealing with people."

"What do you mean exactly?"

"To put it precisely I believe he suffers from Dependent Personality Disorder because of the Separation Anxiety Disorder he may have developed as a child."

"Mmm…I'm not the smartest girl with psychological terms, could you put that in laymen terms?"

"Okay look at this way, I think from what I have gathered, Justin is very clingy to friends or any kind of relationship because of how he was abandon by his father years ago when we were little."

"Oh that is truly sad. So that is why he picks on others?"

"Perhaps that might be him trying to exert his independence to show he doesn't need anybody, but deep down he truly is lonely and wants somebody to be there for him."

"Didn't you say it was a dependent disorder? So wouldn't that mean he wants people to be around a bunch?"

"Yeah, but anything can happen when it comes to psychological scenarios. So he might try to go against those thoughts he keeps to himself. So in essence, I am trying to be a good friend to him."

"Wow Tom, that is amazing that you would be his friend even after all the times he beat you up."

With some shock to his voice, Tom said, "Really you knew how he would beat me up?"

Tara giggled saying, "Did you really think that nobody knew about it?"

"No, I just hoped you didn't know. I didn't want you to think I was weak."

"Tom, what should it matter if I thought you were weak."

"I don't know, for some reason I thought you might not want to be my friend if you thought I was a pathetic loser."

"Tom I will be friends with anybody regardless of who they are or what they have been through. Man, the human mind it sure is complex."

Tom chuckled and said, "Yeah it sure is. But part of Justin feeling lonely might have something to do as well with never having somebody by his side, like a brother. For instance, I and my brother share a great bond. Martin is a wonderful little brother and looks up to me for support and I am there for him, but Justin never had anybody like that in his life."

"Martin is a cute little kid."

"He also is very good at drawing pictures. And he is very creative, which is unique in the sense that he loves to play Soccer."

"Wow, an artistic athlete that's something you don't see every day as a stereotype."

"Yeah, I try to be a good example to him and give him some guidance so maybe he will be a good person when he is older."

"I'm sure you do a great job being there for him Tom."

"Thanks Tara, you're so kind and sweet," Tom said as they looked into each other's eyes.

Then all the little soccer kids rushed onto the field cheering with excitement. Tom's family watched Martin's game with excitement. But at one point Tom got a message on his Hallow Watch phone telling him how they were doing the interviews for the applicants who applied at SpotOn later that day. Martin's team won after putting up quite a good defense with a score of 6 to 4. So after the game Tom thought he should ask his parent's to drive him to the store so he could do the interview.

The near future
Sunday, March 22nd, 4:12 P.M.
SpotOn Retail Store, Smithsonian Valley, Texas

Justin parked his pickup truck as he reached the SpotOn parking lot. Once he was comfortably parked, he headed on into the store. Little did he know though of what awaited him in the coming minutes. In a not too surprising turn of events, Justin had applied at the same retail store Tom had applied, thinking he would have a friend who could give him some occasional guidance if he wasn't acting properly around people (clearly he didn't consider the fact this was Tom's first time to apply for a job, but probably didn't even know that).

But oh boy was Justin so excited for this new job. He looked at it as a new way to start his life again without having to deal with his dark past. Maybe over time he too could find a girlfriend for himself like most of the kids at school. Well, at least that's what he thought without considering for one second people would remember that he was renowned for being a jerk and a bully.

As Justin walked up to customer service with his shoulders held high assuring himself that everything was headed for the better. Asking the young man at the counter where to go for his interview, He headed where the guy told him to go in the middle of the front of the store seeing the interview room label, he opened the door with hope that he would make a good impression.

When he opened the door Justin saw some guy sitting next to Tom who was shocked to see Justin there. Obviously, Tom didn't expect him to be there. Being little perplexed he requested Justin to come sit next to him.

"So, Justin what are you doing here?"

"I decided to get a job here like you did, so you could give me pointers when we are working since I haven't been in a work environment before and it will be cool cause I will be around here with you, my new friend."

"Well, thanks for the thought Justin, but I am not that informative myself how to work here as this is my first job as well. Plus logically, for this interview they will pick between the three of us who will get the job."

"Well, that sucks. Wish it wasn't that way."

"Yeah, well that's the point of doing the interviews to see who is that best for the job and the most qualified. Remember the other night when we were talking about seeming too obsessed?"

"Yeah, I do, why?"

"Well, okay, I honestly think I figured out from a psychological view why you're so sad and clingy as a friend. I know it's not the best place to discuss it Justin, I think having your father leave you caused all this despair. You needed him and he should've needed you. But he disregarded you which no man should do to their child. I think that has caused you deep down to fear anybody that you try to connect with on an emotional level like a good friend or a lover. You fear they might leave you too,"

Tears started to well up in Justin as he said, "You're right! That's exactly what has happened and what I am scared of."

"Well then don't worry; I won't just randomly leave you as a friend for nothing. Don't fear that everyone you try to befriend is going to despise you and abandon you like your father did. But how you have treated others in the past might bring some baggage, so my best suggestion, if you want to make friends is to move on from your past and let there be a new Justin people can appreciate."

"It's funny you say that because I already was feeling like this job was like a symbolic way of me moving on to be a better person."

"That's good! See you're already being a better person."

Justin wiped away his tears to try to get in a better looking mood. Then a few seconds later a woman came in the room announcing something that was going to change everything for them the rest of their lives. The lady announced to all three of them that before they could start the interview, they would need to take a drug test. And if any of them tried to run, the police would instantly be notified to come and arrest them. Since they lived in the near future laws had buckled down about job's doing drug testing, arresting anybody who even applied that had drugs in their system.

Instantly, a gaping spear of fear and dread hit Justin hard in his chest. He wondered how he could have been so stupid to not think of this before he came to the interview. But then he realized he hadn't even known that drug tests were required, it wasn't as if his mother ever told him about them. What was he going to do now except accept the test and hope he didn't get into too much trouble for it.

Then the lady handed each of the boys a little cup and told them to go pee in the bathroom to their left. First the guy sitting next to them went in there and came back out, then Tom and finally Justin. As each one came out the lady poured them into the phial with their names individually not making any mistakes like Justin was hoping she would. As Justin handed over his cup the fear filled up from within him that soon enough he wouldn't have any friends but just be stuck in juvenile prison or something.

So now they had to wait for her to return to tell them who was going to be going on to do the interview. But, of course, they never told newcomers about their drug testing habits of pulling it as a surprise because it was the only way to catch criminals in the act (well what the government considered criminals). As Justin sat down, though, he was so worried about what was going to happen. Hopefulness had turned to total worry.

Tom looked over at Justin with concern wondering why he had such a freaked out look on his face. But Tom was excited getting this job because in a few weeks after his birthday he could get a license and possibly work a deal with his parents to get a vehicle of some kind. Then, maybe he and Tara could go places, maybe Enchanted Rock or the Guadalupe River or Canyon Lake or for the sake of it, exploring the beautiful Texas scenery in their area. The possibilities were practically endless in Tom's mind.

But although Tom was so inspired by these thoughts he couldn't help but wonder if Justin was doing okay measuring the look on his face. He noticed how Justin's feet kept tapping the ground and his hands were looking clammy, sweat was starting to come down his face a little. He figured he should investigate.

"Hey, Justin you okay? You look really paranoid right now?"

"Oh…I do? Mmm…yeah, I am fine I guess?"

"No need to be nervous Justin I am sure you will do fine."

"Yeah, I am sure you're right Tom, but mmm…let's just say I have good reasons that I am feeling nervous."

"Okay, but try not to worry and just make a good impression."

Tom sat there rather curious what was going through Justin's mind. His mood looked like it wasn't changing one bit even after trying to cheer him up some. He began to think maybe he could buy some lab equipment with some of the money he might earn from this job. Maybe he could get some magnets to make his own enhanced plants for a small garden. Tom had so many ideas about what he could do with that money. He knew he didn't need it to be friends with Tara but thought it would be a big help like Jessica had suggested.

Tom felt pretty secure in his chances of getting the job since he considered himself to be a good person with decent values. He was a really good people person and not such a downer like Justin was being lately. He didn't have a clue what the other guy was like who seemed pretty quiet and reserved for the most part. Not too long after overthinking every possible outcome while he was daydreaming, Tom still noticed Justin looking severely stressed and wondered what was going through his head.

⌐ ⌐ △ ☼ ◌ △ ⟩ ⌐ △ △

Justin knew his end was coming or the beginning of a very painful experience. He didn't want to have to deal with all the crazy nuts in Juvie. In his mind they were way crazier than he could have ever been. Justin began to realize he had taken his mother for granted in the past but should have been nicer to her over the years while she raised him without a father.

Now he really wished he had done more with his life instead of just going around school beating up kids smaller than him for drug money. But, then again he was only in high school. He still had his whole life ahead of him to do things. Well, he would have if he hadn't done so many drugs to get himself arrested. So things were definitely not looking good for Justin.

Justin began to worry about what Tom would think of him because of this. Did it mean he would stop being his friend just because he did drugs to feel better in life? Then he thought about how Tom said he wouldn't just randomly stop being his friend. But what if this was enough of a good reason? Then Justin told himself if Tom could forgive him for this as a friend then he would try to stop doing drugs and throwing pity parties for himself. After that Justin felt he was being too clingy again worrying about Tom's opinion.

With every passing moment Justin grew more tense waiting for the employee to come back for him or for the police to show up. The pressure was building and he just wanted it to be over already. He knew the time was coming he would have to deal with the consequences of his actions. Very soon things were about to get rough in ways Justin couldn't begin to comprehend. Justin sat there wishing he had never come to apply for the job or that the labels would have been mislabeled. If only the woman put their evidence into the wrong cup, but Justin was not going to get away free it was now time for him to suffer for his actions.

The door swung open as two officers walked in. Justin's heart nearly stopped in its place as the coppers walked in. Tom wondered why they were there or which one of the other guys they came for. Then the cop pointed in their direction speaking loudly.

"Thomas Turner, you are under arrest for the violation of drug possession and consumption."

The other officer who went to Tom's church then said, "You won't need a pastor, since you were at church earlier. We'll just take you straight to the chair."

Confusion swept across Justin's and Tom's face as they read him his Miranda rights and walked him out to their car. Tom was worried now what was going to happen to him and why he was even arrested. He knew he had never once done drugs and never would since what the dangers could be scientifically implemented to the human mind.

But Tom and Justin both had wanted more out of life and from this point on they both were going to definitely get it. Tom wanted more non clichéd moments for something new and surprising, as well spending Time with Tara. Maybe even be more than friends with her. Justin wanted a friend somebody he could count on to be there for him. He wanted to be happy with things and not be so upset by life; he wanted the loving family Tom had that he had envied since they were children. Justin wanted this because he felt they were a family of love. Hopefully, they loved Tom enough to be there for him in this hour of darkness. If only they knew what was to come for the both of them from this one moment that would forever change their destinies…

Chapter 4
Forgiveness Can Be Hard

The near future
Monday, March 23rd, 6:14 P.M.
Smithsonian Valley High School, Texas

Justin had to make some hard decisions now that he wanted to change to be a better person because of the miracle that had occurred the day before. He never thought that such great things could happen for him, but also he was concerned about Tom and how he had been taken away by the police. Why did Tom have to be the one to suffer for his actions?

Regardless of all his thoughts one thing was for sure, he needed to keep his crowd following him or they would try to get revenge if they thought he had grown weak. So Justin shoved one kid to the ground for his money with his crowd of followers watching. But he had a feeling of pain in his heart because he didn't want to continue doing this to the poor children who probably already had enough suffering in their lives.

As soon as the kid hit the dirt bemused by the situation, Tom and Tara noticed it as they were walking down the stairs from the gym. Clearly they weren't happy about what they were seeing. Quickly the two of them ran down to see if the kid was okay. Obviously, Tom had something important he wanted to express to Justin.

"Justin, what are you doing? I thought you were going to stop this?!"

With a vehement look of desperation on his face Justin mumbled, "Tom, I want to change I really do. But I can't look weak in front of my group because then they will want revenge for the things I have done to them."

"You just showed them you're willing to change. I am sure some of them are going to be willing to forgive you if you just apologize to them."

Justin lately had been thinking about forgiving his father for what he had done to him when he was a child. He wondered if any of these fellow students would forgive him for the atrocities he had committed. Even though he was trying, it was hard for him to forgive since it left him so emotionally unbalanced. But Justin thought it would be the right thing to do and finally change to be a better person.

"Okay guys, Tom is right I want to be a better person and I hope all of you can forgive me for all the crap I have put you through."

Some of them seemed like they were okay with it. But one of them decided to mock him and call him a wuss. Igniting a flame of anger, Justin grew very tense. Now he truly was being put onto the spot to either be given the chance to fight or take flight. The anxiety raced through him deciding what to do.

"You really are a pitiful loser aren't you!? You're nothing but a worthless druggy!", The one boy who clearly had been hurt emotionally to resort to taunting said.

Justin's anger boiled to the surface as he remembered how much he hated his father. Forgiveness was clearly not an option for him at this point. He felt the only thing to do now was to prove himself a leader among the crowd, aka the top dog. Tara had stood there witnessing the words of cruelty the one boy had said. She gave a look of pity towards him. But Justin saw out of his peripheral vision this look on her face, totally misunderstanding her.

With adrenaline and furry rushing through his veins, Justin's feelings all boiled to the surface in a moment that would change his friendship with Tom forever. His jealousy of Tom talking about Tara started to emerge in his mind. Why did Tom always want to invite Tara and Benny to things, but not him? With these ideals running through his mind he took the next step in his life to define whether he would become a force for good or a force for evil.

Stepping forth with his fist rushing forth he bashed the taunting teen to the ground as he yelled with rage. Then he let go of all his inhibitions as he turned quickly giving Tara a look of envy. Worried what was happening Tara stepped back tripping backwards on a wooden stick. As she fell to the ground, Justin had already walked up to her with something he felt he really needed to say and get off his mind.

"You stupid girl, because of you I have lost the only friend I ever had! All Tom ever wants to do is hang out with you now! He only likes inviting you and Benny to things but never me!"

"Well look at you and the way you're acting. Do you honestly think he is going to be keen on hanging out with you if this is how you treat people?"

As Justin was lunging his fist forward toward Tara, Tom yelled "Stop it now Justin!"

Tom grabbed onto him by the shoulder of his arm. Justin glanced back using his left arm to elbow Tom, then quickly turned, grabbing him and throwing Tom to the ground. Tara got up and rushed over to Tom with concern in her eyes for him as she kneeled next to him. But then Justin saw Tom on the ground, realizing it was Tom that he had thrown and not the other kid, then Justin had a look of sympathy on his face.

"Tom I didn't mean to hurt you like that I'm sorry." Justin said as a tear went down his face.

"Yet, you are more than willing to hurt Tara!?"

"I'm sorry, I just am really angry right now. I didn't know how to stop myself."

"Justin, you can apologize all you want but it doesn't change what you have done. Just leave us alone right now."

Both Tom and Tara looked up at Justin. As she wrapped her arms around Tom's shoulders to help him up, she had a look on her face expressing towards Justin, "Look what you have done." Clearly Justin was feeling like he had lost everything in life that had meaning. He truly felt like he was worthless not remembering how he was spared from going to prison for doing drugs. But, why was he spared?

Seeing the look on Tara's face just made Justin more angry. Now he felt he had nothing left to live for since his friendship with Tom was ruined he should get Tara for what she did. Tara saw the look of rage on Justin's face; quickly she turned around running fast as Justin started rushing towards her.

As Justin chased her towards the stairs, Tom and Tara had come down earlier He yelled, "You think you're safe just because you have Tom, well then you better think again! No matter how far you run, I will make you pay for what you have done!"

Running for her life Tara ran into the gym once she was up the stairs. Then she glanced back for one second to see how far behind Justin was, he was closing in. Some of the girls who hadn't left the gym, saw Justin chasing her across the bleachers. Justin yelled more at her as she passed the concession stand running out one of the two main doors of the gym.

"Get back here you stupid brat!"

Justin saw her turn left as she had gone out and continued running down the side walk of the gym entrance. Pursuing her into the main hall of the school, he gave all he got to pay back what he felt she deserved for taking Tom away from him, not realizing he was the one ruining their friendship by his very actions. Once she was fully down the entrance of the main hall in the middle of the cross roads, Tara stopped briefly to see where Justin was.

As she saw him coming through the main door, she thought she should get back to Tom to have some protection. So with fast haste and lots of intense fear she quickly turned to her right which would have been Justin's left heading down the hall. She ran fast almost reaching the door but had slipped on the recently cleansed floor falling down sliding forward toward the door. Justin was almost caught up to her.

Just as Justin was coming up on her directly she had gotten up and went out the door. Tara came to a halt quickly, not wanting to fall down the steps that led to the middle side entrance of the gym. But just as she was putting one foot down, Justin grabbed her by the shoulder pulling her back.

"Where do you think you're going little miss perfect?" Justin said with a devious smirk on his face.

Fearfully, Tara said, "Please, leave me alone, you giant jerk!"

"You really think I am going to let you off the hook that easily, just because you said "Please"?"

"I'm hoping if you value your friendship with Tom then you will come to your senses and stop this chaos before you fully ruin it.

My friendship is already ruined so it doesn't matter what I do at this point. I see how some of you girls can be always thinking you can manipulate us men and sometimes we are very dumb to fall for it, but saying please and trying to use logic isn't going to save you now! So, dream on!"

Justin pulled back his fist, launching it straight at her. As Justin was throwing his right hook punch Tom came running through the middle door at the side of the gym near the bottom of the steps.

Tom yelled, "No Tara!!!"

The blow caught her off balance making her fall down the stairs. Quickly she fell down the stairs tumbling at every step as her arms hit some of the railings and her legs were banging around against the cement. Tom kneeled down to Tara to see if she was okay just as she had done for him a few minutes prior. He put his hand under her backside holding her head in one hand and her back in another. But Tom just couldn't tell if she was okay. Then he looked up with an evil angry glare at Justin and yelled at him.

"Justin! You monster look what you have done to her! Do you have any idea how important she is to me! You can be sure that I won't be friends with you now! I gave you the chance to be my friend and look what you have done! You're going to pay for what you have done to her!

Then the railing began to rattle a little. But was it from Tom or was it from Justin?

Justin had a scared feeling within himself as he saw that look on Tom's face. He didn't want to get arrested for assault so he figured the only thing he could do was run and get as far away from the crime scene as fast as he could. He knew he had been spared prison once, but felt he needed to save his own skin this time. Scared and concerned, Justin quickly ran off to his pickup truck to get home.

ㄴ ᗰ △ ＞ ᗰ ㄴ ᗰ △

Tom used what little strength he had to carry Tara, who seemed to be unconscious up to the nurse's office near the main hall entrance. He certainly was concerned for Tara but at the same time very angry at Justin for what he had done. Now Tom could think of nothing but the fact that Justin was a danger when around Tara and he should have tried protecting her better.

After dropping Tara off at the nurse's office, Tom headed over to the recreational center where he and Tara were headed originally. He found Jessica waiting there for him. She wondered why Tom looked so down. The whole ride home he didn't want to talk about it. He headed up to his room a bit angry about what Justin had done and thought if he really should go after him for revenge. But, then, he would be just as low as Justin, who wanted revenge for things he had already done.

The moments of the crazy events kept playing over and over again in Tom's mind. Eventually, after a while of thinking about it, Tom remembered how the one dumb kid who denied Justin's apology had called him a druggy, which made Tom recall the events of the day before. Tom remembered how the cops took him into custody and he called his parents. They weren't morose He was arrested but definitely they were shocked and couldn't believe Tom would do drugs at all. They had raised him with such good values, that they would never expect such a thing would happen. So because of what Justin considered a miracle for him, Tom did not get the job and worse yet at that point Tom got arrested for something he didn't even do.

Tom realized (or so he thought but, what was really just a presumption) that somehow, someway Justin must have gotten somebody to switch the labels for him. Now he was angrier than he had been; thinking Justin was doing drugs and was responsible for hurting Tara and also getting him arrested. There was nothing keeping him from wanting to rip down a door. He immediately went up to his attic to get his old baseball bat he hadn't used in a long time. Tom was so determined to go beat Justin to punish him for his betrayal and for hurting Tara he didn't feel like anything could stop him.

While he was in the attic looking for his bat and thinking about all that Justin had done, he came across something very interesting in the old bins and storage containers full of junk. That something was a folded paper inside a glass frame under some folded papers in a trunk. He took the paper out of the frame and unfolded them carefully. Tom was very curious as to what they said. As he read them, he was amazed to find out that his family actually owned property in England.

After Tom found the deed to their property he quickly headed downstairs to show his parents. He told them about how excited he was to have found the papers and was hoping that they would go to England to see the property during the upcoming summer break. But of course he didn't really think that his parents were just going to agree to a family trip halfway across the world instantly. Would they really be that quick to be on board for such an extravagant trip, especially since he had just been arrested the day before for doing drugs (Tom obviously didn't include this thought when he asked them)? They shot the idea down immediately.

Then, out of the blue, Tom had an idea. He tried to make a deal with them. Offering that if during the weekend if he could prove he was not doing drugs, they would go to the newly discovered property in England for the summer. Tom really wanted to go so he could have something new in his life and be far from Justin or Tara so he wouldn't end up hurting her again with his presence. He could only imagine the new adventures waiting for him there. To his surprise, his parents said that they would think about it. Their response wasn't exactly a promise, but at least it was a possibility of things to come, and that was enough to give Tom some hope.

The near future
Sunday, March 08th, 3:40 P.M.
Off the coast of Kuwait, Persian Gulf, Indian Ocean

It was a fine day at sea for the crew of the U.S.S Lincoln; one of the young swabbies was busy cleaning the top deck of the aircraft carrier. He felt very serene just cleaning, not having to deal with anybody else at that moment. Comfort though, never can last for more than a moment, and as that moment passed he began to feel very odd and tingly. Something very abnormal and beyond understanding began to occur as he felt a static discharge running down his spine.

The winds quickly began to brew as the clouds above him grew darker. Lightning and thunder were thrashing to and fro in the heavens above the ship. The young boy checked his watch and looked up watching as the clouds were gathering together into a swirling vortex. With dire concern he quickly climbed the ladder to get up to the bridge. The wind grew faster with haste as more thunder boomed scaring the young soldier. Quickly he opened the door to warn the captain.

"Sir at 1540 hours a singularity began forming sir!"

"I do not understand your concern, swabbie?"

"Sir, if we do not move the ship out away from this singularity it…"

Right as the young swabbie was telling his captain what could happen if they didn't get out of the way it happened…his fears were confirmed. The singularity of clouds came together as did lightning from multiple directions all forming into one big bolt shooting down from the center of the vortex in the sky into the waters below.

The waters began to rumble loudly as lots of electrons pulsated throughout them. The young swabbie hurried back down to the top deck towards the starboard side to get a glimpse of what was happening. As he reached for a rail, he saw there was a vortex forming in the water about three hundred yards away from the ship. He could feel it pulling more and more water into it; with concern he quickly gave hand signals to move the ship back, up towards the captain's deck. But the captain didn't need his hand signal to see the giant whirlpool forming, pulling their boat & crew into it.

With quick haste and fear the captain was getting all the crew's help he could to start getting the carrier safely away from the grip of the whirlpool. The ship was starting to get pulled into the spinning waters as it was trying to pull away. Then there was a loud whirring sound as lightning crackled, going up into the vortex in the sky gathering together again, but this time was different then the first causing the whirlpool.

The young swabbie watched in anticipation as he saw the lightning gathering together after hearing the odd sound, then instantly with a flash of light and a very loud peel of thunder he saw a giant blue beam instead of regular white lightning, burst down straight into the whirlpool. As the flash of blue light hit the whirlpool every fish in that vicinity and every person aboard the ship were blasted back, some hitting walls and others almost falling off the ship as they grabbed railings and other parts of the ship. The soldier got up walking towards the railing to see if the whirlpool had come to a halt, but he thought he saw something in the water where the center of the whirlpool was as the mist was starting to clear.

ᴍ ᶫ ᴍᴍ ᴀ ᴍ ᶫ ◇ ᶫ ◇ ℙ ᶫ ᴍ

"Sir, the anomaly began at 1540 hours and ended within what we presume to be seven to nine minutes. But once the anomaly had dissipated we found something in the water."

"Something agent, what do you mean?"

"Well, it's not really a something but more of a someone or at least that's what we thought at first."

"Please do proceed with your report; why isn't this person considered a real person?"

"We can't seem to figure out this man's age or origins?"

"What do you mean you can't figure out his age or origins?! You know today's technology isn't like the crappy radiometric dating they used to use before they realized they were missing variables. You know how accurate it can be."

"Well, his age seems to jump around when we try to get a reading on him and his genetics don't seem linked to any human on the planet."

"Any human?"

"Sir, we don't know how, but you remember the fossils that were found in the Sumerian Ruins in Russia that we have kept from the public back when we raided that terrorist cell last month?"

"Of course, how could anybody forget those ridiculous bones?"

"Somehow this man's DNA seems genetically linked to whatever those things were."

"What is he like?"

"Well he's not that big sir, he is pretty average, actually."

"Mmm…wonder why he isn't like them?"

"I don't know? What should we do with him?"

"You listen here now, and you better listen well. All this info is classified, this whole event is on a need to know basis. What you are going to do is send him to our 357 task force facility until we can figure out where he comes from and what his intentions are."

Tom's parents weren't happy with him because of what happened but they were willing to prove his innocence through another drug test. Although they did notice that in today's society everyone had something messed up in their lives, and anything could be possible. So, Mr. Turner set up an appointment for them to show they raised their kid right.

When Saturday finally came after what seemed like a long week, Tom and his parents drove to the hospital to get a drug test. As they waited to be seen, Tom watched, as all sorts of strange-looking people were coming and going and thought that most of them looked as if they did do drugs. As he was watching, he noticed Tara sitting across the waiting room alone. The second he saw Tara, anger engulfed him. Her bruise looked worse than the day he saw her in the nurse's office. Immediately, Tom got up and walked over to her.

Tara did not tell her parents that it was Justin's fault for her falling down the stairs. She was afraid that telling them would only cause her more trouble with Justin at school. Her explanation was that she tripped on her shoelace and fell down the steps. That's why she was alone at the doctor's office.

Trying to remain calm and not showing his anger, he asked if she was feeling any better. Tara shook her head and said, "No, it still hurts a lot."

Tom had a noticeable look of guilt on his face, which Tara noticed. She said, with a sympathetic voice, "I would never believe you do drugs, Tom, and I don't blame you for what Justin did."

Tom felt happy that somebody believed him, especially over all of the lies that were being spread at school.

Tom then said caringly, "I am sorry for what Justin did to you."

"It is not your fault; I should not have let Justin see my disgust over his cruelty to you."

"Well, did you even tell your parents what he did to you?" Tom said cautiously.

Tara responded anxiously, "No because he might attack me again if I did."

Tom responded encouragingly, "If you don't tell anyone about what he did, he will continue with his crazy assaults and you will always be prone to his attacks just because I am friends with you."

"Tom, you can't blame yourself for how crazy he is. Eventually, he will have to learn to share friends."

"I have an idea. Why don't you tell your parents about how he punched you? That, combined with my testimony of him doing drugs will get him in lots of trouble, maybe even sent to prison."

Tara responded with lots of interest "That would be a great idea. Maybe he won't attack us anymore if we do this."

Just then, the bell rang and the receptionist called Tom's name. It was his turn to see the doctor.

So, he said with relief, "See you later Tara. I hope you feel better."

"I will Tom, thanks".

Tom waved goodbye and walked into the doctor's office. The doctor made him pee in a cup to see what a drug test would prove.

◇ 🏳 🏳 🏳 ＞ △ 🏳 ⅃

When the results came back, the doctor decided to tell him the good news.

"Tom, I have great news you're just as healthy as most young males your age. There is nothing abnormal about you at all from my readings."

"Why did you even come in for a checkup?"

"Well you see, I was arrested last Sunday for doing drugs and I wanted to prove to my parents and hopefully the store that I wouldn't do them."

"Considering your dedication, I think I can help you with that."

"How are you going to do that?"

"Here take this note with you to the place you were applying to prove your innocence and they should let you try reapplying," The doctor said as he handed Tom a note.

"See Mom, see Dad told y'all I would never do drugs."

"We didn't doubt you for a second, Tom, we had a feeling something was off about that previous drug test." Tom's dad said.

"Your father and I will always have faith in you to do what is right."

"Awe, thanks Mom," Tom said as he hugged his parents."

So the doctor's note declared that he is and was drug-free. Tom's parents would also be able to use the document to clear his name with the police. The Turners waved goodbye to the doctor and headed out the door. As they were walking out of the doctor's office, Tom waved good bye to Tara. So she waved back to Tom, the bell rang and Tara was called in to the doctor's office to have her leg examined.

So in the end Justin wasn't able to forgive his father for the emotional pain he had inflicted on him all those years before. This, in turn, caused a major event for Tom trialing his patience as well as his willingness to forgive Justin for hurting the girl he was certain he was falling for. Only time would tell if he would be able to forgive Justin for what he had done. But could Justin even forgive himself for screwing up his only chance at a friendship? Could the mysterious man forgive the military for taking him prisoner for him doing nothing to them? If any of these people wanted to they could rise like eagles above their personal regressions if they chose to. But ultimately forgiveness can be hard…

Chapter 5
Of Life Lessons

The near future
Friday, April 17th, 4:02 P.M.
357 Task Force SoS secure Prison Facility, Sechura Desert, Peru

For forty nights and forty days it was obvious the mysterious man had been locked up for being different compared to other people of this world. He had sported a beard in his time, separated from most of humanity. The unusual man's patience was waning, but clearly he had a plan devised to escape the high security prison. Certain steps of precision would have to be taken to make a clean getaway. Now was the time for freedom and truth.

Cautiously, as one of the guards turned around starting to walk down the pathway to the main door of the hallway cells, the mysterious man pulled a key from his clothes. Quietly he opened his cell door crouching up to the guard. Just as the guard was turning around to check the noise he had the heard the man backhanded his face knocking the guard unconscious.

With passion, he yelled to the prisoners, "Listen up everyone; I know some of you are only here because of things you witnessed the American government doing. As well I know you're all innocent families, so you shouldn't be here. I am going to help release you, but you will need to follow my lead. If we don't work together then we won't be able to get out of here."

The prisoners all cheered the mysterious man on. Quickly, he started opening cell doors helping them out. Logically, either he had talked to these prisoners himself enough to believe their testimonies were true and that they were innocent or he had another source of knowledge telling him that they hadn't really committed crimes worthy of being locked up. Then he guided them to carry the guard to the main hall door so they could use his eye and hand print to open the door.

As soon as the prisoners opened the next door they rushed through to a hall way where two guards were grabbing their guns, smacking them in their faces. This was no time to slow down just because three of the guards were knocked out. Fast paced, some guards came running around the corners of the hall where it split into a T. The prisoners weren't going down without a fight, some just shoved one of the guards down by knocking him on his back; the other guard though was hit with a left hook to the face.

Now that they were out of the picture, some of the prisoners started grabbing their keys and opening the cells of other people who were locked up. But the mysterious man wasn't happy about the fact they were letting almost everyone out. So he spoke up asking them about their reasoning on freeing everybody. One of the prisoners who knew the man told him how their whole village was locked up because of a temple they guarded that had sacred bones of one of the messengers of their god. He told him also how the American government didn't want people to know about these bones or their ancient Sumerian temple way up north, since the Sumerians were thought to only exist in the Middle East.

Because of this news the mysterious man was fully on board for freeing all of the people in that facility. He wasn't going to let innocent people be locked away just for guarding their beliefs; they didn't deserve this kind of treatment just for something they were brought up in through generations that had lived there.

All the prisoners were starting to really fill up the hallways. Some grabbed the most recent knocked out guards and used them to open the doorway to the stairway and elevator shaft which were the same at both ends of the T-shape hallway. Others decided to lock away some of the guards that had previously been knocked out in the hall way in cells, so they couldn't get to them if they woke back up soon.

The mysterious man quickly ran with some of the prisoners up the left shaft's stairway because he thought the elevators could be monitored or remotely turned off and didn't want anything to slow him down from getting out of there. At the top of the stairs on both sides simultaneously the doors busted open as lots of friends and family members quickly ravished the guards, pinning them to the ground and taking their keys to free the prisoners on this level. At the center of this hall was a route to go forward. Finally they might find an exit to this overly protected place.

After taking out all the guards in the new section on the floor they were on, at the front of the middle hallway there was a door and past that door another hall with two rooms on each side of the hall.

Quickly, with haste, the village prisoners raided their facilities of food and weapons. Some grabbed knives and others thought the guns would be useful. Then, just past the two rooms was an opening, much like a giant room for eating food with two doors at the center. With passion, they were finally going to be free after locking the guards up and pressing the gate button to open getting them get out. They all ran out the main door with the mysterious man leading them. Many of the angry, but desperate villagers held guns ready to fire at any oncoming guards that might block them at the gate exit.

But as soon as they ran out the door many of them noticed when they looked forward there was no plane or mountains or any normal outdoor scenery and they heard a loud siren blazing loudly. All they could see was a giant circular wall made of the earth that encompassed all of their surroundings and it was about three hundred feet tall. Their hearts sank with fear wondering how they would get out of there as they stared up at the sun beaming down through the giant chasm on them. None of them were experienced rock climbers.

While they were trying to get a grasp on their surroundings, twenty guards appeared lined up in front of all them at the gate exit ready to take them down. But the guards all just stood there smirking with devious grins like they somehow knew they had the upper hand even though lots of the village prisoners had guns. With anger and resentment, the villagers ran forth pulling each of their triggers but nothing happened at all with their weapons, and then quickly realizing they were useless they threw them down and kept running forward toward freedom.

The guns were a very special kind of gun designed only to work for those who were authorized to use them. All the guards started pulling their triggers as the prisoners were coming towards them, the guns started to whir making crackling noises. Then the villagers were shot instantly as giant bolts of electricity shot forth from the guns blasting some back to the ground making them twitch and faint.

Together, all the prisoners from that one facility built into the circular wall ran forth punching and knocking down the guards grabbing their guns and throwing them far from the guards so they could not use them again. Some took the guards back into the facility opening access to all doors through the main control room on the right side of the main front hall locking them up in cells. While the prisoners were busy with the guards being locked up the mysterious man and some of them started heading out the gate noticing something very strange in the center of the chasm.

One man said to the mysterious man, "What is that thing, a giant fan? Why is there lightning bolts bouncing around on different parts of it?"

"No, I believe they made electro kinetic guns and this whole place is somewhere very far off of the grid of normal civilization. So that giant fan looking thing in the center must be a generator that powers this whole place," Said the mysterious man.

"So we destroy their power source then they won't have any power to recharge their guns?" The fellow prisoner said with a thick Russian accent.

"Well I don't think they need recharging. The noise they made sounded almost like the same kind of noise that is heard when a standing wave of electricity is turned back to normal," Said the mysterious man.

Scratching his head, one of the prisoners said, "I'm not into electrical engineering, could you explain that better?"

"Basically they have one big generator that gives them unlimited wireless electricity to zap us and to power this whole place. But I haven't seen any manual over-ride switches anywhere so even if we get rid of the electricity doesn't mean we can manually over ride doors to get into places," The mysterious man stated.

"Look, the other gates of the other facilities are closed," A prisoner said.

The mysterious man pointed around saying, "They might be, but I will bet you anything there is a control hub in that center building in the middle of the generator, because they wouldn't make it only accessible from the inside only that would be really stupid of them. As well I think we can get out through the giant air conditioning shafts I see in between the walls of the different facilities, I bet they lead up to the surface."

The man nodded in agreement with the mysterious man, but as soon as they tried to walk forwards towards the long bridge that cut across the big generator they could feel themselves starting to get pulled by the suction of the generator. Quickly each individual walking the bridge grabbed the sides really hard making sure they wouldn't get blown away. With lots of anticipation they took hostages near the front door of the generator control building opening the doors to let them in forcefully. Eventually, they took over all of the main control building turning off the lower vent fans to the giant air conditioner vents and opening all the gates one by one taking over a new prisoner facility with each sweep they were building up their army to free them. They opened all gates except for the one guards were located at which also had a helicopter pad.

The truth had to be exposed for the heinous acts of the government that had been done in secret, all in the name of peace and security. A lie had been told to the world. The mysterious man had become more than an anomaly to their knowledge, but as well a crack in the foundation of the way they ran things. Now, if the guards didn't do something soon their whole empire would crumble under distrust of the truth getting out.

▽ ˃ ◇ ▽ ˃ ♔ △ ˃ ▽

Helicopter blades were spinning fast getting ready for a takeoff as the agent who brought in the mysterious man was about to leave for another mission. Quickly, a uniformed soldier ran up to him with vital news.

"Sir, you can leave now if you want, but there has been a giant breech in security, I am telling you this because it was the same facility that is holding our biggest asset. You know the man you brought in that the public can never know about. We are locked into our own facility."

"Don't worry soldier I will take care of him, I have a plan."

The agent signaled the pilot to take him up but not out. Soon enough the helicopter was airborne climbing in altitude. Then the agent decided to take a look around, noticing how many more facilities had been busted into and how many prisoners were escaping. At his nine o'clock view from the helicopter the agent saw that one of the vents had been busted into.

"Pilot, take us over to that vent so I can stop them from escaping." The agent said.

But as soon as the helicopter started moving towards the vent area a bolt of lightning flew past it zapping one of the people trying to climb up the wall. Then another flew from a different direction hitting a person on another part of the giant chasm's wall.

"What if one of those bolts hit us?" The pilot said with concern.

"Don't be so stupid, the lightning is only going after them because they have trackers in them and the computer sees they are getting too high up the wall. Basically, it's a defense mechanism," The agent told the scared pilot.

"All right…if you say so hombre."

"But we need to hurry before one of the important ones in the vent gets zapped, if he is already in there," said the agent.

When the helicopter was just about to hover over the generator, two giant bolts of electricity came flying straight for the chopper. Instantly the alarm to the helicopter went blazing with a sign of turbulence. Apparently the prisoners figured out a way to give them access to the electro kinetic guns. The agent saw that the helicopter was starting to spin out of control and he quickly jumped out the side and opened his chute. As the draft from the generator carried him upward, he watched below him as the helicopter came crashing down quickly colliding with the generator.

The collision started a massive chain reaction of explosions below him, as some of the walls to the different facilities collapsed from the explosions. The agent guided his chute towards the opened vent. Some of the prisoners below were happy the generator was destroyed and they expressed it by raising their fists with joyful cheering. But that happiness was soon taken from them when the agent pulled a gun from his back side. It was a submachine gun of some sort with real bullets and not restricted by anything but his own will.

The agent wasn't happy at all with them, so he started shooting the ground threatening them that if they didn't get out of his way he would shoot them all. So, once he landed, the agent headed quickly through the vent and began running real fast to catch up with the mysterious man shoving through the crowded vent shaft of prisoners. He knew how much was at stake if he didn't catch the one man that mattered most to their cause.

Finally, he reached the top of the air conditioner built into the side of the giant chasm wall of dirt. The agent found that the fan had stopped and the vent wall had been busted open. He stood there thinking briefly. With haste, not to let others escape, he walked over to his left and pulled a giant lever. Immediately, giant slices of metal came crashing down inside the vent blocking all exits and entrances. The agent decided to call somebody on his hollowatch phone.

"Sir, I'm sorry to inform you that the man I brought in has escaped the STF prison with some of the Terrorist, and other prisoners are running around freely, but I trapped quite a few of them in the vents."

"It's alright agent, don't worry we will figure out from our camera footage how they escaped. But also we have intelligence on where they might be heading. I'm sure if you find just one of them you will find him."

"Yes sir, but what about the rest that are running around freely and all the other guards? They wouldn't have been able to kill since they needed them to escape."

"We shall take care of that with our facility failsafe protocol, you just get out of that vent within the next few minutes and try to catch up with the escaped prisoners if you can track them."

"Sir, yes sir."

Clearly the Agent didn't even know these people were not really terrorist; it was just what he was told. Soon as the agent walked off following the footprints in the sand of the Sechura desert the whole chasm started exploding. The whole Special Task Force prison started to implode leaving some trapped under the rubble while others got blown to bits. Some of the villagers died from the collision with the ground as they were blown out the side of the vents from the distance they had fallen. But anybody caught in the vicinity of the failsafe protocol was not going to get out of there alive. All the lives of those poor innocent people were stolen from them. Stolen just for where they were born and the knowledge of their people. For the Government had its own cruel way of dealing with their dirty secrets.

It was a wonderful sunny day, which would clearly be a nice day to celebrate anybody's birthday. But of course it was Tom's birthday, and he was really excited about the party they were going to have later at his house. The possibilities of being sixteen, he could finally get his license to drive a car or even have a better chance at a job than he would have even at fifteen.

Tom was so excited by these ideals that he sat there staring out the window of the classroom at the nice weather and not paying attention to the teacher. So the teacher got mad trying to confront Tom about his poor etiquette thinking he might be embarrassed, but he wasn't one for getting upset over a teacher making a joke of him just because he was daydreaming. He told the teacher & class how he was sorry for daydreaming but he was just really happy that today was his birthday.

"Well Tom, just because it's your birthday today doesn't mean you can slack off." The teacher said with authority in her voice.

"Yes mam, I understand."

"I will let you off with a warning, but you better get your act together and stick with the program and not your fantasies."

Not wanting to cause any confrontation with the teacher, Tom nodded in agreement as he sat up straight and gave all his focus to the lesson instead of his whimsical ideas that made him capricious in the first place. Even though his teacher thought he had bad etiquette, he considered himself to be a man of good decorum which is the reason why he invited all of his friends to his birthday party. Well all of them except for Justin...

Just as Tom had been busy day dreaming in school, Justin was somewhat in the same kind of mindset; very upset by the fact that police had showed up to arrest him in the drug trial room. Justin had to take the drug test again because Tom had taken a note to the store getting them to reevaluate who really was doing drugs. Now he was going to have a court trial because he did drugs and for the fact he assaulted Tara and her parents reported it to the police after she finally admitted it to them once she had talked to Tom.

Very disgruntled by all that had taken place, Justin sat there in class concerned about his court date on the upcoming Saturday in two weeks. But Justin, sat pondering why neither the employees at SpotOn nor the police officers that arrested him bothered to tell him why he was called in for the drug test again. A sinister warped but true thought began to emerge in Justin's mind. He had an epiphany that obviously they wanted a do over because Tom must have proven himself innocent.

Now Justin was starting to look past his despair of losing Tom as friend, beginning to think of how much he betrayed him by making the police look at him like a criminal. How arrogant could he be to think that he wasn't guilty? He knew that he was the one responsible for doing the drugs to feel better about always being down, with no father figure. Just because he was guilty didn't mean he thought he should be in trouble for it. Justin truly felt Tom should have gotten the blame, he was thinking to himself.

"If I was spared through a miracle, why should Tom try to go around altering what was meant to be?" He thought to himself.

"You know it isn't right how he interfered with you." His conscious spoke to him or what he considered his conscious.

"That's right I am going to teach Tom a lesson he will never forget. Thomas Turner will get the Justice he deserves for what he has done!"

"That's right; make him suffer like he never has before."

"He doesn't know the pain I have been through, always having a perfect family who cares about him."

One of Justin's classmates had been watching him as his disposition went from a look of despair to a very angry looking facial expression of revenge. Justin began to formulate a plan that eventually might pay off. But soon enough, he realized his plan might depend on if he was in or out of jail.

Getting tired of waiting for school to end, he sat there waiting for the rest of the day. Eventually the school day was over for him, so he went home to relax and think things over. Justin didn't know anything about it because he wasn't invited, but Tom still had some fun to come.

The near future
Friday, April 10th, 9:07 P.M.
Tom's house, Smithsonian Valley, Texas

Just as Tom had hoped, his day did got much more exciting later. When he got home, his mother had a party put together in celebration of his birthday. She invited Benny's family, Tara's whole family (since John was dating Christie, Tara's older sister) and many of Tom's other friends from school. It was lots of fun for all of them; there was music, video games, board games along with some interesting activities and lots of appetizers with many kinds of snacks and drinks.

There was no doubt, Tom couldn't have asked for a better birthday party. Not one person got bored with all the things to do. Some of his friends brought gifts right up to him face to face. Tom, being a decent man showed them great thanks for their gifts. He was having so much fun with everyone, but the night was getting late. Then, Tom's father had something important to say.

"Thank you everybody for coming here tonight to express how much you all care about my son. Even though tonight is about Tom, I would like to express not only is he a shining example of what a good son could be but his brothers and sisters are shining examples too. The way some of them have matured from the silly children they once were would make any father proud. Because of this my wife and I have agreed to express our gratitude of this wonderful gift of children by returning to them a wonderful gift."

Tom's dad then handed him an envelope. It became suspenseful because his mind had just quickly engaged his curiosity thinking what this could be. So he grabbed the nearby letter opener, opening the envelope. To his amazement once he opened it, he found many plane tickets to England. In that moment his face lit up with excitement that clearly proved this was the perfect birthday for him.

"Oh boy, thanks Mom, thanks Dad! So are we leaving soon?"

"As soon as school finishes and John graduates. We already arranged it with your mother's restaurant and my office." Tom's dad said kindly.

"I can't wait! We are going to England! Are we going to be staying at the property from those deeds I found?"

"We sure are." His father said with enthusiasm.

Nothing could express how grateful Tom felt for this moment. They all gathered together to sing happy birthday to Tom, then he blew out the candles on his cake. After his father finished cutting Tom and Tara a slice of cake, he decided to go eat his cake with Tara on the stairs in the living room.

"So are you enjoying your birthday?" Tara said nervously.

"Yes it's been a really great one. But I have been feeling guilty lately."

"Oh yeah, why is that?"

"Well, please don't be too upset, but listen, I want you to know I love spending time with you, it's just I'm a risk to be around, so I have been avoiding you. But, I also have been avoiding Justin too."

Tara giggled and said, "You don't have to act like it's a big secret Tom. I think it was pretty obvious you felt responsible for what Justin did to me. But you don't need to go around acting like a clichéd movie character just because he hurt me and avoid me, you know? Besides I can take pretty good care of myself."

"Wow that feels like a load off my shoulders," said Tom.

"See, you have nothing to worry about. Sadly though we won't have too much time to hang out during the summer, because of your trip and because we are leaving for our own vacation the day after my sister graduates."

"Oh, yeah where are you going?" Tom said.

"The Smokey Mountains so we can camp in a cooler environment."

"Well that should be nice and fun. Plus, Texas is a pretty hot place to camp depending on where you're camping."

"I hope it's fun, but I know I will miss hanging out with you and my friends. Our area is okay for camping but, it's too familiar to us."

"At least it isn't crazy hot like west Texas during the summer time. Yeah, I think I will miss you and my friends as well. But I'm sure you will have lots of fun no matter what. Family vacations are very fun to go on."

Then Tom's little brother Martin walked up holding a stuffed teddy bear in his arms; with his innocent childlike disposition he tugged on Tom's pants trying to get his attention. Tara motioned her eyes towards Martin so Tom would see what he wanted.

"Hey Martin, did you want something?"

"Yeah, mmm…Tom is it true we will be gone from home and I won't see my friends ever again or Jessica?"

Martin asked this because of how much he would miss his friends and coloring with them.

"No silly, we are just going to be gone for the summertime only. Once school is about to start again we might return then. But we will be together as a family and Jessica will be here waiting for our return. Plus, even though your friends will all be here you might make some new friends."

"Yay, I hope they love to draw also!" Martin said as he ran off all excited.

"Awe your little brother is so cute Tom." Tara said as she blushed.

"Yeah, Martin is a wonderful little brother. He isn't like the way my friends at school describe their brothers. What

I would give to be innocent minded like him not knowing how messed up some people or even the world can be."

"Who knows, maybe someday we will somehow get that feeling back. But speaking of messed up things, how you feel about Justin? You said you have been avoiding him also."

"I don't want to fight with him anymore so I have been trying not to get near him when school gets out. I tried to be his friend and then he had to go nuts on you and that one kid who kept taunting him. Life lessons are hard but they can make us better people or worse and to me it looks like Justin's have made him a lonely monster that can't trust anybody."

"Sorry Tom, I think I get how you feel. You tried to be there for him and that's all that matters."

"I know you're right. Hopefully things will get better for him and he will learn from his life lessons for once, so maybe he can see that he does have a purpose in life beyond being cruel to others. I am trying hard to learn my own life lesson by trying to forgive Justin of what he did to you."

"You're still stuck on that? Just forgive him and move on. Come on Tom, let's quit with the drama and go hang out with everyone else," Tara said inspiringly.

As they were all just hanging out talking, Benny asked Tom about that job he applied for. Tom told Benny that he did not want to accept it because he thought they might be gone for the summer. His thought was if he was going to be spending all his time at their property in England, why get a job at that point. Benny pointed out though that strategy was a pretty big gamble and Tom was lucky that it turned out good for him. Tom then noticed John talking to Christie and smiling.

"Did you know they are going to prom together?" Tara said to Tom.

"They are, wow, I had no idea. I mean I knew they were dating, but the thought of prom never crossed my mind."

"I wonder if we will ever have prom someday? Well I mean I'm not like one of those superficial girls who gets all obsessed with prom, I just would like to someday share at least one slow dance with somebody I can truly love."

"Believe me I know the feeling. That would be a really great experience. Who knows maybe we both will get an experience like that next year or the year after? Yeah, but tomorrow I am trying to get my driver's license."

"Hope that goes well for you."

It was getting late so many people decided to start heading home from Tom's great birthday party. Tom determined that with the way everything had worked out, that this was one of the best birthdays of his life. Now that he felt sorry for Justin, he no longer wanted to hit him with a baseball bat or to even fight him as he had told Tara.

In the end Tom had to learn life lessons on not fighting revengefully when angry and learning to forgive others when they hurt you or somebody you care about. Justin though had revenge in his heart, wanting to teach Tom a lesson because he was mad that he had gotten him in trouble. Justin didn't learn a life lesson how he should just put his past behind him and be friends with Tom. The mysterious man learned a hard life lesson of freedom and how it always comes at a price. But most importantly, the mysterious man had learned the hard life lesson that not all governments could be trusted or were justified in what they were doing.

The near future
Sunday, May 31ˢᵗ, 6:08 A.M.
SAT airport, SanAntonio, Texas

As the Turners arrived at the airport, they all said their goodbyes to Jessica as she was dropping them off, and scurried on into the terminal with haste. Most were still tired from the early wake up they had just endured, but they were quickly obtaining awareness the more each of them moved into the terminal trying to keep up with each other. They were in a rush because they only had twenty two minutes till their flight was scheduled to leave.

Coming into the terminal they turned to their right heading to the luggage storage counter, so they could make their bags checked-in for departure. The lady at the counter grabbed all of their bags putting the luggage on the conveyer belt. They watched, as all of the luggage was whisked away under the black folds, hoping they would see it again when they got off the airplane.

Quickly they paced towards the security area. But Tom was busy thinking about how he saw Tara leaving for the beautiful Smokey Mountains not too long before that moment when they were leaving their house. He also recollected about seeing Justin on a prison bus as they departed their neighborhood. Even though their friendship was ephemeral, Tom felt guilty for the way things ended with them. He was angry from the pain he remembered feeling in his face from his previous encounter with Justin.

The security area was full of guards which looked very tense. Everyone had to remove their shoes and put all the items they had in the little black plastic bins to be checked for any inconsistencies. The bins full of people's belongings moved along down the conveyor belt to be scanned by a big machine as they passed through it. While their items were scanned, each member of the Turner family had to pass through a machine themselves that would use x-rays along with lasers and sound wave technology to scan them. Pretty quick, each of them passed through the screening without a hitch.

Even though they were past security being cleared to go ahead, the intensity was still with them to be at the gate on time. The Turner's headed toward their departure gate. Tom and his family had to wait at the gate listening for their seats to be called so they could board the plane. While they waited, Tom observed all sorts of different people walking by him and his family. Some of them were wearing clothes that looked like they were from other countries. Although there were lots of people passing them, standing in the terminal's hall was one man who looked at Tom and gave him an odd look as if there was something familiar about Tom to him. Tom felt strange about the look the man gave him. Very soon, Tom and his family's seats were called so all of them boarded the jet that would take them to England.

Tom decided to sit down by the window while in one set of seats in front of him Martin sat in between his parents. John just decided to sit in the seat next to the isle leaving some space between he and Tom in case another guest didn't book the seat in the middle of them.

Now that Tom was settled, he started watching the long line of people boarding the plane. Among the people getting on the plane were a few strange-looking men wearing strange coloured cowboy hats. He thought that their skin color was way too pale for cowboys. But thinking about them more, Tom reminded himself that cowboys were outside a lot in the sun, so he figured they must have been tourists from up north coming to Texas. To him, there was something different about the men in his mind.

Since he was starting to think a bunch, Tom wanted to cut himself off from the outside world while he was thinking about things. He pulled out his wireless ear buds and plugged in their link to his hollowatch phone as he stared off at the beautiful scenery past the airport as he looked out the window. One thought about Justin came to his mind after touching his face where he was bruised; Tom remembered how he had a fight not long ago on May 04th, wondering if his bruise was still there. Justin was really mad at Tom being part of the reason he had to go to a juvenile prison camp for the summer, so he kicked Tom to the ground, pulling him by the hair smacking Tom's face into the dirt. But Tom only felt sorry for how lost Justin was. He had hoped that someday he could learn to properly defend himself in these situations, but that day hadn't come yet for him.

Now that everyone was seated, a flight attendant started showing them what had to be done in case of emergencies. The plane started to move and go slowly making turns at the airport taxying to the runway. After a few minutes, the plane accelerated tremendously causing Tom to look out the window. The ground was moving by so fast. As he sat there mesmerized by the ground rushing by, he felt the nose of the plane tilt upward as it lifted off of the ground. Things on the ground quickly got smaller and smaller, as the jet soared in to the sky Tom wondered where Justin was going on that Bus he saw leaving the neighborhood earlier.

As his bus approached the maglev station, Justin sat there staring out the window thinking about how pitiful his life had become. But as the bus came to a halt he had an epiphany along with a change in attitude. Justin knew he was going to be stuck at Prison Camp for the summer because of what Tom & Tara did, so he figured he should make the best of what he had been dealt in life devising a plan to get back at Tom for what he had done.

The bus driver walked up to put handcuffs on the chain link she was caring and place onto Justin's pair to connect him with the others to be moved to the maglev train. Noticing Justin looked too happy and content with the situation she asked "What's wrong with you child, you are going to prison for summer why you so happy?"

"I'm happy because I will be with my own kind there. Besides what does it matter to you? You dumb old bat!"

"Boy you're lucky it's illegal to physically abuse you because you're a minor, because if it wasn't I would of knocked you out cold right now for what you just said."

"Leave me alone; you're ruining my mood."

Then the bus lady continued on transferring the other teens handcuffs to the chainlink. Once the bus driver was done connecting them, she tapped the back window signaling for the guard up front to guide them all out for transfer. One by one all connected the teens who had committed different but similar crimes. They started walking in formation following the guidelines of the three guards that were there to get them to the prison camp.

All of them entered the maglev station guided up a ramp which led to the back of a magnetic hovering train. Justin felt like this might be something exhilarating maybe even similar to going on a roller-coaster at a theme park, much like he did when he was little. His mother had taken him there not too long after his father had left them thinking it would make him feel better & happier, but the sad truth was and still is money couldn't buy Justin or anybody else love after being abandoned.

He thought about his father leaving them again and his mood went from happy to kind of resentful as he along with the other teens got onto the maglev train. Tom's influence still affected him to the point he figured he should stop dwelling on the past and just pursue the future which ironically was analyzing a plan to hurt the very person who gave him advice to move on. Justin sat down in his assigned seat with a smirk on his face because of what he was thinking about, which were ways to hurt Tom.

Each of the three guards went from teen to teen removing the middle chain connecting them to the long chain link and attaching the middle chain connected to their cuffs onto a metal beam in front of them on the back of each seat. The main guard stood got in the middle at the front of their prison transfer boxcar to give them some advice.

"Okay, listen up kids. Each of you knows exactly why you are here. But because this is a public train we aren't permitted to take any of you to the front cars for any reason. If one of you needs to go to the bathroom then request it and one of us will guide you to the lavatory. None of you are allowed out of your seats to move around like other people on the train. This is why you are chained to the seats in front of you. In case of an accident you must be ready to swiftly be put on the chain link again. If there is any attempt to run if there is an accident you will be held accountable in the court of law and most likely sentenced to further imprisonment."

All of them nodded in agreement at what the guard said. Justin sat there turning his head, looking out the window thinking about how he wanted freedom from being stuck there. Then he gave some thought to his ideas on how to make Tom pay for putting him there.

"Maybe, if I hurt Tara some that will get him to hurt more since he loves her more than anything else."

"Yes, that would be great!" He told himself.

"How could he betray me like that!? He said we would be friends not enemies.

"Maybe you should have kept beating him up. You know you shouldn't have put your trust in anybody." He thought to himself.

"Someday I will find a friend who actually cares about me, even if it wasn't meant to be Tom."

"Maybe I will find somebody to help me take care of him to teach him a lesson of how he shouldn't have played with my emotions like dad did."

"It doesn't matter where I take this road or track, I won't let myself be hurt anymore by those selfish jerks anymore. Even if I don't trust Tom anymore, I definitely still believe some of the advice he gave me was worthwhile on getting over things. Things will get better."

All of a sudden Justin felt exhilarated by the inertia from the momentum of the maglev train zipping off really fast, almost like a bullet. Because he was so deep in thought about things, he didn't even anticipate this rush he got from the train. It was certain though that he was enjoying it and was not letting himself be overcome with fear any more but just turning what he considered betrayals into anger.

ㄴ△ᙏᙏᏩᙏ◇ᙏㄴ

Tom felt odd, like something was not right as he opened his eyes. Seeing a long dark hall with dim lights, he got really confused. Where was he? The last thing he remembered was sitting in the chair on the airplane. Even though he was lost, Tom decided the best thing was to find an exit to this place, so he started moving forward down the hall. At the end of the hall was a door so he went through it to the next room.

Entering the room he got a creepy vibe. It was cold & dark with very little light. Tom saw a chair to sit down in and a glass panel on a desk like surface. He sat down grabbing the telephone he saw on the table to his right. On the other end of the phone line was Justin. As he heard Justin's voice on the phone, he looked up seeing Justin sitting in a prison suit, behind the glass window, with a creepy smirk on his face.

Justin screamed with rage and anger, "I will kill you! I will slaughter you making you wish you were never born! You're going to die, Turner!"

Tom woke up panting & sweating with a fear filled look on his face. Tom was concerned about it for a moment but then realized it was all just a scary nightmare and that there was really nothing that he should worry about. After all, it was just a dream, wasn't it?

"Tom, are you alright?" John said to him with a concerned tone.

"Yeah, I am fine why?"

"Because you were talking in your sleep and your hands were even moving around shaking some."

"Just having a night mare; nothing to be too concerned about."

"Must have been a real scary one."

"Yeah it was."

Tom had an affinity for falling asleep in moving vehicles, whether they were airplanes or cars, but not in boats for some reason. Now, he was very much awake, as he noticed over the seat in front of him his Dad watching cartoons with Martin. A flight attendant walked by, but Tom was still thirsty from waking up panting, so he asked her for some water.

A few minutes later the attendant returned with some water for Tom and said, "Since you were a sleep I didn't want to wake you, but everyone else has been served their complimentary meals. Would you like one?"

"Mmm…what do you have to eat mam?"

"Well, we have chicken with smashed potatoes & okra along with your choice of a drink and we also have fish & chips with your choice of drink as well."

"Could I please have the fish and chips meal with a glass of banana mint soda." Tom sat back and reflected that from childhood banana mint soda had always made him feel good.

"Okay, give me a moment and I will go get that for you."

Then, as the flight attendant was walking away to get Tom's food, Martin reached out grabbing her, and wanted to ask her something.

"Yes young man, what do you need?"

"Can my Mommy help you make cookies for everyone? She makes the best cookies in the world."

"Sorry, but your mother is not allowed to help me cook. It's against flight regulations due to fears of terrorism."

"It's okay, I understand." Mrs. Turner responded with a wink.

"Sorry, your mother can't cook with us. I am sure her cooking would have been great though,"

"It's alright; you have nothing to apologize for. I understand the times are tough and there are reasons to limit people." Mrs. Turner said.

"Awe...thanks. You're such an understanding person. Anyway, sorry for cutting you off, but I need to get back to work."

"It's okay, see you later."

Then the flight attendant walked off.

Martin asked, "Mommy why can't you cook and make your great cookies for everyone, and what are terrorist?"

"Well, sometimes there are bad people that want to do bad things to other people and that scares others into not trusting anybody."

Martin crossed his little arms showing a disgusted look on his face as he sat there quietly thinking as he watched cartoons with their father. Then the flight attendant brought Tom his food. He ate his meal and went back to listening to his music as the flight continued.

About half an hour later, which was about two hours into their three and half hour flight, Tom saw land off in the distance. Upon noticing the land and clouds pass below him, Tom dreamed of how cool it would be if he could fly along outside the plane with no attachments. Or just how amazing it would be to fly like that at all. He wondered how it would feel to do such things.

Then Tom noticed that the flight attendant, who brought him his food, offered some cookies to Martin to compensate for not letting his mother bake cookies. Of course, Tom's parents tried to raise Martin well, so he thanked her kindly for the cookies (even though he would have preferred some from his mother). Seeing Martin acting somewhat more mature than he normally did, gave Tom that warm feeling of brotherly love of being proud, thinking Martin might turn out to be a decent person after all. Then he noticed many of the other flight attendants were going around getting requests for snacks and delivering snacks to others on the flight.

Kindly, the flight attendant who was helping their family asked Tom what he wanted. He wasn't that hungry because he had some food about forty five minutes prior, but he asked for some cookies & peanuts with milk like Martin was given. Then, he asked John if he could read some of the comics he brought with him.

For nearly an hour, Tom read John's comics, occasionally playing some of his games on John's portable game system. But then he felt like he needed to go the bathroom. Not a minute after thinking about it one of the flight attendants got on the intercom to tell everyone that they were about to land in England and that this might be their last chance to use the bathroom before landing.

Tom thought to himself, "How cliché that I have to go the moment she tells us this is our last chance. Guess I will never escape the predictable moments in life."

Quickly, Tom got up, moving passed John hurrying to the lavatory. As he got there he saw one man waiting at the door already. It was one of the strange cowboy-looking men (the ones that he had noticed earlier wearing strange cowboy like clothes) standing there. He noticed Tom had to go, so he motioned towards Tom to go up ahead of him. Then the door opened and one of the other cowboy guys came out of the lavatory allowing Tom to rush in.

After relieving himself, Tom came out of the bathroom noticing more of the cowboy people lining up to go to the bathroom. All of them were at different bathrooms throughout the plane. They had to be the strangest group of tourists he had ever seen. To him, their clothes did not look like they were from England or the U.S.

because he had never seen cowboy clothes that looked so odd. If anything, they looked like their clothes came from Mexico because some were the color of salmon.

As Tom was heading back to his seat, he noticed the cowboys going one by one, in and out of the bathrooms. Then, he noticed them starting to talk in a language that no one understood except some guy sitting in the back.

Then, in one brief moment, they pulled out knives and started stabbing and shanking the flight attendant and other passengers. One ran up and stabbed Tom's mom in her side. They did not stab all of the flight attendants. Tom saw this and quickly got out of his seat pushing past John, rushing at the terrorists.

One of the terrorists threw a knife at him. But Tom dodged it by diving into a seat he was passing. His dad came after the terrorist that had thrown the knife at Tom. Tom's dad grabbed the terrorist using him as a shield against another one of the terrorists throwing knives at him.

Tom chased another terrorist, who dropped his knife, and started punching him. Tom's dad joined him in trying to take the terrorist down. Coming from the back of the plane, the guy who recognized the language spoken by the terrorists, came running down the aisle, pulled out a gun, and shot the terrorist that was fighting with Tom and his dad. When they heard the gun shot, both Tom and his dad grabbed the terrorist they were punching.

One of the flight attendants, seeing the terrorist fall to the ground, jumped up and pulled out a rope from one of the overhead storage bins. As Tom and his dad held the terrorist, the flight attendant proceeded to tie him up. The agent wasn't done yet. As he turned around, he saw a knife hurling at him. He quickly dodged the knife and shot the attacker. The terrorist, seeing the gun being raised, attempted to grab a passenger. However, before he could hide behind the passenger, the agent shot him.

The agent saw the last terrorist, who looked like he was in his fifties, running towards the door of the plane. The terrorist was climbing over seats, stabbing passengers as he headed towards the door. The terrorist read the door looking back at the agent down the aisle. Fortunately for those on the plane, the terrorist couldn't read English very well and was unable to figure out how to open the door. The agent came up to him with the gun pointed right, at him yelled, "Stop where you are right now!"

"No matter how much your government tries to suppress the truth, eventually the truth will be set free upon the world and then we will be remembered as martyrs for your corrupt actions! You shall pay for what you have done to us!"

"I know you're a terrorist and you have committed heinous acts all in the name of your misleading religion. So don't try to make me think otherwise, if you have any intelligence at all you will surrender peacefully right now."

"Is that what they told you? That we are murderers over our beliefs? Look at the people on this plane, I chose not to murder them but only stab them so they wouldn't die because violence for violence is not the answer. But what your people did to my village was horrible. There is nothing peaceful about surrendering to monsters; I will not go down without fighting for my freedom!"

"Your village was a terrorist cell! All my info is valid from intelligence gathered by the CIA of the United States of America." the agent yelled.

Then the terrorist ran straight at the agent with his knife drawn, trying to plunge it into him as he was shot to the ground by the agent who fought for his country in the name of protection and peace.

The agent was telling one of the flight attendants how the American government was watching all planes going to England. This program was started since terrorists were carrying out bombing attacks in England. The uninjured flight attendants began getting blankets and wrapping up anyone who had been stabbed. Meanwhile, Tom and his dad hurried over to his mom who was already looking very pale. While checking on his mom, Tom sensed that the plane was starting to fall with exceeding speed. He looked out the window, determining that the plane was definitely falling towards the rising mist of England.

Up in the front of the plane, one of the flight attendants went into the cockpit and discovered that the pilot and his copilot had been accidently shot, and the autopilot box had been pierced by the bullet as well. No one was flying the plane. She hurried back into the cabin asking if there was anyone onboard who could fly a plane. The agent said that he used to play flight simulators when he was younger while standing next to Mr. Turner.

"Sir, I might need your help pulling the yoke," The agent said to Tom's dad.

Both the agent and Tom's dad went up to the cockpit, where they quickly removed the dead bodies of the flight crew. Both Mr. Turner and the agent familiarized themselves with the cockpit to quickly get the plane under control. "Sir quick, pull back now!" The agent yelled so they could get the vessel stable, as the pressure proved to be too much for one man to handle. With the help of air traffic control, they were able to get the plane lined up with the correct runway so they could land the plane safely in the great mist of England.

As the plane came to a stop out on the tarmac, one of the flight attendants rushed over to the door to open it. Immediately, as the door opened, the inflatable slide popped out, and she slid down to the ground to help passengers as they exited the plane.

Within five minutes, the plane was surrounded by police, emergency workers, and medics. The first priority was to get medical help for the passengers & crew that needed attention. While this was occurring, the police were busy arresting the terrorists that were still alive. It wasn't long before the news crews were there to interview survivors so they could broadcast what had happened. The stories were recorded by many different people. One woman reporter, with an accent he wasn't fully able to understand at first, asked Tom what provoked him to go after the terrorist? Tom responded with, "How would you feel if you saw your mother stabbed?"

The news reporter looked like she felt sorry for Tom. She asked Tom's dad the very same thing.

He replied, "This boy's mother is my wife, and I love her dearly and with all my heart."

The reporter then said, "Your family is brave to do what most people would not do."

Tom's dad said, "Thanks, but I am sure we did just what any other family would do in a moment of fear."

So Tom's family was shown on the news across the world for all to see. After relaxing for a moment, Tom wondered how Tara was doing on her road trip.

$$> \triangle \, \square \, \Diamond \, \text{凶} \, \triangle$$

It had only been four hours since Tara's family had left their house so they were not even out of Texas yet. They were just entering Dallas which has pretty bad traffic no matter what time of day you are traveling through. To avoid looking at all the chaotic traffic Tara was watching the news on the TV on the back of her father's seat. Seeing Tom on the news she was a little shocked at first, but very grateful that Tom had survived the terrorist attack.

After hearing what Tom said, she said to her parents "Tom is a brave boy."

Tara's mom said, "Isn't he the boy across the street?"

"Yes he is and he goes to my school, also. He's the one I went to his little brother's game." Tara said as she blushed at seeing Tom on TV.

Tara wasn't the only one to see Tom as she was traveling across country like Tom was. Other people were noticing what was going on with Tom on the news as well.

∀ △ > ∀ ⌊ ∿ ⩜

Justin stepped off a bus with the same number as the one he had gotten off of back in Texas that they had been transferred to once their maglev train reached its destination. The prison camp looked like a pretty big facility. It sure wasn't appealing for a new place to live even for a few months. Having just arrived at the camp, they made all the kids head through the big main door entrance. As they headed forward walking down the hallway in handcuffs, Justin caught a glimpse of a TV and Tom's face just happened to be on the screen. Justin said out loud, "That idiot always fights with people he shouldn't be standing up to."

The guy in front of him said, "You know him?"

"Yeah, I know him. He is the reason I am here."

"Are we not here because of our own actions?"

Justin replied with anger and fury, "Shut up; don't get smart with me you fool!"

The guards continued to herd them to their rooms. The rooms were more like jail cells with bars. Justin surely didn't like the feel of this place; still he would have to deal with it. He didn't like how he would have to deal with all these cop figures and then have nothing to make him feel happy temporarily, like the drugs he'd used and had gotten him here. But he felt he might make some friends.

Later, after Tom's mom was secured safely at a hospital passed out, Mr. Turner rented a car. The police had asked them to come by the station nearby. When Tom and his family walked into the police station, he saw people in hand cuffs and wondered if all these people were terrorists. He reasoned with himself that, no, not all of them were terrorists.

Many of them were handcuffed with bruises, tattoos, and even some looking like they were drugged. More than likely, they probably weren't terrorists; they just didn't look like the men he had seen on the plane.

As Tom walked down the hall of the police station, he saw the knives that the terrorist had used and the cowboy hats that the terrorist had worn. These things were all displayed on a table. Through a window, Tom saw the two terrorists that had survived. One of the officers asked Tom's dad if his wife was okay.

Mr. Turner said, "At first the doctors weren't sure if she would make it from her blood loss. She was having some cardiac arrest, but it seems they got her under control now. So we aren't sure how it will turn out for her, but hopefully she will make it."

Then Tom asked, "Why do you want our family here?"

"We wanted to explain how the terrorists pulled off all the stuff they did. And, we wanted to show our gratitude more on a personal level since we couldn't at the airport."

Even though Tom didn't understand them well because of their thick accents, he and his family sat down in some not too comfy chairs to listen. The officer said, "Look at this knife."

It was sort of round and slightly bent. The officer pointed out how their hats could easily hold a knife since they were rounded. "See these hats. They're round which makes them perfect for slipping in a knife. He proceeded to warn them that the terrorists might come after you for revenge."

Then one of the other officers said, "That is where agent Sizer comes in handy."

"Yeah, he will be here in a minute. Please just wait right here for him."

The officers left the room while the Turners waited for the agent to come in.

A minute later, the door opened, and the agent, from the plane, came in and said, "Hello! My name is agent Dale Sizer." He had an American accent like Tom's family… not at all English-sounding like the other officers.

Then, agent Sizer said with a mellow look on his face, "But it's okay for you to call me Dale. For your protection, I have been assigned to protect your family while you are at your home here in England… if that is okay with y'all?"

Tom's dad responded, "Yes, I think that would be a great idea considering the circumstances."

The rest of the family all agreed this was okay with them.

Agent Dale then said, "The two of you did not look like you were trained for protection against those terrorist. I know a place for you, along with your kids to train outside of London in a town called Bexley Ledger if you would like to learn more about how to protect yourself and your family. Would that be of any interest to you?"

"Yes, that could help if there ever is another scenario like this again. But, I probably won't join you or the kids there," Said Mr. Turner.

Tom thought to himself this might come in handy against Justin.

Tom said, "Yeah, that would be great."

"Okay, tomorrow I will come to your property to take you to your training," Said Agent Dale.

Then, Tom's family got up and went out into the main office.

While Tom and his family walked to the main office, agent Dale asked the officer, "What will be done to the terrorists?"

The officer replied, "I will arrange for the dead ones to be sent back to their home countries."

"What about the living one's?"

"We will get answers out of them and then decide what to do with them in a couple of days."

Agent Dale left the office, got in his rental car, and drove to a hotel nearby. Tom went with his family to their rental car and headed for the cabin they owned out in the countryside. While they were driving, Tom's dad said, with some concern in his voice and thinking the house would be dirty, "Boys we are going to want the cabin to look good for your mother, when she gets out of the hospital. So we are going to stop and get some cleaning utensils, okay?"

So, they stopped at what looked like any old regular retail store back in the states. The store was called Tesco's. When they got out and went inside, they noticed Tesco's was just like the big retail stores on every corner in America. Mr. Turner bought cleaning items and some food, then checked out with John and Martin by his side.

Once the Turners were done shopping, they drove south for about thirty minutes. Their route took them by Stone Henge. Tom wished they had time to stop and see more of it. But, everyone was ready to get to the cabin. It only took another thirty minutes to arrive. The cabin looked like it was right out of a fairy tale. Built of wood with a stone fireplace, it was very interesting. Tom wondered what kind of place this would be to stay at and if his mother would be alright or get better any time soon. He was also wondering what Justin was up to…

So, in the end, each group may have come to conclusions with their transits and some may have still been traveling, but no matter what each of them thought, they were on their way to new things in life. Tom may have felt some things were cliché on the airline, but he still loved the new aspect of being in a country he had never been to before. Justin didn't like where he ended up, but figured he might make some new friends in this place filled with people just like him. Each of their lives would now begin a-new in the transitions they had made across the globe.

Chapter 7
The Cabin

The Near Future
Sunday, May 31ˢᵗ, 5:05 P.M.
On the outskirts of Brighton, West Sussex, England

The Turners arrived at their inherited cabin which looked like an old cabin made of ancient yew wood. It had a nostalgic feel to it, like it could be something out of a fairy tale. Full of peace & serenity, it was like a dream. Not only just calm but also it had that creepy vibe to it. The kind of feeling that one might feel while visiting a grave yard on a misty, foggy evening.

They walked inside to find the cabin full of dust, spider webs and, dirt. Clearly the Turners thought that it could use some freshening and cleansing. It wasn't exactly how one might want to live, considering how long they were planning to stay there for the summer.

Tom's dad then said "Okay, honey you are going to stay here with John and Martin, while me and Tom go see if this place I found called Stronger Walls is still open or willing to come work on our cabin today."

"That sounds like a good plan, don't worry I will make good use of the kids to help clean up the place while y'all are gone."

"Tom, is that all right with you?" His dad said.

Tom responded excitingly "Sure it would be nice to get a lay out of the town we will be training at."

"Alright, let's get going then. Bet they won't be willing to work once it gets dark here."

So, the two of them set off on their family adventure driving towards Bexley Ledger to get to Stronger Walls. It took them a good hour of driving to get there. It didn't matter how long the trip took since the scenery was gorgeous. In Tom's eyes, England turned out to be really appealing to him. He hoped the appeal of this place might last since they were going to be there a long time.

"Tom I wanted you to come with me for more than just travel or protection. His dad said, "I wanted to know if you were okay from what happened on the airplane? But I didn't want to stir up any negative emotions within the rest of the family by asking you in front of them."

"Yeah, I'm fine. It was just scary, as well it really angered me seeing them stab mom like they did. In a way, I feel like if I hadn't had some of the fights at school I have then I wouldn't have been able to take on the terrorists."

"What fights at school?" his dad said concerned.

"Well that one guy named Justin, who somehow framed me. He has been mad at me for years because of something I said when we were younger, but he was even madder because the night I hurt his feelings, his father left him. Justin had a grudge against me for so long because the two memories were connected."

"Well, Tom I'm proud of you for taking on those terrorists even when it seemed they had the upper hand. It's a shame the world we live in today has people fighting over their beliefs not letting others believe what they want to believe. And fathers abandoning the kids they helped give birth to. I guess our family truly is an anomaly in today's society."

Tom was feeling really sentimental from what his dad just said. "I totally agree with what you said. But at the same time I don't think those terrorists were fighting for their beliefs."

"What you mean?" Tom's dad said with confusion.

"Well I ran up to agent Dale on the plane when he was taking care of the last terrorist and to me it seemed like the terrorist was trying to make agent Dale understand that they weren't really criminals, but the he (the terrorist) came from a village that our country attacked in secret or something like that. It sounded like he wanted the world to know the truth of what our country had done to his people. I don't think agent Dale even knew about that though, from the way he reacted to what the terrorist said."

"Well, that makes you think about them in a whole new way. Regardless though, if they were trying to show the truth to world they weren't doing it the right way by causing pain & suffering to people and high jacking a plane stabbing people that had nothing to do with them."

"You're right, but why would our government do something to his village? People wouldn't do something so crazy unless something bad actually happened to them."

"Well, in the past it has been known the CIA has done corrupt things all in the name of freedom. But listen carefully Tom; people have done crazier things throughout all of history. Some for their beliefs and for others belief's, just so they could be free to live how they wanted. When you have that patriotic feeling within you to do what is necessary to survive against the tyranny of other human beings, nothing will stop you from being suppressed even if they cover things up with lies. In the end the truth will prevail into the world somehow."

"That makes a lot of sense. Hopefully there won't be war over this, but I do hope the truth will be exposed if our government did do something to those people's village."

Tom got a warm fuzzy feeling within himself from what his father had just said as they continued traveling up the English country side. As the conversation was ending, Tom just sat there staring at the beautiful scenery till they got to the hospital.

Entering the room where Tom's mom was being kept, Mr. Turner, and Tom saw her lying down in a magnetic hyperbaric chamber, it was increasing the rate of her healing and enriching her cells with oxygen. Then she opened her chamber saying, "Oh I'm so glad to see you here. Did you like the cabin?"

Mr. Turner responded, "Yes, it's beautiful and amazing. John and Martin are there right now doing some chores. Are you feeling better, we were so concerned about you from the last we saw of you being rushed off."

"I'm doing quite better now, once they got my blood stabilized from me bleeding out they put me here in this chamber. So it's looking better, but I'm so sorry I couldn't be there with you & the kids to see the cabin for the first time," Tom's mom said with regret.

"It's alright honey; don't be sad, it was something you couldn't help. I'm sure we will build many more great memories while we're here anyways." Mr. Turner said lovingly to his wife.

"Well I need some rest, the doctors say even when I get out of here I will need to be cautious in how much activity I do because it could reopen my wound."

"We shall let you get some rest then. Speak to you later, and hope you feel better, goodbye love you," Mr. Turner said kissing her on the cheek. "Goodbye, love you mom," Tom added.

Walking to their vehicle Mr. Turner looked at his hollowatch looking something up on the skylink, and then he said to Tom, "Well it looks like the only place open after 5:30 PM is this place down the road called Stronger Walls. Let's go see if they will help modernize our house a little, since it's an ancient cabin. It is imperative we handle all the hard work since your mother will be bed ridden for a while, and we want this to be easier for her."

"Okay Dad, let's get going since everything around here seems to close early, we don't want to miss our chance while we're here."

When they arrived, the two of them walked inside noticing a stocky but not too tall white man. As soon as they walked in, the man said "Welcome to Stronger Walls I am Tony Simmons, how can I help you today?" Tom knew he'd struggle to understand a lot more than just the police officers in England after hearing Tony's accent.

Mr. Turner said, "We need plumbing, skylink and television hooked up at our house. Can you do that?"

Tony replied enthusiastically, "Sure… me and my boy can help you with that. We do any kind of house improvements needed."

Tom looked over at Tony's son and wondered "Why does he look so different from his dad?" While Mr. Turner talked with Tony about how to get to the cabin, Tom walked over to Tony's son, who was nearly his age asking, "Do you have a restroom I could use?"

The boy responded, "What's a restroom?"

Tom, puzzled by his response, replied "You know, a place you go to urinate?"

The boy responded, "Oh, you mean the toilet where you go to take a piss."

Tom, needing a restroom badly sarcastically said, "Well, I wouldn't have put it that way, but yeah."

The boy replied, "Yeah, it's down the hall to the left."

Tom ran off quickly as time was crucial. After a couple of minutes, he came back from the bathroom. He wanted to spend more time talking to the boy.

Tom introduced himself to Tony's boy by saying, "Hi, my name is Thomas Turner, but everyone calls me Tom."

"Hi my name is Kevin, but sometimes my mates call me Kev."

Tom asked a bit confused, "Mates? What are mates in your country?"

Kevin said in a laughing kind of way, "Mates are your friends that you hang out with."

Tom said rhetorically, "Wow, you guys sure are different over here, aren't y'all?"

Kevin laughed like a hyena saying, "Y'all? Yeah, I guess we are, but so are you from the sounds of it."

"Y'all means all of you. So, is there anything fun to do in Bexley Ledger?"

"Yeah, well there is this gym right by my school. I go to Bexley Ledger School for secondary education. Going to the cinema is nice and hanging out at the park with friends is lots of fun when it's not too cold or rainy outside."

"Wow, it seems like a whole different life style to what we do in Texas."

"Whoa, that's amazing you're all the way from Texas? Is it nice there?"

"Yeah, it can be, but it gets hot a lot. But still, it's a real clean place with some very nice people and lots of places to go and things to do. I like swimming at Canyon Lake and sometimes the creek."

"Yeah, well that does sound nice. We have some pools here as well as ponds were we swim. But, people prefer the indoor pools more. Just wondering, why don't you sound like a cowboy?"

"That might be a stereotype for us, but only if you are raised on a farm or possibly by a "redneck" would actually sound like that. I think in all reality it just matters who you hang out with. Because I have even met a few nerds who have the accent you're describing."

Tom's dad then said, "Come on Tom. It's time to get back to the cabin so they can do their stuff to get everything running."

So, Tom and his dad started heading back to the cabin. Their new friends, Kevin and Tony, were not far behind them. Even though Tony could easily have found his way to their address, he tried to drive close behind Mr. Turner so Tom's dad would feel he was a dedicated worker like he felt himself to be.

The Near Future
Sunday, May 31st, 12:47 P.M.
Oklahoma Juvenile Prison Camp, Lawton, Oklahoma

Justin sat there at the lunch table sweating; ever so often he would look over his shoulder. This was no place to be for teens, the whole atmosphere was tense. Rows of teens had other kids sitting by them, while Justin was soloing and eating his food alone. As Justin looked across the table at the one in front of him, he saw a black kid raising his eye brows, and squinting his eyes, looking directly toward him.

Not very happy with the kids' expression, Justin decided to look back at him in the same manner. The boy's eyes grew more tense as he slammed his knuckles down at the table.

"You want to mess with me! Do ya, you stupid fat loser!" the boy said unwisely.

"Don't you dare call me fat, you stupid piece of crap! Bet you are in for nothing more than stealing!"

"Wrong you fat idiot, I'm in here for assault! Want me to take you down, because I will!"

"Bring it you dumb little brat!"

Quickly the boy climbed up onto the table about to jump at Justin when a tray flew at his stomach knocking him down off the table. Justin quickly came around the side of his table punching at the kid who tried to take him on. Prison guards quickly ran up to them trying to break up the fight, pulling Justin off of the kid.

The guards dragged both of them to the warden's office so they could be dealt with properly. With a smirk as the door opened, the warden set down his cup of coffee.

The warden said with a rough voice. "So why did you two goons think you could get away with assaults in a prison?" Justin tried to speak but was interrupted by the warden. "I don't care why you were fighting and, I don't want to know if it was something stupid. Like you wanted to prove you should be feared, or some dumb self-esteem thing. That was a rhetorical question. The point is, you both tried to assault each other. Because of these actions for the next two weeks you both will be assigned some task of labor each individually and will not be allowed in the courtyard recreational center when everyone else gets their free time there. Tomorrow I will assign each of you your labor jobs for the next two weeks."

Both Justin and the other kid sighed then nodded in agreement with the warden.

They were sent back to their cells instead of the cafeteria. Justin sat there on his bed staring at the ceiling bored out of his mind. For quite some time he thought about why was he even deserving of being in this place? After a while, he began to contemplate what kind of friend he would want to make at the prison so that he could try to get revenge on Tom.

The Near Future
Sunday, May 31ˢᵗ, 6:12 P.M.
On the outskirts of Brighton, West Sussex, England

Once they arrived back at the cabin, Tom decided to have a banana mint soda. Tony soon follwed right after them. Getting a good view of the cabin, Tony started drawing a layout of the house. Kevin, walking around, was talking to Tom's family as he went about from room to room.

While Kevin was busy talking to Tom's family, Tom was in the backyard looking around. He couldn't help but notice a weird looking stone. Looking at it carefully, he noticed odd writings on it; he took a moment to go inside asking Martin for some paper and a pencil. With paper and pencil in hand, Tom went back outside writing down everything that looked like words on the stone.

Inside the cabin, Mr. Turner walked and talked with Tony as he worked hard on the cabin installing the items the family wanted. Tony pulled out his auto install tools, which made his job quicker than having to install it all manually, which could take days without his auto install tools. They would zip around the room he was in at the time setting things up.

Tom and Kevin were busy getting acquainted with each other.

With a puzzled look on his face, Tom asked Kevin, "So what's your mom do?"

Kevin responded sorrowfully, "My mom died then Tony adopted me."

Tom said with regret, "Sorry, that sucks. So did your real dad die as well?"

"No, I never knew him and my mom never told me who he was or how to find him."

"Who knows, maybe someday you will get to know him or meet him."

Kevin said, with a little optimism, "Yeah, you never know, anything could happen, I guess."

Once Tony was done working, he came outside and said, "Kev it's time to go. I got all their stuff taken care of."

Kevin & Tony said goodbye to everyone as they left to go home. During dinner that Mr. Turner made, they all discussed what they thought of England from what they had seen so far, and their opinions of Kevin & Tony.

After dinner, Tom tried out the new shower that Tony had installed. Feeling his hairs standing up, Tom enjoyed the warm water running down his body. Eventually, the whole family settled into the normal routines that they did before bedtime. Somehow it all felt different to them. Even the sheets felt different from what they had at home. It would take some real getting used to the different materials on their bodies. Falling asleep the first few nights might not be as easy as it was back at home, especially since none of the boys had their mother around.

Uncomfortable, by the strange materials, Tom laid in bed thinking about Tara, Benny, and Justin. He wondered where Tara was, and if she was enjoying her trip. Then, he thought about what

Benny was up to since it was still earlier in the day back in Texas. Last of all, before he dozed off were thoughts of Justin. Tom kept wondering if maybe he should forgive him for what he did to Tara or still even be upset with him. He figured when he and Justin got back to Texas that maybe he should try to work things out with him.

So, it seemed everyone was getting used to their new homes. The Turners clearly loved their quaint cozy cabin. Justin may have been bored but he was starting to grasp where he was going to have to live for a while. Some people say home is where the heart is, but what could that mean for Justin if he had a corrupt heart, always plotting revenge? Clearly, Tom's family had good hearts to go with their new home in the cabin.

Chapter 8
New Friends & New Places

The Near Future
Monday, June 01ˢᵗ, 6:40 A.M.
Dragon fire inn, Brighton, West Sussex, England

Being a moist morning, Agent Dale indeed felt like it had a melancholy atmosphere to it, as he awoke pressing his hand to his forehead. He leaned over the side of his bed hunching his back as he stared out the window with dew on it, holding a locket in his hand thinking about the night before with his head pounding.

An adorable black British girl kept giving Agent Dale cute flirty looks, but she didn't know about his personal status as he sat there drinking at the pub counter. Trying to ignore her because he wasn't interested in her, he looked down at the pint in his hand and watched the suds fizzle to nothing.

Normally, Agent Dale wouldn't drink only every now and again. But to him, this time he was drinking to wash away his loneliness. With one last gulp to finish his drink, he wobbled back to his room at the inn. Obviously, the locket he held in his hand contained a great significance to him involving someone he loved. Suddenly his head burst with more pain as the hotel phone rang loudly pulling him from his thoughts of the night before.

"Ugh…Hello?" he said with a resentful voice.

"Agent Sizer have you been drinking?"

"Sorry sir if I am not totally with it, I'm a little hungover."

"Well lay off the booze. I was calling to find out if you have gathered any more Intel on you know who?" the general said curiously.

"Well, I have a feeling when I go for that interrogation tomorrow I will get more info out of them about our mystery man who helped them escape. Just make sure that I have access to that interrogation. I also have some other leads, but I need time to see if they pan out."

"Will do Agent Sizer, you just make sure you don't go in there drunk tomorrow."

"It won't happen again Sir. Sorry, see you later." Agent Dale said rolling his eyes.

"Goodbye."

Once he hung up, Agent Dale headed down to the lobby to eat. Grabbing an English muffin with some butter and jam, he quickly went back upstairs to grab a shower & brush his teeth before heading out to the Turner's address which was close by. Arriving in his electric rental car, Agent Dale walked up to the Turner's door knocking kindly.

Mr. Turner opened the door saying, "Why don't you come in agent Sizer."

"It's alright if you want to call me Dale", he said looking over his shoulder at John messing around on the SkyLink, while Martin watched the news from their new couch.

Smelling food, as he walked in, Mr. Turner offered him something to eat. "Thanks for the offer. I only had an English muffin before I came here."

So Agent Dale sat down as Mr. Turner brought over the breakfast he had prepared for everyone.

Agent Dale asked, "So where is your family from?"

Mr. Turner said, "We are from Smithsonian Valley, Texas."

Agent Dale chuckled then said, in a somewhat surprised manner, "I went to high school there, but lived in Autumn Limb. It's a small town outside of Smithsonian Valley. That's the reason I was on that plane y'all were on. I was stationed at Lackland Air Force Base for a while, also."

Mr. Turner responded, "I know, some of my kids have friends from there."

"That's good. So Tom, you want to learn to protect yourself? How come you're interested in it?"

"I get beat up all the time by this mean kid named Justin."

Dale said, "Well, you should be able to fend off jerks like that."

Tom asked, just to be sure if it was the same town, "So, where are we going to train?"

"It's a fitness gym in Bexley Ledger. It also teaches sword fighting like I learned in the Marines."

"Cool, when are we going?" Tom asked enthusiastically.

"Whenever you feel like it."

Tom said with excitement, "Okay, why don't we go right now!"

So, with his father's blessing, Tom, Agent Dale, and John headed out of the cabin and got into Dale's rental car. It was going take an hour and a half drive to Bexley Ledger.

ᨒ ᨒ ❯ ❯ ᨋ ◇ ❯ △

When Dale's car arrived at the training center, they got out of the car and walked inside the gym. Tom noticed that it was just a gym, not some government or military-style building. Inside the building, Tom saw boxing, a wrestling mat, martial arts, a swimming pool, many workout machines, and people fencing.

An old man came up to Dale and said, "So is this another helpless boy who needs training?"

Tom was a little mad at that statement. In his mind, he wasn't completely helpless. Tom looked at the man and wondered why he looked vaguely familiar.

Dale responded "Yes, I think he really needs the training."

The old man said "Okay, you make good choices at picking out trainees most of the time Dale. So, I will teach this boy."

Tom thought, kind of annoyed, "What does this old guy think? I'm not a boy. I'm practically a man already!"

Then the old man said "What is your name?"

Tom told the old man his name and the old man said "Everybody calls me Paulo, but my full name is Paulo Andes."

Tom thought, "What kind of name was that?" Tom asked Paulo, "Was your family from the Andes Mountains in South America?"

"No it's a local village name from where I was born. Who is this other boy?"

"He is Tom's older brother John."

Paulo said, welcomingly, "Well, nice to meet you. So, should we get started?" and they shook hands.

Tom then asked Paulo, "How come you sound American, but you live here in England?"

Paulo responded with a chuckle, "I am from California."

Then Paulo asked Tom what he wanted to learn first and Tom said, "I would like to learn martial arts."

"I am real good with martial arts, especially Taekwondo."

Tom arrogantly thought, "This old man can't be good with martial arts, he is really scrawny looking."

Shortly thereafter, Tom got on the wrestling mat to practice; Paulo moved so fast that Tom could not begin to counter him.

Tom thought to himself, "Maybe I was wrong about this old guy. He has a lot better moves than I thought."

Then for quite a while what seemed challenging to Tom's skill, Paulo trained Tom as Dale and John watched. During some of Tom's training, John got bored and used the workout machines.

Busy folding clothes, Justin stood there in agony, wishing he could be outside at the recreational facility instead of inside folding clothes for charity services. Clearly chores weren't something he had any interest in doing. Then one of the other teens from the prison camp came up to talk to him.

"You know, I thought it was pretty epic how you took down that one idiot yesterday." The boy said to him.

"Thanks, I like to prove to people I can handle my own most of the time." Justin replied with a smirk.

"Well you certainly did that in my opinion."

"So why you locked up in here anyways?"

"For doing drugs and assaulting a girl. What about you?"

"Breaking and entering, took some of their stuff also. Most people are dumb leaving their windows unlocked."

"So how did they catch you then?" Justin said with curiosity.

"Well, first I used black pages to see where they were in that moment by entering their hollowatch number. Sure it didn't give me their id or name but it showed me they weren't home. Little did I know that they had cameras in their house, and a clever silent alarm system. So the police came for me without me knowing they were on their way."

"Well well, aren't you a clever boy? My name is Justin what is yours?

"My name is Cassidy."

"I think we are going to make great friends. Maybe since we are stuck in here doing chores we should discuss each other's good techniques for getting what we want." Justin said, with a devious smile on his face.

"Sounds like a great idea to me."

So, for the next hour or so the two criminals discussed ways to commit crimes of different kinds, teaching one another arts that should never be practiced. Eventually, they discussed how Justin wanted to look into the habits of some of the kids once his chore duty was over. For those two weeks he wanted to see which of them might be useful to his crowd of criminals he was wanting to develop.

> ⟩ 𝔊 𝔊 △ 𝕄 𝔊 𝔊 ↳

After hours of exhaustive wrestling practice, Tom went outside to rest from all the workout training he'd accomplished. Tom looked at his hollowatch noticing it was around the time school usually let out in Texas. Then he noticed something intriguing was going on when he saw kids coming out of the school and gathering in a crowd.

Tom walked over to see what was going on; something bad was happening. He wasn't happy when he saw some big kid shoving a smaller boy around while the crowd stood around them watching.

Tom saw Kevin and asked, "Hey Kev is this where you go to school? Looks like y'all suffer from the same issues my school does."

Kevin replied with a chuckle, "Obviously, it's where we go to school. What are you on about issues?"

Tom perplexed about how he could not know what he was talking about said, "You know, a big guy that beats up on teens smaller than himself for money?"

"Oh, he is not beating him up cause he is little or for money, it's cause Johnny Rodger is a total sod who thinks the Truth to the world is hidden and thinks that Jason is some secret government experiment."

Tom, now super confused and shocked asked, "First, what's a sod and secondly, why would he think he is a secret government experiment?"

"A sod is like what you would call a jerk. Johnny thinks he is that cause of the way he talks different than most people and how Jason is smart and witty and good looking."

"That doesn't make sense! Johnny sounds insane!"

"Oh, he is totally mental. He usually is not a very violent person, but people say he might be doing this to express his anger of how his parents always abuse him for being bad."

Then, a blond curly hair boy said laughing, "Not as mental as them girls."

Tom said angrily, "They're not all that way. Some are very sweet, just like this girl I know from my hometown."

Kevin said, "Tom, this is Thomas Mandarin."

Thomas responded, "Yeah, well around here, there are some nice ones but they go mental sometimes! You know really bonkers for no reason at all."

Tom responded with hope, "You never know. They might have a reason to go all out rage mode, like something you may have said or done. You should be careful of your actions and saying these things could have more severe side effects than you realize."

Thomas said, "Who knows, maybe you're right. Maybe you're not, but it still is nice to meet you Tom. But, I still think they are just total nutters, even if what you said sort of makes sense."

Tom responded kindly, even though he thought Thomas was being unwise not listening to his idea, "Nice to meet you as well Thomas."

Tom noticed the fight was getting bad and no one was doing anything except cheering Johnny on.

Tom couldn't take watching Jason get beat up anymore. So he rushed in between them and yelled at Johnny, "Stop bullying him, he hasn't done anything to you!"

Johnny, big bold and arrogantly proud responded back saying, "He may have not done anything yet, but I know people like him. They are going to be used to take over the world. They are designed to be perfect and the way he talks, it's obvious he has secrets!"

Tom with a look on his face that expressed the thought "Like what in the world?" said to Johnny, "Jeez Johnny, who knocked you off your rocker?"

Everyone laughed at Johnny as he ran off, beginning to get teary-eyed. Clearly, the way they handled situations in England was different than how Tom imagined those same situations would have been handled in America. But, at least Jason wasn't being bullied anymore.

Jason, who had a high-pitched voice, responded to Tom's actions and said, "Thanks for getting Johnny to leave me alone."

"You're welcome. Besides, what kind of person would I be if I didn't stand up for what is right? I've always heard that if you don't stand for something, you'll fall for anything… just like how that Johnny guy has obviously fallen for some very misleading skylink websites."

"Well you sure are a nice and brave person. Most people wouldn't do anything to help. They would just let me get beat up watching it all happen. Anyway, it is nice to meet you. My name is Jason Steward."

"My name is Thomas Turner, but everyone calls me Tom."

Jason smiled and walked off to talk to some other people. Apparently, he was very grateful never anticipating a stranger being there for him like Tom was. Who knows how Tom's actions could have affected Jason and how he would treat others in the future.

Kevin came up to Tom and said, "Yeah, well Tom let me introduce you to all my friends. By the way is that the way you always introduce yourself?"

"Yeah, I guess I have a habit of saying that as an introduction for myself, it must be like a catchphrase for me."

Kevin started pointing out people and introducing each of them to Tom. "Tom, this here is Charles Smith, but he prefers to be called Charlie." Charlie was a slim boy with blond hair and blue eyes.

"This is Louie Worthington" Louie was sort of slim. He wore glasses and had brown hair and hazel eyes.

"Over here is Jamie Pidgeon and Reece Morison". Jamie was a small boy with long blond hair. Reece was similar, except his hair was brown and cut in a bowl shape.

Reece was arguing with Jamie saying, "No. No Reece, Lord Dribble Mouth is an excellent name for our Character".

"No, it's not like we want people to think we are retarded or something."

Tom asked, "Why are they fighting over the name of somebody?"

Kevin said, "They are trying to make a comic book character and they're clearly not agreeing with each other."

Tom said, "Oh, I see. Well, they both will have to find a compromise to come up with a good name for it."

Tom then said to Kevin, "Well, now that the whole fight thing is over, I wanted to ask you something since our conversation was cut short yesterday. Do you have any idea where your dad is from?"

"My Mom said that he was from the Philippines and that she lost contact with him when she moved."

"Oh, I am sorry Kevin. That sucks for you." Tom said with a feeling of guilt.

Charlie then said, "I can't believe how Jason just kept taking the beating and didn't fight back?"

Tom responded, "Maybe he knew how to handle the kind of situation when there just may not be any right response? Perhaps, if you don't have any cause, there will be no effect."

Charlie said jokingly, "Careful mate. If you're too brainy, Johnny might come after you too."

They all broke out with laughter. Clearly, Johnny had issues if he would beat up people just because they were smarter than him. Apparently, his logic was all messed up if he justified his actions with the dumbest, governmental conspiracies. At least some of the conspiracies going around on Skylink seemed reasonable, but the one mentioned by Johnny, was so ridiculous it made them laugh.

Louie spoke up, "Hey Kev, is it alright if me and Charlie hang out at your place tonight?"

"Sure, see you guys there."

Tom said, "Well, it is getting late. I need to get back to my place...see y'all later."

Everyone said goodbye to Tom and he quickly ran back to the Gym. Tom clearly had had a great time with some of the new friends he had made, but didn't want his family too upset.

Once he got back over to the Gym, Paulo said "Wow, where have you been and why were you gone so long?"

"Sorry, got caught up in talking to people and stuff."

"It's okay. There will be more time to do your training later. So, I'll see you guys later." Everybody said goodbye to Paulo.

Tom, John, and Dale headed back to the cabin. When the three of them arrived at the cabin, Dale left for his hotel. Because John and Tom were driving home from the training center, they arrived a little late at the cabin for their dinner. Since they were late, they had to eat dinner a past the normal time for dinner in England, which is usually around six pm. Mr. Turner had made British-style hamburgers, for dinner while they were gone. The hamburgers tasted vastly different from the ones they were used to in America.

After dinner, Tom and John talked a little about how John was looking into colleges he should go to. John told Tom that there were many great choices to check out. Tom smiled seeing his brother so enthusiastic about education and learning, and then he decided to head off to bed.

That night, as Tom slept, he continued the same dream he had dreamt during the trip to England. The only difference was that it started out sooner than before (where he had walked through the hall). This time, in the dream, he had seen the bus Justin was on and the number on it. Following the bus vision, he went inside a building that looked like a prison and experienced the same dream as before.

The next morning, when Tom woke up, everyone else was still asleep. To pass the time, he got on the SkyLink using his hollowatch to lookup information about the bus system in Oklahoma. He had a dream about a bus number, so he wanted to find out in what city the bus number would be located. After a while, he discovered that the bus number actually belonged to the Oklahoma juvenile prison camp.

Tom thought it was very strange that the bus number in his dream belonged to a bus used by the juvenile detention center where Justin was sent. Tom tried to remember if he had seen the bus number on the day that he and his family pulled out of the neighborhood on their way to England.

After he searched his memory, he noticed that his family was getting up. So, he got off the skylink on his hollowatch. He did this quickly so that his parent's would not know he was looking into that bus number, he thought they might find it odd.

Tom went to the kitchen for breakfast, but it wasn't ready yet.

Having to kill some time, he went outside to the mysterious rock he had seen the day they arrived in England. As he walked to the place where he had seen the rock, and still being a little dark outside, he saw the rock off in the distance and it looked like it was glowing. As he drew closer, he could see that it was actually glowing in many different colors making a faint, humming sound.

Tom found it very peculiar. He had never seen a rock that glowed, let alone make a strange noise. Still, looking at the rock, he made a mental note to look up the words he saw etched into the rock. After staring at the rock for a while, he made his way back to the cabin.

Back again, while his dad finished making breakfast, he sat there thinking about the strange rock. Soon, breakfast was ready and they all sat down to eat.

While eating breakfast his dad said to the family, "Why don't we go fishing later today, after we pick up your mother from the hospital. I already talked it over with your mom. So, is anybody all for that?" They all agreed that it would be fun.

After breakfast was finished, the men of the Turner family got into their rental car and drove to pick up Mrs.Turner. Once they were all strapped in they headed down to the south coast of England. They passed many fishing docks and swimming areas. At a place they stopped, was a beach, dunes to the west with grass growing from them, a swimming area, and a bath house and restrooms near the road.

Tom looked to his left on the beach, which would have been east from his view, and saw a big hill. He thought that maybe after he caught his fish, he would go up on the hill to explore. Everyone got out their fishing supplies and started fishing.

After hours of just sitting around waiting for a fish, Martin's line clicked as he started reeling one in. He struggled to catch it, and finally he got it. Once Martin had caught his fish, he headed off to the swimming area.

Not long after Martin had reeled in his fish, Tom caught his. Once he put the fish away, and cleaned up, he took off for the hill that he had seen a few hours prior as they arrived. Tom got on top of the hill, and looked to his left seeing a cliff. He walked up to the edge of the cliff. It was rocky, with a reddish orange color.

Looking down, he saw a hole in the wall below him. Curious, he walked back down the hill and circled back around to the hole in the cliff which turned out to be a cave entrance. He ran back to the car to get a flash light.

As he returned to the cave entrance, he slowly went inside. Inside the cave was very dark and gloomy. It was full of moss among other green things. In the feint glow of the flashlight, he could make out a smallish-looking lake off in the distance. He explored up to the lake, around the lake, even beyond the lake until it came to an end.

Looking around, Tom noticed how the roof of the cave was a strange arch-shaped ceiling made of rocks and other stones that looked ancient. It almost felt more like a room than a cave or like a hall or courtroom or something of the kind. Since there was nothing more to explore, or so he thought, he went back to his family and decided to come back to the cave some other time. He would need much more time to see all that there was to see. As Tom arrived back where his family had been, he found them still fishing and doing the activities as before.

Throughout the day, the Turners all eventually caught at least one fish. It was turning out to be quite a fun adventure for the whole family.

Tensions were high as the villager from the plane sat there in the cold interrogation room of the Gatwick police station. He felt at any moment they might bust in to beat him up or to hold a gun to his head. Who knows what methods they would use to get info out of him? With sweat rolling down his face, he sat there in the chair playing with his hands to take his mind off of things, but he was right in fearing what they might do.

The door flung open making the villager jump a little, as a British officer came in to interview him. With a tall, thin frame the officer twirled a chair around up to the table so he could sit down. The lights flickered a little making the villager blink with a horrible feeling in his gut about what was going to happen.

"Now listen here, we can do this the easy way or the hard way." The officer said.

"What do you want me to tell you?"

"Good…good, I see you know your place. Why did you along with many of your people hijack an airplane?"

"We wanted the truth to come out, but your agent that you probably have in the non-see through glass mirror room, already knows this. My quarrel…I mean my people's quarrel has nothing to do with you." The villager said sympathetically as he remembered seeing the agent have a conversation with another villager.

"Well I am not the agent, so you better start explaining things before you make me even angrier. This info is for London not for America, so tell me! "

"You aren't even going to let me go, so why should I tell you anything?"

"I don't get why you look like an Assyrian when you sound like you are from Russia, so if you want your kid to be okay then you will give me the answers I request now!"

The man gasped as the officer showed him a mug shot of his son from his hollowatch, "How do you have him, he was safely hidden in America?"

"I won't bother spilling our secrets. So are you going to tell me or not?" The officer said with a serious but curious tone.

"No...no I can't tell you anything...my quarrel isn't with you." The villager said with concern.

Instantly, in rage the officer lunged forward punching the terrorist in the face. "Tell me why you killed so many innocent people, you monster! What are you hiding?! We will make your son spill it if you don't. Maybe he will give more info than you have after we use some methods on him we aren't permitted to use on you!"

"If you hurt my..." the door busted open again before he could finish his first sentence even quicker than the first time, just as the officer was dragged out instantly by other officers.

Then in the mirror room the officer was getting a massive lecture from Agent Dale on protocol, while the terrorist remained in his chair concerned now about the wellbeing of his son. Agent Dale looked into the room thinking about how that man beat up the poor terrorist and how Tom had wanted to take lessons for defending himself, which made him think that he wouldn't hurt the man like the officer did because he felt that he was a better person than that.

"What were you thinking? How could you let your emotions get in the way of interviewing him?" Agent dale said dumbfounded by the officer's actions.

"It's just he has caused me lots of trouble, and I never have had to interrogate a terrorist before. I figured this might be the way to do it?" The officer said.

Agent Dale responded "What do you think this is a movie or something? Seriously, let met talk to him for a moment he made it seem like his problem was with the US government, not with you."

"Fine, but you better be good at this for England's sake."

Calmly, agent Dale walked into the interrogation room to try to talk things over with the villager or as he believed, the terrorist. Quickly, he sat down in front of the worried father, trying to have a good relationship with him so that they could talk.

"Sorry about that, don't worry, I won't be water boarding you or threatening you with physical violence or hurting your family."

Getting a kick out of the change in peoples attitude, the villager said, "What is this good cop, bad cop?

"No, I just felt that man didn't give you any mercy and that I should."

"Well fine, you want to be merciful then tell me where my son is!"

"That was a picture our government gave him. Don't worry he has no hold on your son."

"But clearly you do, since you have a mug shot that we didn't have to take any when you rounded up our village's population like a pack of animals?!"

"Maybe the American government has him or maybe somebody else does, I am not authorized, nor do I even know who has him, only that we were given a photo of him to instill fear into you. But you said your quarrel wasn't with the officer or did you mean with the British or who are you referencing?"

"I remember you from that day when you came upon our village leading all those soldiers to get us. We did nothing at all to deserve what you did to us, taking us to a prison in the middle of nowhere."

"Listen, I had nothing against you personally at all. I was ordered from somebody way higher in the chain of command that your village was a terrorist cell, which needed to be captured but not killed."

"I get it, you were just doing your duty, but you don't realize that you have been deceived by whoever is giving you your orders."

"The man I gunned down on the plane said the same thing. He never explained why all of you tried to take the plane?

The man began to weep with tears as soon as Agent Dale said these words. "Oh my... hold on one second." He said as he raised his finger. "We wanted to attract the media's attention so we could be broadcast live to tell the world how we had our lives taken from us on that horrific day."

"I'm only going to say this to you because part of me feels like you need some justice while the other part of me whole heartedly believes that you are a terrorist. You never will get your direct words publically broadcasted since there are people in every country, very high up in power, that control what goes on the air and what doesn't. Not too long ago in the early 21st century people in Pakistan were told by their media that American soldiers were in the middle east to do nothing more than to kill innocent people. People in England were told they were there for oil, and finally, just to get my point across, people in America were told they were there to find people responsible for the same kind of injustice that you claim has happened to you which cost lots of innocent people their lives in New York City. So, no matter what you do, the media won't come out with how you want it to sound because of the way things are run by the people in control."

"No man is innocent, but we can try to be good people if we want to. We knew it was wrong but we had no other way to get the public's attention. Somehow we knew the media wouldn't just put us on by request, which is why we did what we had to. Had our new leader been wiser in his choices, mayb we wouldn't all be here." The villager said breaking down into tears.

"What are you referring to?"

"Long ago we were brought over to Southern Russia by our ancient ancestors to protect the origins of a deep long-forgotten secret.

One day our recent leader, who was or is fascinated by science, thought maybe he should go to the scientific community about the secret we had harbored for so long. Not long after that an archeology team came to our village. Then, not much over a month later after they left; you arrived with your team to take us all."

"Okay…that is enough…we don't need to hear anymore right now." Agent Dale said with a cautious voice and a concerned look on his face as he left the room quietly.

Dale headed back into the see-through mirror room to talk with the officer who had been dragged out. He was very curious about one final detail that he should get before he left. Figuring that he had gathered enough info already, this one last thing would be enough to take back to the American government.

As he stepped through the door, Agent Dale said, "Well that went better than your movie style of interrogating. I assume only me and you heard that conversation since we were the only two to receive headphone listening devices?"

"Well, this young man with the headphones also heard it, but the info probably was already put into the electronic system and will be printed for the record vault at the end of the evening." The officer said as he pointed down at a young guy listening to the recording device.

"What are your plans in dealing with this guy and the other terrorist once you guys are done with them? I am asking because the American government might be interested in having them come to one of our places to do more interrogating for gaining more info."

"We are going to send them to Scotland Yard Prison very soon, within the next couple of days probably. But Agent Sizer, I must warn you, we recorded their conversation the other day. Our suspicion is that they have help on the outside or maybe even that there are more of them out there."

"Well, thank you for your good time and your info. Hopefully you are satisfied with them now for your report. I guess I will be headed out now."

"Goodbye Agent Sizer, you truly were more of a help than I was."

Agent Dale waved goodbye as he headed out towards his car getting ready to leave, when suddenly he got a phone call. Quickly he pulled up his hollow watch phone in front of his face to receive the call.

"Agent Sizer, thank you for your cooperation in figuring out info on how much the Terrorist actually knew about their capture."

"Glad to be of service in being your eyes and ears, sorry I couldn't think of a way for you to hear what the officer said to him."

"It's okay. From the looks of it, he didn't get anything important out of him.

"I do consider it somewhat of great concern though what he said about us just popping up after some archeological checkup. Would we truly do that for some old secret?"

"No no...don't be ridiculous, if you would like when you get back to America, I will show you the intelligence report myself and why we went after them. They might have had some secret we weren't aware of just like he said why they moved to Russia long ago, but I'll bet it's just a coincidence that a month before we came in on them they had some archeologist visit them. I think he was just looking in the wrong places for why things happened."

"Okay sir, I trust you to be honest. I am curious to see these files you told me of."

"You are a great agent Dale. Now remember that box I said would be in your car, be sure to keep it with you?"

"Yes sir."

"I was just given orders to have you put any electronic devices you can in there within the next five minutes, plus you might want to start walking towards the bus stop." Instantly a creepy vibe shot down Agent Dale's back.

"What?!"

"I don't know why they are doing this maybe it's to contain the spread of false info. You better get going or it might be too late for you. See you later Agent Sizer."

"Goodbye sir."

Quickly Agent Dale pulled out the box placed in his rental car putting all of his electronic devices into it as he hung up with the man giving him commands. He shut the box tightly then started walking towards the nearest bus stop. As he started walking off he saw a strange stick-looking thing come twirling down with wings on the top to slow its dissension. The device flew into the top of the police building's roof, and then it beeped a little right before it went off. Instantly, Agent Dale looked around as the lights in stores, on cars, as well as the cars themselves including a three block radius, went out losing power. Agent Dale walked to a bus stop carrying the box with all the other important things he had brought in the car.

The Turners packed their fishing gear away and brought the fish back with them to the cabin. Martin caught a catfish, Tom caught a bass, John caught a Moat Carp, and their parents both caught trout. When they got back to the cabin they fired up the grill and started cooking the fish they had caught. Everyone ate the fresh fish that they had caught that day. All in all, it had been a good day finished off by a great meal together.

In the end Tom made new friends that probably could help him understand English culture better than he had before. Justin's new friend though, might only lead to more trouble or maybe something better not yet known? Their new places came with new adventures, but what secrets did the cave have, or the rock in his yard that Tom had found? What secrets were hidden for so long from the outside world of the village?

After dinner, Tom went on the Skylink using his Hollowatch to do so. He quickly looked up the words that he had seen etched into the rock as it read…

The near future
Thursday, June 04th, 7:07 A.M.
On the outskirts of Brighton, West Sussex, England

Gasping for his breath Tom suddenly awoke by the same fiendish dream he had endured twice already, making for a third compelling escapade with a strange beginning. As he wiped away the sweat from his forehead, Tom pondered why he had kept waking up really warm with an elevated heart beat every time he'd experienced one of these horrid nightmares. "Sitting here in our new air controlled home isn't going to cool me off anytime soon." He thought to himself as he started to head to the back door of the house.

Stepping out the door of the cabin with a glass of water in his hand, Tom felt mesmerized by an enigmatic feeling that the cold damp morning was giving. The moment he gazed upon the strange stone, racing his heart had stopped as he became allured by the rock he had seen, making him remember looking up the words he had seen etched into it. Which were "Ostendo mei liber libri" which meant (Reveal my book). Tom thought to himself, "Why would some rock have this written on it?"

Thinking about all the torment he had to deal with because of these nightmares, Tom sat down on the patio to contemplate things a little about the reasons he was losing sleep.

"Why can't these dumb nightmares just end, I have nothing to fear with Justin. He is all the way across the ocean, it just doesn't make sense?" He thought to himself as he sipped some more water. "I know what I did was somewhat right, so am I feeling guilty to some extent for what I did?" Tom pondered.

"Maybe if I try to work out things when I get home with Justin then these ridiculous dreams will end. I bet there is still hope for him even though he gets frustrated a lot in his life."

"None of this is helping, though, dwelling on my problems with Justin. They can't be resolved right now, but that rock sure is interestingly odd. Wonder why that thing glows or makes funny sounds?"

So, to get Justin out of his mind for the time being, Tom decided to go over to the rock so he could observe it some more. When he walked over to the rock from the patio it started glowing brighter than ever before.

Tom said to himself, "Why would some rock say "ostendo mei liber libri" which is Ancient Latin, but this is England?"

Instantly, the stone started whirring with a humming sound, then it flashed a bright bluish light and it was gone. In its place there was a small wooden box just sitting there. Tom bent over to pick up the box but stood for a second in shock at what had just happened. He couldn't believe what he had just seen. It seemed way too unreal to be physically or logically feasible.

Picking up the box, Tom opened it, looking inside he found that there was a book. The book cover had strange words written on it which looked like more ancient Latin words. Tom opened the book to the first page noticing it had the same words as the title cover with one extra word.

"Wonder why this one says "Teneo Liber Sapientiae" instead of just "Liber Sapientiae"?" Tom said to himself. As soon as he uttered these words Tom heard the same ringing hum then he started to have a head ache suddenly making him drop the book right out of his hands.

Bending down to pick the book up, he noticed something strange on the cover. As soon as he saw it in Ancient Latin the words instantly morphed into English words instead of saying "Liber Sapientiae", its wording read "The Book of Wisdom".

Tom opened The Book of Wisdom to the first page which now said "understand the book of curses". He figured somehow the headache he had gotten made it so he could understand anything written in Ancient Latin at this moment, but still see its original dialect a little before it would change.

Maybe Tom could use this book to learn his own secret language to hide any deeds he didn't want people to know about. Flipping through the pages he noticed some of them did not look like they were to be used for conversations. They were more like actions or other things; even like objects. On the first page Tom saw commands for him to do.

It read saying, "Descendant, although my book is written for your Wisdom, you must know some people in society have referred to it as the Book of Curses. I hope you use my teachings wisely. Let us begin. Point your finger at some grass on the ground and say ignis."

Tom thought to himself. "Why would it tell me to do something so ridiculous, as well it didn't change form this time?"

So, Tom pointed his pointer finger at a pile a leaves on the ground that had been raked up saying "ignis"; only for the sake of it.

Instantly, the leaves burst into flames as they started burning some into a little fire. Tom fell backwards, spooked at what just happened; quickly he picked up the book which he had dropped again falling to the ground.

It read saying, "See, bet you liked that. There are many words to learn, so read this book so that you will unlock your true potential to discover all of the great things you can do."

"You bet I liked that!" Tom thought to himself.

Tom kept reading till he thought his family was getting up. Then he went over to his room while grabbing something in the kitchen and decided to try another word.

Tom got out a glass and said "Aqua" but nothing happened.

He thought maybe he should add a little too it so he tried again saying "Fill this glass with aqua."

Once he said that he heard a hum coming from the glass then it flashed with a light coming from within the glass. Water appeared out of nowhere and it looked pretty good; he took a sip thinking it was the freshest water he had ever tasted.

He heard his family getting up. So he went to the kitchen for breakfast. After he finished his last bit of hash browns he headed out to the garden near the rock. He started reading the book and thought he would practice these words on days when he did not train at Paulo's fitness center.

Tom made sure none of his family was nearby to see him practicing these unique words. He looked at a giant boulder that he knew he could not lift with his own hands and said "Extollo the boulder."

The boulder rose into the air for a couple of feet, stopping in its place, and just hovered there.

Tom thought this wouldn't look right to others so he then said "Exertus the boulder."

The boulder went flying forward far out of their yard. Tom was so excited about what was happening that he smirked when he sent the bolder flying. He kept doing groups of words on different objects while nobody was around so he could keep it all a secret...

When lunch came he asked his dad what they were doing the day after tomorrow. His dad said that they might take the day to go back to the beach where they had gone the other day and just swim. So after lunch his dad went with all the family except Tom to the Bexley Ledger Tesco's store, along to other places for shopping so they could get stuff to take with them. Tom stayed behind to practice his new found skills some more. To put it simply, Tom just told the rest of them he did not want to go with them to the store so he could stay behind. Tom got the book back out to read as he headed to the backyard.

It read "Some words can be used in more than one way. Let me demonstrate what I mean. First say voco quercus oak seed."

So Tom said those three words. Once again with a hum & flash of light a seed appeared in his hands.

Tom then read "Okay, now place the seed in the ground and say celer cresco quercus oak seed."

Tom did what the book suggested. Seeing something that looked just like a video he'd seen in science class one time, the seed burst opened then started growing real fast, then in less than half a minute it was a full grown oak tree.

He read the book some more, "Now the second thing you can use is the word "celer" for making yourself faster. Now say "make me celer." And he said it but nothing happened.

But for some reason the moment he moved his whole body felt like he was listening to his favorite music. As he felt the wonderful energy chill go throughout him, he decided to run to his room to grab his Hollowatch phone to see what listening to music would feel like while he felt like this. But as soon as he started running he saw a car on the road by the drive way just sitting. He stopped running and saw the car go by faster than he could see it right. He ran out into the road where the car stopped again, but it was much further than where it was the first time. He stopped and it kept on going. He wondered if he was running so fast that he was outrunning the car, or was it time it self.

Then he ran back to the book to read it some more. It was written in a joking manner, "So like your new speed? Plus, if you want to run slower say make me not celer."

Tom just kept reading and practicing the words it was telling him until his family got home. He did a lot of crazy things that afternoon practicing all these different words with different outcomes.

When his family got back, Tom realized he had summoned many things so he said "Expello all these things I have vocoed today." Then all the things he had summoned and practiced disappeared with another flash. Tom made himself run at a normal speed again so nobody would think he was randomly disappearing. His parents started making dinner, about half an hour later they ate dinner.

Feeling very tired from the long day & late hours, Tom decided to hop into bed. Most of his family was already asleep though. That night Tom had many different dreams, but not the horrible night mare he had been having. In the dreams he was doing many things that one would think are impossible.

Opening his eye's, Kevin could see the neon blue light on his speakers: they were still playing the indie soft rock band, Weekend Runner, that he had put on the night before. Rushing out the door heading down the street Kevin tried to avoid bumping into other people along the way to the bus stop trying not to be late as he tried to catch his breath from the crisp morning air. Luckily, he made it just in time to get on the next dark red bus just past the crowd that thronged his way.

Kevin seemed bemused that today's bus was a one story instead of a two story bus. He didn't let the colour of the bus deviate him from his goal of getting a hot & spicy sausage roll to go from Craig's Bakery once the bus came to a stop. Approaching the school, hurriedly he ate his food heading to class.

Four periods later of switching classes and occasionally talking to his friends between classes, Kevin and his friends headed to King Finnegan's (an international restaurant) for lunch. Kevin decided on the Fish & Chip platter, while Louie and Charlie got Irish King Burger meals. Reece & Jamie just got kid meals since it didn't take much to fill their small frames.

Sitting down, with a disgruntled look on his face, Kevin sat there eating his food thinking about a girl he had a crush on along with some issues he'd harbored since his childhood. Louie, noticing Kevin's lack communication with them, decided to engage him.

"Hey Kev, why you so glum today?"

"Awe, it's nothing important, just some silly personal things. Anyways how's Molly doing?"

"Well, the other night at her father's house her father said I have a dirty mouth. Well, I'll tell you what, if I want to have a dirty mouth I will be cursing my head off while I'm having my way with that stupid old..." Kevin quickly interrupted, knowing no good words were about to come out of Louie's mouth. "Louie just because he doesn't like you doesn't mean anything bad with you and Molly."

"Nah it doesn't, but I don't want him to put any bad ideas in her head. Besides I got my eye on another pretty bird anyways, because Molly just isn't willing to have much fun."

Charlie said, "So, who's this new girl ya fancy?"

"Oh, no, no, I am not telling you guys anymore, because then you would just try to cause issues." Louie said.

Reese then said "Great job Louie, get in there bruv!"

"Ya, man." Jamie said.

Kevin wasn't so impressed at the idea though. He figured that Louie should be more dedicated to Molly. Even though some of Kevin's ideals of right & wrong were blurred, in his mind one thing remained the same. If ever in a relationship a man should be honorable to that girl for as long as they are together. Not wanting to be obvious about his opinion, Kevin headed to the toilet.

Louie then said "Where you going Kev?"

"To the toilet, care to join me?" Kevin responded with a snarky attitude, making Louie roll his eyes.

Once lunch was over, Kevin and his friends headed back to school for fifth period. Sitting there, in history with a serious contemplative look on his face, Kevin was staring off into space thinking about how life seemed unfair for different reasons. He thought to himself, "Why do all the wrong type of guys get the girl? Molly deserves better than Louie." The teacher then said, "So Kevin do you know when the Romans started looking into taking over the British Isles?"

"No mam…sorry I don't." Kevin replied shyly.

"What were you even contemplating a moment ago, then? I was certain you looked like you were giving something some serious thought and had hoped it was the answer to my question."

"Nothing, just personal stuff…" He said just as he had told his friends at lunch.

Kevin had been around his friend's and teacher's long enough to know that none of them really cared about anybody but themselves. Not one moment of his life did anybody actually show any sign of consideration, except Tony who took him in after his mother died. Sure, he felt like he had plenty of friends, but nobody ever really tried to be there for one another in his circle of friends.

Hearing the bell ring, Kevin's mood elevated as the school day had come to an end. Quickly running into the hallway he hopped around some people trying to avoid bumping into them as they lingered around the announcement board. Stuck in this cluster Kevin just wanted to get to his locker so he could get home. After cleaning out his locker Kevin headed out the door and saw Tom in the distance running up to the courtyard from across the street headed right for him.

Kevin raised his hand waving at Tom so excited he was visiting. Instantly, discouragement filled within Kevin as he saw Johnny Rodger popping out in front of Tom putting out his arms to stop him. Tom, who now was stronger in more ways than one put out his arms to stop Johnny from shoving him down to the ground, braced himself.

Johnny said angrily at Tom "You embarrassed me the other day. Now you're going to have to pay for what you did!"

Tom responded calmly because of how Paulo had told him "One must never use their fighting skills for violence, but only for protection." So Tom, thinking about how discipline helps, calmly said. "I know about how your parents discipline you, but that is no reason to take it out on others. Violence won't resolve anything for you Johnny."

"Discipline! Abusing me when I don't do what they want isn't discipline, its child abuse!" Johnny yelled with rage.

"Johnny, you need to understand when I was little my parents did the same to me, but as I got older I realized they did it to make me understand I was being bad when I did things I shouldn't. They did it because they loved me trying to make me a better person. Sometimes you just need to have faith that things will get better and maybe try being better yourself."

Now very angry Johnny yelled "Faith! Faith isn't going to stop my dad from getting drunk every night beating me! Faith is an absurd ideal made up by people that are hopeless!"

Tom, not knowing about the drunken daddy factor said, "Sorry I didn't know that's why you were beaten."

Kevin stood there with many others watching a battle unfold in ways they hadn't really thought of till now. Much of it because of the way they lived their lives. Johnny said more calmly now, "Sorry, why are you sorry? They used to discipline me but mom divorced dad because he wouldn't stop drinking. Now their discipline is gone and pointless like their marriage."

"I know it's hard to accept it, but Faith can be useful sometimes even when you don't know it is. I am sorry because I know what it's like to go through hard times. I hope life gets better for you. Because I'm not your enemy."

Johnny now confused said, "Alright, guess I won't attack you then."

Johnny walked off as Kevin came up and said, "Man I can't believe you just talked Johnny Rodger out of a fight?"

"Yeah, neither can I, but I came here looking for you so I could show you some interesting things or at least I think it will be interesting."

Kevin was very curious with what Tom had said. "What kind of things?"

"You will see just come with me."

Kevin's eyes widened as he said "Where?"

Tom waved over his shoulder as he ran off quickly saying, "Across the street over at the gym where I have been working out."

"I wondered why you looked more musciley over these past couple of days." Tom chuckled at the thought of this because he mumbled some words from his book to give him more strength while training earlier that day with Agent Dale and Paulo. "Oh brother, don't worry about that, come on lets go over there so you can meet him." Tom said.

Together they ran real fast back over towards the gym trying to make sure cars weren't coming at them. Kevin was so excited for whatever it was Tom was going to show him. He wondered why Tom was being so elusive about this, as well what any of it had to do with him.

Tom walked up first to Paulo saying, "Paulo, I think I know somebody you want to meet."

Kevin walked out from behind Tom and said with curiousness, "Who's this?"

"My name is Paulo, what's your name?"

"My name is Kevin Andes"

Paulo's jaw dropped as he said, "Is that really you, my son?" Paulo almost looked like he was about to break out in tears saying "Oh, my, it is you. You have the same name me & your mother agreed upon. We have so much catching up to do and mysteries to resolve."

Agent Dale then said, "Maybe we should go, so y'all can get to know each other more."

Paulo then responded saying, "Yes, that would be a great idea."

Agent Dale, John and Tom headed out the door to head home; as Kevin stayed behind to talk to the father there he had never known. Kevin was so excited to finally meet his father he had been looking for all his life, but bitterness swelled up inside him as well.

All day he had been thinking about why his father left him. He even wondered if his dad even cared about him at all. Clinching his fist resisting to punch Paulo, he now could finally get answers he never wanted to acknowledge out of fear he buried deep down within himself.

"Why did you leave me and mom, Dad?" Kevin asked with a cold attitude.

"Kevin, I never meant to hurt you. I was a typical young male, always thinking I was in love with this girl who lived where I did, who is your mother. As we got older we grew closer and eventually at the age of seventeen one thing led to another. She was pregnant with you, but she had to move to England with her family. We talked all the time over the hollowatch until you were born, then my mom got married to an American guy from California, so we moved to California. I called her one day, and it gave me an automatic message saying the number had been disconnected. Then, I spent a few years in California saving up for money to move here, but eventually I found somebody I actually had true love for. It was so much more than how I felt about your mother. Now I'm sorry to have to say this, but I do love your mother in a sort of different kind of way than I do my wife. Eventually my wife & I got married and had some children. But I had a responsibility as a father to find you to be the father I should be. So, because I knew she moved to England, I decided to move again from California temporarily just to find her and you. I knew you probably grew up without a father figure. But, when I tried to find her I couldn't find any record of your mom. It was like she had never existed?"

"You probably couldn't find her because she changed her last name to Barnett when this one guy wouldn't stop stalking her years ago."

"That's why the council wouldn't grant me access to her; it all makes sense now."

"It doesn't matter anymore anyhow…because she is dead now…" Kevin said sorrowfully.

"Oh Kevin, I'm so sorry…I didn't mean for you to have this kind of life. I will always try to be here for you and I will always love you. I'm just sorry I couldn't be a better father for you.

"It's okay. Now I know you actually did care." Kevin said as he broke down crying and stepped forward hugging his long lost father.

In the time span of a few days, Tom had training of his body and his mind as to what wasn't even possible to conceive as reality. Never did he expect there to be things he couldn't just give a simple scientific explanation for; sure he could come up with hypothesized ideas, but that wouldn't have proved how his new found abilities worked scientifically. To figure that out, he would need to do science experiments. Kevin had training of the heart, finding out that two people did care for him, one being Tom, willing to tell him about his father and his father who truly cared for him all those years he was missing. So, in the end both were trained in new ways for things that would change the rest of their lives.

Chapter 10
Somewhere Beyond the Stars

The Near future
Sunday, June 07th, 11:25 A.M.
The Beach on the outskirts of Brighton, England

Individually each of the Turners got out of their rented vehicle and headed down to beach. Tom stepped forth thinking the sand felt pleasantly warm today. The serene beach setting was instantly disrupted as he tried to catch himself from falling, just as Martin ran past him almost knocking him over. Tom instantly had a warm feeling of brotherly love as he saw how joyful Martin was jumping into the water.

"Better watch out for the little speedster, Tom, he might knock you off your flops." John said with a smirk as he and their dad were getting into the fishing boat.

"Yeah Tom, John has a point. So are you going to join us for fishing?" Tom's dad said.

"I can take good care of myself thank you, and no I might just read, swim or go exploring some." Tom said, while walking towards Martin who was playing in the water as he looked to his left at the hills by the cliff. "Whatever suits you son." His father said.

Walking, with a very curious look on his face, Tom asked Martin, "What are you doing splashing around while throwing dirt?" Martin responded "I just want to dig a hole here, but the water keeps filling it up making it where I can't keep my hole and it goes away."

"Well, Martin if you want to keep the hole you should dig it further up the beach so it won't get filled by the tide."

"I know that, but this is more challenging." Martin said rolling his eyes.

"It won't work no matter how much you try to change it Martin. Come here, I will help you dig a hole." Tom said while motioning his hand to come closer, as he walked up the beach. Martin hurried to catch up to Tom dripping sand and water off his shorts. Shoveling sand with his hands, Tom said, "See this is a much better place to dig out a hole, maybe it will even fill up much later if we dig it deeper."

Tom kept looking over his right shoulder while shoveling sand with his hands, so Martin asked, "Tom, why do you keep looking over at those hills?"

"Awe, it's just that I sort of want to go over to this cave place I found. I like to go to explore and think about things."

"What kind of things are you thinking about?" Martin said curiously.

"Just about how mad I probably made Justin causing him to end up in that prison camp. I figure the future is going to be a certain way because of these nightmares I have had at least three times."

"If that's the case, try to change the future so it won't be that way. You never know it just might all be a dream."

With lots of excitement at this new idea, Tom said, "You are a genius, Martin! Who would think kids your age could have shared so much wisdom. In the past I tried to be friends with him and that just resulted in him being so insecure he tried to hurt Tara."

Martin placed his little hand on Tom's shoulder saying, "Tom, when I'm at school with all my classmates and somebody gets mean with people for whatever reason they do it, I forgive them of what they did and just keep trying to be that person's friend so that they might eventually change themselves." Tom felt a sense of serenity. This might be the right thing to do when Justin got home once this summer was over.

"You are right, Martin, maybe that's what I will do. Well, looks like we are hitting the water underneath the sand. I guess this is as far as we can dig for now. Let it fill up with water when the tide comes in and enjoy the show, but for now I am going to do some cave exploring. What are you going to do?"

"I'm going to swim!" Martin shouted as he ran off into the water.

Tom paced off, grabbing "The Book of Curses" (he thought it was way cooler sounding than the Book of Wisdom) out of his backpack he had on the table by the chairs his mother set up. Walking to the cave by the sea, Tom was enjoying the nice warm weather England was getting.

Stepping foot in the cave Tom felt as if the atmosphere had just changed to a more damp, cold feeling. Folding his arms, he felt like this place needed cleaning up that would make it better suited as a place for his own private get away from his family if he ever had problems with them. "I can also use this place to read whenever I want or to do experiments." He thought to himself.

Astounded by the mystery of this place, Tom explored the cave. Finding a back cavern (or what he thought was just a cavern) he walked in curiously vocoing some furnishings for his hide away as well as some tools. So, with dedication and perseverance he installed torches into the walls in the back cave and the main chamber with the lake in it. Finally, when he was done, he said "Ignis all these torches."

The torches all lit up making the place feel much warmer. Tom then said, "Expello all this dirt and dust in this area." He could hear that hum again then the place started rumbling with a nice shiny look to it. Then he noticed the whole place looked different. It looked like some old temple eques place that was meant for some sort ancient office or something. There were more torches that appeared out of nowhere just from cleaning up the place they began to lighten up. By Tom's logic he could tell that this place must originally have been made from the old English Knight Templars.

Sitting down in a chair he just vocoed; Tom opened the book of curses searching for two specific words for an idea he had. A few minutes later he found the words he was looking for and thought what he had planned next was going to make for quite an adventure.

Then Tom walked up to the cave wall and placed his hand on it saying, "Make me a vermis cavus that goes from here to where I expello my voco items." Instantly out of nowhere, the harmonic sounding hum came again as part of the wall began to vibrate morphing into a crystal emerald looking stone. Each piece of stone,

one by one and at different rates, started backing deeper into the wall as the whole area started spinning like clockwork or a whirlpool, and then the emerald crystal rocks emptied into what looked like a giant swirling vortex of energy.

Stepping forward, checking it out, Tom started to feel all strange inside as if he was being pulled closer to the vortex. Before he could step back, he quickly felt a sense of rushing water or as if everything around him was fading away. Trying to look back, he saw the beach below him disappearing...then the earth & moon itself was looking smaller. All around him he could see lights moving in darkness in circular motion, like the galaxy. Feeling his sides to see if he was wet, he looked forward and a green light getting stronger with each passing moment as his world faded away.

Before Tom knew it he was aimlessly staring up at the green sky that constantly was shifting colors like the aurora borealis. He wasn't sure if he was lying down or standing up or even sitting down. Staring at the stars, in a hazy state of mind, he wondered to himself, "Why am I here? How did I get here? What am I? Who am I?" It felt like he was in a dream; as if he didn't know how it began or how it would end. Somehow, though, he felt like he knew this place; like he had always been there; like it was home...

"Where is the sun or the wind?" he thought to himself as he scanned the sky but only seeing it lit up with colors & stars yet no sun, but plenty of light. "Why do I feel complete, but have so many questions?" He asked himself.

Over to his right he noticed lots of random objects floating in the air. Tom got up off the ground to see what they were. Peeking at them with interest they looked familiar to him; like he knew them already. Reaching out his hand with curiosity, Tom touched the giant boulder, instantly remembering everything he'd forgotten when he first appeared there. Immediately, his clouded mind became clearer focusing on his goals.

Turning away from the floating vocoed objects, Tom noticed a grassy mesa with rich looking scenery; the whole place was giving him shock & awe. Standing there on the plateau, he looked back at the hovering objects thinking "Man something must be wrong with the gravity or magnetivity of this place. Maybe, somehow, those objects have become diamagnetic?" Surely, now Tom was getting something new out of life, just like he wanted a few months prior.

"Okay, maybe I should establish a home base or a fortress in case I decide to go exploring this place a lot." Tom thought to himself as he walked over to some bushes of a plant species he didn't recognize. "Alright here we go, Voco a small but not too big Arcis." He said. Again the hum came that accompanied Tom anytime he summoned something or made something. Just then the ground began to shake.

Tom looked around as walls of Sapphire rose up; at each of its four corners there was Chrysoprase (green looking stone) obelisk posts. The ground below him felt like it was moving, so he stepped back, as golden bricks began forming a pattern for a path. Looking to his left down the path he saw three Aquamarine pillars shooting up out of the ground diagonally towards one another. More humming resumed as a spire made of quartz crystal emerged at the top side of the pillars, leaving then the tips of the three pillars on the very top of the point of the spire.

Tom looked up in amazement at the base of spire as more bricks of Quartz crystal formed going all the way down the side of the pillars creating what looked somewhat like a triangular pyramid teepee with a spire at the top. "Man, whatever force listens to me creating things sure has some odd taste in architecture." Tom said as he looked at the unusual structure that had formed. He looked to his right down the golden brick path and saw a gate made from some odd colored material.

"Maybe I should close this gate and get back to my parents before they notice I have been gone too long." He said as he walked up to the gateway of the strange fortress. "Where is the control to this gate thing? Oh well, occludo this gate." He said as the only gateway on the east wall closed shut so nobody could get in or out of the fort and nobody from earth would be able to explore the world too much beyond the gate.

Tom tried to dig out a gold brick from the side of the path that looked like dirt but as soon as he pulled the brick out it flew right out of his hand, and back to the path conneting in its place. "Strange, gold usually isn't strong magnetically so why is it connecting with the other gold bricks like that?" Tom thought to himself as he moved towards the entrance. Heading into the strange building, he scratched his head wondering why the walls in the main hall were made of quartz crystal. To his left he saw a doorway with a spiraling stair case, so he went down to find cells in a dungeon like room.

Tom looked down to the end of the dungeon corridor as he said, "Make a vermis cavus from there to the old English knight's temple in the cave by the sea and merge it with the one that exist so they are one." After the usual hum the quartz crystal wall turned yellow like citrine and the brick started to fall back into the ground spinning like the first wormhole. He stepped through it, this time seeing the universe below him getting bigger with each moment. As stars began passing him by he noticed the moon as he passed it. Then he saw England coming into view with its nice beach. Next thing Tom knew he was back standing in the cave by the sea.

Walking up to his family on the beach casually trying not to seem too excited about his discovery, Tom said "Hey, what's going on?"

"We are just making some fish. John and I got lucky about 20 minutes ago." Tom's dad said while putting some fish on the fire pit. John then said "Yeah, it was so strange because the water went from murky to clear all of a sudden and then the fish were easy to spot." Tom chuckled; thinking about how he was responsible for their lucky catch.

"Why are you laughing, Tom?" Mr. Turner said.

"Oh, it's just funny how something weird like that would happen."

"So Tom, where have you been?" John said while getting plates out of the vehicle.

"I was just exploring this cave over there past the hills." Tom said pointing towards the Templar cave.

"Oh yeah, find anything interesting?" John said.

"Nope, nothing much really." Tom said feeling guilty he semi lied.

"Tom, you should be careful. If you slipped in there and hit your head on some rocks, none of us would have known where to find you." Their mom said with a concerned voice, leaning over her chair's armrest.

"Mom, if that happened, you could use ELO (Earth Locating Operations) on my hollowatch to locate me or my body. Still I do know how to take care of myself, thank you very much." Tom said rolling his eyes.

"Kids always think they're so wise, don't they honey?" Mr. Turner said to Mrs. Turner. "Yeah, but someday he will understand the concern of being a parent." Mrs. Turner said getting up putting some fish on the plates that John had gotten out. "That's true. Maybe then he will appreciate all the times we looked out for him." Mr. Turner responded.

"You guys know I can hear you, right?" Tom said.

"Yes, but sometimes we like to talk between the two of us about things we don't think you would understand yet." Tom's mom said.

"Mom, Dad, I'm 16 now, I think I can fully get why you would be concerned about your loved ones. It's not like I'm Martin's age." Tom said with a bold voice.

"Hey! I'm not stupid Tom, I love Mommy and Daddy and everyone else in our family also." Martin yelled with his high pitched voice.

"I know Martin; I'm not saying you're dumb, I'm just saying I'm old enough to know how things can be hard on people."

Mr. Turner then said, "Tom until you lose somebody you love or have somebody to lose whether it be a child of yours or even your wife, you won't fully understand why some people get overly worried for their loved ones."

"Yeah, I guess both of you are right," Tom said earnestly. "But, still, I do think I should try to fix things with Justin so we won't have any issues in the future. That's a sign I'm getting more mature right?"

Tom's dad laughed, "Yeah, it is Tom, but this isn't about how mature you are. It's just about your mother being concerned for you."

"Yeah, I get what you mean." Tom said as they all sat down to eat lunch together.

"So Mom, Dad, are we going to go anywhere else while we are here besides this beach?" John said, "You know it would be nice to see some other parts of Europe."

"Well John, your father and I have been planning some other excursions while we're here. The problem is I can't do much traveling because my wound is healing, have you noticed how I haven't gotten in the water at all?"

"Awe, that sucks. Still, I do want to check out some colleges soon. Maybe Tom could come with me to look at them."

"Yeah, I would really like that." Tom said.

"Well John, your mother and I will talk it over and once we figure out if you two can do some college site seeing before we need to go on the excursions when your mother's wounds are good enough, then we will give the two of you the go ahead."

"Sounds like a plan." John said happily taking a bite of his food.

△ ▷ ◇ ◇ ▷ 〉 ˪ ◇ 〉

Sneaking out quietly late at night after everyone had gone to bed Tom tried not to wake anybody up. He snuck out the back door pacing quickly to the road in front of their cabin. Treading down the road next to the field, he thought to himself, "Man this adventure could go a lot quicker if I had a way to travel faster, or maybe if I vocoed me vehicle or made myself speed up some." While scratching his head he said, "Oh wait…make me celer, duh."

Speeding down the road, Tom quickly approached the beach they went to casually. It was a cloudy night, with very little moonlight making it hard to to see where he was headed. Carefully, he made his way into the cave by the sea trying not to fall off the rocks. Noticing the torches were still lit on the walls, he walked past the lake cove. He wondered why they hadn't gone out yet. He looked down at his hollowatch, checking the time so he would know how long he'd have to explore this strange world again. It said 12:22 AM as he approached the wall with the wormhole.

Stepping once more into the doorway between the archaic void and the mysterious world of wonders, Tom was sent off to see the exhilarating universe again. No matter how many times he had this experience it never seemed to get old or remotely boring to him. He couldn't help but look around in amazement as stars, planets, and galaxies moving around and passing him by.

Trying not to fall down from the sudden darkness of arriving in the underground dungeon corridor, Tom was excited to check out more places outside the citadel. He scratched his head, wondering why the place still made him feel complete, but this time he didn't forget things. Climbing the dungeon stairs, he opened the main hall doors of the fortress and saw bright sunlight again. "What is going on? There shouldn't be any sunlight, it's only twelve something?" Tom said dumbfounded. It was still bright, showing star constellations he didn't recognize, but still showing light everywhere in the sky all coming from no source. "Wonder if the sun ever sets here or if the light goes away? For that matter, I wonder if any of this is real light or just a powerful magnetic field causing the illusion of light?"

Walking down the gold brick path Tom said, "Open the Porta". Immediately the gate of the structure opened letting him get out to explore the place more. He was excited the very moment he began running out of courtyard on the grassy plains surrounding his structure. The wind was blowing hard as he ran with enjoyment looking at all the beautiful scenery.

"That's strange. Earlier I remember it felt like there was no wind here? Maybe that was because I was so entranced, not knowing anything about when I had gotten here." He thought to himself. "Wait a second, why am I not running really fast like I did before when I was trying to get to the wormhole? Guess I'm not meant to run really fast here." He said perplexed. "Hey, that looks like a nice place to check out." He thought with a perplexed look, staring off into the distance at a majestic looking forest to the left of the citadel.

Upon reaching the forest, Tom felt as though it had a very odd presence about it. The whole place just seemed to send shivers down his spine as if there was an enigmatic force running the place. The trunks were so big, and the leaves so close together that hardly any light proceeded down onto him. The only light that did proceed was a warm green light. "There it is again, no wind here." He said to himself walking deeper into the mysterious forest.

Once very deep in the woods, Tom saw unusually wide ponds of water next to trees. It was the strangest of woods, very quiet; possibly there were no animals to mess with anything. "Wonder what those strange looking ponds are about? This has to be the strangest forest I have ever seen." He thought. Looking around he could hardly get a sense of any signs of life. The area seemed like the only thing that took place there was the trees growing and soaking up sun light & water from the odd ponds; without a breeze even. This was the kind of place anybody who didn't know where they were going just might get lost in if they explored it too much. So he walked out back to the plains of grass.

While Tom had been in the forest some clouds had rolled in blocking the view of the unusual star alignments, but the clouds made it obvious to him some interesting geography in the distance way north of the forest pond. Heading to his right and trekking onward towards a mountain in the distance, Tom wanted to check out the area surrounding the mountain. Wind was starting to pick up blowing in his face as he started to climb up a group of hills. He hoped soon he would get a better view of the area.

Reaching the top of the hill on this set of Great Plains, Tom got a much clearer view of the geography of this odd world. Gazing forth below him off the steep side of the hill he found out that he was on a ravine. Strangely, though there was no river directly below him at the bottom of the steep wall of dirt, just another giant forest.

Looking down into the valley he saw mist among the trees that made another forest. The trees looked to be a different kind than the ones in the pond forest. A glorious feeling filled him as he saw the mist as if it were clouds below his feet. Across the misty valley at the foot of the mountain he was wanting to see, there he saw a river near the end of the forest.

Looking up at the clouds that were passing part of the mountain he couldn't fully see, Tom thought, "What's with this place, it feels as if there were some kind of harmonic convergence of energy or emotions, as if I should be here. But I also feel like that mountain is calling out to me to be there." Then he snapped out of the trance that the view of the mountain had given him, "Why don't I feel tired at all? It must be getting late. Maybe I will go see what is in the other direction." He thought looking at his hollowatch.

It may have been the tallest mountain he ever saw, seeming to allure him with how they kept going so he couldn't see the top of them, but Tom felt conflicted that the mountain was calling out to his very being. A feeling as if it wasn't time yet to see what was up on this strange rock, yet he wanted to. So he quickly walked back to his fortress, then headed what he thought was west, but was really south, towards a direction he had not yet gone to explore.

Upon reaching a new less grassy like area of the plains he saw mountains with weird shapes. "Okay, this place just keeps getting weirder and weirder." He said looking up at the one that looked like a Lion, the other was shaped like a lamb, but they were lying down together. Tom thought this to be very unreasonable, given his knowledge of wildlife on earth. "Who would cut a monolith of a Lion and a lamb together?" Tom thought.

In Tom eyes, these clearly were made by some sentient life that had been here at some point. But they had moss along with other plant life growing on them, so they must have been old. Tom wondered where the intelligent life had gone. Had they made these monoliths as he saw another one that looked like an Eagle next to a Dove.

The next one he saw made him have more questions about this place, because there was one like a pyramid. Tom gave it some thought; maybe the Egyptians had once been here or who ever made pyramids on earth, but something seemed off about this pyramid to him and with good reason. He walked around it then realized it only had three sides at its base, and not just four like a pyramid. It kind of looked like a giant three dimensional triangle.

Tom wondered if this Triangle pyramid had been made from the same materials back home. Tom wasn't even sure if any of these materials were on earth at all. There were also ones in the shapes of creatures he had never seen before. In his perspective, this place was very strange with all of the qualities it had, because of what he was used to seeing while being on earth.

Semi tired of exploring and not wanting to be perplexed by the monoliths much longer, Tom thought, "I better get home to take a nap at least. I may have energy here, but not sure if I will back at the cabin." Once back in the dungeon, Tom went back to the cave by the sea through the wormhole.

Looking down at his watch as he stood in the Knights Templar cave, Tom saw it was already 4:13 in the morning. Strangely the hollowatch made a little beep as if it had an error and instantly changed to say 12:23 AM. Scratching his head he thought, "What's going on? Does Time stand still or not exist in that one world or place I keep checking out? Well guess this gives me some free time to explore this place a little."

Wanting to check it out, Tom walked through a door frame into some sort of a hall, and then had to take a left. In front of his view on the right side of the wall were two doorways, one was a room with some degraded tables and chairs, the other looked like some form of barracks with rotten wooden framed beds made of really stale degraded hay. The room with chairs and tables didn't seem that interesting to him. "Maybe I will go home after I check this place out some." He thought.

Walking into the barracks, Tom thought, "Man, this place seems really old. Oh, is that an ancient cupboard over there?" He moved the door that had come off its hinges; throwing it to its side as it busted on the floor because it was so old. Shelves on the cupboard walls had broken, leaving glass jars and clay vases busted on the floor. Seeing this mess, he said, "Resarcio all these broken objects." Instantly, with a little hum, everything that was shattered or withered lifted into the air and came back together in the places they had remained. "Well that looks better."

Tom couldn't help but notice, though, something seemed odd about the back wall of the cupboard (he had a knack for spotting flaws in patterns). One of the bricks looked a little out of place with the pattern of other bricks, and sticking out of the wall too much. With all his might he pushed the brick back with both palms of his hands, pushing it deeper into the wall. Then he heard an odd click as the rest of the wall began to go back, then to the right opening a door way.

A passage way opened up as dust fell all around Tom. A sudden drafty breeze made some of the torches flicker. This sent chills down his spine as an ominous feeling came over him. It wasn't a bad feeling, just as if there was an enigmatic presence of some kind. Stepping slowly forward he saw something not too far ahead of him that seemed more like a dusty old cave than a room. The strange feeling started to increase as he stepped forward hearing water drip down some of the rocky walls.

After walking thirteen cubits from the secret doorway he reached a strange mural built into the end of the cavern. In the mural, men were pictured standing together on a hill holding a strange looking large golden box with what looked like two winged creatures on the top. Surrounding the men were other people frightened by the strange rays of light emanating from the box and the mural itself.

Getting up from working out on the weight lifting machines, Justin and Cassidy headed over to the stands in the prison yard to sit around looking for ideal people that might have the skills they were looking for. They were trying to choose who could best help with Justin's plan of revenge against Tom, as well as make more criminal buddies for their group. One young man couldn't help but notice the way they sat there observing people constantly.

"Why are you guys just staring at different people?" the teenager said.

"Why do you look middle eastern, yet you sound like a Russian?" Justin said back sarcastically.

"Well, it's a long story, but essentially my ancestors came from the Middle East, but we lived in Russia for hundreds of years."

"Mmm…okay. Anyhow, so what are you in here for?"

"That too is a long story, one that ties into our village's secret. One day our newly appointed leader told an archeologist some things we had been hiding for centuries. Then, not too long ago, in the future, our whole village was raided and kidnapped by the American government. So we escaped the facility, but a lot of the village's people died when they self-destructed the place, so we wouldn't get out a-live to tell the world what they had done. Thankfully some of us managed to escape. Once we got into America we separated into groups and my group was found. So they put me here so I wouldn't be able to tell the public what they had done. It was the only legal way to handle me since they had arrested me in public." The teenager said.

"Yeah, but this is a prison camp for public teens. Wouldn't they be trying to make sure their secret is secure by not letting you live or monitoring things you say?" Cassidy responded.

"Come on, you really think they would do something that might attract more attention to them? They probably aren't doing anything drastic because they think nobody will believe me or because they don't want people to figure out my dad was the terrorist on that plane."

"Wait…your dad was that one guy who survived the terrorist attempted hijacking?" Justin said.

"Yeah, he is. They even made up a fake ID for me so people think I'm a legal citizen if anybody comes snooping about me."

"I still don't get it though, what secret is so important that they would do all of this stuff you are talking about?" Justin said.

"Well, my village had one goal when it was founded long ago. We came from Sumer in south Mesopotamia long before it had become Iraq. The goal of our exodus was to head back north to the land where Arba's origins came from who was our forefather that had headed west into the land now known as Israel, so we went up north to make a temple and hide some sacred bones. Then my ancestors traveled for a long time to the mountains of what is now known as Russia where Arba's ancestors had come from before they moved to Sumer. Eventually, our goal by each succeeding generation seemed less and less important. They thought they were just dumb old bones.

Some of us migrated to other parts of the world. But my family was one of the many that stuck by why we had moved there. Even if it was centuries prior and our tale is passed down to every kid we might have, it is never forgotten or changed."

Justin said, "I don't get it, all that over some dumb bones that were sacred to them or something? Sounds like a very silly reason."

They weren't just ordinary bones they carried to the temple; they were carrying giant bones with them."

"What like dinosaur bones?" Cassidy said.

"No…they were bones of giants." The young man said.

"Well, we were looking for people with certain skills. Do you have any useful skills?" Justin said.

"I might not have committed the crimes that got me here, but our village during my entire life had training centers to learn how to defend ourselves and protect our secret. Until we reached a certain age we were just taught that we had a secret, but didn't know what it was until we were old enough to hide it. Not everybody considered it important. Like I said, not everyone was well trained when your government came for us."

"Well, nice to meet you. My name is Justin and this is Cassidy."

"Nice to meet you too; my name is Sacra." He said with a suave smirk on his face.

The sun was setting on Agent Dale Sizer while he was busy practicing pistol shooting with his boss. It had been quite a nice afternoon just getting to spend time together bonding as work partners. Since it was getting dark though, their time for practicing now would have to come to an end; but not before Agent Sizer could get some answers to what was going on with some of the things he had been dealing with recently.

"Sir, I have some question regarding the terrorist cell I have been dealing with the last few months." The agent said.

"Yes, I figured you would be bringing up some of this stuff." His boss said.

"Well, for one thing, how did they manage to get knives in hats past airport security?"

"We discovered through some investigation that one of the terrorist's brothers worked for airport security and got him to look the other way so they might get by when their hats went through the scanners."

"Why was Director Ford so elusive the day of the interrogation of the terrorist? Just as he told me, he would show me the files when I got back to America. But something seemed off in how he didn't want any info spread about the interrogation and somebody above him sent an EMP device on the rooftop of the police station I assume. Then two days later I saw in the newspaper how the officer who did poorly interrogating had died in a car crash. Doesn't that seem fishy to you?"

Immediately Agent Sizer's boss looked down at Agent Sizer's wrist angle then twisted his left wrist sideways so the hollowatch camera was out of sight of his facial view. Putting his right hand up to his neck and sliding it sideways, he tried implying "Shut up now." He said. "Why Director Ford has been like this is beyond my knowledge. You should try talking to him about this stuff when you get back to America. Maybe he can give you better answers, but I already showed you my own files on the intelligence of the terrorist cell. Agent Sizer's boss used his right hand to open the flap on his suit jacket. There it was, on his white shirt next to his tie a sticky note reading "Dig deeper for more info…"

Agent Sizer realizing his own boss was trying to be elusive and realized there must have been something hidden going on here that he shouldn't be speaking about out loud. But the question remained how were they being heard and how deep did this secret go?

"Well, I shall speak to him about that stuff I guess. I'm sure he can give me some guidance. It is getting late though; I need to head back over towards Brighton's area. It's been a pleasure practicing with you."

"See you later Agent Sizer, keep up the good work and keep looking for Intel on these escaped Terrorist."

The Near Future
Wednesday, June 17th, 1:16 A.M.
Stonehenge, 2 miles west of Amesbury, Wiltshire, England

Agent Dale had trouble getting through the traffic of Birmingham, causing him some major delay in getting back to Brighton. He wanted to get back quickly so he could go to bed, that way he could help Tom the next day. He looked around, as he could see fog coming over the nearby mountains with the moonlight shining down on them just as he was approaching Stonehenge. It had been a long ride, but getting to see this structure was well worth the time.

Dale wanted to check out the famous monument, so he got out of his car to check it out. The stone felt so old and cold to him full of mystery. Who could have made such a thing centuries before? A strange shiver came over him as he felt a breeze coming down on him at that moment.

The whole place seemed to get an odd vibe momentarily, suddenly lights beamed down from above. Quickly, the lights moved around in odd arrangements as they flew over some fields nearby. As the lights got further from him, so did the strange noise that accompanied them.

Agent Dale felt semi spooked by the quick encounter. He hurried to get back into his car to get back to his hotel before those things tried to do anything else to him besides scare him. The ride home was fueled with speculation as to what that thing was or why it was messing with him. Concerning him, he thought he might get abducted or taken just like old myths of strange lights proposed.

Somewhere beyond the stars there were answers to what that strange world Tom found was and why he had found it at all. Somewhere beyond the stars were answers to whatever Justin was planning with his friends. Somewhere beyond the stars were answers to the mysteries surrounding Agent Dale's career and what those lights were about that he had just seen. For only somewhere in time remained the answers each of them was searching for in life.

Chapter 11
The Nightmare Comes to Life.

The Near Future
Friday, June 19th, 4:08 P.M.
The Cliff by the sea, Outskirts of Brighton, West Sussex, England

It was a sunny nice day at the beach by the sea. This was probably their last trip to this cove since Mrs. Turner was almost fully recovered, and they had other parts of Europe they wanted to visit while they were staying there for summer. Tom though wanted to head up the hill that led to the cliff above the cave to try a new word he learned.

Standing there gazing at the amazing glory of the sea, Tom admired the beauty of the sea as waves swayed back and forth. "There must be a reason for all this beautiful scenery to exist." He thought in his mind being very excited watching the waves move as they glimmered with the sun hitting them. He decided it was time to try what most would consider impossible.

Looking down there from the Cliffside the wind was blowing fast pushing up against his body blowing his hair around. In that moment he prepped himself in his mind with pride, honor and faith as he said "Please make me able to Volo!"

Tom felt a rush of emotional feeling with comfort go through him that made him feel warm, like all boundaries were lifted off of him, like there was an unimaginable peace upon him. This was like an emotion he never once had felt in his life ever before surprisingly it felt almost as extreme as his Love for Tara, if not more.

As Tom walked forward one step his right foot felt tingly like it was pulsating or vibrating. He took another step then one more and continued then looked down and noticed he was walking on air. Amazed by the way it felt with what was happening Tom looked up willing himself to go up. Then he could feel vibrations coming out of his feet pushing him forward higher into the heavens. The thrill was amazing and spectacular in words that can't even begin to describe the essence of the moment for anybody who experienced this.

Tom decided to travel more East up the coast to explore things which he did for quite a while, but then noticing the time on his hollowatch he thought he needed to get back to his family. So he flew back over to the cliff where he came landing back down onto it. He walked back down the hill to see his family was swimming while having a wonderful day at the beach.

Tom decided to walk past a dune on the beach to a little grove separated from their cove. Walking over there he began practicing by growing trees quickly and setting them on fire. Little did he know on top of the dune John was watching him with curiosity.

John quietly walked up behind him and said, "You have got some big secrets, don't you little brother?"

Tom freaked out quickly responding, "Secrets, what secrets what are you talking about?"

John responded with a chuckle, "Oh come on, don't act like I didn't just see you set a tree on fire that you made appear out of nowhere in the first place."

"Drats…I was hoping you didn't see that"

"Well I did, not like there is anything wrong with me knowing is there? So what are you a freaky mutant or some kind of wizard?"

"No I don't think there is anything wrong with you knowing as long as you don't go blurting it out to everyone. Plus I don't know why I can do these things, it's just when I say the words in this book, I accidently found out that interesting things can happen when I say certain words."

So Tom explained everything that had happened so far on his adventures to John. He decided to show John some of the amazing things he could do. After showing John his abilities John asked "So is there like an invisible mana bar only you can see on the top left of your eyesight?"

Tom laughed saying, "No don't be ridiculous, I'm not a living RPG video game. If you are trying to ask how far I know I can go, well I honestly can't say how I would know or if it would ever run out?"

"Maybe you should try to test your limits."

"Well I had a great idea, when we go on those college tours we talked about to mom the other week I could practice my abilities as well go exploring some more while we are away. How does that sound?"

"Sounds like a great plan to me."

"Yeah, but don't tell mom, dad, or anybody about my strange abilities please."

"Don't worry, I won't I promise." John said as they walked back over the dune as the sun was setting.

The Near Future
Saturday, July 04th, 1:09 P.M.
On the outskirts of Brighton, West Sussex, England

Today being July 04th Tom wanted to right his wrongs with Justin and resolve their differences because he didn't want things to turn into the nightmare he had endured three times already. John said goodbye to his parents just as Tom said, "Bye mom, bye dad, love y'all, see you later." Their parents waved good bye as they drove off towards London.

Tom remembered how the previous weeks they had many escapades & adventures together since Mrs. Turner was still recovering. One time John told their parents they were going to check out Oxford. When John drove them to spend the night to check out the college at Oxford, John checked it out and went off to an arcade, while Tom flew off to see the beautiful Cardiff Mountains in Wales.

There was another time their entire family decided to go on an excursion. They visited France, staying there for two days and a night, so Tom flew off late at night to see the Eiffel Tower in Paris. He was having so much fun escaping his family and checking out so many different places in Europe leading up to the 4th of July. He saw the Scotland Highlands, and Neuschwanstein Castle in Germany. It was all because John was willing to put his preferences aside to help Tom out, so that Tom would have the chance to explore these amazing places.

Half a mile from their cabin John stopped the car saying goodbye to Tom, and told him what hotel and room they would be at later. Tom got out of the car, flying up into the sky going about sixty miles per hour. Then he flew backwards going towards the cabin which was west. As he went over the cabin fireworks were shooting off all around him into the sky as he flew past and unnoticed by his family (even though it was still day time Martin wanted to see the fireworks before the sun set). For another two hours he was flying over England until he hit the sea boarder.

The Near Future
Saturday, July 04th, 1:37 P.M.
Somewhere out at sea, Atlantic Ocean, International waters.

Agent Dale felt very tense knowing July 04th was usually a prime suspect day for terrorist attacks. He decided to go with some of his old Navy & Marine buddies to celebrate the 4th of July on the aircraft carrier where they were assigned. To relieve himself of any anxiety of a possible attack, Agent Dale decided to talk casually to his friend. "So Jonas, received any good news or commands lately?"

"No not really. All they keep giving me is dumb orders to be on the lookout for odd activity from ships passing through this part of the Atlantic. You know, like if anybody is off course or off route from what all the schedules say. What about you, have you been given any new Intel on that stuff, or are you not permitted to talk about it?"

"Not really, just more mystery at the moment. Did resolve some stuff, but still feels like something is off. I'm sure I will figure it out eventually. So how's your family doing?" Agent Dale said.

"They're fine; my daughter is doing well making some okay grades. Of course, my wife misses me a whole bunch. What about you, how's your love life going?" Jonas asked curiously.

"Just the usual, they miss me a bunch. Wish I would be home instead of stationed in England. So, we have our ups and our downs." Agent Dale said while rubbing the locket in his pocket. "So how was your recent leave visit with your wife and kids?"

"My leave was great we went on a three hour tour in a..." Immediately alarms went off blazing with lots of noise.

"Captain Hale, there is a fast moving bogey coming from the east on radar; its moving fast sir!" an officer yelled trying to talk over the alarm.

"It's our duty not to let anything get into American waters that might cause danger. Lt. Elliot fire two heat seekers at that bogey now." Captain Jonas fearfully said.

Agent Dale headed outside to the outer deck of the island hub to see what they were trying to take down. Instantly he watched two missiles launch out of the RIM-9 Sea Hawk while quickly curving fast towards the object the radar picked up. Agent Dale thought he was seeing things when he observed the fast moving object. He thought it looked like a human body figure.

As the bogey got closer to the carrier Agent Dale noticed the human figure looked like it had Tom's stature, as well his face, but the sun blurred his view when he tried to look up at it. Ironically he didn't know that it actually was Tom.

Tom was starting to feel the missile's heat, panicking he yelled, "Exertus this missile away from me!" The missile oddly pushed away from Tom, and then it almost went fully into the water, but came back at him very fast. The other one was still tracking him, getting closer on his tail trying to attack him.

Quickly, he put his feet down in a standing position, spun around flying backwards; then holding out the palm of his hand quickly he said, "Exertus this missile to attack the other missile coming at me." He stopped midair as the missile's middle vertical thruster ignited sending it up, then its side thruster came out from its side making it do an elliptical u-turn. The missile on Tom's tail swerved fast going off course until it collided with the other missile which caused a big explosion.

Tom kept heading west saying, "Let me volo more celer." He blasted off creating a sonic boom near the aircraft carrying Agent Dale. The sonic boom caused the carrier to bounce around swaying in the ocean. Agent Dale tried to grab onto the rail as he saw Tom flying off very fast. The crew got a little woozy from Tom's actions; still he managed to escape which was all that mattered. Quite a few of them, though, were perplexed with what had just taken down their missiles.

About an hour later Tom was soaring over the smoky mountains of North Carolina. Tara looked up into the sky seeing a giant line of smoke coming out of nowhere above her camp. She didn't know it was Tom. He was so small up in the air that nobody could actually notice him, but they did notice the trail of smoke he left behind.

The Near Future
Saturday, July 04th, 9:09 AM Central Time
Oklahoma Juvenile Prison Camp, Lawton, Oklahoma

It was a very warm day in Lawton for all the kids who had broken the law by being put in juvie for the summer. Justin wasn't willing to let anybody believe he wasn't top dog. He gathered his group of friends to watch him take down a 14 year old kid who thought he could talk smack to him.

Punching the smaller boy to the ground to show people who was boss Justin said, "You really think you can make dumb remarks to me, you little brat?"

The kid responded, "It isn't that hard to rile you up, you big dumb idiot."

"Listen here, you are going to have to suffer if you want to survive while staying here, you better respect me or I will make you suffer so much you won't want to go home." Justin said as he threw a left hook knocking the kid down again.

Over the loud speaker a voice said, "Justin Phelps, please report to the Warden's Office."

The gate to the workout courtyard opened up letting Justin head inside with Sacra following behind. He pondered why he was going to the Warden's Office. They didn't call in the kid he just took down, so it must have not had anything to do with that situation.

"Sacra, stay here while I see what the Warden wants." He said as he entered the office.

"Phelps, you obviously have issues you never try to get past, but I feel somebody actually came here today to visit you and you should get some chance to speak with them. So go to the visitor's room to meet your guest." The warden said.

"I have a visitor?" Justin said.

"Yes, now go talk to them before I change my mind."

"Okay, thanks see you later." Justin said as he waved goodbye.

Justin motioned at Sacra, implying to Sacra to follow him, as he came out of the office heading down the hall with haste & curiosity. Entering the dark visitor's room he couldn't be more surprised for who was there.

Justin sat down then spoke into the phone saying, "Well, I never expected a visit from you Tom. You know, especially since I thought you were still in England."

"Yeah, came all the way here from a faraway place so we could resolve our issues."

"What do you mean, we both live in Smithsonian Valley you dumb idiot?"

"How did you know where I have been?"

Justin smirked and sarcastically said, "I saw you on TV genius."

Tom looked surprised as he remembered that one day on the plane. This definitely made Tom feel uncomfortable as if something wasn't right.

Justin said, "Besides that is all beyond the point of what I want to talk about."

"What do you mean? What do you want to talk about? Do you want to try to resolve our issues so we can just be friends?"

"Are you kidding me? After you got me put in this prison you want to be friends? You must be some kind of special stupid, Turner."

"I didn't get you put here; you did that all on your own by being obsessed with drugs. I wanted to give you another chance so we don't keep having all this back & forth fighting when you get home."

Justin responded with anger, "You are really pissing me off right now. I have been saving some words for you."

Tom started to feel really creepy inside dreading what Justin was going to say next. Tom knew this gut wrenching feeling was the result of him knowing what was coming.

He looked up and Justin started yelling, "I will kill you! I will slaughter you and make you wish you were never born!! You're going to die, Turner!!!"

He pulled out a knife then stood up as he started plunging at the glass nearly breaking it; loud alarms started going off.

Tom yelled, "Ignis!" Holding his hands together in a ball-like shape facing Justin, flames burst out turning the glass into sand and smoke. The flames hit Justin setting him on fire. Tom looked up to see if there was enough room to say something as he was flying.

So he quickly yelled, "Cavus." Looking up, a hole in the ceiling appeared. Tom flew back up into the air so fast he created another sonic boom blowing out the fire he started first all while knocking Justin and his friend down to the floor. Sacra got up off of the floor saying, "Why did the kid that got my father arrested visit you?"

"I don't know, but I will kill that idiot someday."

"Do you know that kid personally?"

Justin responded aggravated, "Yeah, he lives in my neighborhood and goes to my school."

Sacra said with excitement, "Well that was strange, yet interesting; it's also interesting you know him personally."

"Yeah, who would think two guys could end up in the same place together and both know the same guy who has wronged them? Still, I will get my vengeance on that brat someday."

"How are you going to do that? I don't think it would be very easy to take down a guy who can fly around like a superhero."

"Every man has a weakness of some kind. I'm pretty sure he won't be hard to exploit and take down." Justin said with a grin.

♛ ♛ ◇ △ △

Tom went flying back towards the hotel where John and he were staying. It took him two hours to fly there at a supersonic pace. He landed on top of the hotel and got into the elevator to go down to the 3rd floor where they were staying.

On his way down Tom thought about how his nightmare had come to life. "Why didn't the outcome change like I tried to make it change?" He wasn't worried one bit about Justin saying he would kill him. This new found confidence was going to his head. "I try to be friends with him and he threatens to try to take me down. Seriously, how does he even think he can fight me?" He thought to himself.

Then Tom remembered how he hit a pigeon on his way home then he thought, "I'm so tired of all this dumb drama, Just wish it would all be over with Justin. Why do I even bother trying to be the better man? It's obvious he doesn't want to change. Maybe I can put him in his place a little, then try to work things out with him once he is back from prison." Then Tom laughed about hitting the pigeon on his way home.

Walking into Paulo's gym, Tom & John found Agent Dale sword fighting with Paulo, or as some would put it, fencing. Finishing the duel, Agent Dale asked Tom where he had been two days before. To cover the truth, Tom lied saying, "I was with John at the college and arcade."

"Oh you were, were you? I could have sworn I saw you get hit by a missile the other day."

Tom chuckled and said, "Wouldn't I be dead then?"

Paulo said, "Even though this is a humorous conversation, let's get to work on the sword fighting".

So, instead of goofing around talking too much they fenced with each other for several hours. Tom was getting really good at countering Paulo's attacks. He wasn't too cocky about it either, since he knew Paulo clearly had lots more experience in these things.

Around lunch time Kevin came over with Paulo and the group. They had some fish & chips from Seabreams. Kevin told Tom how Paulo had come over to Tony's the other night. While Paulo was there, Kevin found out that he had brothers and a new mom waiting for him back in California. "But my mother can never be replaced."

Tom said, "You ever going to meet them?"

Kevin dipped some fish in ketchup responding, "Yeah, my dad, Paulo, is requesting from Tony that he will let him take me over there to visit them for like a month or more and see where our father/son relationship goes from there since school is about to have its normal break for us."

"That is great Kevin; I hope it works out for you. Funny, I was wondering why y'all were still at school in July."

"Yeah, ours doesn't let out till later in the year than yours, I think."

They all talked about their day; then Kevin had to get back to school so he wouldn't get in trouble.

After Three hours of weight training, Tom decided to have a break and visit Kevin, since school was ending. He walked over to the courtyard as all the kids were leaving school. Once he arrived, Tom saw Kevin with his group of friends and walked up towards them and said, "Hey, Kevin how was the rest of your day?"

"It was quite boring. Science really isn't my strong suit and our teacher was telling us all sorts of ridiculous theories for how the world would be different if our magnetic field was stronger."

"Well, you never know it could be different due to all the qualities a strong magnetic field can bring to things like the bending of light or suspended water, which is diamagnetic or can increase your health, you just never know?"

"Yeah, so anyhow, was the training with my Dad hard?"

"Not reall…" Out of nowhere and out of the corner of his eye, Tom saw a fist coming at him. Quickly Tom put up the palm of his hand stopping it.

Johnny said with anger, "You really shouldn't try to make me look like a fool all the time!"

Tom, with his snarky attitude said, "Well, I don't really need to do that at all. You're already doing a fine job at that all on your own."

Tom chuckled for a moment; till he remembered that he shouldn't try to resolve this by fighting or doing anything negative. He then said, "Sorry, Johnny that wasn't nice of me to say."

Johnny filling with rage, threw another punch while saying, "You're not going to talk me out of this one; I knew I should have taken you down last time, but I wasn't thinking right that day."

"Johnny, you're not going to resolve your problems by beating people up. Maybe you should get into boxing or do something safe to relieve your stress from your parents." Tom dodged Johnny's punch as he said all this.

Johnny, now furious yelled, "Stop bringing up my parents. They will never change!"

Johnny threw another punch as Tom flip-jumped over him to avoid it saying, "If you have faith Johnny, anything is possible."

"Ahh here you go again with your stupid faith talk. Well faith isn't going to save you today!"

Tom, with his quick wit had a whim of an idea. Johnny came running forwards to fumble Tom, but Tom had other ideas. Quickly avoiding getting hit, Tom swooshed up real fast twenty feet above the courtyard. As usual, there was a crowd watching the fight in the Bexley ledger courtyard. The kids who were there at the school stood speechless, hearing the voice but seeing no one. Until they all looked up in amazement like they had never seen something so unreal.

Tom talked, but it sounded loud like a yell saying, "So still think Faith won't save me now, Johnny? You see, I don't want to fight you and I won't bother if I can just avoid you. Hopefully someday you will understand why I have done the things I have done. Some things are better left alone just like reacting to your anger in ways that hurt others."

As he said these words, the crowd started to cheer Tom on as he flew off back to the gym. He left Johnny there very confused and perplexed by what had just happened. He had become the talk of the day for everyone at the school. The rest of the day who spent departing to their homes.

Once back at the Gym, Tom & the crew all said goodbye to each other and started heading to the places where they were staying. Trying to fall asleep, Tom was glad he stopped the fight before it got out of hand, but he was concerned about how much he desired wanting to finish the fight instead of just running away from it.

The Near Future
Wednesday, July 08ᵗʰ, 8:09 A.M.
Dragon fire inn, Brighton, West Sussex, England

Agent Dale was hoping this call would end soon so he could get to Paulo's gym to meet up with Tom and John. "Yes sir, I shall keep an eye out for any info on them." said Agent Dale.

"We almost snagged some more of the escaped terrorists the other day, ones that weren't on the plane. Sadly though, they had already begun running by the time our forces got there."

"How did you find them, sir?" Agent dale asked curiously.

"One of them was dumb enough to try using an old fashioned pay phone to call their relative in jail."

"Well…that didn't sound like a smart plan. I'm sure one of them will slip up again."

"Let's count on it, Agent Sizer."

"I will tell you if I figure anymore out about the others."

"Okay, see you later."

"Goodbye, sir." Agent Dale said as he was getting into his car.

Agent Dale arrived not too long after that at Paulo's gym. Tom and John were lifting weights with Kevin. "What's Kevin doing here; doesn't he have school?" Agent Dale asked. "Nope, schools out for summer vacation for them this Friday, but I asked if he could get out three days early because we have a plane to catch this afternoon." Paulo responded.

"Cool sounds like fun, where are you going?"

"We will have to end today's training lesson early, this might be the last one we can do for a while."

"It's okay, Paulo; you have taught me a lot. I think I will be able to handle anybody who tries to take me down with the self-defense you have taught me," Tom said as John tried to suppress a smile from the irony of what Tom was saying.

"Yeah, Tom I'm sure you could take on anybody from what Paulo has taught you." John said with a semi sarcastic voice. Then Tom acted like he was dropping the dumbbell in his hand, but really was elbowing John's side.

"So why are y'all traveling?" Agent Dale asked.

"We are headed to Cali, to visit my wife and kids, that way Kevin can get to know his brothers and his new mother."

"Well, hope it's a great bonding experience for y'all." Agent Dale said.

"I'm sure it will be."

For the next couple of hours once they were done weight lifting they started swimming for cardio. Then around 11:14 Paulo said they would have to be leaving soon, so they should say their goodbyes.

Kevin went with Tom outside asking curiously, "How did you pull that off the other day? Everyone at school is questioning how it was possible, even some are questioning the very essence of what they thought was reality."

"I won't be able to explain it in the little time I have now, but maybe later when you get back or something. Hey, why don't you just add me on facespace or skylink network then I can keep in touch while you're gone and explain it to you."

"That sounds brilliant, yeah, I think I will."

"In fact, let's add each other now." Tom said as he lifted his wrist opening his facespace PSI on his Hollowatch (PSI meaning program software interface). Then, Kevin opened his, and they pressed each other's hollowatches together causing it to beep notifying they had added each other.

"Well, guess this is goodbye till y'all get back or next time we visit? You have been a very good friend." Tom said.

"Cheers mate, you have as well, but this will be exciting getting to meet my new mother and little brothers. I also just wanted to tell you that I never really got to say thanks for helping find my real father. It feels so good to know that he wanted to be with me all along and he came this far to find me."

With a warm smile Tom said, "What are friends for?"

"Yeah, who would have thought they were for finding missing parents. Well, I guess I will see you later then, goodbye Tom".

They both laughed, then Paulo came out to ask Kevin if he was ready to go. Kevin said he was ready.

Tom said to Paulo, "Thanks for all your help training. It meant a lot to learn how to take care of myself and when to use that ability."

"You're welcome. Hope you use it wisely cause sometimes good lessons are taught to bad people, but I am sure you will use them with caution and only when needed."

"I will try to use them for defense only and when the time is right. That way I am not using them in the wrong manor or for the wrong reasons."

"Good, that is wise of you. Well, I guess this is good bye buddy."

Tom smirked as he said, "We may meet again someday soon enough who knows? Goodbye Paulo."

They waved goodbye as Paulo and Kevin headed for the airport driving down the road. It was a fitting goodbye to Kevin and Paulo in Tom's eyes as well as Agent Dale's. When Tom and John tried to get in their car to leave they found out it was out of power. "Crap, I forgot to recharge it this morning." John said.

"You guys need a ride?" Agent Dale said.

"It would help. Just let me grab the battery to recharge it back at the cabin." John said.

"Okay."

"Crap, it's been stolen!" John said looking under the hood for the battery.

"Come on guys, let's get out of here." Agent Dale suggested. They all got in Agent Dale's car and headed back to the cabin.

When they got back to the cabin and walked through the front door a man looking like one of the terrorist from the plane, popped out from behind the door and quickly whacked Agent Dale in the back of the head. Right as he saw the Turners tied up sitting in chairs. Tom ran back out the door trying not to be caught, but another terrorist jumped out of the bushes punching Tom to the ground...

The Near Future
Wednesday, July 08th, 1:24 P.M.
Cove by the sea, Outskirts of Brighton, West Sussex, England

Tom awoke feeling really hot and sweaty as his arms were tied up laying in the backseat of a car parked at the beach where his family went sometimes on their vacation. Whoever it was that knocked him out, had also wrapped a bandana around his mouth. He felt light headed, but figured out what he needed to do to help his family. Hopefully, he could pull it off without revealing himself to his parents.

Tom, said under his breath, "Expello the bandana on my mouth." The bandana vanished from around his face.

Then he said, "Expellpo these ropes tied around me." The ropes disappeared; he cautiously tried to open the door only to find the terrorist waiting to grab him. His parents were within the terrorists hands, as they walked them up the hill to the cliff by the sea. Tom's family was walking slowly up the hill, worrying about what was going to happen next. All of them knew in a scenario like this it would take a miracle and they didn't expect one to come.

Once they reached the cliff on top of the hill by the sea the Terrorist from the airplane said, "You stupid Americans are always ruining things for us devoted followers. Why do you always get in our way?"

Agent Dale yelled, "It's you that committed crimes and got yourself locked up in the first place. Then you tried to high jack an airplane!"

"We committed no crimes to be locked up like animals!" the terrorist yelled.

"How did you escape the prison I was tasked to escort you to?" Agent Dale asked,

"There was a man there who seemed like he was…"

"Like he was special with a personality that seemed spiritual?" The agent interrupted saying.

"Yes…yes, how do you know that?"

"I met him, he wasn't like most people."

"But you, you are like most people; a total selfish human being who just does what he's told." The terrorist said. "You killed my brother! This wasn't about anything personal before, we just wanted the truth to be known to the world! Now you have this personal vendetta to deal with…and now you shall die for what you have done to my family! But first watch this boy suffer for your actions!"

He pulled out a gun pointing it at Tom. He cocked the gun saying with a chuckle, "Have any good last words?"

Tom said in a cocky manner, "I have just two words to say Lobores Solis." The hum began once more as the ground started to shake; rocks came falling off the cliff; then the moon started to rush by them unknowingly (well Tom knew why). As it started to cover the sun, a giant shadow was crossing over the sea and all the tides going in towards the land went outwards.

The Terrorist said, "What are you doing?!"

Tom said, "I am not doing anything. I think somebody greater than you is angry at the silly mistakes in your life and is just scaring you."

"No, this is you...you evil child." The lead terrorist said frightened.

"I'm not evil." said Tom with confusion.

The Terrorist told his men to let go of the family and the agent so they could get out their guns to shoot all of them. So they did, but the moon was now making such a big eclipse so that the sun was darkened with no light given.

Agent Dale quickly yelled, "Let's all jump, we might live the fall into the water!" The entire group of Terrorists started firing their guns as the Turners and Agent Dale jumped off the edge of the cliff. They all fell into the sea except, Tom who had to make himself fly down vertically.

Tom yelled, "I know a cave; follow me!" Each of them grabbed the closest person they could feel coming from the direction they heard Tom yell. Together they swam towards the cave, but the current caused by the moon was sweeping them outward towards the ocean. So Tom thought logically if the water was moved because of the solar eclipse then changing the current of the water or the position of the moon would make it go towards the cave.

Tom said under his breath, "Exertus the current to let us be carried towards the cave". After he had said this all of them started getting pulled towards the cave along with the current of the water.

Tom knew it would be dark so before they could get there he said under his breath, "Ignis the torches in the cave."

Once inside the cave's lake Tom said, "Come on this way, there is a room in the back of the cave."

Torches were lit up everywhere when they got out of the water. Tom watched as shadows of body figures were getting closer to the cave entrance, but luckily Tom also noticed the earth was still shaking from the sudden solar eclipse. So he whispered, "dissimulo this cave." Rumbling was still going on, then the cave started to close as the entrance vanished which meant there was no exit. Tom's family members freaked out and were scared that the solar eclipse had affected gravity so much that they were trapped.

Tom told the rest of his family to go into the back part of the cave where the knight's quarters were so they could hide there while he and John could look around for an escape. The Turners and Agent Dale went into the back room while Tom and John stayed in the room with the lake in the middle.

John asked, "So got any more bright ideas?"

"Yes, but first let me take care of those Terrorists.

Tom said with a bold voice, "Give me the Validus of ten men and Ostendo this cave." He felt the energy of becoming very strong rush through him, then the cave walls started to go back to normal being an opening.

Flying fast out of the cave Tom said, "Stop this labors solis." Quickly, the moon went flying back over the mountain side next to the hill by the sea causing the tides to rush at the cliff. As water burst up against the cliff, Tom landed down on its edge as the shadow of the moon disappeared causing the earth to reappear; revealing Tom. Analyzing the situation, he looked down upon the men at the bottom of the hill.

The Terrorists saw Tom up at the cliff then came running up the hill at him from their cars. Quickly, he flew off the hill by the cliff really fast yelling, "Ignis" He started shooting fire out of the palms of his hands setting trees near them on fire, just to scare them. He landed on the ground, quickly starting to use some of the moves Paulo had taught him to fight with, on all of them.

Tom had a great advantage. He was able to push them around with his strength. He banged them around like light objects as if they were toys. He punched one guy into the sand then threw another at one of the trees that were not on fire. One was left, so Tom asked where the leader was. The terrorist said he went back to the cabin.

Tom went soaring back to the cabin looking for the terrorist asking him in a snarky manner, "Why are you running from me?"

The terrorist responded instead of going inside the house, "I want you dead, you evil freak of nature."

Tom, mad at his mean comment said, "How many times do I have to say I'm not evil, and I'm not a freak. I'm just different." The terrorist yelled back, "Hope you love dying and suffering as much as you like causing issues." The terrorist pulled out what looked like a bomb trigger. Obviously Tom knew what was going to come next for his summer get away they were living in. He yelled, "Expello all my family's belongings from the cabin." So the terrorist pressed the button. Then the cabin exploded from a blast as Tom went flying up into the sky to out fly the explosion.

Tom came back down saying, "Voco all my family's belongings back here to the cabin that I Expelloed." Everything that was not part of the cabin design reappeared. Then he flew back to the cave telling his family that the cave wall had collapsed again so they were free to leave. Dale jump-started the terrorist's cars and called the police.

Then they drove back to the cabin. Tom's family was shocked that everything at the cabin was destroyed, except their personal belongings.

Tom's mom said, "How could everything be destroyed except our belongings?"

"I don't know. It is very bizarre?" Tom's dad said.

Tom's mom then said, "It doesn't make any logical sense; there wouldn't have been enough time for them to mess with it, then put it back once the house blew up. Why would they put it all back just where it was?" Tom blushed as he tried to keep himself from laughing at the wacky situation that had been created by his actions. Clearly John had an idea about what had happened, so he smirked over at Tom.

Dale then said, "Regardless of the odd circumstances, I think your whole family should head back over to America tomorrow."

Mr. Turner with worry said, "Okay, but let us get our bags packed and then head to Brighton for tonight so we can stay close by you."

"That's a great idea Mr. Turner." Agent Dale said.

So Agent Dale helped them pack their bags, then they headed to Brighton for the night. They got to the Dragon Fire Inn to stay close to Agent Dale. Agent Dale called Paulo's hollowatch phone to tell him they would not be there when Paulo and Kevin returned. Tom and John said good bye to Paulo and Dale told Paulo why they were leaving. Then he said goodbye to him. Tom's dad used his hollowatch to find out when there would be another flight the next day. That night Tom slept well knowing he stopped the evil Terrorists from killing him along with his family.

Chapter 12
The Book of Curses

The Near Future
Friday, July 10th, 8:17 A.M.
The Turner's house, Smithsonian Valley, Texas

Hovering outside his own window, making sure Benny wasn't awake yet, Tom looked inside. The enjoyment of having gone for a sunrise flight over Canyon Lake and taking in the beauty that could only be seen from above, was something he treasured seeing. Being sneaky he quietly hovered in through the window then walked down stairs finding his brother on the computer.

Sitting at the desk in the den, John saw Tom in the reflection of the screen and said "So, where did you go?"

Looking around to make sure his parents weren't awake Tom responded, "Just for a flight around Canyon Lake; enjoying the sunrise It's something real spectacular and you should see it some time."

"Don't worry; mom and dad aren't up yet. Besides, shouldn't you be more concerned about Benny seeing you fly out your window?"

"Nah, I'm not that concerned since he looked like a log when I left and when I got back. I'm pretty sure he's fast asleep on my couch. Tom responded with a smirk.

"Yeah, Benny always has slept like that; even if we were yelling he wouldn't notice. Ever since you two were little he has been that way."

"So what are you looking at on the computer?" Tom said curiously.

"Well I was trying to figure out from what you told me on how your book says that people refer to it as the book of curses. But, all I could really find that seemed like something more than a gimmick or conspiracy theory or myth was this one skylink page on the locate engine. Also Martin saw me looking things up earlier as he walked by…"

"What!" Tom said softly but abruptly.

"Don't worry, are you kidding me, it wouldn't matter if he saw it, he is still just a kid after all. He wouldn't be able to comprehend it." John said rolling his eyes.

"Yeah, I guess you're right. Anyway, show it to me before Mom & Dad get up."

John enlarged the skylink page that looked like it had something about their ancestor on it.

The legend on the page read:

The book of Curses was a legendary mythical book that was written by a powerful witch doctor many centuries ago in ancient Spain. It was rumored to have magical curses in it that would harm others at her will; it was believed by locals the witch who made the book could grant wishes of anything the person requesting desired. The Book of Curses was very important to the witch doctor; she never let it loose of her grip. It has been told that she took it with her when she escaped to a foreign country for being put on trial to be burned at the stake for being a witch, but nobody ever was able to track her location again. One legend suggests she fled north towards ancient France even curing some of them with health issues. It is a mystery to this day why it is named (The Book of Curses) or how she was able to help people across Western Europe with the strange things she did.

Perplexed at the possibility, Tom asked curiously, "So are we descendants of some old Spanish witch doctor? But, we don't even have any parts of us that look Spaniard, do we?"

"Well, if it's positively true that's interesting to know? But some genes are stronger than others; maybe her genes got blurred along the way and were not as strong as her descendants. Possibly some family branches migrate to different places in the world getting new looks as they adapt."

"Then, why did I have to say, "Reveal my book" in ancient Latin to find it if it was not mine in the first place, but our ancestor's?"

John said assured of his knowledge, "I learned in history class that if something belongs to a person it is always passed down to the next generation of family members. So, that book is technically our family's book."

"Okay, let's delete this so our family doesn't think we are into witch craft" Tom said as he deleted the skylink page from the history of the computer.

John said with much concern, "I think if I were you, I would be more worried about Mom & Dad finding out that you are speaking ancient Latin words, and causing witch craft to happen more than them seeing that skylink page."

"What I do is not like witch craft. I have studied it once for a project back when I didn't even know the info I needed for the project. So I found out that witch craft is using a bunch of herbs as well as certain colored candles, and then repeating words in a ritual-like manner to cause things to happen. Some things I read, said you call upon demons to help you, not just saying one word and then something happens, so there must be a difference? Another old definition of witch craft was pretty much the art of rebellion."

"Well, if it's not magic then I don't know what to call it?" John said.

Tom then responded, "You know some time long ago they would think if you knew too much you were a witch, so maybe there is more to that story about her than we know?"

"Well, until you know the whole story behind it I would be very careful with those abilities, because you don't even know if they have bad side effects."

△ ＞ ⌇ ◇ ▽ ⚼

Agent Dale got out of his car pulling up to his parent's house while he talked on the phone with his boss about important matters. "Sir, I just don't think it's the greatest idea. Certainly, you might be taking care of two birds with one stone, but the risks are very high in doing so."

"Agent Sizer, you listen well. It's the best way for us to maintain things till we get more leads. If there ends up being any issues, then we shall try to find an alternative way to handle things when the moment arises. But, until then, just follow protocol making sure things are alright."

"Yes Sir, I shall. Goodbye sir, my family is waiting for me." Agent Dale said getting off the phone walking up onto his parent's porch.

Knocking on their door he said, "Mom, Dad, I'm here. Anybody home?" With a fast pitter net of feet, the door flew open as his son yelled, "Daddy! You're here!" Agent Dale bent down lifting up his son into his arms, holding him and hugging him, then putting him down. "You bet I am, son."

Then his wife, Kathryne, came around the corner from the kitchen holding their little girl saying, "Hey honey, glad you finally made it home."

"I'm back, baby." Agent Dale said with a smirk

"See, you're still wearing that locket." Kat said holding his locket a little by the chain.

"You know how much it means to me, how it always has a picture of the four of us that I can hold close to my heart when I miss you." He said as he kissed his wife Kat on the lips.

"Well, I missed you too, and so has Daniel. You know Jackie is too young to express how she missed you but she did."

"Yeah, I'm sorry I was stuck on duty in England for so long. I don't think I will have any out of town missions for a while. Right now I just have to keep my eyes on a few people locally to make sure they are safe. In fact they are the family I have been protecting since the airplane incident. I also need to look for leads on some certain people, too."

"Work is work and life is life; at least you're here now and that's all that matters."

"I know it just seems unfair for me not being able to be here constantly for Danny. He shouldn't have to grow up with me being absent most of the time."

"Well somebody has to pay the bills."

"You're right, but still a boy needs their father. Sorry, I wasn't able to get over here to the house last night or yesterday; I had a lot of debriefing to do back at the center from some of the things that took place in England."

"It's okay Dale, let's just have a nice afternoon while we visit your parents."

"Speaking of my parents, where are they, as well how are they?"

"Your dad's off on one of his motorcycle rides and your mom is out back finishing up some gardening with Daniel." Agent Dale walked out back talking to his mother and son, Danny telling them a lot about the crazy adventures in England that he had endured.

The Near Future
Sunday, July 12th, 12:31 P.M.
The Turner's house, Smithsonian valley, Texas

Coming over to Tom's after he'd gotten back from Church, Benny was glad to be done with the chores that he had just finished doing for his parents. For a while they played Ring of Mystery on Tom's Z-Triad. Once they played a few games on the skylink Tom wanted to see if Benny could beat him at chess. Tom wanted to test his own skills to see if they had gone down in his absence.

Benny opened up his high school's PSI, looking into the sports section on his hollowatch. "Knight to E5" Tom said with a smirk, as he moved his knight. Benny randomly moved another one then said "Hey, Tom, did you know that back in the early twenty first century basketball season didn't even start their try outs until November at our school?" Tom remained silent, because his attention had been drawn away by Tara's car pulling up across the street.

"Tom, are you even listening to me?" Benny said with a frustrated look on his face.

"Huh...oh sorry, I just saw that Tara finally got home. I have been wondering when she would be back."

"Oh, so Tara is back." Benny said rolling his eyes. "Well, no wonder you're so distracted talking with me about sports."

"You ever feel weird seeing girls?" Tom asked feeling weird again; seeing Tara get out of her family's car.

Benny responded with a chuckle, "You really shouldn't always say what's on your mind Tom. You might say the wrong thing to the wrong person. Besides, that's just how boys feel when they see a girl they think is hot."

Offended, Tom abruptly responded, "No that's not what I meant at all Benny, I'm not talking about lust. It's more of a feeling that irradiates through your whole body, but it starts in the stomach then it moves through your chest expanding throughout your whole body, much like an emotion, not an I got to go to the bathroom feeling."

"Whatever, everybody has their different, weird feelings Tom. Like look at me for example; when I listen to music I feel like I'm getting electrocuted, but it also feels good because I'm listening to my favorite songs. The strange thing though, is I enjoy that feeling and it's not a bad feeling to me even though it feels like electricity."

"Yeah, well that's sort of the way I'm trying to describe my feelings for Tara. It's like something about her just makes me feel like I'm listening to music, but like that music feeling is maximized throughout all of me."

"Well, why don't you ask her out if you like her so much? Before school ended for the summer it looked like you were about to be a real couple, what happened."

"Ah, well because of all that stuff with Justin I felt like she wasn't safe around me. But now that school is starting again I think I might try to ask her out."

"What's with this new found confidence?"

"Remember that training I told you about the other night when we got back? That is one reason; another is, I can't just live in fear of

Justin always being an issue. I'm sure eventually he will realize not to mess with me. So, I will try to see where things go with Tara, I guess."

"Well, glad you are manning up. So you're thinking about joining the basketball team this year?"

"Yeah, actually I am."

"You certainly look like you have been working out some getting semi toned and all. You look like you grew some over the summer a little too. Hopefully, you will make the team."

"Yeah, I hope so to." Tom said as he got up out of his seat by the window. "Be right back, I'm going to go grab a snack." He headed down stairs to the kitchen grabbing an apple from the fridge, then saw John alone in the den.

"Hey John, what are you up to?" he said.

"Ahh, nothing much, just waiting for mom and dad to get back from the grocery store. I'm finalizing everything for going to college at CalTech."

"So, you really are going to move to California to go there for college?"

"Yeah, England in my opinion is too far. They have great programs at CalTech that I want to be a part of, and a good basketball sports college team."

"Mmm…that sounds interesting."

"Well, don't worry! Guess you could always just fly over to me if you miss me much." John said with a chuckle.

Tom laughed saying, "Don't worry I'm not too concerned about you going to college. Just don't get too crazy if you join a fraternity."

"I'm sure I will be fine." John said.

Tom walked back upstairs playing games and hanging out with Benny the rest of the day.

The Near Future
Monday, August 24th, 07:22 A.M.
Highway 617, Smithsonian valley, Texas

It was a humid morning and Tom was glad the bus he rode to school had air conditioning. Plugging in his wireless headphones to his ears, he put on some of his favorite music from his hollowatch while he waited to get to school. As he sat there, flipping through pages in the book of curses, he tried to figure out new words. Very excited, his mind raced, thinking of how this school year would be great and he wouldn't have to put up with Justin's bullying anymore.

Walking through the school door, many people saw Tom, but they were all in shock that he looked somewhat taller and more muscularly toned now. Some girls were going gaga for his profound new look that he gave. (He only grew a little but he looked much taller because he walked with his back straight instead of hunched). Once he stopped noticing people staring at him, he began to put his books in his locker before heading to English class.

As he stood there, he could hear some girl nearby talking about him to another girl saying, "Wow, can you believe it. Look at Tom; he is so much sexier this year. Especially, those blue eyes and his soft looking brown hair."

"I know, right? I can't believe it either. Who would think such a nerd could become such a hottie." Although Tom had always had brown hair and blue eyes, sadly enough these girls were shallow. This was the first time they really noticed his eyes, only because he was more muscular and defined.

Tom chuckled when he heard them talking about him and then he walked off to English class. Later on in the day, around lunch time, he headed to the lunch room and grabbed his food. He decided to walk outside to the courtyard. Approaching the tables, he saw Tara. Tom though maybe he should check on how she was and check up on the things that were going on in her life. Then He sat down and asked her how her summer was?

Tara said, "It was fun and full of adventure."

"So was mine, it was lots of fun."

Tara laughed then said with a smirk, "I doubt getting attacked by terrorist qualifies as fun."

He chuckled a little and Tara giggled. Clearly, they were enjoying their conversation as well as the close comfort of one another.

Then, she said with a warm look on her face, "I saw you on TV a few months ago when we were on our way to Cherokee, North Carolina."

"Yeah, isn't that place in the Smokey Mountains? I have seen those mountains before and they look really nice or at least they did from where I saw them."

"Where did you see them?"

"Oh yeah, well let's just say I have never set foot there, but I have seen it." Tara felt puzzled knowing he wasn't referring to an air plane or car trip. Tom though, saw their beauty when he flew over Tara without either realizing they were both in the same area at the same time.

"Okay? Well, we did so many things just like the time we went hiking. That was so gorgeous. Once we got to the top of the mountain and the view was amazing. We did lots of river tubing, as well, and different things even some fishing and seeing different things. We even saw this one cave that had many different rock formations in it, which was real cool."

"Sounds like you had lots of fun. Yeah, we went fishing a lot. I saw some different and famous landmarks while we were staying in England. We did lots of swimming and I checked out some colleges in England with John." They talked about their summer vacations till the bell rang. Then they left for Chemistry class.

△ ▷ △ ◇ ⚛

Later on that day, walking down the stairs on the backside of the gym leading down to the courtyard area where they came across each other frequently, Tom saw the strange boy that was with Justin in the juvenile prison camp. He wondered what that kid was doing there with Justin, or more of why he was there. Before they could see him, remembering he didn't want any of Justin's teeny bop drama this year, he walked back up towards the concrete balcony to go wait for Jessica in front of the gym.

◇ ▷ ↳ △ ▷ ↳ ◇ ▷ ▷ ♔

Entering the CIA center in SanAntonio, Agent Dale was hoping to find some more answers to the matters that were perplexing him. He felt like things were tense there today, though. Some of his fellow coworkers had a sense they were being pressured into doing the work. Then again, things could always be tense considering they were somewhat like their own counter terrorist unit.

"Agent Myers, why is everyone so tense today?"

"Because some of those terrorists we are searching for are still out there, or at least they could be forming another cell. Plus there are the ones still unaccounted for that escaped the prison facility right before it exploded when you were there."

"Speaking of which; I was coming in today to give a follow up report on some of my Intel on the things that took place in England. I was wondering though, if you could help me search for more Intel by telling me who supplied you the details of the terrorist cell back when we had to raid & capture them?"

"The intel I received came from Agent Bishop. Still, Agent Sizer, what's the point of figuring out where it originated?"

"I just need to figure out its source point to know the exact reference of the terrorist's origins so I can get some insight as to why we went after them in the first place." Agent Dale said arching his eye brows as he walked away.

Looking around talking from one agent to another, he climbed the corporate ladder figuring out the origins of the Intel given to attack the terrorist in their cell. Occasionally he started making phone calls all around even to other bureaus or branches of the United States government to find out where they had gathered their intelligence.

One thing became clear, that there were a lot of routes this knowledge took before it actually reached Agent Dale's office. After hours and lots of researching he finally found what he was looking for as the origin of the actual Intel of data on the terrorist cell found in Russia. Finding out that this should be the final person to talk to really made him feel liberated. He finally could get the proper answers he was seeking in a young lieutenant stationed in Russia.

Calling the lieutenant on his hollowatch, Agent Dale said, "Hello Lieutenant Clancy, this is Agent Sizer from the CIA center over here in SanAntonio, Texas. I'm calling about intelligence you gave out on January 16th."

"What do you want to know?"

"I would like to know the events surrounding your Intel, such as how you came to obtain the evidence that convinced us to go after the terrorist cell that we did."

"Well, Monday on the thirteenth we received our orders just like we do every Monday to search for info in a certain location. This time we started looking within the vicinity of the Caucasus Mountains. Then, later on that Thursday, I overheard a phone call being made by Nioklay Serzynkov, about how he wanted supplies for his training camp for the Kafir Dunya brotherhood. He wasn't just asking for food, he was ordering in all sorts of guns from a weapons dealer so his village could get away with their plans. Poor fellow seemed like he was really trying to convince the dealer he actually had a village of soldiers who needed the guns. So we checked out where he was wanting these things to be sent and then sent off the intel back up through the chain of command."

"Well that was an interesting tale. Where might I be able to find this Serzynkov guy? Was he rounded up when we went into their camp a few weeks later in February?"

"No no…he was arrested immediately so he couldn't warn his camp that he might have been compromised. In fact, the Russian government had him picked up by the local police then escorted to a prison in Moldova."

"Moldova? That's quite a long distance from the Caucasus Mountains." Agent Dale said perplexed.

"Yeah, well those Russians sure are odd in how they deal with things. Plus he was in a fairly big town when we overheard him. He thought making these transactions outside of his village would help, but he was dumb enough to tell the dealer the location on the phone."

"Something seems fishy about all this, like it was too easy. Well thanks for your info Lieutenant Clancy; it has shed a little light on the situation."

Ending the call, Agent Dale thought he should get some more info on this Serzynkov guy. Walking up to a desk he said, "Agent Myers, can you please do some research on Nikolay Serzynkov? It won't be hard to figure out who I'm referencing if you look at the Intel from the terrorist cell scenario."

"What do you want me to find precisely, Agent Sizer?"

"I need you to check all of this guy's transactions, then give me the bank number."

"Alright, I will get right on that. Once I have gathered your request I will contact you."

"Thank you, Agent Myers, have a good day. See you later." Agent Dale said as he walked off heading for his boss's room.

Walking into the room, sweating and a little concerned over the possibilities of issues of this being a set-up, Agent Dale needed to ask his boss some stuff that didn't quite seem reasonable.

"Sir, I was hoping you could explain to me the logic of allowing the Asrar family to live so close to the Turners when they have ties to them. You know, their household's father who apparently from DNA evidence, blew himself up in their house. All right after he had kidnapped us. It just seems dangerous, especially if they realize they aren't too far away to reach their family. If they want revenge or something, such as how Sacra is going to school at the same place that one of the Turner kids goes. I know they are staying in my neighborhood, but still isn't it a risky move?"

"There may be lots of risks, but there is lots of value in giving them a temporary American home. We can monitor them trying to reach out to any of their friends that escaped all while they think they have freedom. Also, we will be able to determine if they have any devious plans or who they consult on a daily basis. Don't worry too much about the Turners. We have you checking in on them and occasionally other cops and agents are sent out to keep an eye on them. Plus, the school already has detectors for any weapon shaped objects that might pass through one of the main doors."

"Fine, hope you are right. But that family has already been through so much. I really don't want to see them become victims to any more of those Kafir Dunya terrorists. So, got any interesting leads on the other terrorists?"

"Yes, right now we are tracking somebody up north we think might have connections to some of the ones that escaped. But this guy is elusive; he's very good at covering his tracks."

"Seems a little odd for a guy who might have come from a tribal terrorist cell."

"They aren't exactly tribal like Agent Sizer. According to some reports these people would train their kids to defend themselves at young ages. Something tells me they have lots of things they don't want us to find out and I wouldn't be surprised if they also trained them to keep their agendas hidden. Oh, by the way, I just remembered director Ford is here today from DC, and he wanted to speak with you about some things you requested from him."

"Okay, Thank you sir. Have a wonderful day; I shouldn't hold up director Ford any longer."

Agent Dale quickly headed out the door towards the guest office to see if director Ford was there. Dale walked in calmly greeting Director Ford with enthusiasm.

"You look a little shaky Agent Sizer, is everything all right?"

"Yes, I am fine, but how did you know?"

"Even though you tried to cover it with a smile & enthusiasm, it was too obvious something was troubling your mind by the way you were tapping your pants with your finger and your face was one of anxiousness. Right before you saw me." Director Ford said lowering his eye brows.

"Sorry, just lots of work details have been bugging me lately. As well, it's not as if I usually have to meet you in person, because we were working over the mic the other month."

"Well, no need to be scared just because I'm like your boss's boss. Still, what's bothering you with work? I came here to give you those files that I told you I would."

"Oh thanks, for hand delivering them. Couldn't you have just skylinked them or mailed them to me? Occasionally I keep coming across claims from those terrorists that they were never terrorists at all. Like from multiple ones, not just one of them. Like the one at interview interrogation when you heard the recording."

"I had other reasons to be here today and thought I should also give them to you, but Agent Sizer, anybody will say things to justify their deeds or to try to formulate a lie to save their skin. But in the end the truth will always prevail. It would take a lot of work and conspiring to make somebody look like a terrorist if they weren't one. Here, maybe these files will help put your mind at ease." Director Ford said handing lots of files on the terrorist cell to Agent Dale.

"But sir, what about how they or somebody above you ordered you to send down that EMPAP (AP standing for air projectile)? Or the fact one of the British interrogators who heard what the terrorist said, died a few days later according to a newspaper I read?"

"It was a car accident, Agent Sizer…I heard about that too and found it very fishy. Still, I'm sure whatever reason was needed not to let the English have that Intel was a good one. I will try to talk to my bosses about that info and see if it could help you; how does that sound?"

"Okay, thanks for your help, Director Ford."

"Alright, I will be seeing you later; I need to get back to DC now that I'm all done here."

Tom had discovered more about the Book of Curses even though it was very little info. Maybe one day he would be able to figure out more. Still it made him ponder what his ancestor was, or where she came from. Agent Dale had tried to solve his own book of mysteries, but only found out there was still compelling info to be found or fully known. Hopefully the truth would be known to the both of them very soon.

Chapter 13
The Hidden Diary

The Near Future
Friday, August 28th, 4:13 P.M.
Smithsonian Valley High school, Smithsonian Valley, Texas

Standing in the gym while he waited in line, Tom couldn't wait to try out for the basketball team. The room full of sweaty boys anxiously awaiting for the try outs, wasn't helping. Even though it was a hot day, he had hoped that he would be able to outdo some of them on the court. Some were doing well, while many were failing to amount to anything even considering low standards. A few people had angry looks on their faces, others were sad, and many were smiling with enthusiasm thinking they might make the team.

Wiping some sweat from his forehead, Tom asked, "Hey Benny, you think I will be good enough to make the team?"

"Maybe you will if you put a lot of effort into it and give it your best. The only way to really know is to try."

Now it was Tom's turn to try to demonstrate how to throw the ball into the hoop. He tried by throwing it just like John would, which paid off because he made the shot. He hoped this would earn him favor with the coach.

A little while later it was his turn to try making a slam dunk. Running forward towards the hoop, he jumped up barely making himself fly to the hoop. He looked like he made a three foot leap up to the hoop. Everybody around him look surprised he could jump that far. Once everyone was done trying out, the coach said, "Tomorrow when I'm home I will analyze all of your qualities, then when I have made my decisions, I will put the list of people that made it on the team on the board Monday. You are all dismissed."

Grabbing his bag, Tom headed off to the extra bus that was provided for try outs. Sitting down, he got out the Book of Curses to read some more and to learn more words. While reading it, he found in the back of the book there was a hidden pouch that had a paper written with more ancient Latin words on it. Being perplexed at why it was hidden there in the back, he unfolded it to see that it said... Ostendo mei proprius liber libri." Tom thought, "Oh boy here we go again with almost the same words."

Tom decided to check the Book of Curses first to find out what they meant. "Proprius" meant one's own self like persona, "Liber libri" meant book. So he said, "ostendo mei proprius liber libri." But nothing happened or appeared on the bus so he wondered what was going on. "Man, where is that persona book." He thought to himself. Then he wondered if it might be where he found the Book of Curses at their property in England.

Curious to find this new book, Tom wondered if their might be a word in the Book of Curses similar to teleport. Then he said, "Ostendo to me a word similar to Teleport." The wind picked up then the book pages started to move quickly, like an invisible hand was moving them. Then it stopped at a page that said "inflecto". The word morphed in his eyesight into "Warp". Not wanting to attract any attention though, he needed to wait till he got off the bus.

Getting off the bus in his neighborhood, he stood there for moment making sure nobody was watching him or could see what he was doing to find this missing persona book. Once the coast was clear he curiously said, "Inflecto me to the cave in England."

Hearing the hum that always came when he made odd things happen, the words he learned made him feel all tingly inside like he was being filled with lots of energy. It felt different to him than when he made himself run fast saying "celer" though. This amazing feeling continued to radiate through him until he turned to nothing but the silhouette of a man enveloped in a flash of light as he vanished at the bus stop.

Randomly appearing in the entrance of a cave in England, Tom wondered where he was. Looking around very puzzled, it confused him because he didn't emerge at the one by the sea. Walking into the dark forest nearby he decided to fly up into the air to figure out where he was. But he only kept seeing forest for many miles under the pale moon light. It seemed like the sun was just setting in England because of the time & latitude difference.

High enough into the sky, Tom could see an outline of the land. Quickly he zoomed off towards the Southside of the country so he could get to the cabin. Upon arriving, unpleasant thoughts arose seeing it all broken into pieces as he walked through the debris. Heading to the back yard where he first found the book of curses and the glowing rock, he landed down noticing a box that was smoking with little lightning bolts moving around on it. He said, "Make my hands lentus to electricity."

Picking up the box his hands began to feel all warm and tingly as if he had not heard his favorite music in a long time. So he figured saying "lentus" worked making his hand resistant to the electricity. Opening the box he found another book ready to be read. On the front cover it showed Ancient Latin again that morphed into the words "The diary of Alida."

Sitting down under the moon light on a burnt tree stump, Tom set the box down as he opened the diary. As he opened it, he hoped it might have dates to tell when it was written; but sadly it was just split up into different days or events that took place in Alida's life instead of some form of time.

Tom read the first page seeing each word morph into English except a few certain ones. *"This is day one in my diary, but it has been one year since the great son of The Master has returned to the caelum saecula saeculorum or the sky of eternity. I am writing this diary because I am going to have been sent out of the concero regnum onto the planet called Earth for wanting to help heal people on Earth. I asked The Master if I could and The Master has granted me my desire. So they threw me out here onto the concero regnum from the sky of eternity where I am now. I am trying to figure a way to get to Earth so I can help people there that are falling ill to many different famines. I have found my way to the Hall of Connection here in the Northern air temple which is at the tip of the western peak of Mt Ó'Asavard which is on top of Mt. Iam which rest on top of Mt Yemeway. Which all is in the Connecting Realm, it is a palace of many minerals as well it is of great wonder that it has been made to* connect to any place livable for ones who breathe The Master's air. The People here say that for many years there was no connection to earth yet recently the gate way has been active. So I am taking the gate way to Earth now, I will write what has happened after I pass through."

Tom turned the page to the second one reading it. "*I have just passed the Gate way to earth it was amazing leaving that place to find out that I could come back to Earth to see its beauty with mesmerizing views. The air seems different here on Earth then the last time I was here as well as the sky seems to look very different, but it is a great place to live with such caring creatures. I believe that I now am in a place called Solomon's Temple. The people here call the Gateway the Ark of the Covenant in their own language I am merely translating. I don't get why it is such an important relic to them because it's just a pretty looking Golden box. I assume they don't know what true potential it holds since they keep it locked up from others. Well now I must be leaving for Hispania that is near where the ill are mostly right now in the Rivers of Time. I will write more tomorrow."*

Tom wondered why the Ark of the Covenant was a Gateway to a land that in some way connected to other Realms that his own ancestor came from.

He turned the page to the third as it read saying "*It is day two for me on earth, I have learned from some Roman centurions how to get to Hispania so I have flown my way across a very beautiful sea arriving here to heal people, but some seem reluctant and worried that I might bring great Evil upon them for being what they think is a* sorceress or a practitioner of evil crafts conjured by what they refer to as the bearer of darkness or the tempter but we know I am no such things. I was hoping that my actions here would convince the people of the Connecting Realm to let me back in, so far I am not reading any signs that I can come back yet. But then again I was sent out for wanting to help people talk about irony. Plus the fact that the people here in Hispania all speak the Latin language is a good bonus to my living and being able to deal with them since I use it all the time to help them."

"It is day twenty three I have been led by my heart here crying out to me, but I don't want anything right now. I have found a beautiful green pasture by a still water. I want to do what is right but sometimes this body feels plagued by something in this world like it is not properly functioning maybe I can restore it if I return to the sky of eternity. Eventually then things will be better for me. Even though I have seen death many times I don't fear anything in this world because I know I am always protected all the time from deaths grip."

"Day twenty seven I have made some friend's that accept me for who I am and what I do for others. I even found a wonderful peaceful man to call my true love named Josinaldo. I hope soon enough we can be married. I will write again when I feel like I should."

"Day one hundred and seven I am getting married today. I am very happy today because this is one of the biggest days of my life. I will no longer just be alone in my journey of life. Our love shall last *forever. I am so excited about spending the rest of our lives together because Josinaldo is a wonderful man to be with."*

"Day three hundred and sixteen It has been almost a whole year on earth, I have been married to Josinaldo for nearly seven months as well I am with child which shall be born in a couple of months. I don't know a name for him yet, but I will think of one. I made sure that all my kids and their kids so forth and so on will always have at least one boy in their family so me and my husband's legacy will live on."

"Day three hundred and seventy six I have given birth to a boy and have named him Joseph. He is such a cute little baby. He is such a sweet and kind child I love him so much. I hope he can be protected from the troubles in this world."

Tom skipped a lot of pages since this started sounding like what he figured to be typical talk of a newlywed. The next thing he read said *"It has now been seven wonderful years here on Earth. I am happy with my wonderful family."*

Tom skipped many more pages.

"It has been 1190 years sense I moved here. But I am not happy that my Children have died over the years just like my first husband who I thought was my true love. But luckily my children had children and their life cycles have gone on for many generations. Plus I have heard news that in Jerusalem the Ark has been taken by knights of the Templar Order so if I ever want to go back to the Connecting Realm I need to go to Britannia. Things in this land have changed drastically since I arrived here and the Romans don't have much

influence here anymore as I previously wrote. Life is hard to watch your loved ones die. I don't see why I have not aged much but I am heading to Britannia to get to the Gate way back to the Connecting Realm. I am leaving earth because I have an unknown disease but the river of time does not pass everywhere in the Connecting Realm so I can heal there to figure out what is wrong with me. Joseph's descendants will stay in Hispania even though some have moved more up north. I will leave my diary, my book of Wisdom for my heirs to read someday as well as my pet companion Dragon Viridiso at my property I purchased in Britannia it shall be concealed so only my descendants can call them forth to read them and spend time with Viridiso to get to know me better since he and I spent so much time together. I am leaving for the gateway at the Ark now so goodbye Earth."

Tom flinched then said to himself confused, "She had a pet Dragon and its name was Viridiso how strange?" With a look of regret on his face at the memory that Viridiso means green in Ancient Latin he said. "Oh brother, why did I say that? I can be so stupid sometimes"

The box that was lying on the ground flashed then where the Diary was there was a weird egg glowing in many different colors appeared.

"I really need to learn how to hold my tongue." He said chuckling. "Oh the Copperony of that phrase" he thought in his mind. He gave it a lot of thought then wondered when it would hatch or how he would be able to take care of it? Then he inflectoed back to his house putting the Egg on his book shelf along with the Book of Curses and the Diary of Alida.

The Near Future
Saturday, August 29ᵗʰ, 3:10 P.M. or 1510 military time
Russian Prison facility, Chisinau, Moldova

Placing his hollowatch onto his wife's wrist, Agent Dale said "Okay honey, I will be seeing you soon. Like I said I need to go talk with this source on info; I'm glad you came with me." Earlier on they had worked out details about why he was putting the hollowatch on her wrist.

"Bye, Dale, see you soon. Love you.

"Love you too." He said kissing her as he got out of the rental car.

Heading into the facility, Agent Dale asked the guards if he could speak with Nikolay Serzynkov. He walked with the guards to a visiting room and then sat down waiting for them to bring in Nikolay.

As he was being wheeled in, Nikolay had lots of hair missing. Nikolay saw the shocked look on Agent Dale's face and said, "What, not what you were expecting for a man in a high security prison? Hello, I'm Nikolay Seryznkov."

"Well, you can't deny this is odd to me. are you alright? Oh, and my name is Agent Sizer, I am here on behalf of the CIA."

"It's just terminal cancer, and I'm sure you know international terrorist don't get treatments, especially ones they can't afford."

Pulling out his APpen (all-purpose pen), Agent Dale turned the clip on it to set it to the record mode then pressed the button to start recording their conversation. He asked, "Just terminal cancer huh? Well, I am here to figure out why you were trying to order weapons for the terrorist cell near the Caucasus Mountains. As well how did you become affiliated with them?

"I met the leader one day at a café in Beslan…"

Agent Dale rudely interrupted, "Beslan really? I am usually more kind towards people with terminal illnesses, but you are pushing my patience. In the fact, I have traveled half way across the planet to get answers. If it were a real terrorist cell do you think they would just go about gathering regular people for their causes in cafés? According to your records, you have never lived in that village prior to this year. Which, from all other sources, is seeming to me like you had to be born in their town to be involved with any defense training they did. You moved there right after New Years, which seems odd given the fact that around that time we found the evidence on you. I also found out that you didn't bring much with you when you moved. So why don't you just tell me the real story about why you made that phone call?"

"Well you certainly are a clever man, Agent Sizer. I will give you that. Clearly you did your homework on the subject. It all started last October when my wife and I were both diagnosed with cancer. As you might guess with the Russian economy failing as a result of us going back to our roots of socialism, instead of the experimental economy of democracy we had for a while. It makes cancer treatment impossible for the little money we earn around here. I was desperately searching for jobs in a coffee shop in Beslan one day in December when an old man came up offering me a deal."

"What was this man's nationality and what kind of deal was he proposing?"

"Ha, you Americans always seem to have little patience; I am getting there. He definitely was American. How he knew about my health issues seemed somewhat odd. He told me how he knew that my wife and I needed help and that he would provide it' as long as I did one single thing for him. But, he told me that it would cost me the rest of my life in prison. I knew I didn't have much longer. And I didn't care what I had to do as long as it would save my wife's life. Not having much money to begin with I gave him my bank account number and money appeared in that account within a week. The instructions he gave me were odd. He wanted me to give my wife the healing treatment immediately and then move alone to that village. He told me specifically to call the weapons dealer to ship weapons to my new home on that week in January. My wife was cured and we said our goodbyes, then she moved to Tenerife to start a new life. He didn't give us enough money for my cure as you can see."

"Do you even know about the village secret?"

"That they are terrorist? What secret are you talking about?"

"Apparently according to past interviews with them the only reason they teach kids defense is to protect some secret. So apparently, you literally have no affiliation with them prior to your story."

"No agent, I don't. Now that my wife is safe, I will die knowing I helped her. You are lucky to have asked me these things now; I probably don't have much time left.

"Can I have your bank account number so I can look into who gave you the money? I had a feeling this was a setup, because the intelligence just seemed too easy to have gained. Plus, the terrorists themselves didn't seem like terrorists every time I have come across them. Thank you for your help in this investigation."

"You are welcome. Here, give me a note pad so I can give you my bank account # so you see if it can help you get the info you need." Nikolay said reaching out his hand.

Agent Dale handed the man his APpen and note pad saying, "Who knows if I can get enough evidence. Then, maybe you will be sipping maitais in Tenerife with your wife."

"I would appreciate that, but I doubt they will let me go after this."

"Not if you were just coursed into all this, then you might be freed." He said and was gone.

△ ᨇ ＞ ◇ ᖇ ᖇ

Getting quite warm during midafternoon, Tom decided to go swimming at Canyon Lake taking the egg with him to give it some sunshine and get himself some cooling time in the water. He took it with him because every now and again he would see it shake as well move a little.

Sitting there for a while, Tom jumped into the water splashing it everywhere. He even swam imaginary laps to keep up his fitness skills. He looked over towards the egg's direction because the wind was starting to pick up as massive stormy clouds were gathering towards the east.

Freaking out, Tom quickly ran out of the shallow water onto the shore not wanting to get struck by lightning. He reached out to grab the egg so he could run away. But just as he was about to grab the egg two clouds came together; lightning came bursting up from the ground surging through the egg. Fire flew from the surface of the egg hitting the forest trees near the lake.

As the trees burst into flames, Tom yelled, "Oh no!" He aimed his hands at the water in the lake saying, "Extollo lots of water." Moving his hands towards the directions of the trees he said, "Exertus all this water onto the trees that are burning." Then, a massive amount of water went flying all over the burning trees so the fire was put out instantly.

Tom figured that he had prevented a massive forest fire for all of Texas. Sadly, he definitely didn't realize the repercussions of his actions, because now the dragon that was in the egg had hatched. It went soaring over him, shooting lightning from its mouth back at him.

The lightning that it shot scared him so he ran back into the water. Quickly, he blasted out of the water creating a sonic boom as he chased after the new born dragon.

Catching up to it, the dragon blasted more lightning at him making him plummet to the ground (Apparently Tom's resistance to lightning wasn't permanent. Even though he had used it to get the diary). He thought maybe the Book of Curses might have a word for "tame". He said "Voco me the Book of Curses from my bed room."

Emerging in his hand, he opened the book as he looked up the word "tame" in it. He found the word which read saying, "Domito means to tame." Now, he had the word he needed he had to get to the Dragon before it did any real damage to people.

So he said, "Inflecto me to the newest born Dragon and Inflecto my book back to my room."

Appearing at a forest in the middle of some very rocky humid place, Tom wondered where he was and how he appeared in the wrong cave that one day. For a while he wandered around through this mysterious forest then he started yelling, "Veridiso are you here?"

After looking around for a while Tom heard loud thumping sounds. Naturally, he was worried about what it was. But, as soon as he came around a tree, he was very shocked to see what he had just found. Walking in loud rumbles with each step they took herded together were herbivore dinosaurs (Well at least Tom assumed they were since they were eating grass). Then a flock of pterodactyls flew over him as he heard a roar nearby in the forest.

Tom freaked out about how he had somehow inflectoed himself to a place on the earth that had dinosaurs still roaming it. He gave it some thought, but he had to assimilate an idea. Why would he end up with dinosaurs if he wanted to get to a dragon?

After a moment of thinking, he remembered how in 1841 Sir Richard Owen coined the word "dinosauria" from the Greek words "deinos" meaning fearfully great or potent and "sauros" meaning lizard. And, how prior to that the only English term for the fossils found in the record was known as dragons. As well he remembered how many cultures had different names for them in different languages. Stories of their history in the world and how they eventually died off, becoming extinct. There were many reasons not fully known to science but often theorized by men in the science department.

Then, Tom thought to himself, "Guess they aren't quite so extinct like they say? I should have a look around to see where I am?" Flying up into the sky looking around from a great height he didn't recognize any of the land mass and then he saw what he dreaded was coming. Quickly he yelled, "Where am I!?"

Tom blasted off into the sky again. Following fast behind him with a dead tyrannosaurus in one of their mouth's, was the kind of dragons people typically think of. They were chasing him, shooting fire, lighting, rocks, and acid along with many different elements. Getting closer, near the outer space of the planet, he looked down, not recognizing any of the continents on the planet's surface. Looking out across the expanse of space, he didn't even recognize the star constellations. Just as one of the dragons was about to eat him alive he said, "Inflecto me to Veridiso the dragon."

Appearing out of nowhere he saw the Cabin that was destroyed. Then looking around, he noticed where he was and thought to himself, "Of course this is where Veridiso would go because Alida lived here."

Then the dragon came swooshing down at him with rage. Tom yelled, "Domito Veridiso" The dragon stopped attacking and finally landed. It was such an odd creature to see. Why it even existed, perplexed Tom.

Then with a sarcastic chuckle, Tom said, "Geese none of those dragon books I ever read ever told me that they started out this wild." He wondered if anything from those books held true facts about dragons, but then again he did remember how they were thought to be mythical by most people with closed minds.

So he thought to himself, "Can you read my thoughts? Some people think dogs do, or are you wise like some people think?" The dragon just stood there as if there was nothing happening; then gave a funny look to Tom like there was something wrong with the way Tom was looking at him.

He said to the dragon, "Let's go home boy or at least I think you're a boy." Then he picked it up while saying, "Inflecto me to my bedroom."

Emerging in his bedroom, the dragon started making weird noises like it was trying to talk, but Tom did not understand what it was trying to say. He got out his book, looking for a word such as "understand".

"Oh yeah, Teneo helped me know what the book even says in it in the first place." He said when he found the word "Teneo". "Help me Teneo the words of this dragon." He said, then hearing the ringing hum he started to have a head ache all of a sudden. Then the dragon was speaking English to him all of a sudden, or at least that's the way Tom heard it.

It said, "Please, let me have something to eat."

"Mmm…yeah, okay, hold on."

Tom was shocked as he ran down stairs and went to get some turkey and carrots with a boll of water to go with it for the dragon.

The dragon said, "Thanks for getting me some water on my egg. I have been waiting a little less than a thousand years, perhaps more like nine hundred to be more correct. She waited for some ancestor to summon me and give that egg the water it needed so I could be free. Tom said, "You have been in that egg for that long?"

"Yeah, bet you humans don't have that much patience."

Puzzled Tom asked, "You really want to be called Veridiso?"

It replied, somewhat annoyed by the thought saying, "No, Alida, never tried to be improper so she referred to me as my real name and she wanted to use that name as the word an ancestor would say to summon me so I could tell them more about her."

"So what do you want your name to be?"

"Please call me "Todd", because I like to hunt foxes."

Later on that night, as he slept Tom began having a weird dream. In the dream he was flying above the atmosphere of the earth while many jet streams were passing each other. Then, he noticed lots of explosions going off everywhere all over the globe. They were big ones in the shapes of giant mushrooms all around him; much like nuclear bombs of some kind.

Tom was growing more tense by the second…soon enough the whole planet was consumed in this horrible glowing green mist; but then the planet started to burn like it was all set on fire at an instant. He woke up panting and sweating a whole bunch. Quietly, he went down to the kitchen to get some water.

Once back in his room Todd said, "That was a horrible nightmare you just had, was it not?"

"Wait, how did you know about that nightmare?" Tom asked curiously.

"A pet always has its owner's dreams. Have you humans not figured that out yet?"

"No, you pets are a mystery to people sometimes since you can't usually talk to us."

"Well, now you know, plus I thought people could talk to animals and pets?"

"I don't know what kind of world you've been living in but no, animals can't talk normally." So, Tom and Todd went back to sleep, both were pondering great details. They were perplexed about many of them as they drifted off into more rem cycles.

The Near Future
Friday, September 11th, 4:01 P.M.
Smithsonian Valley High school, Smithsonian Valley, Texas

Two weeks prior, on Monday the 31'st of august, as the bell rang, Tom ran through the hallways excited with many other boys who were attempting to get on the basketball team. Arriving and surrounding the board, many boys were mad they did not make it, and some were cheering with excitement.

Tom was stunned to see that he was accepted on the team as he read the board. Tom ran outside with excitement and saw Jessica there to pick him up. He told her that he made the Team as they went back to Tom's house celebrating. Jessica stayed for dinner and invited her husband Robbie over to have dinner with their baby Josh, when they came over to celebrate with all of their family who was proud of Tom for doing so well making the team.

Today though, was practice for Tom and Benny who also made the team. They were practicing in the gym. On the other side of the gym the girls were practicing gymnastics. When it wasn't Tara's turn to do stunts she watched Tom practicing along with the other boys.

Then quietly, trying not to arouse suspicion, Justin came into the gym waiting near the end of the bleachers and hiding behind them. He stayed there till after the practice ended and Tom left for the showers. He walked out from behind the bleachers while Tara was alone putting stuff in her gym bag.

Justin said to her stirringly, "Did you really think it would end with you falling down some stairs?"

She freaked out and was about to run when Justin hit her to the ground. Half an hour later Tom came out of the shower room wearing a plaid shirt with brown linen pants. He looked at his hollowatch, noticing there was a text message saying, "If you ever want to see Tara alive again meet me at the neighborhood park."

Quickly running out the door Tom did not even take time to look around if anybody was nearby watching him. He soared into the air flying off to the neighborhood park. Landing, he ran towards Justin who had a pistol looking gun to Tara's head. He was worried with intense fear; worried she would die with that gun to her head?

Stopping in front of Justin, Tom yelled, "What are you doing!?"

Justin gave a strange look with his eye brows in Tom's direction. Then Tom looked over his shoulder to see Sacra shooting him with a gun of some sort. Passing out really fast, he fell to the ground.

Chapter 14
A Nightmare in the Making

The Near Future
Friday, September 11th, 5:38 P.M.
Guadalupe River, Smithsonian Valley, Texas

Hearing water rushing past him nearby, Tom thought it sounded like it was falling a great distance. He felt kind of drowsy. He opened his eyes to see that he was tied to a chair and the water he had heard was coming from the river next to him. The river water was rushing by him off a cliff and looked like a waterfall edge.

On the edge of the river's waterfall, Justin was holding Tara in the same way Tom had seen at the park. Justin said with an angry voice, "So were you dumb enough to really think that a new school year would mean a new outlook with all the crap you have put us through in the past? Well, if you did, you were wrong!"

Tom concerned yelled, "Let her go now! I didn't want to deal with any of your teeny bop drama this year, and I figured you might mature a little since you are getting older."

Justin responded with a smirk, "Do you think you can just pull off some more of your magic crap, and get yourself out of this?! Well think again you stupid brat! We aren't going to let you get away with anything anymore."

Tom responded, "No, it's not magic it's something else..." Turning his head to see Sacra pointing a gun at him he got scared a little. Yelling with a vengeful fury in his voice Sacra screamed, "You're going to pay for what you did to my Dad!"

"Your father? I don't even know you, who are you?"

Raising his palm above Tara's shoulder towards Sacra, Justin said, "Wait Sacra, just calm down, we don't want to kill him yet. First we need to kill him in the heart."

Tara wittingly knew what he meant by what he had just said. She decided to bite Justin, which in return he quickly retaliated by punching her. Justin then grabbed her again using all of his thrust to push her off the edge of the water fall.

While Tara bit Justin, Tom quickly said, "Make me lentus to fire."

Then Tom with haste said "Ignis". Flames came out of the palm of his hand destroying the rope wrapped around his hands. He burst off with a sonic boom, knocking Sacra and Justin onto the ground that they were standing on. As he went soaring down into the waterfall he picked up Tara as she was falling.

Flying up into the air with her in his arms and holding her tightly close to his chest Tom flew away diagonally from the water fall gulf. Justin and Sacra looked up as he was getting away from the area, wishing they had just taken him down for good and unhappy their guns fell into the river going down stream when they were knocked over.

Tara looked at him with amazement at what he could do then asked him, "Tom, how are you able to be do all of this?"

He responded with a warm smile on his face "I don't know; I just know how to make myself fly and do some other things, but I don't know how it fully works from an empirical scientific view?"

Tom decided to show Tara some nice scenery by flying her past Canyon Lake then back towards their neighborhood. Landing in front of Tara's house he worked up the courage to ask her if she was dating anybody. Tara responded in a joking manner, "Oh you think because you saved my life, and you have super powers I should just randomly choose to date you like a clichéd story? Oh, but to answer your question, I am not seeing anybody at all right now."

Tom responded with a chuckle, "Well that's good. You're single and no I don't think that gives me any rights. I just wanted to know if you were single since I really like you to the point that I would want to get you to be my girlfriend or at least try going out with me?"

She had the cutest blush as she smirked saying, "You have no idea how long I have wanted you to say that."

"Okay, well how about next Friday after practice. We can go see a movie or something?" He said smiling at her.

"Sounds like a great plan."

"Okay, can't wait for our first date." He said floating up into the air. Looking down he blew her an imaginary kiss with his hands with his eye brows raised as he went back to his house. He felt a little ridiculous that he flew off from Tara's since he lived across the street from her. "I could of just walked home." he thought. Being so over whelmed by his affection & love for her he wasn't thinking clearly.

Walking into his house, Tom began to think about everything that had just transpired. But as soon as he got into his bedroom he forgot all about his feelings for Tara with what she had just said, because he felt a sudden urge to attack Justin and Sacra for what they had done to them. Nearly killing Tara, he thought they should pay with death themselves. Then he told Todd about everything that had just happened at the park and the river waterfall.

He said to Todd, "What do you think I should do about them?"

"Maybe scare them with your abilities some more or try to work out your issues with them. In the end it is up to you."

Tom, not thinking rationally from his anger said, "All right, I will be right back in a little while once I deal with them."

Tom flew out the window and through his neighborhood back to the park to see if Justin and Sacra went back there. Landing in the park, he noticed that they were walking together back out of the forest near the park. He started running towards them. As Justin and Sacra saw him they quickly freaked out.

Standing there Tom said, "Why are you always trying to hurt me and Tara all the time you jerks?"

Justin replied in a mean way saying, "Because Tom, you claimed to be my friend, but you lied. All you really wanted was Tara as your girlfriend. You only tried to be my friend because you had some stupid pity for me and my life. Then you decided to betray me by turning me over to the police."

Tom yelled, "You think all that gives you the right to try and murder us? It isn't my fault you were a drug addict; I just gave them an idea it could be you or the other kid since it wasn't me. You're going to pay for what you did to Tara!"

"But Tom, you saved her. So, we did nothing to her really." Justin said with a sarcastic taunting chuckle.

"You nearly killed her!"

Justin said while motioning for Sacra to follow, "Well, your stupid tricks don't scare me Tom, time for you to die!"

Tom filled with pride and thinking he could take on anybody raised his arms up saying, "Bring it, show me what you got."

Justin started running toward Tom with Sacra by his side ready to battle. In their minds, the two of them thought they would make it where Tom wouldn't be able to get back up.

Quickly, Tom yelled as he started running towards them not wanting to take on two at a time, "Modus sacra and dissimulo his mouth." Suddenly Sacra was bound to the dirt on the ground as his mouth started to close and his lips started coming together sealing on him, making it were he could only breathe through his nose. Now his lips looked like they were nothing except just normal skin as he tried to scream but no sound could escape his sealed mouth.

Tom said sarcastically with much pride blocking one of Justin's punches, "So want me to undo your new best friend's problem or you want to end up just like him?"

Justin yelled with lots of anger, "You jerk! What have you done to him!?" Instantly he plunged at Tom trying to punch him again with all his might. Standing his ground, Tom made himself stable for Justin's plunge at him.

Stopping Justin from hitting him by blocking his punches, Tom fought back giving Justin a black eye and some bruises on the arms. Then he said, "Undo sacra's dissimulo on his mouth." Sacra's lips went back to normal instead of being like regular skin.

Sacra, still bound to the ground started yelling, "This child is Evil!"

Tom said with a grin, "Funny, that's the same thing that dumb terrorist said to me right before he tried to kill me. Well, his final words were, "Well, hope you love dying and suffering as much as you do causing issues." But the other sentence was near the end of his life."

"That dumb terrorist, as you just put it, was my father, you moron!" Sacra said.

Truly saddened by this revelation, Tom put his arms down, lowering his eye brows saying, "I'm truly sorry, I had no idea that he was also your father." Having an epiphany he said, "Wait a second, you just happened to be the son of the man who tried to kill me. You met Justin in a prison camp and he's the exact same person I have had issues with for years?"

"Well, yeah?" Sacra responded.

"Something isn't right here, it all seems too coincidental. Almost like it was some strange plan…" before Tom could continue anymore with what he was thinking, Justin punched his side saying, "You really thought Sacra was just going to help me fight you for no reason, Turner? Are you that dumb? Because of what you have done, we both have reasons to take you down."

"I didn't know what to think." Tom said puzzled with much intrigue "Considering the police wouldn't reveal our identities to the terrorist, I presume that you had something to do with telling Sacra who I was and he probably told his father. So, Justin how did you or Sacra's father figure out where I was living in England?"

Justin, bruised with pain, and anger said, "It's not hard to convince your sister I am your friend Matt, just to squirm some info from her stupid mouth."

Tom yelled back angrily, "Don't you dare talk about my sister like that! You don't even know her. At least my mom is smart enough not to let me be friends with terrorist's children."

Justin responded with a smirk, "Could have fooled me. And my mom doesn't have a clue. She thinks he is just some foreign exchange student. Still doesn't change the fact everyone in your family is gullible since you idiots think nicely of everyone, you all are just a bunch of dumb idiots."

Tom ran at him with a punch, knocking him to the ground again. Then he turned from Justin towards Sacra pointing at him and yelling, "In addition to that, you tried to get his dad to kill me and my family! It's your fault his father is dead. Unless, of course you count the fact he did pretty much blow himself up trying to take me down."

Sacra tried plunging at Tom angry as all get out. But couldn't since he was stuck to the ground. Falling to the ground, he started yelling in the same strange language from the people on the plane on the flight to England. It was strange to Tom since he didn't speak it, but it was normal to many other people from their land.

Getting up, Justin brushed off the dirt from his pants saying, "Tom, no matter how many magic tricks you do to me or Sacra, like I said before you don't scare me and this will be the end of you."

Tom, filled with hysterical rage, started to grin then yelled, "Labores solis." As soon as he spoke the trees in the park and the forest all around started to bend; moving in one direction like they were being forced that way. Suddenly the moon came into view then started to cover the sun again.

Then, to scare Justin he said, "Ostendo the sun light on Sacra and set him on ignis then inflecto him to a prison cell in my vocoed dungeon." Suddenly the moon had a hole in it as the sunlight was shining on Sacra through the moon, then he burst into flames vanishing right in front of Justin.

Justin yelled, "No Sacra!!! What did you do to him!?"

"Wouldn't you like to know." Tom responded arrogantly.

"You're going to pay for this, you worthless piece of trash!"

"Make an ignis ring around me and Justin." With an eerie howling wind a giant ring of burning flames burst up surrounding them in a circle of fire. Tom started running at Justin; quickly Justin turned around running through the flames back into the forest to escape.

Deep in the forest, seeing Justin in the distance, Tom yelled, "Make Justin doleo!"

Suffering severe pain, Justin stopped where he was and fell to the ground wrapping his body up with his arms & hands. Parts of his body started pulsing with boils bumping up and down into his skin.

Catching up to Justin, Tom saw the results of his actions. Where Justin's skin had burst open it was bleeding all over the dirt on the ground. He thought this was too pernicious and realized that if he didn't heal Justin that he was going to be responsible for killing him from bleeding to death.

So, in a hurry Tom said, "Sano Justin." All the blood that had burst out of Justin went running back up his body back into his veins and he healed from the wounds Tom had inflicted on him. He was back to normal.

Justin yelled, "I'm going to kill you and Tara you monster!"

Filled with pride and anger, Tom yelled "Modus Justin!"

In desperation, hoping to get Tom to come to his senses Justin pleaded, "Tom, why are you trying to kill me and Sacra!?"

"Because, both of you keep trying to kill the two of us! I love her too much to let you do that. I wasn't trying to kill either of you. I just wanted to stop you from bullying on us. I just want to have a normal year at school where I don't have to put up with the crap you keep giving me!"

"Either you die or I do!" Justin responded back jumping forth to attack Tom, but he was stuck to the dirt on the ground.

Smirking at how Justin was trapped, Tom walked up to his side then pointed his hand at the ground right behind Justin saying, "Make a cavus with spikes." The ground burst down-wards creating a giant hole in the ground with spikes at the bottom of the pit.

Bound to the edge of the cliff that was on top of the hole in the ground, Justin yelled, "I don't know how I'm going to do it, but I will kill both of y'all!"

Tom, amused that Justin couldn't do anything responded, "Oh really? How exactly are you going to do that?"

"By crushing her frail thin body as I'm on top of her beating her to death while you sit there trapped. If you kill me now, I'm sure Sacra will finish the job." Justin said dripping sweat from his face.

Enraged by Justin's remark and with a very angered face Tom yelled, "You aren't going to do anything to her or to me; not any more, I won't ever let you hurt her again voco lighting!"

The air became dry very fast, instead of moist. The pressure of the air changed and all the clouds' surrounding them began to spin in a giant circle like vortex. Light was appearing in the middle of the vortex and in the sky in the shape of a giant fist. Tom looked down at his hand noticing it was crunched up like the fist of light in the sky.

Justin said, "What are doing now? Preparing to kill me in some weird light fixture?"

Moving his fist forward real fast, Tom made the lightning come down out of the eye of the spinning clouds plunging into Justin's chest, blowing him out of the ground that he was bound to and taking the ground with him, falling backwards into the pit with spikes.

Justin yelled very profane words as he fell backwards, meaning to insult Tom one last time before he died. He plunged down into the pit falling onto the bed of spikes at the bottom. As the spikes blasted through his chest & legs blood busted out all over the spikes. Laying there coughing up blood and twitching like he was having a seizure, Justin seemed incapacitated.

Standing there seeing Justin severely hurt, Tom wondered what he was going to do now because he had really damaged Justin most this time. Possibly even making it to where he might be actually dead very soon. Guilt consumed him and made him decide to make things right or go back to being as normal as he could make them.

Tom said, "Stop this labores solis and inflecto Justin to my voco dungeon while undoing the modus ground from him." Justin disappeared as the solar eclipse went away.

Tom said, "Inflecto me to my voco dungeon."

Appearing in front of the dungeon cell that had the worm hole next to it on the wall, Tom saw Justin laying there twitching in the cell. Justin was watching out of his cell seeing a body figure disappear into the worm hole. So did Tom, out of the corner of his eye.

Tom walked over to the other cells to find Sacra, but could not find him anywhere, and the door was open to it. He thought the body figure he saw walk through the worm hole was not Sacra because it was too tall to be him. Then he walked back to Justin's cell saying "Sano Justin." The spikes that were in Justin pushed out of his body, then all of his wounds healed up again.

Tom said, "Inflecto me and Justin back to the forest in our neighborhood." Figuring it wouldn't be right to hold either of them hostage and somebody else had already let Sacra out letting him go to

England through the wormhole. So, he brought Justin back to their area instead of leaving him there just to be freed.

Emerging in the forest again, Tom quickly said, "I'm not going to fight you anymore because it would be pointless and just lead to more fighting. But I will have you out of my life." Then he said, "Did you see who that tall figure was that freed Sacra?"

Dazed and confused Justin responded, "What are you talking about; where are we? Why am I healed and I'm not in that pit thing you made?"

Then it struck Tom's mind that the same thing happened when he first went to the other world where he didn't know who he was when he got there. So, there must have been a time laps in Justin's mind not even remembering their trip there.

Tom said with a smirk on his face, "Never mind how you got here, I still need to make a phone call." Then he used his hollowatch to call Agent Dale saying, "Hey Agent Dale, I really need your help to get Justin out of my life. He keeps attacking me and my girlfriend. I also found out he is the one responsible us being attacked by terrorist."

"Yeah that's interesting; it's kind of busy here right now, though. I shall see what I can do. And if he has been assaulting you and breeching the law that landed him in that juvenile camp in the first place then we probably have rights to detain him and put him far from Texas so he can't bother you."

"Thank you so much Agent Dale, I wanted to do what is right so I called you instead of just trying to keep fighting with him like

Paulo trained me. Basically, I am just tired of dealing with all of the issues he throws into my life."

"You are welcome, see you later."

With pride and thinking he could always take on Justin but wanting to do things right, he flew off and headed home wondering how all this trouble with Justin would work out.

After dinner, Tom called Benny and asked him if he wanted to come over and spend the night like he usually did on weekends. While he waited for Benny to get there, he told Todd to sleep on the roof so Benny would not be scared or confused by Todd.

Todd responded saying, "Okay, but someday he will discover me if I remain a dragon" as he flew out Tom's window.

When Benny got there they started to play Ring of Mystery Three together which was multiplayer. While playing Ring of Mystery Three, Tom told Benny how he and Tara were going to be considered an actual couple now and had a date next Friday.

Benny surprised said, "How did you manage to get one of the prettiest girls in the whole school to date you?"

With a very cocky attitude, Tom responded, "I was just being myself. So you think you can beat me on Tír na nÓg?"

"Are you kidding me Tom, you know I could beat you on any map if I wanted to. What's with all this new found confidence you have been having lately?"

"Nothing really, just felt like I can take on anything that comes my way."

"Well Tom, don't be too confident. Some girls like a humble man. Also you won't be able to beat me on this map."

"Fine if you say so, but let's play just to make sure you're not in over your head. Thanks for the advice though, you make a good point." Tom and Benny played Ring of Mystery Three till it was really late. Then they went to bed after they were done with a map called "final outcome".

Walking in from a long drive from his house to work, Agent Dale headed directly into his office, getting ready for a day of investigating. First he thought he should follow up with Agent Myers though on those bank numbers. Getting on his hollowatch phone he called Agent Myers saying, "Hello, how are things going in England with that Asrar kid?"

"Well, he claims to not know how he got here. He said one minute that he was with his friend in the woods then the next he was in a cave near Brighton."

"Strange, wonder how he got there? Also I was calling about that bank number you were going to look into. Did you find anything new on it?"

"Yes I did, but I found out all their skylink connections have been erased. It's strange to think that who ever sent money to Serzynkov had an American bank account from what those numbers you found from Serzynkov's account show. And I found out they bounced around through multiple accounts, all of which have been deleted of course. But I finally found the bank where they originated. So that might be able to give us a hint if we could get access to the printed records to identify the actual person they belonged to."

"Well, Agent Myers, I shall see what I can do to get a hold of them. Just text me the name & location of the bank and I will pay them a visit next Friday when my schedule is more cleared up."

"Okay, I will send it to you. The location might surprise you though."

"Thanks, but yeah that was real crazy yesterday when all the alarms went off from Sacra Asrar randomly appearing in England. I also wanted to say thank you for going instead of me. Kathryne wouldn't have been happy with me having to leave home again so soon."

"Well, I figured you might need to stick around there for some unknown reason. I will be back shortly with Sacra Asrar, we do need to figure out how he ended up here though."

"I don't know Agent Myers, how can we explain a guy randomly teleporting halfway across the planet? I just don't think this is an answer we will easily find?

"Maybe you're right Agent Sizer, but I believe there is an answer for everything even if at first we don't understand it."

"Guess that is a nice outlook. Still, while you were leaving for the airport yesterday I found out that Justin Phelps kid was bullying the Turner's kid and was responsible for the terrorists kidnapping in July. Now, he has been moved with his mother to Kentucky so he can't terrorize the Turners anymore. Well I better be going. Got a lot of stuff to do. See you later."

"Goodbye Agent Sizer."

Chapter 15
Tom's First Date

The near future
Thursday, September 17ᵗʰ, 10:10 A.M.
SARB National Bank, San Antonio, Texas

Pulling up to the bank hasting seven masked men emptied out of their old fashion van that ran on oil they rushed inside packing guns with silencers on them. The short one went to the right shooting out the camera on the east wall. The average height, fairly skinny one, headed over to the west wall to take out its camera. The others were taking out the cameras with the leader along and two other guys shooting the regular employees to the ground before they could access their hollowatch phones.

Quickly running two of them ran into the banker's little offices and tried to stop them from clicking the alarm buttons under their desks. Making all the people on the first floor pile into the main room up front, the short one said with an odd accent to the leader, "Sir, one of the employees managed to press their button. I think we should get out of here, we have been compromised."

Smiling underneath his mask, the leader said with a distorted voice, "Don't worry. Remember that device that beeped right before we decided to get out of the van?"

"Yeah?"

"Well, that was my notification that the two guys I sent to spend the night in that old office building next door disabled the alarm system on the roof putting it on a loop, so we shouldn't have to deal with any cops."

"Then, why are we wearing masks, gloves, and why do you have a voice distorter?"

"Because one can never be too careful in case there is something we may have overlooked. Speaking of things not to overlook, everyone give me your hollowatch phones now!" he yelled at the hostages.

All together the hostages started to take off their hollowatch phones and handed them over to the robbers. The two guys on the roof rapped grappling hook ropes around an air vent on the roof and then climbed down the side into the alley. Making sure nobody was watching them, they peeked around the edge of the alley, then headed into the bank to join in with their co-robbers while turning on the closed sign & locking the front door.

The Leader said with a cocky attitude, "Okay, which one of you is the manager? Let's get down to business."

"I am," a balding man said with an anxious voice as he looked up at the leader and turned his eyes, trying hard not look at the criminal too much.

"We have already disabled your security system, so even if you pressed your buttons repeatedly nobody would come for you. Hence this is why we took your hollowatch phones, as well. So, you better listen intently, if you want to live. You will take me into the main vault right now so I can see where you keep all your money.

You know, nobody can see you since you have tented windows and the closed sign has been turned on near the door and locked."

"Why should I help you? I would just lose my job."

To let the manager know he wasn't going to tolerate anything and wasn't going to let the manager screw around with him, he instantly shot the manager in his foot, then said, "The next one goes into your employees head, and then after all of them are dead into yours. All I need is your hand or eye for the main vault door. So you really want to keep trying my patience?"

Screaming in pain and agony the manager said, "Fine I will open it for you, you nutcase."

Holding the gun to the manager's head, together they headed for the main vault door. The manager took off his glasses while placing his hand on the scanner. As the vault door opened the leader looked around feeling weary that this was all going too easy for him. Two other guys followed into the vault carrying garbage bags ready to fill them up with cash.

"Here is the money." The manager said, opening a drawer filled with lots of stacked one hundred dollar bills with tracking bands around them. "You won't be able to keep that money. If you try to take off those bands it will spray a substance onto you that is hard to get off and the bands have trackers in them." The manager said.

The leader then said, "I don't care about that crap very much; open up your records vault now!"

The Manager had an epiphany that this guy had a lot of other things going on if he only wanted some bank records. "Okay, hold on a moment and let me open it for you."

Using his key, the manager opened up a locked file holder asking, "There is a lot of records in here, are you looking for a particular one?"

"Yes, all the records from December of last year are here." The leader wearing the mask said with a distorted voice.

Handing him the paper records from December, instantly they heard gun shots and glass shattering in the main room as the other six guys watching the hostages dropped their guns after being shot in the hands. They quickly tried to reach down to grab them but were shot in the legs as a swat team rushed in, grabbing them and freeing the other hostages.

"No! How were the police alerted?" The short robber with one of the bags of money said.

"I don't know, but this manager is our only leverage." The leader said grabbing the manager by the collar of his shirt lifting him up from a squatting position to open the record holder.

Walking the manager to the vault door with a gun to his head, the leader said, "You try to arrest us this man will be shot!" Then the short robber and the skinny guy got in front of the leader holding the manager in front of him to give them a circle of protection.

"Where is a way out of here?" The leader mumbled in the manager's ear.

"To our left is a hallway with a back door to the alley." He replied.

With the wall to their backs, they walked sideways leading their only leverage to the hallway. "We will be in an office down this hall if you want to send one negotiator in without any weapons," The leader said as they backed themselves down the hallway. "This short guy here will be standing guard at the corner. If you shoot him, then the manager dies. The skinny guy will be guarding the door to the office, so if you shoot him, then the manager will die. Do we have an understanding?"

"Yes, we understand," A voice said in the distance from the main door of the bank.

Carrying their money bags, the men got into their positions as the leader went further down the hall. Then, he walked past the office he referenced talking with the swat team. Quickly, he shoved the hostage to the skinny robber saying, "He's your problem now." Then he bolted for the back door and into the alley way. First he looked out to make sure no officers could see him going that way.

Lucky for leader, the officers didn't have a clue there was a back door, so he ran to the end of the alley looking around its corners to see if anybody was there. The coast was clear, so he decided to take off his mask to get some fresh air. As he started pulling off his mask, from around the corner of the dumpster, Agent Dale came running punching him to the ground and knocking the leader's gun out of his hand. He grabbed the records concealing them in his jacket pouch. "Did you really think you could rob a bank without there being something to connect you to the crime? Well, you forgot one detail, human intuition." Agent Dale said as he put hand cuffs on the robber.

"How did you know I would be here?"

"Because I traced the call of the man who hired you, asking you to hurry up with the job. As well I called the cops on you warning them about your big group of eight other guys. You won't be going to jail or the police precinct right now. First we need to interrogate you where I work, so let the thought of that settle with you for a while." Agent Dale said putting the leader of the robbers away in the cop car telling them where to send him.

Then he got out his hollowatch phone from his car and called Agent Myers, "Hey, Agent Myers. Turns out your idea of installing that PSI really panned out along with the other leads you have given me. I just can't believe it's him who has orchestrated all of this."

"Are you sure this is wise taking on somebody with so much power? Don't we need more concrete evidence against him?

"Don't worry; I think I got just the thing we need to finalize our evidence. We just need to find the right guy with the right talent."

Now that Justin was out of Tom's life, he was able to sit there at the lunch table thinking a lot about things that were happening that day instead of worrying about Justin. Just like that morning how he had stood in his bathroom thinking about shaving. Sadly, he realized that he didn't even need to shave yet since his hair wasn't known for growing crazy fast. Then he chuckled, remembering his thought about taking breath mints to school so his breath would be good if Tara and he kissed on their first date later.

Benny was trying to get his attention, "Earth to Tom!"

"Huh what? Sorry. What did you say?"

Benny chuckled saying, "You are always day dreaming Tom. What's it about this time?"

"Sorry, I was just thinking about how this is the first time I will have ever gone on a date before and if I should have brought breath mints to school for our first date tonight."

"Dude, don't worry. I'm sure everything will be alright."

"Believe me, I'm not worried at all. I just hope things go over smoothly since I have never been on a date before." Tom responded with confidence.

"Just put on some charm & suave attitude. Trust me, you will have all sorts of girls begging for your hollowatch number," Benny said looking back over at the table where Tara was sitting with other girls who were giggling and looking over at the boys grouped together.

"Benny, I don't want a bunch of girls to be with, I just want to be with Tara. I have always liked her and she apparently has liked me since last school year from the way things sounded the other week."

"Then, just be yourself if that is what pulls her in."

"Yeah, so why were you trying to get my attention?" Tom asked taking a bite of his sandwich.

"Just was wondering if you were excited for our first game tomorrow?"

"Oh, I am. Do you think we will do good?"

"No, the team mates keep missing their shots during practice. It would be nice, but I find it highly unlikely that we will win."

"Never know. We just might do well and you are only looking at the odds through the view of our practice shots."

"Well, we shall see."

$$\triangle > \lrcorner \triangle$$

During practice after school, Tom was sweating hardcore as he ran down the court with the ball and threw it to Benny. Then, Benny would either throw it to somebody else or try to make his own shot. Benny thought the team was doing much better than at their previous practices. Giving this gave him a little hope for the next day's game. When their practice ended different players either went to get showers or go home. Tom stayed to get a shower so he would smell good for his date.

Tom did an odd handshake/fist bump and said goodbye to Benny as he headed to other side of the gym to watch Tara finish her gymnastics. She was doing pretty good from his point of view. She even managed to do one of the highest double jumps she had ever done in her life. He admired almost anything she would do, though, just because it was the girl he loved.

Tom waited for her to come out of the girl's locker room once their practice has ended. Seeing her come out of the locker room, he got excited thinking it was time for their adventure to begin. He walked up to her asking, "So where do you want to go tonight? Or what would you want to do? I got my parents to let me borrow my dad's car for our first date."

"How about we go see a movie at Northwoods movie theatre on 1604 by the Gameplayers store?"

"You shop at Gameplayers?"

"Yeah. What did you think I do for fun? Sit around the house playing with dolls & makeup? Or, did you think I just like to try on dresses all the time? She said in a joking manner.

"Oh, no, not at all." Tom responded, laughing, "I just didn't expect you to be a gamer girl." He said smirking at the idea she played games just like he did, which was appealing to him.

"I might occasionally do girly things, but I'm not that feminine to the extent that I feel I can sometimes be a little repulsive towards some guys."

"Well, I like you just the way you are."

"Come on. Could you get any more clichéd sounding?"

"Sorry, bad habit I guess. Let's get going." Tom said walking with her towards his parent's car.

On the way to the movie, Tom & Tara talked about how their days went as Tom tried to keep his focus on the road so he wouldn't drive poorly. Then, as they were getting close to town he asked Tara what she wanted to see.

Tara replied, "How about that movie based on that book from the 1900's?"

"That sounds like a good one. I kind of wonder what life was like back then for those people."

"Who knows? Still, I think we have a pretty good lifestyle all our own."

Parking the car, Tom said, "Okay, let's go get our tickets."

Together, they walked up to the ticket booth to get their tickets, then they looked around noticing lots of people were gathered together for a Friday night out. "I forgot how crowded it gets here on Fridays." Tom said.

"Yeah, it certainly does have lots of people. I wonder how long going to movies has been a thing for Friday nights at this theatre? You know like when everyone came here on Fridays."

"I don't know. I guess it's just everyone looked forward to the weekend."

"You're probably right."

Tom asked the guy in the ticket booth for two tickets, and then he and Tara headed inside to get their seats. She was very happy that Tom had paid for both of their tickets. After getting some drinks & popcorn from the dispenser machines, they got two nice seats up towards the middle of the theatre. Tom didn't like sitting on the lower seats too close to the screen.

Sitting there, as the movie was starting, Tom wondered if he should kiss Tara while the movie was playing. But, then he thought, "No it might take months of dating before I should try to make those kinds of moves." He thought that because he had never dated anybody before his whole life and not knowing what to do and what not to do.

Tara was wondering if maybe he would kiss her, but hoped that he wasn't one of those boys that were desperate for kissing all the time; especially on a first date. Still, she wondered what it would be like to kiss him for the first time. She wondered if it would be something special.

After the movie ended, they headed out the door at the back of the theater near the screen. No one else came out that door with them, so they were all alone behind the theater. Tom started to talk to Tara as they walked down the pathway at the back of the theater. Just then, five weird and rough gangster-looking guys came out of the bushes from the road connecting the parking lot nearby. They were wearing hoodies, jeans, and had weird hair styles. The gangsters came running at Tom, then quickly pushed him to the ground. Two of them grabbed Tara, then held her against the wall of the theater.

Tom came rushing at them yelling, "You guys just made your biggest mistake!"

One gangster replied with a smirk on his face, "Oh yeah ya stupid teen, what you going to do about it? She's ours for the taking?"

Tom yelled, "No she will never be somebody's object you jerk!!!" The lead gangster pulled out a knife and threw it at Tom.

But Tom, pointed the palm of his hand in the direction of the oncoming knife to block or catch it saying, "Voco lightning." A bolt of lightning went thrusting at the knife and made it fly right back at the leader, hitting him in the leg. Two of the four other gangsters surrounding Tara, started to pull down their zippers looking as if they were about to pull down their pants. Then, Tom realized what they were about to try to do to Tara.

Quickly, while the gangsters were distracted, Tara unleashed some surprising moves of her own and kicked one of them in the loins. Then she punched the other one in the face who was holding her other arm, this freed her from his grip.

Tom quickly said, "Give my kick the praevaleo of the sonic boom." Tom came running at the gangsters and released a martial arts kick he'd learned from Paulo. As he started kicking the gangsters, they went flying against the walls of the theater just as they were beginning to pull the boxers down that they were wearing. Then he held out the palm of his hand and pointed it towards the gangsters that were holding Tara and at the ones that were pulling down their pants.

Tara jumped out of the way to let Tom finish them off as he said "Ignis." Two flames came bursting out from his hands burning the four gangsters that were messing with Tara. They hastily ran into the bushes, running for their lives, while the fith one was limping from the knife to his knee. Tom grabbed Tara as they hugged each other.

Tom asked, "Are you okay, Tara?"

"Well are you?"

Then both at the same time they replied, "Yeah I am fine."

Tara giggled that they had both said the same thing.

Then Tom said, a little concerned by her answer, "Really? You're fine after what those guys just tried to do, with you, or should I say to you?"

"Yeah, don't worry Tom, I'm not some damsel in distress that you always need to rescue. I can handle a fight. I learned some defense moves when I was camping this summer. At least we stopped them together. Besides, I have to admit, this is pretty exciting for a first date."

Tom, being a little shocked at her feisty outlook and somewhat excited by it, said "Man, you sure are a wild card." She smirked as they walked off towards the car they came in.

Once in the car, Tom drove them off to Alamo Café to have a nice Mexican meal. They were in town already and this was the best place to go for Mexican food from Tom's point of view (even though there are lots of good Mexican restaurants around San Antonio). When they arrived, they got a small table for two. Tom pulled out the seat for Tara then asked, "So, what did you think of the movie?"

"Glad you are asking since our conversation was cut short. I thought it was pretty good and really close to the book."

"Yeah, that ending though. Who would have seen that coming?"

"Still, it was pretty decent. So, what are you thinking of getting to eat?"

"I'm not sure; I love nachos but I'm also in the mood for enchiladas."

"I like burritos, but the ones here are really big and filling; don't want to overstuff myself.

As the waitress walked up, she asked what they wanted to eat, drink, and if they wanted to split an appetizer. Tom got a banana mint soda and Tara got an orange cayenne soda. Tom decided he was much more in the mood for enchiladas instead of nachos; Tara got three soft Chicken fajita tacos with rice & beans. For an appetizer they shared some queso & chips. As he ate some of the queso on a chip, Tom thought that this was the best queso you could get anywhere.

As they waited for their meals to arrive, Tom said "So think we will win tomorrow or get clobbered?"

Taking a bite of queso on a chip, Tara said in a warm-hearted manor, "I think you'll after seeing today's practice. Y'all looked pretty good out there."

"Thanks. You are a really sweet girl."

Tom didn't know what else really to say. He thought in his mind that girls could be so more complex than guys. Maybe even a bit mysterious since they were known to be the most complex mysteries of the universe. To him, physics made more sense than the actions of girls or how guys should talk to a girlfriend.

For a while, they visited about different things while they ate. Once they were done eating, the waitress came to cash their check, and Tom held up his hollowatch to the waitress's hollowatch and bumped them together to pay for their meal after choosing a tip amount. "This has been a great date Tom; I have had a really great time." Tara said smiling as they were getting up to leave to go to Tara's house.

Pulling up to her house in his parent's car, Tom asked, "Tara, I was wondering if you would you like to go with me to Canyon Lake tomorrow before the big game just to hang out and stuff?"

"I sure would, that would be lots of fun."

"Well, I will see you in the morning then. Good night sleep well."

"You, too, Tom. Sweet dreams." Tara said as she winked walking into her house.

The near future
Saturday, September 19ᵗʰ, 10:12 A.M.
Tom's house, Smithsonian Valley, Texas

Moseying on over to Tara's, Tom knocked on the door as he held his triad speaker in his left hand. Tara opened the door and Tom said, "Good morning, how are you?"

"I'm good. Good morning to you too. Did you sleep well?"

"I sure did." Tom responded with enthusiasm.

"Oh yeah, I wonder why you slept so well." Tara said flirtatiously, grabbing Tom's right hand.

Smiling, Tom said, "I don't know…I kind of had a great time with a really wonderful girl last night. Then I thought about spending some more time with her again today."

"She must be one lucky lady to have a guy like you." Tara said holding his hand up in between their chests.

"I told my parents I was going to go with you to Canyon Lake today. How do you want to get there? By teleportation or flying?"

"They didn't bother asking how we were getting there?"

"Luckily, no, I guess they just assumed your parents were taking me."

"Good thing your parents aren't presumptuous. How about we go there by flight, since I would like to get some good views of the scenery surrounding our area?"

"Okay, flight it is. Here, hold onto this and hold onto me tight." Tom said, handing over his Triad speaker to Tara as he grabbed her waist.

"What about my swimsuit, though?"

"Want a new one or you want to go grab yours?"

"I will be right back. Just hold on a minute." She ran back inside then came back saying, "I'm ready, let's go."

"Alright, but don't get too scared because I am the one holding you."

"Oh, come on, Tom. If I did not trust you, do you really think I would let you hold me at those kinds of heights in the sky?" Tom chuckled putting his arms around her waist in a locked position.

Holding onto her with all his strength, Tom blasted off soaring high into the clouds. Enjoying the brisk air Tara felt Tom lifting her up and placing her back on his arms so he could hold her up instead of around her waist. With a better view of the scenery, not stuck facing each other, Tara looked to her right and watched the clouds moving below them faster than they were traveling.

Descending through the moist clouds passing by, Tom felt so happy to finally have some peace in his life so he could relax and enjoy the day with Tara. Looking down at the beautiful hill country of Texas, Tara said, "I can't believe there is so much green down there and look at the big trees to the west of the lake." Lowering his right wrist and pointing down at the tall trees, Tom said, "Back in the early twenty first century there was a crazy writer who thought one day Texas's climate would rapidly change. So he started using his money to create magnetically enhanced habitats to grow redwood trees in the neighborhood that he grew up in."

"Man, I can't believe that somebody would do something so crazy." Tara said looking all around at the different views."

"Well, long ago, during nearly the same period as the development of those redwoods, we used to have lots of juniper trees which annoyed people's allergies too much and would suck up most of the water preventing other plants from producing. Locals called them cedar trees, but they were really juniper trees. Eventually, once the environmental activists weren't able to control the government anymore with fear of non-proven hypothesizes; they chopped down all the cedar trees and prevented them from growing anymore, the cedars weren't even native to the area originally. Then they shipped them to countries for people who needed regular homes instead of living in cardboard boxes or on the streets."

"So in essence, they traded all the Junipers for the redwoods." Tara responded jokingly.

Tom laughed saying, "Well technically the redwoods are only moderated to that one neighborhood, while the junipers were all over the place over populating other plants across a lot of the state."

Holding Tara in his arms and landing by the shore at the beach Tom said, "I will be right back. I need to go change. Voco me a new pair of swimming trunks in my size." After his vocoed trunks came he walked into the bathroom to change and came outside grabbing the triad speaker Tara had left on a table as she walked into change.

Using the green tongue feature of his hollowatch and triad speaker, Tom put on some nice music for them to listen to while they were going to hang out at the beach. They ran off into the sparkling water having a great time talking and swimming; even playing Frisbee with each other till it was lunch time.

When lunch came around for the love doves sitting at the bench Tom said, "Okay, so what do you want for lunch Tara? Just name whatever you want and I promise it will come out being the best food you could ever imagine."

Smirkingly, she responded, "Mmm…how about a large gyro with mozzarella cheese and tzatziki sauce with some french fries."

Tom raised his hand in the air opening his palm and said, "Voco me and Tara two large gyros with mozzarella cheese and tzatziki sauce and some french fries and a side of sliced tomatoes." After the typical hum, two gyros appeared on paper plates on the bench, and the french fries on top of some paper like material in two baskets made of wood.

"Wow, that is amazing, Tom, why did you ask for tomatoes, though?" she said eating her gyro some.

"Thought you might like some on those gyros, but I don't care for tomatoes that much because of their weird texture and taste." He said taking a bite of his gyro.

"Well, it's okay, but I have never eaten tomatoes on gyros before. I don't mind them, though. How did you get your powers or abilities as you call them?"

"It all started in England and it's a long story from there."

"Well, I'm pretty sure I have plenty of time to hear about it today."

So, for a long portion of the day, Tom told Tara his story about everything that had happened with him on his vacation. He even teleported the both of them to England to show her the remains of their Cabin. Then he showed her the ancients Knights Templar cave and the beach they visited frequently when they were there. To him, it was lots of fun to show her some of the key parts of their vacation so she could experience the same places where they had been.

Emerging back at the beach as the sun was about to set; Tom reached down toward his left arm with his right hand turning on some romantic music from the early twenty first century in his triad speaker and said, "So what do you think of this kind of music?" Tara looked over from the foot of the beach standing in the sand responding, "Sounds quite classical, but also very romantic."

"So you do like it? I thought this might really set the mood for us, especially since there is a sunset starting." Tom said reaching out both of his hands grabbing Tara's. "Well, you've got great taste in music. Who would think for a guy who has never been on a single date before yesterday, that you would be so romantic?" She responded.

Smiling at each other, they twirled around for a moment falling to the ground by the edge of the forest. Trying to catch their breath and laying in the sand in opposite directions they turned their heads towards the lake watching the sun start to fall over the horizon. As the beautiful song continued, Tom started to float upside down hovering over Tara's body. Looking up at him, Tom reached out with his hand to her saying, "Here, come with me."

Grabbing his hand she responded, "Come with you, where?"

Holding her hand warm heartedly, Tom said, "You will see."

Muttering some soft words under his breath, Tom started to stare into Tara's eyes. Staring into his blue eyes, Tara began to float up into the air with him as the water in the lake began changing color. It began to become very tropical with a crystal clear tint to it as though it had been cleaned or purified.

Holding each other's hands, they moved in closer, and Tom placed his right hand on her waist and his left hand on her shoulder. Tara grabbed Tom's side and his face as they moved forward spinning in a circle in the air together kissing each other's faces.

Wrapping their arms around each other and completely spinning under the sunset while they were kissing, exotic plants began to sprout up all around them. Plants that nobody had ever seen before. Some of them had fruits growing while others had vegetables growing but neither of the love doves recognized any of them.

Holding their legs in the air behind their backs and spinning in a circle, kissing as the sun was setting, the plants that grew started to glow making the moment even more special for the two of them. As the music played in the background, they landed down on the ground on their feet. They could barely stand from the feeling they were getting from each other. Then he said, "Oh boy, that sure was refreshing."

"You're right it sure was. You're the best kisser I ever met." Then she said embarrassed, "Let me correct myself, you're the only guy I have ever kissed, but still the best from my view."

Jokingly, Tom responded, "Well there are billions of other guys to try."

Tara responded sincerely, "Sorry Tom, but there isn't any other guys I even want to test the waters with. You are the only guy I know that makes me feel the way I do. I just love everything about the way you think and the way you are there for anybody. You are always trying to do things right even when the odds are against you."

Tom's face felt warm from the sun burn and from what Tara had just said, so he responded, "Awe...I love you too, Tara and I'm glad we have each other. You're very important in my life. I will always do what I can to protect you."

Giggling she responded, "Come on, obviously I don't always need saving. Only when the guys grabbing me the other night showed up did I need it."

"Yeah, that was pretty hot seeing you fight those guys off. Never thought I would be able to tell my friends I have a girlfriend who can kick butt like that."

Rolling her eyes, she responded, "But, you can't really tell anybody about that because then you would have to tell them about the part where you kicked two guys against a wall and lit them on fire. I'm pretty sure they might find that a little ridiculous."

"You're right. Oh well, at least we have each other to share these memories." Tom said light heartedly. "It's getting late and we need to get to the game. Come on lets go."

"Should we teleport to get there since its starting soon?" Tara said looking at her hollowatch.

"Yeah totally, Inflecto me and Tara to our school for the basketball game, and inflecto my triad speaker to my bedroom."

Emerging at the school, Tara said, "Good luck, I will be watching from the stadium."

Tom quickly ran off to the locker room to change for the game. Then he realized he didn't really practice most of the day with Benny like he should. After all the team mates were done changing, the coach gave a pep talk so they would probably play better, and then they all yelled together, "Let's go Rangers!"

Tom, Benny and the rest of the team came running through the banner out onto the court. Tara went to sit down by the front of the stage, Tom's family got on the bleachers and sat down to watch him play his first big game. Agent Dale even came to the game. He found himself a seat on one of the bleachers.

For the first quarter, Tom did not do much and Smithsonian Valley was losing when it ended with a score of 18 to 25. Near the end of the second quarter until half time, Tom scored a 3 pointer and got them up by 2 points with a score of 51 to 49.

When half time came, Tom went to talk to Agent Dale in the stands.

Tom asked, "Why do you look so down, Agent Dale?"

"Well, the past couple of days have been hard gripping with some evidence from one investigation. And then there is the guy I have been trying to find for many months now. Tomorrow I have to fly all the way to Washington, and I only have been home for about two months. My wife doesn't like it when I go on trips for my job; she is always afraid I will get hurt or have to stay there longer like I did with your family. Then, on a whole separate account I'm trying to find an old friend of mine."

"Sorry about the trouble my family caused your marriage. How hard have you looked for your friend?"

"Practically every way that is known to mankind. And it isn't your fault y'all needed protection. So don't blame yourself."

"Well, maybe I can help find them?"

Dale chuckled and asked, "How are you going to do that? You don't have any idea how complicated the situation of finding him is. Do you?"

"Nope, but I have my ways."

"Maybe someday he will be back like he was."

"Like he was?"

"Yeah, he was a man of great virtue and wonderful ideals."

"What kind of ideals?"

Dale answered, "He really wanted to get away from the civilization we met each other in. For some reason he feared the way they operated things for some reason, he had great ideas that could even change the world for the better."

"I don't see why anybody would want to be alone just because they didn't get along with a civilization they were in?"

Dale responded, "Well, that's not the reason he isn't here right now. It's way more complex than that. He had his reasons for not getting along with other people by certain things they were doing. But it doesn't really matter now that he is gone."

"That sucks. I am sorry. I hope you can find him even if he is gone. Talk to you later, I have a game to play and good luck finding your friend."

Agent Dale waved goodbye as Tom went to sit down. Then, when half time was over, Tom thought later he would try to find Agent Dale's old friend.

The third quarter began and Tom was put right back into the game. Twelve minutes later the score was 71 to 75 and then the quarter was over. Tom went to get some bottled water to drink because he was out of breath and feeling real hot.

When the fourth quarter started, Coach Morel devised a plan so they could do better. They played for about fifteen minutes and time running short and they needed 5 points to get ahead. Luke threw the ball to Drew who bounced it and ran, who dribbled it down a little then passed it to Benny and Benny threw it in the hoop and scored 2 points. Coach Morel, being a retired NBA player, had a great plan to win the game and told them to take a time out with 5 seconds left. Drew took the ball from one of the other school's team members and passed it to Benny then Benny passed it to Tom who was in the middle of the court. Tom looked around seeing two guys coming at him from both sides and saw he had only 2 seconds to make a shot. He jumped up, flying diagonally to the hoop and made a 3 pointer slam-dunk.

Lots of Smithsonian valley high school students and families in the bleachers yelled with happiness that they won, except a few people. But it was really obvious that one guy that was staring at Tom that was wearing a weird coat and sunglasses didn't seem to give a real reaction to the win. The crowd picked up Tom carrying him to the locker room with Coach Morel behind them and The Rangers rejoicing over winning 103 to 100.

After they were done talking and changing in the locker room, Tom and Benny came out and found Tara, Tom and Benny's parents, Martin and Agent Dale all waiting for them. Tom said, "Mom, Dad I have big news. As you know, last night I went on a date and today I did not get to practice with Benny. I was busy spending time with that girl standing next to y'all and she is my girlfriend, her name is Tara."

Tom's mom said, "Well, nice to meet you Tara."

Mr. Turner said, "Yeah, you seem like a nice girl for Tom. Now, let's go home to celebrate Tom and Benny's victory."

Tara, Tom and Benny's families drove off to the Turner's house. When they arrived, they all got out and headed inside to celebrate their victory. They made appetizers to eat with the party they were having. Some other families from the team came over to join them for their party.

After hours of listening to music and playing board games, Tom headed up to his room after saying goodbye to the other families.

He was about to go to bed, when he heard somebody throwing rocks at his window. He opened the window seeing some of the gangsters from the movie theater from the other night. He jumped out the window landing on one of them, knocking them to the ground. Tom stabilized himself saying annoyed, "How did you find me and what do you want?"

The leader replied, "Geese, you really think all we did last night was hurt you and your silly girl."

"No, I believe you were attempting to do much worse things to her but you did not succeed because we stopped you." Tom responded.

The lead gangster said, "We also stole your wallet if you did not notice."

With a feeling of remorse, Tom felt his pocket, then thought, "So that's how they found me." Tom then said, "Well guess I will have to erase your memories then."

Throwing Tom his wallet, the lead gangster said, "Wait a second dude. We want you to join us and help us with our plans to become the most powerful gang in all of San Antonio!"

"Sorry, but I try not to do bad things. As well I am not the type to commit crimes on a daily basis."

The lead gangster said, "Well then, if that is what you wish we will find you again. I have your info hidden at my apartment."

Very peeved Tom responded by saying, "Listen, I am not in the mood to deal with any dramatic fights or annoyances right now. So ignis inflecto all of the gang members, except the leader to my citadel dungeon and voco me any info he has on me." They flashed with a blazing fire then disappeared leaving nothing but the shadow of their body's behind. Then a paper with Tom's info appeared in his hand.

The lead gangster started yelling at Tom, "Whad ya do with my crew, bro?! How did you get my info on you?"

"The same thing I'm going to do with you. But first, oblivio the past seven years from the lead gangster's memory. Thankfully, the other world place will make you forget how you got there once you go through the wormhole, so inflecto the lead gangster to join his friends in the dungeon." Then he thought to himself as he crumbled the gangster's info on him, "Good thing I never lock those gates in the dungeon so they can just walk out of there."

Walking into his house, Tom wondered where Agent Dale's friend was, so he went back inside to talk to him about his friend. "So, why do you think your friend is still alive if he is gone, Agent Dale? And if he's alive where would he be?" Tom asked with an anxious expression on his face.

"Well Tom, he could be anywhere but I think he is alive by some of the things he once told me about are unraveling every now and again. Plus I never said he was dead but said he was gone," agent Dale said with a worried look on his face.

"But, why would that mean he is alive?"

Agent Dale said, "Because only he had such crazy ideas and told me in the ways that he did."

Tom went back upstairs to his room thinking about how he should go looking for Agent Dale's missing friend. As he stood there in his room he wondered how he would find him. Then he said "Inflecto me somewhere near Agent Dales missing friend."

Then something happened that would affect Tom in the long run. Nothing happened, as he just stood there in his room. Very puzzled and confused why nothing happened or why he was still there, Tom started to rapidly worry thinking very fast about what was wrong. Tom said to himself, "Okay, let's see if I can still do anything?"

So, Tom decided to make himself hover up in his room, but before he could, instantly he saw the door knob twisting causing him to trip backwards, and fall. Agent Dale walked in the door and saw the worry on Tom's face and said, "You alright Tom? You look petrified, like you're really scared?"

Tom responded anxiously, "Yeah, I am good. Just some personal issues." Then he said more inspiringly like he was trying to cover his mood, "So what brings you up to my room?"

"I thought about what you asked a couple minutes ago and thought I should tell you something my friend once said to me."

Tom was now very curious and asked, "What did he say?"

"He said I would never fully understand the world we live in for its massiveness of mysteries; but anything could happen so I should always be ready for anything."

Tom felt moved by these words, like they meant something important. Then he said softly, "So he was a great man, I take it?"

Dale responded morosely, "He helped me get through some really tough challenges when it seemed like the odds were against us."

Tom responded with honor for this friend, "Wow, sounds like the best kind of friend a person could have."

"He sure was for the little time I knew him." Tom then remembered the task he had made in his mind and thought, "Maybe if I ask Dale where he lived I could find him?"

So Tom asked Agent Dale, "Where did your friend live?"

Agent Dale responded, confused at what to say, "I actually never knew where he lived? To be honest, our knowing each other was short and his departure from my life was very quick. I believe it was unintended. Even more weird though, I am not sure what happened to him?"

Tom wondered how he could not know what happened to his own friend. But, he thought it would be too emotional to ask him about his departure. So Tom said, "Well, who knows, maybe you will see him again someday? On the contrary, where do you live or where did you grow up?"

"I live with my wife near the neighborhood of Native Hills in Autumn Limb and that is where I grew up."

Tom thought with a good feeling in his chest, "This may be a good place to start looking for Agent Dale's missing friend." Tom said, "Yeah, well it is getting late maybe I should go to bed soon."

Agent Dale responded with a smile of enthusiasm, "Yeah, who knows what the future holds and thanks for the good conversation."

Tom said with a cheerful smile, "You're welcome. Good night."

"Good night Tom," Agent Dale said as he walked out the door and shutting it. Tom laid down on his bed and thought about how he was going to be able to find Agent Dale's friend without his abilities, or why his abilities weren't even working anymore...

Chapter 16
The Search for a Friend

The Near Future
Sunday, September 20th, 2:17 P.M.
Rolling Oak Hills, Smithsonian Valley, Texas

Feeling somewhat paranoid, Tom stopped, taking the foot off of the pedal of the bike thinking about how he would reach Agent Dale's old neighborhood, but it was going to be a long ride. He couldn't stop thinking about the horrible nightmare he had the night before revolving about how he felt his abilities weren't working for him anymore. Checking the ELO PSI on his hollowatch, he realized he needed to head down highway 617 to reach highway 218 and reach Agent Dale's old neighborhood.

Enjoying the brisk breeze, Tom peddled fast, heading down highway 617 loving the fact that it wasn't excruciatingly hot. That didn't change the fact he was trying to avoid the crazy traffic Texas presented absolutely full of maniacs that seemed dangerous at times. Whenever he heard a car pulling up close to him he turned his head, looking back, pulling off to the side even more.

After his courageousness with the tenseness of highway 616, Tom finally reached 218. Heading north from the cross over for about five miles, he pulled up to a King Finnegan's restaurant in front of the Guadalupe River Bridge. Feeling hungry from all the bike riding, Tom ordered a shepherds burger with a side of Finnegan's wild mushroom bisque. He sat down, trying to cool off as it was starting to get really hot outside.

Five miles later after riding into the Native Hills entrance, Tom wondered what street he should head towards. "Maybe if I call Agent Dale he can tell me where he used to live." He thought.

Driving up to the parking lot as rain poured down, Agent Dale sat there for a moment in a trance thinking about how he should deal with things as his windshield wipers kept going back and forth. He didn't want to scare off the guy he needed to catch on his mission, since he might have ties to the Kafir Dunya extremist that escaped their prison cells and tried to high jack the air plane. Hearing his hollowatch ring and feeling its vibration as he was about to open the door of his car and go inside the apartment building, Agent Dale answered without looking to see who was calling, "Hello, this is Agent Sizer."

"Hey Agent Dale, it's me, Tom."

Surprised by Tom's calling he responded, "Oh…hey Tom, what's going on?"

"I'm good; I was just calling to ask you what street you lived on in Native Hills when you were growing up?

Sounding very perplexed, Agent Dale replied, "Well, I don't know why you want to know that. I will tell you though, I lived on 0316 Gogh drive."

Tom responded cheerfully, "Thanks I will talk to you later."

"Later Tom…" Agent said scratching his head, "Well that was weird and very unusual." Agent Dale said to himself as he got out of his rental car.

"Okay, time to focus on the mission at hand." He thought to himself walking up to the doorway to the main hall of the apartments.

Getting out of the elevator on the third floor of the apartment complex, Agent Dale looked down and noticed his hollowatch glitching out with static like images on its main screen. Figuring this guy wasn't going to leave easily, he pulled his gun from his holster and ran fast towards apartment 3F where the man resided. Kicking down the door, Agent Dale yelled, "Steven O'Brian, you are under arrest for abetting terrorists in a plot to high jack transcontinental flight 851." Running into the room, Agent Dale noticed the lights in the room were flickering.

Shutting the door, Agent Dale came in. Steven stepped forward saying, "I didn't do anything wrong. You guys have been after me ever since I uploaded that stupid video that I saved from Flutter. You know the one the government tried to take down within one minute of it airing."

"What are you talking about? It was reported that you helped one of the terrorists relatives who worked at the airport put the security on a loop so they would be able to get their knives past everyone?"

"No, I'm not a criminal. They are setting me up just to shut me up. I developed my own PSI that instantly saves any flutter videos or anything broadcasted from high altitudes. Also when the government instantly took it off the Skynet, my PSI took note of that and it warned me that I was being traced. So I did everything I could to get away from them."

"How am I supposed to know this isn't some elaborate hoax on your part?" Agent Dale responded, looking straight at Steven pressingly.

"See how your hollowatch is showing nothing except static right now?"

"Yeah, so whats that got to do with anything?"

"I also developed some EMI emitters to keep the government from seeing me on anybody's nearby video feeds or skylink connections of their hollowatches. Let me show you this video inside my faraday glass box." He said setting a glass box with a hollowatch in it on the kitchen table.

"You know this is nuts, right? The government only taps into hollowatches of actual criminals that they know have committed a crime or they have a lead on. So you can just turn off the connections on your phone if you didn't want them to trace you. It's not like we actually watch everyone from every possible way like that twentieth century book."

"There are forces at work you can't even imagine. Trust me; I am not just some nutty, paranoid idiot," Steven said pressing the button on the hollowatch closing the faraday glass box it was in.

Agent Dale watched as he saw himself on its screen, aiming his gun at the terrorist who was trying to make a public statement about how they were locked up. "It was broadcast live directly on an account that was only ten minutes old." Steven responded sounding somewhat saddened about the possibility that the people in the video weren't really terrorists, only just kidnapped victims.

"Maybe you are right about this being a set up to shut you up. I have found recently when I keep trying to find out the sources on certain intelligence, that there are odd circumstances behind them. Are you truly a good hacker, though?"

"If I wasn't a good hacker, I might not have gotten away from the government in the first place." Steven said smirking. "Then again, I probably wouldn't have had this issue if I didn't hack the mainframe of Flutter as well…" He said regretfully.

Putting his hand on Steven's shoulder, Agent Dale said, "Well, I might need your help finding some concrete evidence on the person who has set you up and the people in the video you just showed me. In fact, I think I know just the way to resolve these things. If you will work with me I give you my word that I will help clear your name."

Reaching out his hand, Agent Dale said, "Do we have a deal?"

With a skeptical face Steven responded shaking Agent Dale's hand, "Deal. Still I need to get out of here first."

"That won't be too hard, I will just say I couldn't find you. But to reach me for further details on our operation here is a safe hollowatch number where you can reach me." He said writing down a specific number on a note pad with his all-purpose pen.

"All right, but where should I go?"

"Head down to San Antonio Texas. I know some safe places down there. Don't try to attract too much attention getting there, though, since I need your help."

"Okay, I will speak to you later, then. What should I call you?" Steven asked opening the window to the apartment's fire escape.

"Just call me "Agent Sizer".

Wandering through the streets following his ELO PSI, Tom finally reached Gogh drive. Rolling down the street, sweating from all the pedaling, he looked around for the Sizer name on multiple mail boxes. Finding Agent Dale's old home, he looked around pondering where he could find some clues. Then, he went from house to house asking neighbors if they knew anything about Agent Dale or any close friends he might have had when he was younger. Most of them didn't even know about Agent Dale and none knew of any close friends he might have.

Growing tired from all his searching, Tom walked down the street giving up hope he would actually find Agent Dale's friend or that any of this had a real purpose. Thinking about how ridiculous it must have seemed going on this pointless adventure, he laughed remembering how he got off the phone. He thought, "Man I am lucky Agent Dale didn't question me about why I wanted to know his old address. Funny too, how he said Native Hills, but his home technically was in Redwood Hills."

It had been practically almost an hour since he arrived at Agent Dale's street and it was getting dark as the sun was setting over the horizon of the giant redwood trees. Walking west and holding his bike as he got to the end of the long street, there was an interception with another street at the end. Looking up, and noticing a strange alluring star, he stepped forward, following it into the bushes at the end of Gogh Drive. Not recognizing this big star, made it seem that if you did not follow it, it would make you feel like you were missing out on something important.

Past the bushes there wasn't much grass, just quite a bit of aloe vera plants along with a few cactuses in what looked like a miniature desert on the face of some very steep cliff-like hills. Following his own unorthodox path and trying not to hurt himself by touching the spikey plants, Tom made his way to the base of the cliff-like hills. He couldn't help noticing that they were made up of caliche soil and had steps going up it. Somehow they looked natural and a bit designed at the same time. Walking up the steps carrying his bike, he thought to himself, "I must be crazy following a star then finding steps up a hill that looks natural but also look like stairs, which were invented by the ancient Babylonians. Babylon, though wasn't anywhere near here thousands of years ago? Maybe they were made by locals in this neighborhood or ancient Indians…who really knows? Still, why do they look so natural?"

Reaching the top of the caliche cliffs, Tom realized he had come across a new problem. He saw that he was walking right into a giant forest made of redwoods and oak trees. Treading on, in the direction he saw the star, he wandered through the forest not knowing where he was going. The glowing star with its radiance couldn't be seen anymore because of the tall trees. Eventually he found what he thought to be a large drainage pipe by a big rock coming out of a hill to his left. Leaving his bike there by a big rock because it was so steep, he climbed the hill finding it led to a road where he could see the star again and the moon beaming down on him.

Going back down to the big rock something caught Tom's eyes. It was a strange symbol etched onto the stone. Feeling led here by the star & mysterious circumstance, he crawled into the drainage pipe to see if Agent Dale's missing friend was inside it. He might be dead and had never been found. Inside the pipe he came to a dead end. Then feeling a strange triangle sticking out of the circumference of the pipe he pressed it, then the dead end opened up with a breeze coming through it.

Tom crawled out of the pipe and found out he was in some strange old cave-looking place, with a giant octagon stone table in the middle of it with weird symbols and carvings all over. He looked around the odd place noticing three strange crystals on different walls that seemed like rectangles of carved rock, instead of the natural stony cave-like walls enveloping the rest of the room. Grabbing the crystals, he noticed they could fit into each other making up what looked like a solid triangle. But the middle rectangular wall, unlike the others, had three steps to climb to reach the crystal it held.

Tom felt the octagon table's center and noticed it was like an indention of a triangle in its center. So he put the crystals together in the center of the monolithic table, fitting it into the right dimensions. The crystals lit up with glowing water, it looked like microscopic life pouring out from them. The glowing water flowed through the carvings on the stone table. It even made the room light up with a nostalgic hair raising feel to it.

Tom could see things better now that the glowing water was in all the carvings. The three giant rectangles he had seen started to open up vertically, revealing they were really doors. He was wondering if he was still on earth because this place seemed too bizarre to have been made by any normal human. Walking through the door on his left that led through an odd passage with another odd cut off room he found a big alter. There, sitting in the middle of the stone pad like alter, was the Ark of Covenant. His jaw dropped as he thought, "What's this doing here!"

He thought it was a fake after examining it for a moment. Tom then headed back to the main cave-like room. Curious about what the door on the left held, he walked on through it to find another odd room cut off with a flat stone pad and a giant triangular stone structure against the wall. It was strange at the top of the triangle-like structure since it had a round arch to it instead of pointed lines at the top.

Tom was curious by this thing he saw. The pad had some English writing on it from what he could see. Walking closer to read it, he could feel something invisible trying to pull him closer to the wall. It felt almost like the rapids of a river. Looking up he noticed there, against the wall, was a swirling vortex much like his worm hole in England. He read the stone pad with it saying "The gate way to Auqisitus".

Tom thought he would check that place out some other time. So he headed back to the main stone monolith room and then walked through the giant door in the middle finding something very peculiar.

It was a giant chamber-like place with a unique design. The chamber room had two beds of glowing aqua colored water. Then down the pathway of the giant chamber was a wall of ice shards hanging off a giant wall that looked like it was made of dirt combined with rock.

Standing there mesmerized by its mysteriousness, Tom decided to step forth going down the pathway which was made of cobblestone. Confused by the walls of this place looking natural, yet the rest of it looked like it was made by someone. At the end of the pathway looking like a ladder on the rock wall, there were some metal bars to climb up.

Tom started climbing the ladder made of metal bars. As he went higher, he could feel the coldness of the ice shards getting closer as the dirt of the wall began to blend with the ice itself. Even though he had put on some muscle over the summer, he still felt very cold as he put another hand on another freezing cold metal bar climbing up the cold wall. Not being able to take much more of this climbing because of the coldness his hands started to feel very numb. They started shriveling up with blisters and his skin hurt, with all his being, he knew he had to get to the top of this crazy wall.

Reaching the top, (which was very high) Tom saw a little stone room about three cubits in front of him. Before those three cubits cut off into one room, there was a balcony that went from one side of the cave chamber to the other. Getting up the ladder onto the balcony, turning around, he looked down noticing how high up he was. It was not a place you would want to fall off of even with the glowing ponds of water below. There seemed to be a bunch of tree roots growing in from the ceiling above the pathway which could not be reached by hand nor from where he was standing.

From Tom's view, this place seemed mysterious with an odd, yet alluring vibe to it. He wondered where and what this place was or who had made it. Still, he felt like he should push onwards to the next part of this mystery that he had become involved in, so he turned around towards the odd room.

The room looked strange in architecture as its measurements in design were odd in number. It was a room of nine cubits by nine cubits. Noticing a door way on the right side of the room with light coming through it, along with snow flurrying through the construction of the doorway, he decided to check it out. He was puzzled to see snow blowing in. Watching the snow he felt this odd feeling that he wasn't in Texas anymore.

Walking through the door-way into the light, Tom found himself outside on top of a very windy mountain cliff with snow blowing everywhere as a moon shined down brightly upon him. This moon was looking bigger than he had ever noticed the earth's moon before. It shined so bright & big that he thought it definitely wasn't earth's moon. Standing there, as the wind blew; he looked out in front to the giant cliff. Below he noticed there was a big gorge. He thought anybody who fell off would die. Stepping back a little, so he wouldn't fall, he looked to his right seeing a wall of dirt.

Turning left, Tom found another trail of snow he could follow which had a wall of dirt on his left and the gorge of certain death on his right. Moving onward about twenty one cubits he found the mountain path ended with a giant wall of ice. Desperately hoping for some form of resolution he found a wooden door next to him on the left that looked very old fashion, much like something from a medieval tale. To the right there was nowhere to go except toward the giant gorge. No creature would want to fall off into it, so he decided to open the wooden door to his left.

As he opened the door, Tom saw a person sitting in a chair at the end of what looked like a nice underground cave-home. He was sitting in a chair between a bunk bed and a desk with a light next to it. The man said, "Come on in, you look really cold." Tom didn't hesitate for a second to go in since he was so cold from being out in the freezing snow. It seemed to have a nice warm feeling in there compared to outside in all the coldness, yet somehow this place felt quaint and cozy to him. Then he asked, "Are you the missing friend of Agent Dale?"

The man said, "Agent Dale?" As if he was confused that Dale was an agent or at least that's how it came across to Tom. "Well, a long time ago he once was my friend."

Tom replied as he paced forward some towards the man, "Well then, are you him?"

"I guess so, but I don't see why he would be looking for me at all?"

Tom curiously asked "Why not?"

"Because in my mind, the circumstances are very complex. He shouldn't be looking for me. He wouldn't know where to begin his search, let alone why he can't get a hold of me, since we were forced apart."

Tom stated in confusion, "What, why would he look for you then?"

"Because he probably found proof that I am not as gone as he might have thought I was. He probably wants to be my friend just like how he used to be."

"Why don't you tell him that you're alive?"

"You see it's really hard to explain. And even if I did it might change everything that I have worked for so hard. And the government might want to put me in jail or kill me for misunderstanding things that have occurred. They might think I am avoiding them, even though that is not the reason I gave up my old life."

"Then why in the world did you stop being his friend?" Tom asked.

The man then changed the subject and said in a mysterious elusive attitude, "I never wanted to stop being his friend…and I didn't really have a choice on how we were separated. I definitely had no choice when certain, very gruesome events took place when I was younger…when we were separated as good friends by obstacles in our lives."

Tom was a little annoyed by this answer and wanted to know more. The man continued his story, "I knew this was my chance to go out to do better things in other countries and make a new start in life and fulfill my destiny." Tom said in confusion and sarcasm, "Really destiny, come on? What do you mean "destiny". Does anybody even really have a destiny?"

The man replied in his bold voice, "Yes Tom, even you have an amazing destiny you never knew. Everyone exists for a reason, otherwise you wouldn't exist at all."

Tom, scared out his mind exclaimed, "How do you know my name!?"

"I know a lot about you, some that you don't even know. And I how you have a long journey ahead of you."

"How would you know all this and why do you claim to know so much about me?"

The man responded very confident of what he was saying. "Tom, I also know about your abilities and let's just say a voice inside my head told me about you."

Tom got very defensive, "A voice inside your head!? You really expect me to believe you learned about me through a voice in your head which sounds insane in the first place? Besides everyone has abilities, so who knows what you're talking about."

"Oh, come on Tom, you know very well what I am talking about, so don't even act like you don't have a clue."

"Okay, let's say theoretically I did have some abilities…what, would you say they were magic, natural, maybe even super powers?"

"You see Tom everyone carries on traits and habits that are in their genetics because of the things their families did or could do in the past. Your family was more capable of doing things. Things like you do, because of Alida being what she was or is….I am not really sure on that one at the moment. Even though most humans are capable of doing these things, not many would know it because their ancestors didn't know about it or ever try to work on their talents like your ancestors did."

Tom stood there amazed at what he just had heard then asked, "How would you know about Alida being related to me or even who she was, neither me nor my brother have ever spoken to you that I know of. Maybe John did?"

"Tom, I have been following your own history much longer than you have or at least I think so. Although I can't be sure when you started.

"Why would you want to know about me or my family?"

"Because I have my own reasons for the things I have done or even been hired to do." Having what he thought was an epiphany Tom asked, "Wait a second are you that guy that was wearing sunglasses and a black suit at my basketball game the other night?"

"No, that wasn't me at all. Still I could see why you would think that was me."

"Okay, besides all your creepiness about knowing about me as you claim you do, how am I to know what my purpose is?"

"I didn't find out my own purpose very easily. It was a hard time for me to start a new life alone not knowing anyone or being able to talk to or trust anyone, since Dale and I were forced apart as friends. It has not been a very simple life. Then again, whose life ever truly is easy. You will find your way Tom. I am sure everyone eventually does."

Tom, too annoyed by this guy's elusiveness thought he should bring up how agent Dales life had gotten better since he had been gone. Then he said, "Yeah, well Agent Dale made a new friend named Paulo and his life is way better now."

The man replied with a chuckle, "Yeah, I know. Paulo holds a special place in my heart and is a good friend to me and Dale."

"Is the Paulo you are speaking of look Asian and has a son?"

"Yes, that is him; actually he has a total of three sons and is looking for the third one." Tom replied surprised, "Wow, God does work in mysterious ways; you must have kept up with him if you knew about Kevin."

The man said confusingly, "Who is Kevin?"

"Kevin is Paulo's missing son who he found."

"Oh yeah, is that his name, Kevin? That's nice. So is he a good kid?"

"Yeah, he is a nice kid. I met him, too." The man responded chuckling, "Ahh, I see, probably while you were in England, I bet."

"You know it's creepy that you know where I have been." The man rolled his eyes then said, "You were on TV from that airplane incident; it isn't hard to put two and two together. That is where Paulo said his old girlfriend moved."

"Still, I saw Paulo once at an event where Dale was. Or at least I think it was Paulo. He looked like him but he had a goatee/beard line. Never thought Paulo would come all the way from California or England to see that event." Tom replied "Guess that's where Dale and Paulo met each other."

"Might have been, because I never really did understand why some random Filipino guy, I didn't know, would show up at that event. I thought it was some random guy, but I guess it could have been Paulo. I just wasn't sure, even though he looked so much like him. Still, I don't think for sure it was Paulo there because there were reasons he could not have come to that event, so it must have been somebody else."

"Well, who else could it have been, then?"

"I don't know. Maybe somebody related to Paulo?" Tom asked "Why would a relative of Paulo's show up at this event and not Paulo?"

"I don't know. It was just a guess. Sorry guess that sounded like a dumb scenario."

"Yeah, it sure did. You won't explain the only reason why you gave up your life, was it a complex scenario or circumstance?" The man responded, "No, there are other reasons I can't fully acknowledge. The government I was involved in was very corrupt. They were doing very horrible things. I honestly feel they are going to influence other governments someday to do very dastardly things as well. It was my destiny to leave that life behind, putting me where I am today."

Tom rhetorically said, "So, Dale was not the only reason? It sounds like to me you used to be a government agent."

The man responded "Maybe I was...and nope, had lots of other issues that made life so hard. I wanted to just be gone from those people's view of how to deal with things. I even made a lot of choices that I regret. Soon I realized that if I continued with my ways in life, that my actions could have disastrous results. So I moved onto a less harmful life. Totally different than from what I was doing at the time. I found a path in life that did not involve my past. Later on I learned there were lots of people you can trust in the world. More than the bad government's followers. Some who I could have great friendships with, and that's when I became a much better person. Still, you could say I used to work with Dale as well as the government."

"Wow, that is one big story. But I can tell you Dale really misses you and he is a great friend. You should never give up that friendship. For all you know, he thinks you just had other issues and disappeared and not that you stopped being his friend."

The man said, "Well, I have a question for you. How prepared are you for something very emotional of a great loss?"

Tom briefly thought about how his abilities were not working and how Tara might leave him then he said, "I would..." The man interrupted, "Be devastated and emotionally unbalanced to the point you would go mad with pain over losing her?"

Tom surprised asked sarcastically, "Wait, how did you know what I was going to say? Did the voice in your head say that to you as well?"

"Maybe it did...maybe it didn't, still anybody with a heart would know losing somebody you love would be hard on you. And another way to answer that is...well, I am just good at knowing what people are about to say. I do know about your girlfriend. Part of my old job was to prevent bad things from occurring so we had to think ahead of events taking place." Obviously, the man knew something that he didn't want Tom to fully know.

Tom, so perplexed by this man, asked, "What's your name?" The man responded with a very stern look on his face saying, "My name is not of any importance to you, how did you manage to find this place?"

"I have my ways of getting to places. For one thing, where are we?"

Then the man asked as if he was curious, even though he already knew, "How could you not know where you are? Did you run from your parents or something, and then get lost?"

Tom responded, "That's hard for me to explain. Just tell me where I am please?"

The man stated, "Well, you're in Autumn Limb, Texas." Tom had asked this because he felt that wormhole and saw snowy mountains, so he was worried he might not be where he was when he crawled into the tunnel.

Tom asked, "Wait, how did you know that I might have been wondering what state I am in?" The man chuckled saying, "Well guess I am just too good at knowing some things. Plus I didn't know that's what you were wondering, usually when people ask where they are you should tell them everything to be informative. You know in case they are lost. It's getting pretty late, shouldn't you get home?"

Tom laughed then asked in amazement, "Yeah, maybe I will soon, but what I would like to know is what is with that weird underground route that leads to a snowy mountain and then to here all about?"

The man responded, "Well, for one thing the snowy mountain is not even real. That is a holographic room that I made. In fact everything you have seen since entering the underground entrance was made up by me in a dream I once had when I was little. I added some extra stuff."

Tom then thought to himself, "That is strange to make a whole place similar to a dream you once had."

Remembering he saw the Ark of the Covenant, he then asked with real interest "Is that even the real Ark of the Covenant?"

The man replied with a tone like he was hinting at something else, "Nope, it's just a replica I had made. The real ark, could not be found simply because of certain circumstances and mysteries surrounding its whereabouts." Tom had presumed what he said had something to do with this guy's studies on his family.

Tom then asked, "Okay, what about that wormhole that leads to a place called Auqisitus?"

The man responded with curiosity, "Well, I found it in some Sumerian ruins near the coast of Kuwait, and then I had it brought over here. Still, how do you know it's a worm hole and not a portal?"

"I like to study these kinds of things, but it has all the math features of a worm hole and not just a portal."

The man said with a chuckle, "Okay, I guess I will believe you even though I know there is more to the story than you are telling."

Tom responded humorously, "Well the same could be said for you, Mr. Mystery man that looks around Dale's age." The man gave a strange look like he was puzzled when Tom said this.

Placing his hand on Tom's shoulder, the man said, "Tom, we may never fully understand the world we live in. It is full of massive mysteries. To which we may never have the answers, but the most important thing you can do is be prepared for the coming future for anything could happen.

Tom remembered Agent Dale said something similar and it felt very important to him. Then the man rhetorically said, "I take it you don't need a ride home?"

Tom puzzled by what the man just said asked, "Well is there a quicker way then out the long underground tunnel?"

"Yes, just follow me and I will guide you out of here."

"Okay, lead the way."

Tom followed him up to the top of the bunk bed on the right side of the room, and then Agent Dale's elusive friend opened a shaft on the ceiling revealing some more ladder bars. Then, they both climbed up the bars. After climbing up they were both oddly in an air vent so they crawled through till they popped out of the vent into a room full of games, movies, and a skylink computer center which included a television built into it.

Tom, seeing the skylink computer center, wondered how Agent Dale couldn't find his friend if he worked for the government. He probably had access to anybody's devices, so he asked the elusive friend why Agent Dale couldn't find him.

The elusive friend said, "Probably because they didn't have any idea where to look for me here, and details might have changed from what he was looking for. It has been a long time since he saw me and has no frame of reference for what he is looking for. Come on this way."

Tom and the man walked up some stairs into a hall way then they turned right as the man opened his front door to let Tom out of his home. Tom said, "Well, thanks for the info. Should I tell Agent Dale where you live now?"

"Well okay, but do try to come back some time in the future."

Tom replied, "I will. You still have too many mysteries surrounding you."

The person said, "Well as if you don't or do you?"

Tom said perplexed by what the man had just said, "Goodbye. You're the one that has mystery's not me."

The man chuckled again saying, "Goodbye. See you later."

Tom walked out of the person's yard confused why the man said what he just did a moment prior. Then he noticed he was on top of a hill and at the bottom of that hill was the street with the hill down at the bottom where the forest was and where he entered into the cave.

Walking down the hill, Tom grabbed his bike by the big rock & fake drainage pipe getting back up on the street to head to his friend Matt's house, just like he told his parents he would. Riding back over towards his neighborhood he thought a lot about the things the elusive man said. "Why did he say I could do what I can because of what Alida is, or was as he put it?" He questioned to himself.

"Does that mean she is still alive?" Then he thought "There is no way she was still alive. That is highly illogical and impossible? How did that guy know so much? Could it really have been from a voice in his head or just lots of research he did on me or when he was in the government?"

As much as his scientific mind tried to make sense of things, none of it really made sense to him. In the end, Tom's search for a friend yielded great results, giving him much more insight than he could have ever hoped. What did it all mean though? And how was he going to figure out the rest of this deep mystery? In the end, who was the elusive man…?

Chapter 17
Things Nobody Wants to See

The near future
Friday, October 30th, 6:12 P.M.
CIA Headquarters, Langley, Mclean, Virginia

Walking through the halls of the CIA headquarters, Agent Dale was happy he had convinced Director Ford to speak with him regarding the conspiracy he had managed to uncover. He knew that he needed to speak with Director Ford if he wanted to gain any ground in convincing Congress about how deep this conspiracy had gone. Approaching a desk outside the director's office, he told the secretary why he was there. "Director Ford will be with you in a moment." She responded.

Waiting for seven minutes, Agent Dale read some news articles on his hollowatch trying to endure the wait. Feeling a little nervous that this wouldn't work out, he sat there sweating a little, and then decided to grab a small cup of water from a dispenser near the wall. Taking one sip of the water, the door to Director Ford's office opened up and he said, "Come on in Agent Sizer."

Walking into the room with a tense look on his face, Agent Dale said, "Sir, what I need to speak to you about is a really obscure hidden matter. We need the best discretion we can from being viewed or heard."

Chuckling Director Ford walked to the windows of his office and closed the blinds responding, "What's this all about Agent Sizer?"

"Well Sir, I discovered that there was a massive cover up going on. They could even be listening in right now, so I have taken extra measures to make sure that our conversation won't be over heard." Agent Dale said, as he took out a small triangle device from his pocket pressing its button making the lights flicker.

"Don't you think you're in over your head a little bit? How could people be listening into our conversation? You might as well put on a tinfoil hat and say the Native Martians are out to get us. But don't worry my windows are sound and bullet proof."

"Sir, I need for you to take me seriously here. This isn't just some paranoid delusion. I have actually found lots of evidence on that whole situation. It involved the supposed terrorist cell from Russia full of Kafir Dunyas that proves they were just an innocent village with an ancient secret. You are my only hope of convincing Congress who is behind all of this."

"Did you bring any of this evidence with you? As well, do you actually have anything solid to prove these things? Because you know, none of this will hold up if you don't have any solid evidence."

"Yes, indeed I do. I brought with me a typed copy of my interviews with the many terrorists, and the one interview I conducted when I went to Nikolay Serzynkov who was paid to set up fake intelligence to make the villagers look guilty. Also I got reports from Lieutenant Clancy who was the one to find out the intelligence."

"This is all nice you have built up a case, but it doesn't change the fact that you need something solid that actually incriminates whoever is behind this. Do you have anything to show who is behind it?"

"Yes, here are some papers showing the bank numbers showing transfers to Nikolay's account. Somebody tried to delete the sender's accounts and their history. Luckily for us, I know some good hackers, and I did some other things to get a hold of the paper printed versions with the ID of the original bank account owner."

"Did you bring those with you also to show me who is behind it all?

"No I didn't." Agent Dale responded, pulling a gun with a silencer attached out of his holster. "I knew you weren't going to come clean even with me stock piling evidence against you."

"Ah…I see we're beyond formalities now. You know killing a man like me is probably a capital punishment. Besides, some papers you could have easily printed yourself, so you really don't have anything solid against me. Investigators could also think I was sending that man money for his cancer."

"It's funny you say that. You see, I figured since my own boss was being elusive, he must have thought somebody was listening to him. So, luckily for me, later on Agent Myers told me about a PSI I could install to see if people were listening to my conversations on my hollowatch. It's a good thing we left our hollowatches in our cars while we went swimming with both our families that weekend at Canyon Lake so she could tell me about it in secret. Then, one week later, on the twelfth of September, she called me and you just happened to be listening, which confirmed it was you all along. So I checked your phone records from October and your bank numbers. The next week I got the papers from the guy you hired to rob the bank. I know all about the drug lord transporter you hired to put chemicals in the Sernynkov couple's air vents to give them cancer."

"All you really have is your word Agent Sizer. It doesn't seem like you have that much against me. You're insured to be alone. Conversation will remain that way since nobody else is listening and you blocked it with a small EMI generator. I was the only one keeping an eye on your group's interactions, so you don't need to worry about others always watching you. You are of no significance to them."

"Them? Who are you referencing and what is so important about some bones you tried to keep from the general public?" Agent Dale responded, angrily holding the gun more firmly to spook him. "Tell me now?!"

With black foreboding eyes he responded, "There are forces at work far beyond the United States government; things you wouldn't fully understand. They live in the shadows, keeping things hidden from humanity. For many years they kept themselves where nobody could mess with them. Only when things are fully right will you ever have a clue of what you are dealing with. You cannot know what the bones are, because then it might make you question everything that you thought you knew about the history of our world."

Having a horrible, ominous feeling in the pit of his stomach, agent Dale retorted, "You really think some elusive talk is going to save you now for what you have done? The whole world will know about whatever it is you have been trying to hide."

"In a world of ants, you aren't really anything except a pawn Agent Sizer." He said with pride scoffing.

"Yeah, well you best hope that those pawns don't start rebelling against whoever is trying to mess with them. I got it all on camera using a glass faraday box. I had my new hacker friend you were trying to catch install it this morning under a custodian's fake id. So, now the whole world will be exposed to what you have been trying to keep a tight lid on. Now that I got all I wanted out of you, the truth is my gun is empty."

Looking real paranoid Director Ford yelled, "Do you have any idea what you have done?! The world isn't ready for them yet! Delete that footage now!"

Patriotically Agent Dale said, "Some things are inevitable Director Ford. Whether you like it or not. You cannot hope to run mankind as you please, or take away people's right to live and believe what they want. Eventually the truth will come out."

"You don't get it. I am not going to stick around for the aftermath of what you have done. This will affect the whole world changing it into a whole new era." Director Ford said hurrying for a pill in his upper left pocket.

Agent Dale freaked out running towards the old man to stop him from taking the pill; still he was too late. Director Ford fell to the ground gagging up foam and saliva and twitching on the floor. Feeling like he was too late, and had lost a lead in a global mystery Agent Dale quickly opened the door calling for help.

> ⌐ ⌐ ⌐ 🏳 ⋈ ◇ 🏳 > ◇ >

Sweating from working out and being nervous that he didn't have his powers anymore, Tom threw the ball to a team mate at school practice. "Maybe I should tell Tara how I don't have my abilities anymore." He thought to himself catching the ball. Shrugging those thoughts off, his mind started to contemplate how fun the next night would be since it meant lots of free candy.

Heading towards the changing room, Tom saw his friend Matt who had been waiting for him to finish with practice. Matt said to him sincerely, "Hey Tom, you sure it's okay for me to be going with y'all tomorrow night?"

"Yeah, of course it is. Benny told me Thursday he had invited you. I think he was trying to make sure it was okay, even though I don't see why inviting anybody else would make it any less fun."

"Thanks Tom. You sure are a good friend."

"You're welcome. It's no problem Matt; so what you going to dress up as tomorrow?"

"I am thinking that I want to dress up as a 1940's jazz player with a suit and all."

Tom chuckled thinking, "Well, that certainly will bring some class." Then said, "I'm thinking about being a wizard or maybe a super hero and I think Benny is going to be a ninja; not sure yet about Tara."

"Yeah, well I am going to catch the late buss since I stayed to talk to you, so see ya tomorrow evening Tom. Goodbye."

"I could give you a ride if you want?"

"Sure that would be great."

"Okay, let me just go get my regular clothes, then we will leave."

Wiping the sweat from his forehead, Tom released the pressure rod of the lawn mower and turned it off. Putting it away, he headed inside for a glass of lemonade to cool off for a moment since it was so hot outside. Feeling very exhausted from working hard on their yard all afternoon, he was glad to be done so he could finally get ready for the nights big events.

Walking into his room, Tom heard Todd say, "Geese you really reek right now."

"Well, hello to you too."

"Sorry, it's just when you humans sweat, it really smells bad, as if your natural odors weren't odd enough already."

"Well then, fear not, because I am going to go get ready for tonight's Halloween adventure."

"Oh, that is good; otherwise, bet Tara would puke at the smell of you." Todd said chuckling.

"That's not funny, Todd." Tom responded with arched eyebrows.

"Oh, come on Tom lighten up, I wanted to ask something. May I please go with you tonight? Since it's Halloween, I am sure nobody will notice the oddness of having a green dragon with you."

"Sorry Todd, but they would notice a dragon, then think what in the world, even if it is Halloween."

"I could walk on my two feet instead of flying, you know, like one of those little people."

"No Todd, it's too risky I don't want to lose you like I did my abilities."

"Are you even sure you really lost those or do you just assume you did because you did not warp that one time?"

"I am not fully sure. But I have pretty much lost all faith in them even working again. I have got to go get ready; so see you once I'm done with that."

Walking out of the shower, Tom thought he should shave since he hadn't done it in a while (even though he only started shaving when he started dating Tara one month prior). So he shaved and brushed his teeth. He used mouth wash, while he hoped Tara might kiss him later if she didn't leave him for being so boring lately. Putting on his deodorant and cologne he headed back to his room to get some shorts and a t-shirt, and then he put on his wizard robe and wizard hat along with his shoes.

Todd said jokingly, "Well don't you look spiffy."

"Thanks, I think? But still Todd, do you think Tara will break up with me tonight?"

"Why would she do that? That girl is too crazy to dump you."

"Well some high school girls are strange and choose to break up with their boyfriends on special occasions like holidays."

"Dude, if she was that kind of girl she wouldn't be worth dating for anybody except a boy who would want to dump her and play stupid mind games. Besides I am sure Tara is more mature than those naughty girls that think relationships are games."

"Yeah, you're right. She is nothing like those kind of girls. Don't see why I questioned it in the first place. Oh wait, I thought she may not like me without my abilities."

"Tom! If a person was willing to leave you or you leave them for those reasons, then they don't deserve you or you don't even deserve them. A relationship is about you loving them selflessly for who they are and not for what they can or can't do. You should both be in love, not just one and the other is not. I'm pretty sure you both love each other equally."

"I know, I am just thinking that she won't be that way, but still she might break up with me just because I am different now."

"You can't live your life anxious about things that might or might never be true Tom, tomorrow has enough problems of its own. Does she even know you don't have theses abilities anymore? Like I said, you assume you don't have your abilities, or does she still think you have them?"

"No, I have not told her yet, but I feel like I am lying to her just by not telling her. Maybe I should tell her tonight."

"It's your choice, but I am sure if she really loves you then she will stick by your side even if you're not able to do things you once could."

"Yeah, you're right Todd; well I got to go so see ya later."

"Goodbye Tom, have a fun night and try not to worry too much about these things."

Raising his eyes and nodding his head in agreement, Tom shut the door heading down stairs to grab an apple to eat as a snack, since he hadn't had any food since lunch time. While eating his apple he called Tara, Benny, and Matt telling them he would be waiting for them to arrive so they could all head out together. Then he heard Martin running down the stairs really fast and turned his head to see that Martin was wearing a little Native American outfit.

Tom's mom walked up asking, "Tom would you please take Martin with you and all your friends so he isn't out wandering the streets all alone?"

Tom responded kindly, "Sure thing mom, I know it definitely would be better than him being all on his own."

"Good, just don't stay out too late."

"Don't worry we won't. Hope you and Dad have a nice time at that annual Halloween party. By the way is Jess not going with y'all to the party?"

"No she, Robbie, and Josh are going to be going on their own candy walk in their neighborhood. You should see how cute little Joshy looks in his little sailor outfit," She said pulling up a photo on her hollowatch phone.

"Yeah, he does look adorable, mom."

"See you later, Tom. Love you, but remember to keep Martin safe."

"I will. Love you mom. Goodbye."

Tom's mom and Dad said goodbye to Martin then walked out the garage door and drove off. So, Tom sat down and continued to eat the apple he had grabbed enjoying its bitter sweet taste.

A couple minutes later Tom heard somebody knocking at the front door. He threw the apple core into the trash can heading into the living room from the kitchen to see who it was. Opening the door while the sun was setting into Twilight, he saw Tara standing there in her beautiful cowgirl costume. She looked so gorgeous with the sun setting in the back ground.

Tom, being ridiculous as most teenage star crossed lovers could be became speechless at the sight of her. After being unresponsive for a moment of intense staring, he invited her to come in. Tara came in as Tom made a gesture for her to sit down on the couch. Both of them went to Tom's couch sitting down, staring at each other.

"Hi mmm…how are you?" Tom said with a big nervous smile on his face.

Tara kind of smirking, responded, "I'm good. Are you okay though? You seem kind of pale or nervous?"

"Yeah, I'm fine. So mmm…yeah you think tonight will be fun?"

"I would assume so, since I am spending it with you."

"Awe, you're so sweet Tara."

Blushing, she responded, "Yeah, but you are even nicer than I am. You're always trying to help people and be there for them and not just some of the time."

They started to stare at each other again. Then they started moving their lips closer towards each other…then right as they were about to kiss each other they jumped hearing a loud knock at the door. Tom got up and with a sort of anger like expression on his face marching over to the door. He yanked it open quickly. There he saw Benny and Matthew waiting with a confused look on their faces.

Benny puzzled said, "Why do you look so angry Tom? Is something wrong?"

Matt then added sarcastically, "Yeah, Tom, why do you seem really peeved? Is it cause we are here?" Tara over-heard the conversation then blushed that Tom was upset over Matt and Benny interrupting them, thinking it was funny how Tom was responding to them.

Tom responded calmly, "Sorry, I was just getting mad over some silly stuff in my head."

Benny said, "It's okay. We understand everyone has issues." Then Benny and Matthew both chuckled over what Benny had just said. They all went to different chairs in the living room while Tom sat back down on the couch with Tara.

Benny asked, "So what routes do y'all think we should take tonight?"

Mathew said with enthusiasm, "How about we go down to the park then loop around back up in a giant circle or square or however you want to imagine it?"

Tom responded, "Nah, that might take way too long on foot. It is 2.2 miles and my mother doesn't want Martin out too late. How about we go right down towards Mrs. Chaffin's house, I am sure she has some great things. She always does. Maybe when we get back from that route and drop Martin off, we can head down the longer one if you want, Matt."

Tara said, interested in Tom's idea, "That sounds like a great idea. I like that route, plus it's not as far away from our houses."

Benny smirked and said, "Alright fine. I'm good with that idea. But if we don't have enough candy and goods then we are definitely going further later."

"That all sounds like a great plan." said Matt.

"Martin, are you ready to go trick or treating?!" Tom yelled to get Martin's attention.

Quickly Martin came running back down the stairs screaming with excitement. "I can't wait. This is going to be so much fun! I also can't wait for all the free candy!"

Getting up, they started heading out the door with enthusiasm, thinking tonight they would all get candy and have a wonderful time together. Tom turned off the lights and locked the door. As he shut the door, Tom turned and saw that the moon was full and very bright. It was beautifully illuminating the area for them so see where they were headed. Matthews outfit shined a little from what seemed to be sparkles on the suit he was wearing. It was all part of his Jazz outfit, Benny covered his face with his Ninja mask so nobody could fully see his face. Together, they walked over towards the neighbor's house to the right of Tom's house stopping to get some candy.

Once the door opened, they held out their bags and yelled, "Trick or Treat!" Tom's neighbor gave them some candy; they said "thank you" and continued down the road towards the next house.

As they were walking, Benny said, "Hey, how about we spice tonight up a little and tell some spooky stories to set the mood for the night?"

Tom was worried because he thought he saw the man in the black suit that was at his basketball game a month before coming up behind them passing Tom and Tara's house. Tom responded saying, "Alright I guess that would be good."

Benny said, "Well, have any of you ever heard of the tale of the giant bird creature here in Texas?" Matt responded, "Since, I am from Georgia originally, no?"

Benny continued. "Alright, so the legend goes that back in the late 1800's there were stories of people occasionally seeing a giant bird-like humanoid figure with a wingspan of twelve feet wide on each side."

Freaking out, but interested, Matt asked, "What else did this thing look like and has it ever done anything besides appear?"

"Yeah, it certainly has. But to answer your first question it is said to have the face of an ape or a gorilla with blood red eyes. And it's five feet tall with black bird-like wings. Some say it has a reptilian look to its wings much like bat skin. One time a man, who barely spoke any English, claims to have seen it snatching up a little girl. So, many different legends say it likes to sweep down then take away little children kid-napping them into the sky." Martin got scared and started shivering at the thought of that happening. As they walked down the dark street some clouds were starting to come over the moon.

To calm Martin down a little since he noticed Martin was shivering Tom said, "I don't know, but a giant bird sounds a little crazy to me." Thinking to himself about all the crazy things he had been through....who was he to judge what was possible or impossible?

Benny said, "Well there are so many different people who claim to have seen this legend. I don't doubt it for a moment. My old pal, Michael, who lives in the other neighborhood claims to have seen it fly off one day from on top of his car."

Tara had a look on her face that implied she had found this story humorous. Reaching the next house, they got some candy. Then, after a few feet they arrived at Mrs. Chaffin's house.

Once they had knocked, she opened the door and greeted them happily. "Well well, don't all you children look adorable tonight?"

Tom said kindly, "Thanks Mrs. Chaffin. You look like you have a nice apron you're wearing."

"Oh Tom, don't be so modest." Mrs. Chaffin said, giggling.

They all did their trick or treat routine then Mrs. Chaffin gave them candy then said, "Y'all have a nice evening and see all of you tomorrow at Church."

They were now a few feet from the edge of the street and sidewalk. Looking across the street at an old long drive way, Benny said with concern, "Oh yeah, we might want to avoid that house."

"Why would you want to avoid that one, Benny?" Matthew asked curiously.

"Because Matt, that place has some really bad history and nobody has lived there for a very long time."

Matthew asked, "Why has nobody lived there for a long time, and besides, what's so bad about it? It's just a house."

With a real look of worry and fear Benny responded, "Many years ago it was rumored that a single woman lived there with her three children. She was an alcoholic and neighbors around here would say sometimes they would hear screaming coming from that house because she did horrible things to them when she got drunk. But she supposedly stopped drinking and the screams were not heard as often, but that's not where it gets really bad."

Regretfully Matthew said, "How could it have gotten any worse than that?"

Cautiously Benny said with worry, "One night the neighbors grew anxious because they heard them all screaming again. Then they heard a female laughing psychotically. The neighbors panicked and called 911 when they all saw the house had been set on fire. The children were still screaming and she was still laughing as they all burned together in the house before the fire department along with the cops could even get there."

Tara looked pale, shocked and freaked out at what she had just heard. But to some degree, they all seemed a little bit concerned with the story. Even Matt was trying to come off not scared by the story.

Frightened, Tom asked rhetorically, "What could cause a mother to go that mad and do so much crazy stuff to her own children?"

Even though Tom didn't really want an answer, Benny responded, "It is said by some of the kids from school that knew her kids, that she was looking for a cure to her alcoholism. And then she started practicing mystical arts such as witchcraft. Some of the other kids from school heard this story from their parents who had gone to school with her kids. They claim that eventually it led to her going insane and killing her already broken family by tying each of them up to the master bed and setting their house on fire."

Tom gulped at the thought that doing magic could lead to people going insane. He was never sure if his abilities were magic or natural or maybe a scientific thing. He didn't fully understand even if they were fully gone now. Tom thought, "Oh dear what if she was like me and when she lost her powers she went crazy and hurt everyone around her. I don't want to end up like her."

Tara said to Tom, "You okay, Tom, you look very worried?"

"Yeah I am fine. Maybe it is best we avoid that house. It sure does seem like that place could be evil from the sounds of that story."

Martin stood there speechless, but Matthew being the tough type, always trying to prove his worth in the world said, "Well I ain't gona let some old wives tale ruin an adventure!"

Matthew ran off quickly across the street and up the drive way headed towards the house. Tom worried about what problems could arise from having his abilities in the first place and not wanting to let

Matthew go to the evil house alone. He quickly darted off and ran after him, after Matt was out of sight. Tara, Benny, and Martin soon followed. The group of friends wanted to stick by each other on this horrible fright night. There were clearly things nobody would ever want to see, but that didn't stop them from wondering what was there. Little did they know what truly awaited them in their own near future...

Chapter 18
Reality Meets Fiction

The Near Future
Saturday, October 31st, 8:18 P.M.
The Edge of Taggart Street, Rolling Oak Hills, Smithsonian Valley,
Texas

On this particular all Hallows eve, it was getting cold for an October in Texas. The pace was changing quickly for Tom and his friends as the dark clouds had already covered the moon. Now the wind was picking up and the clouds looked like they were moving quickly as the wind howled. Thus it was getting colder, with more of an eerie feeling as they moved onward to find where Matthew had run off to.

Tom, Benny and Tara ran down the long drive way while Martin held onto Tara's hand. The trees were swaying and rumbling in the wind as they kept moving more toward the house assuming Matthew would be inside.

Tara asked worried, "Tom, you really think he would go inside that house after that scary story? He would have to be mad to go in a place that horrible."

"I don't doubt it for a minute, Tara. Matt is always trying to be a macho man to prove he is above others in all categories just so he can make his self-esteem feel better, or at least I think that's why he does that."

"Yeah, Tom has a great point, Tara. He would do something so outrageous because he is insecure and thinks this will prove him to be a man." Benny said.

"You boys are such ego maniacs some times."

Tom responded, "We are not all like that, just the arrogant ones that want to prove themselves because they have too much pride."

"Yeah, Tara, we are not all that crazy. Some of us have values and are real men."

"I rest my case. You just proved even y'all can be like that." Tara laughed at what she had just said while Martin remained quiet, trying to keep up.

As the leaves were being blown around everywhere they approached the house but were shocked at what they saw once they got close.

Fearfully Tom said, "Guess the rumors are true and it did get burned a bunch at some point?"

Tom said this as he stared at the rotten, dead looking, burned house as Tara commented, "Yeah, it sure did get burned. Why don't we try to yell for Matt, and maybe he will come back if we do?"

They all started to yell for Matthew. Benny yelled, "Hey Matt! Stop being a wuss and show yourself already!"

Tara yelled, "Matt where are you?!"

Tom then yelled, "Come on Matt! Enough with your mind games already!" Saying this he figured Matthew was trying to play some kind of joke on all of them.

They waited a minute, but still heard no response. Their concern grew with every moment that Matt didn't respond to them. It caused more fear to plague their minds. Hopefully, Matt was alright. Only time would tell if he was.

Cautiously Tom then said, "Looks like we might have to go inside to look for him."

Martin screamed loudly with fright, "No! No! No! I am not going in the house with the bad witch!" So he crossed his little arms putting his legs together scared sitting on the ground in fear.

Warmly Tom said to him with kindness, "Don't worry Martin. Benny, Tara and I are here and we will keep you safe."

Sarcastically Benny said, "I don't know, I believe the screamer on this one. Maybe we should just stay out of that witch house."

As Benny rolled his eyes, Tara stomped on his foot and said, "Geese, you idiot, you're not helping with this matter. You're only making it worse for Martin by feeding his fear."

Tom gave Benny a stern look, then said, "Everything is going to be okay. Let's just go inside where it might be warmer, Martin. We might find Matt in there so we can move on from this creepy place."

Calmly Martin said, "Alright, but we better leave as soon as we find him." Then he crossed his little arms again as he stood there firmly.

Tara chuckled and looked around saying, "Come on, let's get inside. This place is already creepy enough outside."

Tom, along with the group started to approach the big tall, dead looking house as they walked slowly up the creaking broken down steps.

Tara said, "Wow, look at how old and rotten the wood looks. There are vines growing on different parts."

Calmly Tom replied, "Yeah, it must have been abandoned a long time ago if there are branches of vines growing on this place."

Jokingly Benny then said, "Look out Martin, the vines might get you."

Martin shuddered, then chuckled saying, "That won't matter. I will rip them with my hands."

Tom opened the broken burned down door while they all walked through the door and viewed their surroundings.

Tara said as she looked up the stairs, "Is it just me or did this place just get colder?"

"Yeah, actually I felt it as well. I also have this horrible feeling in my chest and a chill running down my back" Benny responded.

Then Tom said, "I do too."

Abruptly the door behind them closed fast. Quickly they all turned around as Martin started screaming, "Ahh! Ahh!! Ahh!!! Crap we are all going to die!!!"

They turned back towards the stairs as they saw a shimmery tall shadowy figure rush across the hall into another room. Benny yelled, "What the heck was that!"

Tom responded shivering, "I don't know. But I bet it wasn't a good thing."

Tara gulped saying, "This is crazy maybe we should leave this place. It just keeps getting creepier and creepier."

Then Tom said, "Calm down Martin. Don't worry. Everything is going to be okay. Just hold Tara's hand some more, just like you would Mom."

Martin grabbed her hand and started to shake with fear while clenching her hands. "Tom, I don't think Martin can take much more of this craziness. He is shaking and clenching my hands which is a good sign he is way out of his comfort zone." Tara said very concerned.

Tom said to her, "Well, we need to find Matt before we leave here. It wouldn't be nice to leave him alone in a place like this."

"Tom, we don't even know if he even came into this messed up house." Tara said with anger.

"True, but we do need to find him to make sure he is okay." Benny responded.

"Oh brother, you boys are so arrogant sometimes." Tara said.

Pissed Benny yelled, "At least we got good skills of survival unlike you stupid…"

"Enough both of you. If we don't work together we won't be able to get through this as easily." Tom yelled then calmed down as he finished.

Benny said, "He is right. Plus this is dangerous. Tonight is Halloween, the only night where the dead can come back to life, so we should be cautious of any evil beings that might be here."

Sarcastically Tara said "Where did you get that silly info? From a movie?"

"No, I learned about it in school when we discussed the history of many Holidays."

Tara giggled saying, "Yeah, the Easter Bunny isn't the real reason for Easter. I hope you were not dumb enough to believe that already." Benny gave her a mean look, then Tom gave him a stern look.

Tom said, "I have an idea. I will take the room to the right with Benny and you and Martin can go to the one on the left."

"Okay, but be careful in there Tom I don't want that shadowy figure to get to you." Tara said as she was concerned for their safety.

Tom then walked into the next room while he thought about how he had just split them up for two reasons. His first reason was to separate Tara and Benny from fighting and his second was to cover more ground so they could find Matthew and get out of this crazy place. As Tom walked into this new room with Benny, he took notice of how some of the burnt furnishings looked like stuff you would see in a dining room. There was broken glass that was part of a cabinet that had been ruined of its beauty, it had cups and plates in it that looked ruined too.

Tom chuckled then said to Benny, "Looks like that china isn't going to be useable for anybody."

"Yeah, but who would want such fancy plates in the first place?"

, "Woman, who have good taste in china, I guess? Wow, look at that table. It looks burned and one of its legs broke off."

As they stood there, out of the corner of Tom's peripheral vision, he saw in the reflection of the broken glass of the cabinet a tall shadowy figure that rushed off fast, noticing Tom was looking at it. Tom felt a rush of jittery energy flow through him causing him to flinch at the sight of the creepy being.

Benny asked, "Why did you just flinch like that Tom?"

"Because, I just saw that creature in the reflection of the glass. It was big and very gruesome. It had claws with skin as black as night. But it ran off when I noticed it."

They turned around the corner of the cabinet where they had just been looking as they went through the door way into the kitchen. They both felt really cold all of a sudden. Both of them felt that disturbing feeling down their backs as it got colder.

"Tom, I don't like the feel of this place. It's really freaking me out. You know I'm not one to get creeped out that easily."

"Neither do I, Benny, but we need to…wait did you just hear that?"

"Hear what?"

"Be quiet and listen…"

Both of the young boys emotions grew more intense as they both noticed some strange things. There was some of the burnt wood chips moving around, then the whispering began. From different directions all over the kitchen esque dining room they heard a deep voice whispering from the left to the right all around them saying a different word each time it spoke. In multiple places it was saying, "We shall do to your loved ones what has been done to us! The debt shall be paid by the blood of Tara, Tom...Benny we know your weakness and it will become you, making you suffer...We will make you fall victim to your weakness, Benjamin! Now, she shall die, Tom!"

They were scared that a voice from literally nowhere was threatening them, scaring them with something neither of them had experienced, or had to deal with ever before in all in their life. Then very loudly they both heard what sounded like a female, screaming in terror and agony. Quickly, they ran back from which they came and were running with a trickling feeling picking down their spines just hoping they would get to Tara in time to save her. Running across the hall, Benny and Tom ran straight into Tara and Martin.

Annoyed at them running into her, Tara yelled, "Ouch, what did you goonies do that for?!" Then she noticed the terror in their face and asked, "Hold on, why do y'all look like that?"

Benny said, "Didn't you hear what that thing said?"

"I didn't hear anything. What's going on?" She responded.

Tom said with worry, "We heard something talking to us from all sorts of directions. It said it was going to kill you, then we heard you scream like crazy like something was hurting you. So we ran for our lives to see if you were okay hoping we could save you, or at least I think that was also Benny's intention."

"Yeah it was Tom." Benny said agreeing.

Tara said, "Yeah, I am good, but y'all look devastated and really freaked."

"I saw a door in the hallway earlier. Let's all check that out and if Matt is not in there let's check out the upstairs." Tom said hoping to end this tracheas adventure soon.

They walked out of the living room area and into the hallway again walking up to a door built into the stairs. They opened the door then went inside to find a tight room with stairs that led down to a basement. They walked down the stairs. They were creaking eerily as they went down and noticed a very odd assortment of belongings in this obscure basement.

Tom asked, "Are those jars of hearts and other human body parts?"

They all gulped as Tara said, "Look over here! There is some sage along with other herbs in this cupboard."

Benny said, "Look at all the strange symbols written everywhere. They kind of look Satanic and Evil."

Tom said, "Okay. No doubt with that story line, she was definitely into mysticism and witchcraft."

Martin was clenching Tara's hand again and then Tom said, "Obviously Matt is not down here so let's go to the second floor so we can get out this house for good. We'll see if Matt is up there or not, then we are definitely leaving this evil place."

They all went back up to the first story of the house and walked back down the hall; then started climbing the broken stairs to the second story. On their right was a door. They peaked into for a moment only to see it looked like a burnt out bedroom. Probably one of the children's old rooms from the story. Then to their left they saw a hallway with many doors at one end.

Tom said, "Let's check the one at the end first."

They all nodded and continued to the end of the hall. They were very worried at what would happen next. The emotional baggage this place presented was not one any of them were used to dealing with. Anybody in a house like this would be intensely fearful no matter how brave they claimed to be.

Once they got to the end of the hall they opened the door inside and looked. It was another burnt room which looked like a bathroom but the wall was missing, making it where they could see the tree rustling in the wind in the moonlight. The wind howled as it gave a big breeze, then they all noticed a strange noise. Through the wall on their left they thought they heard a banging noise as if something was hitting the wall or bashing the floor. They weren't sure what is was, but knew for sure it was in the room on their left.

Exiting the burnt bathroom they headed for the door that was on their right and went inside to see what looked like skeletons burnt on a bed. The room was severely damaged with a body figure on the ground in the corner. It was Matthew curled up and every now and again hitting the wall in torment.

Tom quickly yelled, "Matt are you alright?!"

They all ran up to him as he mumbled under his breath "No, this place is Evil and cursed. Get out of here now!"

While putting one arm over Matt's shoulder Benny said sarcastically, "You don't have to say that twice."

Tom put his hands to his own waist saying, "What happened Matt, did you see anything weird like we did?"

"Oh yes, it was so horrible, those scary…no those horrid, evil red eyes!" Matt responded with intense fear in his voice.

Noticing something Tara interrupted, "Hey guys, isn't it a little strange that these skeletons are here? Wouldn't the police or fire department have taken their bodies away from here?"

Tom responded curiously, but regretfully, "Yeah, you're right that is odd?"

The wind began to howl ferociously as Matthew's eyes widened then he yelled, "Oh dear, it's coming back!"

The bones lifted up into the air as dust started blowing in from different directions. Muscles and different things started to form on the skeletons till they were full bodies like a living person would have. However their skin was pale grey with a hint of dark blue. The bodies had red glowing eyes and claws for fingernails.

Tom, along with his friends were now all cornered standing in the corner with Matthew. There, before them were three small body figures of what looked like a teenager and two preteens along with a tall mother figure.

The creepy beings stared at them. Then the mother figure began to speak in a demonic low pitched voice, "You children are going to get to experience the joy of death like my Children and I did.

I shall tie you to this bed and set this house on fire, then you will join us in Hell Burning forever!"

Benny said, "This woman is nuts: who wants to suffer forever?"

"Don't worry Benny, this thing won't get us." Tom said cautiously and slowly.

They all were at max fear and shock at this point.

The demonic mother said, "Come on my dear little children, go tie your selves to the bed and get ready for the ceremony so we can get our friends to possess these new children before they die!"

"Yes, mommy dear." One of the little demonic kids said.

Then the demonic mothered cackled psychotically and manically, endowing fear into Tom along with all his friends and little brother.

Tom said, "It's obvious now what they are guys."

Benny said angrily, "Oh yeah Tom, and what might that be?!"

As the children started tying themselves to the bed, Tom said, "Obviously the kids mom got into witchcraft and summoned Demons to end her problems. But she just got herself possessed instead and now they pose as dead people to trick others into thinking there is no happy afterlife or that we are going to burn in Hell."

Sarcastically Benny said, "No duh genius, let's get out of this crazy place!"

Looking at them sternly the demonic mother grew into a taller figure nearly hitting the ceiling. It looked like it was made out of shadows and had horns with evil black-looking wings and red glowing eyes. Then the mother yelled, "You're not going anywhere you're all going to burn!"

Quickly the bed lit on fire. The fire spread fast as the Demon screamed and growled with a roar at them. So they all quickly ran trying to escape. They ran through the fire and out of the bedroom door and into the hall. Running down the hall, Tara's foot fell through the floor, then Tom turned around to help her up off the broken floor. They continued onwards to the stairs quickly trying to climb down them without stepping too hard as much of the house was on fire again. They ran out the door for their lives not wanting to burn or be near those vile gruesome creatures, whatever they were.

As they ran out the door, pieces of the house started to collapse as the vines growing on it were singed and fell off onto the ground. Then the entire house collapsed in on itself as they ran down the drive way. None looked back except Tara. She had to know what was happening. Then Tara saw it and stopped in amazement. Her eyes widened and she quickly turned around trying to hurry to catch up with Tom and the rest.

Once they approached the road, they could see a fire truck all the way down by Tom and Tara's house coming towards them.

Benny yelled, "Hurry, let's get over to the next street on the left so the police don't think we started the fire."

Tom quickly responded saying, "That sounds like a great idea."

They all nodded in agreement, then ran over to the street where Justin's mom lived and moved quickly to the house behind

Mrs. Chaffin's home to get candy there. As they stood there from a distance, they observed the fire trucks approached the drive way and then drove up it. It was peculiar that this happened so quickly once the fire started.

So, Tom asked, "Why did those fire trucks come so fast when the fire started? That house looked like it hadn't had electricity in it for a long time. There just couldn't have been any alarms." Matthew was still shaking and so was Martin.

Benny said, "I don't know, but I think it has something to do with some guy I saw in a suit down the street across from Mrs. Chaffin's house. I think he saw the fire and called the fire department."

Tom was very worried remembering that he saw that figure earlier that night, and at his game. Then he responded saying, "A guy in a suit; wow that is strange. Lately I think have been followed by a guy with that description…wonder what he wants with me?"

Tara said, with a peculiar look on her face, "I don't know. What would a guy in a suit want with you? And even if he has been following you at least he is not doing anything bad to you?"

"True. Well, let's get moving before the cops start looking for people around here."

They all started moving from house to house down that street, but their "trick or treats" were not as enthusiastic as before the creepy house encounter. Near the end of the street about the second house down, they came across Justin's house.

Tom felt guilty as soon as he saw the house. He remembered how he had Justin sent away with Agent Dale's help to keep Justin from murdering Tara and himself. But still, so not to appear guilty looking, he continued up the small drive way to the door with the rest of them. But, Tara couldn't help but notice the look on his face. They knocked on the door, and then Mrs. Phelps opened the door with a beer in one hand and a bowl of candy in the other. They all dully said, "Trick or Treat."

She responded in a somewhat curious voice, "What are y'all so down about? Not like your child has been banished from the state for being a criminal."

Tom gulped and said, "Sorry, for your loss. Maybe he will not get into trouble and someday return?"

Then Mrs. Phelps said with a sigh, "I don't know, I do miss him and I am concerned for him, but I doubt I will see him anytime soon. But why do you kids look so down on Halloween?"

Martin said in a childish way since he was a child, "We saw big monsters and they were scary."

Mrs. Phelps chuckled as she said, "Well, don't worry now. All the monsters are probably long gone." She gave them all some candy and they said, "Thank you." then waved goodbye as she shut the door. Then they all walked onto the yard, but Tom stopped to talk.

"Well now that we are all less jittery and calmer would you and Matt walk ahead to comfort Martin with some jokes so Tara and I can have a minute to talk?" Tom asked Benny.

Benny and Matthew agreed and they went a little ahead of Tom and Tara down to the next street. Once they got out of close hearing range Tom and Tara started walking together.

Tara said with a giggle, "So Tom, am I just some silly stuff in your head?"

He chuckled remembering what he said back at his house and responded saying, "No no...of course not. I just didn't know if you would be mad if I told my friends we were about to kiss each other when they interrupted. I thought that you might have thought I was bragging. So I didn't want to upset you."

Tara smiled and said, "You are so kind Tom, you're always thinking of others instead of just yourself. It's such a great trait to have in a boyfriend."

"Thanks. I didn't know you thought so nicely of me. Bet you won't think so highly of me once I tell you what I have wanted to tell you for some time now."

"What? Does it have something to do with that look you had at Justin's mom's house?"

"No, it is something bigger, plus I have been worried you will dump me cause of it."

Tara looked with concern in his eye's and asked, "What is it Tom? You can tell me anything."

"For over a month now I have not been able to use my abilities or at least I don't think I could? I was afraid you would like me less cause I wasn't able to do great things, like fly or whatever you wanted me to. So I felt like I wouldn't be able to please you."

With a big look of relief, Tara said calmly, "Tom…what kind of girlfriend would I be if I only liked you for what you could do? I mean, look at somebody who gets injured protecting our country and needs a prosthetic leg. You don't always see their wives leave them because they are crippled. Not only that, but I loved you before you had your abilities, I just never got to tell you before you saved me from Justin and by that point I had already seen your abilities."

"Awe Tara, you're the best girlfriend a boy could ask for."

"It's funny. I was wondering why you were so distant from me and didn't want to really go on any dates lately. And to think this whole time you were just avoiding me in fear of rejection. You're way too modest sometimes, Tom."

"Guess we can look back on this and laugh about it now."

"Yeah we most certainly can, besides never give up hope. Maybe your abilities will come back. Oh, and what did happen to Justin and Sacra?"

"I don't know if they will come back like you said, but I hope at some point they will. But yeah, after I rescued us I had some crazy stuff happen with them. I think Sacra disappeared through my wormhole in the dungeon prison like place that I made in that other world. As for Justin, well, we had a big fight and I had to call Agent Dale to tell him how Justin wouldn't leave us alone. From what Agent Dale told me he had him arrested and sent him to another state."

"Wow, that sounds like real crazy story. Why is it Justin always acts like a ridiculous dog always looking for a fight?"

Tom chuckled and said, "That was funny because you made him sound like an animal, which is kind of how he acts. But still I don't know why he is like that. I even tried to be his friend at one point. Do you remember when you and I first started being friends last school year? That's when I tried being his friend as well?"

"Yeah, I remember. But I don't get it Tom. You're so nice and caring. Even for your enemies, you will try to take care of them and be there for them. Why are you so nice and wonderful? Plus why couldn't you just talk it out with Justin and end his madness with always bullying us like you did that Johnny guy from England you told me about?"

"I tried, but for some reason Justin was unreasonable. He just would not be bothered to take any of it calmly. I guess I am just that nice cause I like to be good with everyone and I try not to cause issues. But I think some of the stuff I have done has caused issues. Just look at Mrs. Phelps; she had beer in her hand. I don't think I ever remember seeing her drinking beer before Justin was taken by the authorities?"

Sympathetically, Tara said, "You can't blame yourself for that. For all you know she has always been that way and you just finally noticed it. You felt guilty for her having to send Justin away. As well it's her choice. Even if it isn't good for her body, she chose to do that stuff and you can't help what she does."

"I know, I just feel like it's my fault. But I am glad you love me and won't leave me for my mistakes. I love you, Tara."

"I love you too Tom."

They stopped walking then grabbed each other's hands, looking into each other's eyes as they started to move closer and closer towards each other to kiss each other, when suddenly Tom was ripped away as his mouth was covered by a quick hand. Then his arms were put behind his back being held by another group of hands. Tara was being grabbed and held against her will, too.

Tom looked around noticing who was there with them. They were all in a circle with some of the gangsters Tom had dealt with before. Some of the men who were there looked like relatives or friends of the terrorists. In the middle was Justin and Sacra with big smirks on their faces.

Justin said in a real cunningly, prideful voice, "Well, well, Tom, how the tables have turned for you now that we have ambushed you. We got your mouth covered before you could cast a spell or whatever it is you do. You won't be able to do anything and I can take care of you and Tara once and for all."

Tom shuddered, and so did Tara along with everyone else being held captive. They all tried yelling and screaming but nobody could get much out with their mouths covered. Martin was kicking and screaming as he was being held up in the air by one of the stronger guys. Martin bit his finger, then tried running as Justin tripped him and covered his mouth lifting him up.

Justin said, "Ahh, is this your stupid little brother, Tom?"

Tom's eyes widened with fear as Justin pulled out a knife putting it up to Martin's throat as he was holding him.

Justin said threatening and angrily, "You listen here you little pipsqueak. You try to run from me, you will have to get past this knife and if you do, that you will end up cutting you. So don't try anything foolish."

Martin looked scared as he looked into Tom's eyes.

Justin said with pride in his voice, "So Tom, how does it feel to know there is nothing you can do to be the hero in this scenario? Do you feel trapped and insecure like you might be locked away, powerless against anything we do to you?"

Then all the terrorists & thugs holding Tom and his friends, chuckled with laughter.

Then Justin said, "Don't worry Tom, I…" Immediately Sirens were heard by everyone and there were flashing lights out of nowhere. Some black cars appeared and Justin slit Martin's throat accidently and yelled, "Hurry, let's get out of here!"

They all let go of everyone then started scattering. Tom freaked out seeing Justin had slit Martin's throat. He quickly ran up to Martin as he started to cry with snot running out his nose. Tom took off his Wizard robe and wrapped Martin's cold little body in it holding him in his arms as the tears were streaming down his face.

Everyone else ran up to Tom, as he held Martin in his arms and cried as he murmured under his breath, "I will fix you Sano Sano Sano…"

Tom held Martin's little body in his arms. Just then, Agent Dale got out of one of the black cars. He looked petrified seeing blood everywhere and Martin in Tom's arms all helpless. He quickly called for an Ambulance. At this horrible moment, that night in Tom's mind, reality met fiction as he realized there was nothing he could do for his little brother except wait patiently for help to come…

Chapter 19
Do the Ends Justify the Means?

The Near Future
Saturday, October 31ˢᵗ, 10:09 P.M.
Rolling Oak Hills, Smithsonian Valley, Texas

Sirens were heard screeching around the usually quiet neighborhood as an ambulance arrived. The medics quickly took notice of the cut on Martin's neck as they put him on a board and into the ambulance. Tom came with them since he was the only family member. Quickly the ambulance's sirens were turned on. It was moving so fast it jerked Tom around with the inertia it created as it blazed out of the neighborhood heading down the highway for the nearest hospital.

One of the medics with the name tag, Joshua, came out from the front of the ambulance into the back after he checked Martin's heart rate saying, "I am going to have to use the hot Iron's to jump start his heart."

Petrified and nodding his head while his little brother lay there with his heart stopped and technically "dead", Tom began to weep a whole lot. Joshua used the shockers to jump start his heart. It didn't work. He tried another time but still nothing. Then the third time the heart rate monitor showed some beeping for a moment as Tom hoped that things were better. Then all of a sudden, as Martin opened his eyes, he had a look of pain as the heart rate monitor flat lined. Joshua kept trying to help him a couple more times, but it didn't work. So he said to Tom and the driver, "Time of death 10:14."

As he said these words, Tom's eye's widened with fear and worry, realizing his little brother was now gone…

Nearly an hour and a half later sitting in a chair at the hospital, Tom looked up at the doors as they opened to see his parents coming in. His mom was crying and his dad looking indistinguishably mad or upset at the same time. Walking up to Tom, his mom said with a stuttering, "Are you okay, Tom?"

"No, mom I'm not. I failed to take care of Martin. It looks like I couldn't keep him safe like you wanted me to."

"Come on now, Tom, it's not your fault. Those monsters did what they did to y'all."

"But, you don't get it mom. It is my fault; it's totally my fault."

"What do you mean?"

"If I had just come to y'all in the first place when I started getting bullied by Justin, maybe Martin would still be alive."

"This was orchestrated by a bully?"

"And a gang, plus some of the terrorists I helped stop."

Looking puzzled his dad asked, "When did you stop a gang?"

"When I was on my first date with Tara we were attacked and I rescued her."

His mom said with concern, "Tom you can't blame yourself. They just wanted revenge because you stopped them in their tracks on their escapades. But in the end you were doing the right thing."

"Yeah, but there is doing things right and then there is just doing them recklessly. If I had not been so reckless, Martin would still be alive! I became so prideful and arrogant taking these people down on my own. I was so selfish and dumb I forgot who I was. I'm just a typical boy who thought he could take on anybody. It is all my fault Martin is dead." Tom said as tears rolled down his cheeks.

As Tom started to cry, his mother came running up to him crying herself. Then leaned against her crying and sobbing as his father joined in and they cried together as a family that loved one another. After filling out the paper work, Tom's mom called John to tell him what had happened and that the funeral would be the following Wednesday. She also told him that she was going to set up a flight for him to come to the funeral. Jessica came in with Robbie and with Josh in her arms. They were crying, so they consoled them for a while.

The Turners all went home that night, sleepy and very sad with their sudden loss.

Walking into his room, Tom heard Todd ask, "Where have you been? It's really late."

"Sorry, we were at the hospital; Martin was murdered."

Now concerned Todd crawled over to Tom saying, "Geese that sounds terrible. Are you alright?"

"Well, I am not hurt physically, but emotionally I am way off the Richter Scale. I feel like I have this giant hole in my chest. Just like my heart has been torn out."

"I am sorry, Tom, this must really suck for you. I remember the times I would fly above you and Martin throwing that ball to each other. It must hurt to have somebody ripped out of your life like that."

Sarcastically Tom said, "Oh, and on top of that, somehow Justin is free from wherever Agent Dale had put him and he's running around with a bunch of nut cases."

"What are you going to do?"

"There is nothing I can do, so I am just going to let the authorities take it from here."

"Well I guess that's a good thing; hopefully there will be redemption for your loss."

"Who knows Todd…who knows? Well, I am getting tired so good night or bad night in my case."

"Good night, Tom. Hope you feel better soon."

Tom layed down and tried to get some sleep. Because of what happened he had trouble sleeping that night. He kept reliving that moment when he saw Martin get sliced in his throat in a repetitive nightmare, so he tossed and turned all night, not getting any good rest.

The Near Future
Sunday, November 01ˢᵗ, 07:11 A.M.
The Turner's house, Smithsonian Valley, Texas

Exhausted from hardly any sleep and lying in bed as the sun was rising, Tom woke up and went down stairs to eat breakfast. Slouching as he came into the kitchen, he poured himself some cereal and milk in a bowl then sat down at the table to watch the news. Still depressed over the loss of Martin, he sat there, but listened intently as he heard something odd on the news.

The reporter said, "Scientists are still stumped over this strange burst of energy and where it came from about three weeks ago. It fried a mountain lion in a local neighborhood. We don't know what it was or how it came about. It severely burned this mountain lion leaving no traces of radioactivity. We are lucky a bird watcher caught it on camera, so we will now show that clip."

Tom watched as they showed the clip. He saw a line of trees as a giant red beam that looked almost like a concentrated pillar of fire come out of the sky going down in an angled position into the forest.

The reporter continued talking, "After the clip went viral on Flutter, scientists went to inspect it; all they could find in the woods was a burned mountain lion. Well, that's all we have on that mysterious story for now. If we have any updates we will inform all our watchers at that time."

Tom clearly had his mind elsewhere. Instead of thinking of Martin, he pondered what could have caused that beam of energy? It somewhat reminded him of a Co2 laser. "But are there any Co2 lasers powerful enough to disintegrate a whole lion?" He wondered?

Sitting there thinking of all the different possibilities, the doorbell rang. He got up, went to the door to answer it, as his parents were still asleep and trying to deal with Martin's death by escaping this world into a dream world. They didn't want to be bothered or to have to think about their loss, so they slept. When Tom opened the door he was surprised to see Matthew, Benny and Tara standing there together.

Tara asked, "Is everything alright, Tom?"

Benny said, "Yeah, last we heard, you got rushed off last night in that ambulance. Is everything okay?"

Tom responded, "Well, Martin didn't make it and we are having a funeral for him on Wednesday."

Having a look of shock on her face, Tara gasped and said, "Sorry Tom, this must be utterly horrible for you."

Tom said morosely, but curiously, "It is, but I will have to deal with it. Everyone dies sometime. Martin just had to die sooner. Whether it is my fault is to be determined, but I think it is. What happened to y'all?"

Tara hastily responded, "Now hold on, Tom, you can't blame yourself. Justin and those maniacs had already tried to kill you and me. Remember all the times Justin had tried to hurt us? We are all lucky that agent friend of yours showed up when he did. If he hadn't we might all be dead."

Benny added, "Yeah, as well we just stayed with your agent friend and the cops while they tried to hunt down Justin and his group."

Thinking about it Tom about it said, "Wait a second. In the midst of all that shock, I forgot. Why was Agent Dale their immediately after that all went down last night?" They all looked hunched and confused.

Tara said, "Who knows. Guess you will have to ask him later."

Matthew said, "All I know is that I am grateful to still be alive and I am sorry for your loss, Tom."

"Well, I will just have to deal with the consequences of my actions." Tara rolled her eyes and sighed as Tom said that.

Kindly Tom said, "Well guys, I was eating breakfast. So I guess I will talk to y'all later."

They all said good bye leaving back to their homes. Tom headed back to the kitchen to finish eating his cereal. Later, his parents woke up so he went to his room, slothing around and playing games to escape thinking about Martin till it was time for church.

At church, Tom sat their trying to focus but kept thinking of other things in Sunday School. Eventually it ended and he went to the sanctuary where he sat down with his family. The service started and they sang a few songs, then the announcements were made. Finally then the Pastor gave his sermon.

By the time it all ended, Tom thought it was ironically amusing that today's Sunday School was about forgiveness and the

Pastor's sermon was about loving your enemies. He wondered why everything spoken at Church always related to something going on in his life. There was some invisible thread tying these events together which seemed odd to him and very illogical.

Later that afternoon after Church as Tom was walking up Tara's porch, he thought he should try to have a proper conversation with her about the sorrows he was feeling, instead of just blowing her off like he had done earlier. As he stood there ringing the bell, her mother opened the door. Asking her mother if he could talk to Tara, he waited for her to come outside to the porch.

Sitting down on the porch bench with him, Tara said, "Hello Tom, are you feeling better than this morning?"

"Yeah, I guess so, but I am still down sort of. I always keep coming up with these reasons in my head that it's all my fault he died. If I wasn't trying to be romantic with you and wasn't selfish, I could have had time to notice Justin with the rest of them and maybe I could have saved Martin. But no, I was too much in love to let it go and it cost me my own brother's life."

Tara sighed as she responded, "Tom I love you. But you can't keep blaming yourself. It's not helping anybody with your "woe is me routine". There is nothing you can do to change the past. What's done is done. I honestly feel how horrible it is for you, but if you just keep living in turmoil it's not going to make things any better for you or anybody in your life."

"You're right, Tara. I just feel like I am a complete danger to you and anybody around me."

"Well, I can take care of myself and I am sure the cops are really hard core on finding Justin and his friends. Now they won't think of coming near you, especially after what Justin did."

"Maybe…who knows? All we can do is hope and have faith things will get better."

"Yeah, so true. And maybe Martin is living a happier life than what's becoming of this world." Tara said placing her hand on his leg trying to console him.

"Maybe, Tara…maybe. Who knows? Only time will tell what becomes of us in the end." Sitting there as they watched the sunset, holding hands, the two of them confided in each other. They talked out things and enjoyed each other's presence.

Approaching Martin's casket, Tom stood there thinking about how prideful he had been. Maybe if he had not lost his abilities that caused pride, he would not have lost the little brother that he loved. He thought to himself, even if Justin was caught, would it even justify the means? The road was going to be hard now. Moving on certainly felt impossible.

Walking up behind him, John said, "I know we didn't talk much when I got to the house this morning. But how are you feeling?"

"I'm alright, I guess…how was your flight?

"Well, at least we weren't nearly killed by terrorist this time."

Tom chuckled as he turned to give John a hug. He was crying a little, and John said, "Sorry, Tom, I know it must feel really horrible to have had Martin literally die in your arms."

"Sometimes life is like that and I know now that we must all go through losing somebody at some point."

"It sounds like this whole situation has really made you mature a lot more from what I can tell."

"You think so?"

"Yeah Tom, I definitely know so, because you can really tell you're taking it way better than anybody would have expected you to."

"Thanks, John, so how is Caltech going for you?"

"It's been going real good and lately we have been having some breakthroughs on the possibility and science of Teleportation that I had already told you about."

"Sounds fascinating. Tell me more, if y'all figure out how it works and all."

"I will, let's sit down, though; I think it's almost time for the memorial sermon from the pastor." John said.

Once the sermon was over they all got in their vehicles. Lots of people from church and, even Benny, who's family weren't really church goers came and drove with them to Martin's burial. It was being held out doors at a nearby grave yard. Getting out of their car, Tom, along with his dad, John, and Benny decided to be pole bearers and carry Martin's casket to his grave. Their mom stood there crying with Tara and Jessica as the men carried her deceased son to where he would be laid to rest.

The Pastor gave a speech on life & death and how we must all let go and just move on. Tom with his family stood there as they lowered the casket into the ground going lower into the earth. With a handkerchief in her hand, his mom continued crying. His father had his arm on her shoulder. John stood next to Tom and Robby next to Jessica, who was standing there holding Josh.

They all paid their respects as they grieved together. Then Tom noticed Agent Dale was there in a back row. He also noticed the guy in the suit that he kept seeing standing over by the vehicles. Tom smirked for a moment thinking, "It's funny how that guy is always dressed for a funeral."

Tom wanted to ask agent Dale some questions that had been brewing through his mind after everyone took a turn walking up to the grave and tombstone. He walked up to agent Dale and asked, "Hey Agent Dale, how did you show up so quickly the other night? Do you know who that guy in the suit is that I keep seeing around different places in my life is?"

"Yeah, actually I do. He is the reason we showed up so quickly Saturday night. He is from the FBI here to investigate, observe and protect you as well."

"Observe, what do you mean?"

"Well he is trying to keep you safe, and make some judgments about why these Terrorists keep coming after you." As Agent Dale said this, Tom looked over at the man in the suit.

Then Agent Dale said, "Like Saturday night, he called the fire department as soon as that old house you were in was set on fire."

"Y'all knew about the fire?"

"Yeah. Don't worry, we are positively sure, due to your personality, that it wasn't you who set it on fire. It might have been Justin or his group. That house hasn't belonged to anybody for a long time."

"You're right, it surely wasn't us who did it, but it was scary trying to escape it before it almost killed us."

"It, what are you talking about? He also saw you getting held up and quickly called me to get us there to save y'all."

"It was something scary; something nobody would want to see, maybe even a demon. Also sounds like this guy is my own guardian angel."

"Does sound strange, but these are the reasons I am here today, you know to protect you. And I wanted to pay my respects to your little brother."

"Thanks, that's nice of you."

"As well I have come to inform you, due to how much we realize Justin and the Terrorists have it out for you, that we are going to have to request that you and your parents come with us into witness protection. The rest of your family should be safe since they live at such great distances from you. Of course, we will still have people watching them for their safety. Are you willing to be put somewhere else."

"I am willing to do that. That way everyone else is safe from the danger my presence has put them in, but you will also have to ask my parents."

"Your presence? Tom, it's more than just you. Remember your dad also helped stop them on the air plane. I will talk to your father about it."

Tom thought, "Yeah, but you don't know about all the other crap that I did to instigate the situation."

Consenting Tom said, "You're right. I just feel like Martin's death is my fault and I am a danger to everyone around me."

"Tom, we all have trials in life and everyone is responsible for their own actions. It isn't your fault all these people are messed up in the head and they keep attacking you. This is a time for you to man-up and deal with these issues. I had to deal with things when I was younger and I know that through my trials I was made a better man because of them."

"Uh huh, I see" Tom responded nonchalantly.

"In fact, my friend you found once told me when I was younger we all have mountains to climb. It's all downhill once you have climbed that mountain."

"You're right Agent Dale. Thanks for your words. They have inspired me some."

"You're welcome, but I have just passed it on. He usually is the one with good advice not me."

Seeing Benny starting to walk away towards his family's car, Tom responded, "Well okay, see you later Agent Dale"

"Good bye, Tom, see you later."

They separated as Agent Dale went to talk with Tom's parents, and then everyone at the funeral headed home. They drove off, leaving the grave yard except for Agent Dale who stayed behind for other reasons.

Agent Dale walked back towards Martin's grave. But out from behind a tall tomb Agent Dale's friend emerged and started talking to him. "It sure is sad he has no idea what's ahead for him, but I am sure he will do fine and overcome those mountains that await him."

"Yeah, well it sure is crazy how things have played out for me. But who knows, maybe things will get better for him."

"Things are always darkest before the dawn, my friend."

"Why did you leave me there without saying goodbye?"

"Really? I thought you drowned?"

"When I came up out of the water you and the others were gone, but eventually I found my way back to shore."

"Ahh, now it makes sense. Dale, I think sometimes there are just times in life where things have to happen certain ways." His mysterious friend said with a foreshadowing attitude.

"Yeah, well sometimes I wish things were different. I have wondered where you have been for so long, but you act like it wasn't much of a burden on you."

"Trust me, it wasn't easy Dale, and try to always remember no matter how crazy things get…keep hoping that things will sort themselves out."

"You know I am not that big on hoping for things to get better. I rather take action and resolve any trouble then let the cards fall where they may."

"I understand where you're coming from. Still, I think things have worked out in extraordinary ways. Just like how Tom found me without even knowing I was one of your targets and not just a friend."

"I just told him the truth, about how I was looking for an old friend. I don't think the government will be trying to lock you up again now that I exposed that conspiracy you hinted at when I dropped you off at the prison facility months ago. I'm pretty sure they have their hands full dealing with details on Director Ford now."

"That's good. Hopefully you will be able to figure out the rest of that conspiracy and stop whoever he was working with…any how I am going to go home, so see you later."

"Goodbye, see you later." Agent Dale said as he and his friend separated, both going back to their homes.

𝕻 𝕻 𝖑 △

Sitting down to eat dinner, all of the Turner's were having a great time conversing with each other. None of them were as sad as they were at the funeral now that it was over. Passing some avocado chili cheese fries to John, Mr. Turner said, "Okay, everybody quiet down. I have some important news to discuss with everyone. Me and y'all's mother have been discussing something important for the past couple of hours. Earlier today Agent Dale told me how the government is offering us a place to stay hidden from Justin or the terrorist in Hoboken, New Jersey if we want to move there temporarily till these criminals are caught. But, knowing how courteous your mother and I are, we have decided to get your opinions first."

Shocked John said, "Man, as if living on my own half way across the country wasn't hard enough, but to have to be separated across the whole country, now that will be a challenge."

Their father responded, "It's okay. If you were that far already it shouldn't be that hard."

Jessica said, "It will be hard not to see you on the weekends, but if it keeps y'all safe till they are locked away, then I will be glad you are all alive and safe."

Tom realized the magnitude of what was going to happen to his family, so he asked, "Hey can I go talk to Tara about this real quick?"

They all agreed and Tom quickly ran out the door across the street to Tara's house. Once he rang the doorbell she came out and he asked her to sit with him on the bench of the porch to talk.

Tom then said warm heartedly, "Tara, I am sorry it has to be this way, but my family is going to have to leave Texas for a while."

Seeming down she responded, "Does this mean you're breaking up with me?"

He responded, "Of course not…I love you and I would never want to leave you but I…I mean my family is a danger to you and the people around us, so we are being put somewhere far away."

"You're not the danger. But I understand it's the way it has to be."

"Don't worry. Eventually Justin will be caught with the rest of them and then we will be home again."

With a sigh of desperation, Tara said, "Just give me one more kiss Tom, before you go so you know I am right here waiting for you."

Moving forward, slowly bringing their lips together, both of them held their breath as they gave each other one long good bye kiss as they looked into each other's eyes. After kissing each other the two of them got up and told each other how much they loved the other and said their goodbyes.

It was a pleasant morning with nice cool air and sunshine all around. Todd glided into Tom's window thinking about the plans they made a few days before. Laying there under Tom's bed, he hoped it would all work out accordingly. Tom quickly busted open his door and rushing in then closing it saying, "Todd, you almost ready to go? We are going to be leaving soon."

"Yeah, I'm pretty much ready. You know I don't really have any belongings to take with me like the rest of your family. I am just concerned about this plan. What if I get lost or wind up somewhere else."

"If you follow the plan, nothing will go wrong. I'm sure you can take care of yourself even if we get separated. Oh, and don't forget to close my window when we leave so rain doesn't get in while we are gone and follow the black government vehicle that I get into."

"Alright, see you on the other side."

"Goodbye Todd, be careful."

Todd watched as Tom grabbed his suitcase and backpack and headed out the door as he turned off the lights. Then he flew over & out the window, grabbing it's edge swinging around it's side with his claws and closing the window so nobody could get in. Resting on the rooftop he waited for the Turners to say their goodbyes. He was getting bored of their cliché moment.

"Well Tom, I don't know how long you will be gone, but it was good to spend the night one last time before you leave." Benny said giving his best friend a hug.

"Yeah, I am going to miss y'all a lot." Tom said looking at Benny and then over to Tara.

Hugging Tara, and not wanting to make things awkward with his whole family was there, he whispered in her ear, "I will miss you the most and I love you."

Crying a little bit, Tara responded, "Goodbye Tom, I love you too."

Once Jessica's family said their goodbyes, the Turners got into the government issued vehicle and drove off with Todd following from the air. So he would not be seen by Tom's loved waving, He stayed high up above their neighborhood. When the vehicle turned a corner he swooped down slowing himself as he glided onto the top of the vehicle Tom was in.

Stopping at the same King Finnegan's restaurant where Tom had been a few months before, the Turners pulled up to the ride through to get some good food. This was making Todd hungry as he hadn't had anything to eat since earlier that morning. Tapping on the window, Todd gestured to Tom to give him some food hoping Tom's family wouldn't notice. Opening the window, Tom slipped him a few sweet zunchinipotato fries.

As he arrived at the airport, Todd flew up staying out of view from any humans as he landed on the roof. Quickly he ran on the roof top to a gateway Tom had suggested so that he would be able to see their family passing through security. After a few moments, he saw Tom with his family coming through the security check with Agent Dale. They had checked their luggage into lay away. Stopping in the middle of the Terminal, Todd could see them stopping to say goodbye to John as he was going in a different direction.

Todd scoffed to himself saying, "Humans. Why do they always have to be so emotional about everything?" John hugged everyone and they said their goodbyes to each other then he walked one direction to board his plane, and the rest went the other way headed for their plane.

Trying to keep up with everyone, Todd would glance through the window making eye contact with Tom to alert him that he was still following. Not paying attention to where he was flying, Todd eventually flew into the side of one of gateways which made Tom laugh when he saw him collide.

After getting to their gateway, they waited twenty minutes to board the flight. Once the gateway opened up, the Turner's and Agent Dale boarded their Plane to New York to reach their new place in Hoboken. When everyone was seated on the plane it started to move, so Todd grabbed onto the vertical stabilizer on the back of the airplane. Holding it tight, the craft began turning corners getting to its runway. When it picked up speed he really had to hold on as the plane ascended. For about an hour they rode the plane till it finally landed in New York. It was much colder there in Hoboken; not your typical warm weather like Texas has.

Todd hopped from the terminal roof onto the back of another black vehicle as they headed for the hotel where they would be living. Riding in the vehicle, Tom stared out the window as he saw the auburn trees in a field with the beauty they held. It was clearly obvious, fall was setting and he could tell they had seasons there in Hoboken, Texas rarely showed signs of the seasons.

As the Turners pulled up to their hotel, Todd flew up to the top of the building, while they started unloading their belongings and getting settled into their new home. While Todd was waiting for Tom to come meet him, Agent Dale said to Tom, "I'm sorry about the other day when I was at your brother's funeral and I told you to just man up and deal with these things. Since I have been through a lot in my life, I have found it easier for me to just move on. But when I was young I did need some therapy."

"Yeah, I could definitely use some therapy from the things going on lately."

"The person I want to recommend to you is a good friend of mine and lives down in New York City. His name is Myles Hernandez."

"Oh yeah, is he the one who gave you therapy when you were younger?"

"No, he is just a friend. Myles would have been like eleven or thirteen when I was doing therapy."

"Alright, that sounds nice. But wouldn't you have to drive me there to meet him since I don't have a car of my own?"

"I would. If you're willing we can go Wednesday. There might be more than driving?"

"Yeah, sure, that sounds nice. See you later Agent Dale." Tom said as Agent Dale was walking off to leave them.

Setting his bags down in their room and remembering he needed to talk to Todd, Tom said to his parents, "I'm going to go explore this place a little. I will see y'all in a few minutes."

Getting impatient waiting for Tom, Todd started tapping his claw on the edge of the roof. Hearing the door fling open, he turned around to see exactly who he had been waiting for. There, on the ledge, he said jokingly, "So, you finally made it up here, did ya?"

Tom, emerging a little short on breath, said, "Sorry, I kind of forgot I was supposed to come up immediately and Agent Dale wanted to ask me something. Did you travel all right on your own?"

"It was good, but it looks like a storm is coming."

"Yeah it sure does. Are you going to be safe with this thunderstorm brewing?"

"I don't know. I guess so. But I wish there was somewhere warmer to go rest?"

Todd watched as Tom looked at the sun hidden behind the clouds and rain was pouring in the distance as it got closer to them. Then, he looked down and noticed the pool was a half pool, which was the kind where half of it was outside and the other half was inside. There was a part you could go under to get outside or inside.

Tom looked down and said to Todd with hope, "Hey, why don't you fly down real quick to see if the water is warm."

Replying with a snarky chuckle, Todd said, "Alright I will. But if it's freezing you will be the one getting toasted." Diving off the building falling vertically, Todd opened his wings then glided in a circle dropping down into the water. Swimming around for a moment and enjoying the cozy water, he then flew back up to Tom. Then enthusiastically he said, "Wow that water is nice. Warm and comfy just like a spa."

"Good, just like I thought. Perfect so you can stay warm in there at night time, and use it to avoid the rain. I will be down there in a little while to meet you and swim some; but try to remain unseen if there are any other people in there. Besides, how would you know what a spa is like?"

"Sounds like a good plan and fun at the same time. When you and your family aren't home I have seen advertisements on your entertainment center."

"See you in a little while."

"Alright, Tom, see you there."

Walking back into their new home, Tom's parents asked how he liked the place. He told them it seemed like it was going to be an interesting place to live. Sure it was far from how Texas was, but it still felt better than having to fear about Justin constantly. Now he could be assured that there wouldn't be any more psycho hostage moments.

Sitting there in the chair and looking out the window, Tom began thinking about how missed Tara and how he knew he would see her again someday. "But Martin can never be seen or replaced again." He thought to himself. Taking off his shoes and sitting there watching the storm get closer, he thought, "Do the ends justify the means? We moved all the way across the country, but has any of this really resolved anything? In the end was it worth it, or was it all for nothing?" Pondering these things, thunder and lightning crackled across the sky as Tom's heart filled with rage and regret.

Regardless of how Tom felt, things surely were about to change for him and his family. At least now there was some serenity to Tom's darkest hour, knowing Justin would eventually be caught by the authorities. What new adventures awaited him there in the northern parts of North America as he settled into a new living standard? In the end, do the ends ever truly justify the means?

Chapter 20
An Uncertain Precedent

The Near Future
Wednesday, November 11ᵗʰ, 6:02 A.M.
The Turner's apartment, Hoboken, New Jersey

Hurrying to get his breakfast eaten because he wanted some time to swim before he had to leave with Agent Dale, Tom turned on the entertainment center to watch the news. He was enjoying the taste of his jellified toast and spice filled beef patties as some horrible news headlined came across the screen saying, "MORE VILLAGES BOMBED IN THE PHILIPENES"

Listening to the news, Tom heard how recently another village had recently been bombed in the Malay Archipelago on one of the remote islands as a result of the new dictatorship taking place in the continent of Asia recently. He really wished there was better things on the news these days. But all they ever showed was bad news and bad events. "Why does it always have to be this instead of something good for once?" He thought to himself.

After eating & changing, Tom hurried down to the pool and jumped right in to do a few laps. Then Todd swam up to him saying with a chuckle "So, Tom, does Tara usually eat fruit while getting ready to go swimming?"

"Todd! You're not supposed to know about that!"

"Hey, it's not my fault that I have the ability to know what you're dreaming."

"Well, still even if you can do that, it would be nice if you kept that kind of stuff to yourself."

"Oh, come on Tom, you have to admit it's a really funny scenario. Why would she eat an apple, a strawberry and a banana all while giving you funny looks as you're swimming?"

Pausing for a moment and concerned Tom responded, "Please don't tell me you feel what I feel, too."

Smirking, Todd said, "Nope. Pets just witness their owners dreams not feel what they feel. But emotions and what you feel could be two different things. Or, at least, I don't necessarily feel your emotions. Maybe the more I grow to liking you as a friend or owner I might experience more empathy for you and feel what you feel and maybe even feel your emotions, eventually."

"Maybe you are right. Who knows?"

"So are you enjoying the water?"

"Yeah, it sure is soothing. Nothing quite like cold air and warm water to really move the senses. Have you enjoyed living here the past few days?"

"Well, this sure beats your cramped bed room back in Texas."

"Hey, it's not that cramped. You just take up a lot of space."

"Not really. If I let myself grow then I might take up a lot of space."

"Speaking of which, I was wondering when you would grow or get bigger?"

"Well Dragons choose when they age or get bigger, but once you have done that there is no going back. Unless of course, something else makes you young again."

"Wow that sounds like an important decision. But what would make you young again?"

"It is very important to the growth of a dragon. It's a long story...let's just say I wasn't always inside that egg."

"Okay, I understand. Does that mean you also choose when you die?"

"Well...no. Nobody knows when their time is up, but everyone dies sometime. Still, you should realize death isn't the end...in fact it's noted in history that death is also just known as a slumber and someday everyone will awaken again."

"How is that in history if it's something that hasn't happened yet? As well I never heard of that in history class, maybe at church, but never in history class."

"The past becomes the future and the future becomes the past and in the grand scale of things there is no telling if time existed in the first place."

"You know you're only confusing me more by what you just said. Plus none of that made sense." Tom said dumbfounded by what he heard.

"Oh trust me Tom, it has plenty of meaning."

"Okay, if you say so..." Tom said as he was cut off by his hollowatch beeping and buzzing. "Quick, get out of view of my video sender." He said.

Picking up the phone Tom answered, "Oh, hi Agent Dale, what's up?"

"I'm here, but you aren't in your room apparently. You ready to go?"

"I will be ready; let me just come up to change."

"See ya soon."

Heading back to his room, Tom told Todd goodbye and went upstairs to change while Agent Dale waited for him in the living room. As they headed off to New York to visit Agent Dale's therapist friend, they pulled up to an FBI building right next to their hotel. Tom asked, "Why are we pulling into this building and this parking lot?"

Agent Dale responded cautiously, "Well Tom, I wanted to tell you myself. I am not allowed to warn you ahead of time, but somebody from high up in the American government wants to talk to you. And they want to talk to you without your consent so you wouldn't choose to run off out of fear. Just try to think of this as a pit stop on our way to my friend. Besides, the chopper to get us to New York quicker is on the roof of this building."

"Fear?" Tom said confused. Then he said, "Well, they should only worry I will run from them in fear, if their deeds are bad."

"Well, let's hope you don't piss them off then. And please be cautious on what you tell them. Sorry for not letting you know sooner."

Walking into the building, Agent Dale flashed his badge while Tom stood next to him allowing them to walk ahead. They got in an elevator and went up several floors. Once they reached a certain floor

Agent Dale escorted Tom to a room that looked a lot like an interrogation room, much like what you would see in a movie or a show for cops or FBI people.

Agent Dale left the room and five minutes later a bald, stocky rough looking guy came in and sat across the table from Tom. He opened the file he was holding to ask Tom some very interesting questions. The bald man said, "So, do you know who I am and what I want?"

Tom replied slowly and curiously, "No. Who are you?"

"Good, good…well, I am the Secretary of Defense and I am here on behalf of the government of the United States of America."

"Well, that is a pretty big title for a guy who wants to question a mere teenager."

He chuckled saying satirically, "A mere teenager huh? Look Turner, you know as well as I do that you are no normal teenager."

Tom shifted his eye's quickly with fear and responded, "What do you mean; I don't know what you're talking about?"

"Now listen here, don't you play ignorant. We have been keeping track of you ever since your family helped stop the terrorists on that plane. We learned a great deal about your attributes. So, don't you even try to be coy with me, boy."

"Alright, so I have had some unusual experiences recently."

"Good. Sounds like you're finally realizing the importance of being honest with us."

"We obviously noticed that you were at the epicenter of the shadow of the moon every time it shifted recently and produced a solar eclipse."

"Well, why does that make you think it was me. It could have been anybody or anything?"

"Cause Turner, you're the only one who was in the middle of its shadow both times it happened. And let's not forget the missile incident in the Atlantic on July 04th. You have any idea the danger you imposed on thousands no...millions of lives from making the moon shift like that? It caused massive tsunamis and floods in various places across the globe. At least you got the planet to tug a little away from the sun increasing its speed some."

Tom thought, "I wonder how much it has increased in speed?" But Tom gave a look of shocked guilt saying, "Geese I had no idea that would happen. Besides, how can you prove it was me who did all that?"

"Really, what kind of a boy can jump nearly half way across a basketball court for a slam dunk? That is just unrealistic unless you had a boost of some kind."

"I don't know, maybe one that could fly..." Tom mumbled under his breath.

The Secretary of Defense scoffed stating, "You certainly have caught the government's eyes with your unique attributes which could be useful if used in the right ways. But we don't even know where your loyalties lie?"

"Hey, I helped stop terrorists on multiple occasions. Obviously I would be there for the American government."

"Yeah, well even if you are, being able to move a whole planet or rock, is some pretty big fire power. Therefore we just have not decided yet whether you would be of use to us or a casualty to the United States of America or the planet. Some said you should be executed immediately. But, obviously some of us figured you could help change the stage for America."

"I would love to help y'all out there, but there is just one problem."

The secretary rolled his eyes asking, "And what is that?"

"My abilities are gone and are not working for me right now, and for all I know they are gone forever?"

"Great. We'll try to get that problem solved before the government changes its mind on how to deal with you."

"I will try, but I don't know if I can help you in any real, useful way."

"Well, at least it's not a device causing this issue and if you don't have your attributes then you're not a casualty. But we will be keeping our eyes on you."

The secretary had already got up to leave the room by the time he said his final words. Sitting there, Tom waited for Agent Dale to come back into the room. When he did, he sat down with Tom to talk briefly. "Sorry you lost your abilities Tom, and your little brother." Agent Dale said sorrowfully.

"Yeah, well it doesn't really matter. At least I won't do any more damage than I have already. So how long have you known?"

"Ever since you lifted those weights in the gym after mumbling something under your breath, I had a feeling and thought it might have been you when I saw somebody fly over the carrier. But when we were on the cliff, that is what convinced me totally that you were not normal."

"Yeah, well without my abilities I am nothing; obviously they are lost or gone."

"Obviously? Well how are they obviously lost?"

"Cause I didn't do something heroic to stop Justin and save my brother's life. If I had been honest with my family from the beginning, then maybe Justin would have been handled more properly and Martin might still be alive."

"Tom, just because you couldn't change how things played out doesn't mean you need to dwell on the bad blaming yourself."

"Yeah, I know. It just feels so bad that I had the power of the universe in my voice and I couldn't do anything to stop Justin."

Agent Dale said with a sarcastic voice, "Really. The power of the universe? So, I guess to you that confirms you don't have your powers now. But nothing truly is ever lost and anything that is missing can be found again."

"I don't know. My abilities seemed pretty universal if they could move a planet. Let me guess those were more inspiring words from your friend?"

Agent Dale chuckled responding, "Yeah, he sure did get me to learn some pretty silly phrases."

"Yeah, so are we going to stay here all day?"

"No, let's get out of here so you can visit my friend, Myles. We are going to need to head up to the roof to get in our chopper since it's quicker than dealing with all the traffic in Manhattan."

Reaching the top of the roof of the FBI building, they got in the helicopter and headed for the Big Apple. On the ride over, Tom thought about how much in deep hot water he was now that the government knew about him. Hoping they wouldn't imprison him for being a danger to the world, he thought of many events that might logically play out and wondered if he would have to escape the government at some point.

Once they landed, they got in a car and drove through the streets for a few minutes. Tom was shocked at something he saw. So he thought to himself, "That is highly unlikely, no way."

He shrugged the thought of what he saw off as they pulled into a parking garage. Walking into the building from the parking garage, Tom scratched his nose a little as Agent Dale just paced on with his usual serious tone till they got into the elevator. Reaching the floor of the glowing button on the elevator panel, there was an office with many doors with names on them. One of the doors read "Myles Hernandez". Agent Dale knocked on the door, then a Cuban Latino looking man opened the door greeting them.

Agent Dale requested, "Please Myles, treat him with care and be nice to help him with his issues."

"Don't worry, I will, see you later Dale."

"Bye guys. Tom I will be waiting in a car on the street outside the first floor when you're ready to leave."

"Alright Agent Dale, see you later." Tom said as he walked into Myles's office shutting the door.

"Well, have a seat Tom."

"Okay." Tom responded sitting down on what he thought to be a clichéd therapy chair.

"So Tom, why exactly is it Dale wants me to give you therapy?"

"Well, he could have many reasons. Some of them I don't think you should know."

"Really? Why not? A therapist is supposed to know every aspect of why their patient is visiting in the first place?"

"Yeah, well how do I know you won't just go blabbing to everyone about my personal stuff, like to my parents?"

"Tom, a therapist is supposed to keep everything a secret, unless it is harmful to the people of the public or you're planning a criminal plot."

"All right…I guess I will tell you everything, then."

Tom spent a long time relaying to Myles about everything that had happened with him over the many months.

>>> 🜚🜚🜚🜚△> ⌐◇🜚🜚

Walking down the hall of the first floor, Agent Dale decided to call Kathryne and talk to her since they would have some free time. Getting in the car, He and Tom traveled in, Agent Dale called his wife. Kathryne picked up and Agent Dale said, "Hello honey. Got some free time right now, so I thought I would try to spend it with you. How are you enjoying our new temporary home?"

"It's alright. You know I am used to moving, but I think it's having a very big emotional effect on Danny. He's really missing his friends from Texas."

"I know…I wish there was something I could do to help with that. But how bad would it have been if I just moved alone like I had to for the summer? You know what I mean?"

"You're right. Still that doesn't change the fact our son now literally has no friends. But having a father there for him is better than being alone with a bunch of kids who could badly influence him without you around to give him guidance."

"I was reading about the school we are sending him to. If we want him to get more involved and make more friends, they are having a program this weekend we could go to."

"That sounds like a good plan. But, it's just annoying that we keep having to move. Or I guess you do and this time you brought us with you."

"Honey, once all this stuff with the Turner family works out I will make sure we are permanently located in our house in Texas."

"That would be great; I really hope that is soon."

"So for dinner tonight you…"Agent Dale's hollowatch started buzzing. "Kat, Agent Myers is calling I will talk to you later. Love you goodbye."

"Goodbye Dale, love you too…" she said morosely as he had to get back to work.

◇ ʮ ◇ ▽ ʮ

Once Tom was finally done telling him everything, Myles said, "Wow that sounds like a lot of crazy moments."

"Yeah, I knew you would think I am insane and probably want to put me away."

"No, not at all Tom. I believe you it's just…wow, so much. Obviously, you blame yourself for your brother and it seems like you feel lonely from the fact you had to put your relationship with Tara on pause. It's just really a big story that sounds out there, and not many would believe you. But since I know Dale brought you here obviously the government aspect is real."

"If you don't believe me, call Tara. She could back me up and Justin definitely could if you could find him or get a hold of him somehow."

"Like I said before, I do believe you. But just for my own sanity I might look into them. Anyhow, I guess I will talk to you soon. I am not meaning to cut you off or anything, I just have another patient scheduled soon. We can talk more about everything next time."

"This has been very interesting and you do seem like a nice guy. Well, see you later Myles. Nice to meet you."

"Same here. Goodbye Tom. I hope to see you soon. Next time we should probably focus more on some of the things that are bringing you down and how to resolve your anger towards Justin."

Tom got up and walked out the door heading for the elevator to go down to meet up with Agent Dale. Standing in the elevator he wondered if these therapy sessions were even going to help. "Sure it was my first time. I just hope to feel good again soon from all this." He thought to himself. Reaching the bottom floor he saw somebody through the window staring in at him.

> ⟩ ▣ ⌐ △ ᗰ ⌐ ᗰ

Answering his hollowatch, Agent Dale said somewhat annoyed, "What do you want right now Agent Myers? Sorry if I am being grumpy. It's just that I was busy talking to my wife?"

"It's alright, I understand. Sometimes my husband and I have our issues, also. I was just calling to tell you I found out that info had come through fully from Steven O'Brian about you wanting him to try to check a lot of Ford's moves the past couple years."

"What did you find out?"

"Apparently Steven found out an interesting pattern in Ford's life. It seems every year, near the beginning of June, for many years Ford would get a message telling him the same thing it always said, "it's time". That isn't the interesting part, though. What was very peculiar was that within the next couple of days, even if he was busy with something in the CIA, he would book a flight to that area of the Caucasus Mountains. It was not too far from the village that we had attacked."

"That is very enlightening. Still, why did he go there is the bigger question?"

"Well, this next part is where things definitely seem like something is being kept secret. Whenever he went there he would leave his hollowatch in the hotel. He booked the room on the 6th of June. Then any space station records Steven and I looked into seemed to be missing info from over that area on those specific hours when he would leave his hotel and return."

"So, do we have literally no way of finding out where he headed?"

"Well, that's the good thing. We can see when he left and when he returned to the hotel and we have a general direction of which way he was heading. So using that knowledge, we have configured only a few possible places he could have gone within the time limit. I shall send you the coordinates of them right now."

Looking at them for a moment, Agent Dale said, "Interesting. When I try to view the ground view on my hollowatch of 43.138824, 41.911010 there is five miles where the trees look odd."

"Well, I am glad you noticed that. I had Steven look into it since it looked off to me and apparently after he hacked the ELO database he found that the images for that area actually had a base point from coordinates in a forest near Horde Mountain in North Carolina."

"Strange. So somebody doesn't want the general public to know what this place actually looks like. The way Ford spoke of things, I'm almost sure this place is the one out of your calculations that he most likely headed to. I won't have time to check this place out for a while, but when things look more open for me, I shall definitely investigate it in person."

"Okay, sounds like a great plan. I recommend when you do, you take somebody as backup in case this place isn't safe to be at alone."

"Oh, don't worry; you can be sure I will have some protection with me. This place might require some serious investigating if we want to figure out who Ford was meeting with there."

"You're probably right in thinking that. By the way how did Tom take that meeting you had sprung on him earlier?"

"He took it really well actually. It kind of surprised me how much he didn't freak out that the government had been keeping tabs on him. Still this is an uncertain precedent. Never before has the American government had to be so cautious over the potential of one young man. One who could change the course of history as we know it."

"Well, with attributes like his, why would he even have much to fear in the first place?"

"Well, according to him his "abilities", as he calls them aren't around anymore or he can't use them. I think Tom is an amazing kid with a lot of talent for doing what is right, so I would presume he thinks we are trying to do what is right since he looks for the good in people.

"Well, we know you and I try to do the right thing, but look at Ford. We thought he was a patriotic loyal man, and he ended up being a major issue for lots of innocent people."

"Agent Myers, it doesn't matter how much you think you know somebody. They could be harboring the darkest secrets and you wouldn't have a clue. No man is innocent and everyone has bad deeds they do at some point in their life. Let's just hope we aren't fooled again in the near future.

"I totally agree. So, do you think Tom is hiding the fact he still has his abilities?"

"The way he spoke to me, I am sure he is just going through a lot of pain and he doesn't have any confidence in himself right now. Maybe he will get over that eventually and get them back or perhaps he is lying to keep himself from the government trying to use him. Speaking of Tom...I got to go, see you later." Agent Dale said finishing their conversation and seeing Tom running down the street chasing somebody.

$$\triangledown \triangle \text{┗} \triangle \text{ᗰ} > \diamond \triangle$$

Quickly running, chasing the guy he saw through the window of the building. Tom was determined not to let him get away. He kept pursuing the person exerting all his energy down the streets of Manhattan. A couple blocks down the street he came to a dead end just as the guy he was chasing turned into a back alley getting stuck where there was a fence in their way. This left the runner trapped for Tom to do whatever he wanted as he approached him.

Tom yelled at him, "You're one of those rats from that gang. What are you doing all the way here in New York!?"

The young man was clearly scared of Tom and responded out of fear, "I just noticed you and figured you could help with Ricky's memory, since you were the one who made him forget seven years of his life."

Tom, still angry yelled, "Where is Justin!?"

"I don't know where or who he is?"

"He is the guy that killed my little brother!"

"Oh him…"

"Where is he!?"

The guy backed up a little as Tom yelled, "Exertus!"

Then the young man went flying backwards hitting the fence and busting it open.

The guy got up, worried for his life and yelling, "Please don't hurt me!"

Tom now had full faith that his abilities were back and said, "I will help your friend. But, first tell me where Justin is?"

"Last I heard he was sneaking out on one of the cargo ships with some of those people he had with him. He was trying to flee the cops here in America. But I don't know where he went. The drug dealers by the docks might know."

"Thank you for your help and remember to tell Ricky I restored his mind for him."

Tom remembered some words for memory and remember, so then he said, "Let Ricky memoria his animus of the past seven years."

"Thank you I think?"

"You're welcome. He should remember his past now."

"Goodbye, see you later, if I even see you at all."

Tom, glad that he could do things again decided to pay a visit to the woman he loved most. He decided her instead of going straight to Justin, because his love for her was stronger than the vengeance that burned in his heart. Excited to visit Tara, he said, "Inflecto me to outside Tara's house!" Within a moment he made a flash disappearing from the streets of New York City to reappear right in front of his home and Tara's house.

An uncertain precedent surely was underway in the sense Tom had his abilities back, which meant he could do whatever he pleased. The government wanted to make use of him, too. Agent Dale was uncertain who wanted to keep everything so secretive, but he was certain he would find out soon enough. Never before had the stakes been so high for the future of humanity with an uncertain precedent looming that could surely make differences in the way people think of themselves and what they are capable of.

Chapter 21
Doing Things Honorably

The Near Future
Wednesday, November 11th, 12:19 P.M.
Tara's house, 5463 Taggart Ln, Smithsonian Valley, Texas

The stage surely was changing again for Tom as he emerged outside of Tara's house with his abilities returned to him. Filled with joy at the thought of how he could do great things and maybe even help people out who needed it, he walked up the steps to the door and he knocked. Waiting for one moment, he was surprised to see it was Tara opening the door instead of one of her parents. Instantly, mesmerized by the sight of him, she jolted forward with giving Tom a kiss on the cheek and a big hug.

Smirking, Tom said with that warm feeling Tara gave him, "Geese, I have only been gone a couple days Tara. What's with all the excitement?"

"I know that's silly. But a couple days away from the person you love can feel like an eternity."

"I know exactly what you mean. I sure have missed you and having to move away from everyone too."

"So why did you and your family come back?"

"Well let's just say my family has not come back and I took a short cut to get here."

"Wait. Does that mean you have your abilities back?"

Hovering a few inches off the ground looking down he responded, "Yeah, it sure does."

Smiling she said, "That's great I knew they weren't gone for good."

"Yeah, let's go sit on the bench while we talk."

Both, sitting down in comfortable positions, reminisced over what had happen the past few days. Apparently Tara had cops outside her house every day and night always protecting her family in case anybody tried to do anything to them. As well according to her follow up, Tara was doing good in volley ball. Tom asked her what he should do with his abilities now that he had them back.

She responded nicely, "Tom, it's up to you how you use your abilities. I would just recommend not doing anything that could bring up more issues in your life."

"Yeah, that's for certain. I won't make that mistake twice."

"That's good. But are you alright from what happened with Martin?"

"Not really…but we all lose our family eventually. I think it's something I am going to have to get used to no matter how old or capable of doing things I seem to be. I will get Justin back eventually for what he did once I find him, though." Then Tom thought how vengeance would not be honorable to Martin's memory.

Tara said, "Mmm…Tom isn't there kind of a giant loop hole in what you just said?"

A little stunned at her, Tom responded saying, "Wait a second what are you talking about?"

"Think about it Tom. You can teleport to me on command of your voice. I don't think it would be that hard to find Justin with your abilities."

"Hey, you're right. Let's see if I can just teleport to Justin right now. If I can resolve this stuff, instead of having to find him that would be great. Inflecto me near Justin, but not too close."

For a moment they both waited and nothing happened. "Well it doesn't look like that is going to work. Did I lose my abilities again?" Tom said a little annoyed and worried he was stuck in Texas.

"Hold on, Tom. You thought you lost them before. Now would be a good time to see if you can use them at all before you freak out and get all worried for nothing."

"You're right, Ignis." Tom said as he held his hands up cupping them together as a ball of flames appeared in them.

"See, you do still have abilities. Wonder why they didn't work for you before or this time either when you wanted to teleport to Justin?"

"Maybe the universe or whatever that governs my abilities in the first place doesn't want me to use them for certain occasions for some unknown reason?"

"It is possible. Still how would you resolve it, even if you could find him now? Maybe this just isn't the right time."

"I believe that is true, because if I were to just teleport to him now, there are so many possibilities as to what could happen. He could be erratic and try to kill me instantly. Or we might get in a fight and I might kill him out of spite. It would not be honorable, nor would it do Martin justice if I tried to end Justin's reign of terror out of vengeance and anger. So, I would like to find him properly. That would take time and it might be good for him to cool off from however Martin's death affected him. Then, maybe we can work things out properly instead of fighting."

"That's very noble, Tom. It does sound like a more mature way of handling things."

"Thanks Tara. I am glad I can visit with you now that I have my abilities back. You're such a wonderful girlfriend."

"Awe, I love you so much, Tom. You are definitely better than most of the people in today's society."

They kissed each other, then Tom said, "Yeah I think I am going to go grow some flowers at Martin's grave and return to New York so Agent Dale doesn't flip out because I've been gone for so long. I have to figure out if I should reveal to the government that I have my abilities back, or think about what they might do with me if I don't tell them?"

"Don't worry Tom, you could deal with them no matter what they throw your way."

"You're right. Well, I guess I will see you later Tara. Goodbye, love you."

"Love you too Tom, goodbye."

Flying over to the grave yard, Tom landed behind the morgue and then walked through the gates over to Martin's tomb stone. As he was getting closer he noticed all the other grave sites around and wondered if everyone buried there had lost their lives due to somebody else's evil deeds. Thinking logically about how that could not be the case, since death was considered to be a natural part of life that everyone eventually has to deal with, unless for some reason not fully known we weren't meant to die.

Once Tom arrived at Martin's tombstone, he stood there looking at it and said, "Martin, I am sorry you died because of my actions. I did not think things through sooner. I am here today to show love and honor for the brave little brother you were and how you always got through hard times like they were nothing. But that's the beauty in kids like you. Y'all don't know yet about all the evil things people in the world are willing to do. So you are bold and brave. I can't promise to fix you now since your dead…but I promise you I will learn from my mistakes."

Feeling the air blow and bellow as it touched his skin, Tom felt he should say a few more words for the mood. With emotion in his voice he said, "Make it Niveus and celer cresco a variety of beautiful flowers for Martin's grave." Then it started to snow all around him as lots of different flowers emerged all around Martin's grave.

Standing there for a moment as the grave yard was engulfed in snow. Surrounding all around him, Tom looked up at the sky remembering how he felt at peace flying. So he decided to fly back to New York instead of warping there. Looking down at Martin's grave, once more rage filled his heart so he looked to the heavens. Yelling as he blasted off, flying into the sky, soaring past the snow coming down as into a higher cloud he flew as he started to head north.

◇△〉ㄴ♨▽〉△△🏳

Getting off the cargo ship feeling somewhat tired from a lack of sleep, Justin snuck behind some of the other fugitives between crates. He didn't sleep well their entire trip across the sea for very definite reasons. Being so slothful he wasn't being cautious as much as he should have been, he walked out from behind a crate where he could have been spotted. Cassidy quickly grabbed him, pulling him back saying quietly with anger, "What are you doing Justin? You almost got us caught!"

"Sorry. Guess I'm not thinking clearly right now. I keep having these horrible nightmares of Tom's little brother that I killed." Justin responded feeling paranoid and guilty from what happened before they fled Texas.

Angry and tired of hearing this, Cassidy responded, "You have been saying that since we left Texas. You don't even know if the kid died. We need to get out of this country if we are going to escape any police forces from America coming after us."

Annoyed by his uncaring response, Sacra said, "Cassidy be nice. You don't have any clue what Justin's going through right now, especially since you haven't killed anybody before. Once we are out of this place we should be safe from the American government. Where we are going, they would never mess with us there. It isn't too much further from here."

"Well, it better be soon. I gave up a nice life with my mother in Kentucky to go with y'all to help Justin and you with this revenge plot." Cassidy said with his loud voice and southern accent.

Rolling his eyes, Sacra said, "Really? You hold your mom up in some special manner? She is just your mom."

"She might be my mom, but she's all I got. My dad got put in prison when I was real little and didn't care about me at all. I'm sure Justin understands how I feel since his dad left him, too."

Justin then interrupted their fight saying, "Guys, be quiet or else we might get..." Before he could finish his sentence a couple of cops showed up to try and arrest all of them. Then Justin yelled, "Everyone, run!"

Quickly, every fugitive that was on the ship dispersed running from the police. Each one taking separate routes knowing where their final destination lay, they managed to confuse the cops enough to get away. He (Justin) wasn't very happy that he kept enduring PTSD while having to avoid any authorities. He hoped eventually they would find a place where they wouldn't have to really hide anymore. According to what Sacra said though, he thought that time would come soon.

△ ▽ ◇ ◇ ◇ ♄

After flying for quite a good while, somewhere over the Midwest Tom heard a strange sound getting closer and closer to him. Quickly, he moved into some clouds so he could avoid whatever was headed his way. He didn't want to be seen, but kept his head in view to where he could observe whatever was making that noise. As he hovered there in the cloud with his head sticking out of the top of it, he saw ripples in the sky being made really fast by what looked like another person moving faster than him through the clouds making some disperse in different directions.

Tom became shocked, wondering in amazement if that was truly another person. He quickly flew off real fast following them. Obviously, they were going way faster than he was, and he didn't like the thought of that as he followed behind their airstream.

Eventually, they reached Cremo, the city of fire on the north side of Chicago just as the sun was setting. Then, the person crashed directly into a small lake below them. Tom tried to avoid attention and then noticed the person hadn't come up in a moment or two. Diving down into the water he noticed that it was a girl. Her foot was tangled in some sea weed, so quickly he untangled her and brought her onto the shore of the beach by the lake.

Tom panicked as he noticed she wasn't breathing. He quickly tried using the Heimlich maneuver on her and giving her CPR. She started to spit up water, coughing a few times, and then he quickly flew off. The girl awoke as she felt a gust of wind, but Tom didn't think she saw anybody there. He stood there, hovering above her and watching to see if she was okay. Then he had to get out of there because it was getting dark. He blasted off really fast and headed east towards New York.

Once he landed on the building Agent Dale had taken him to, he went down the stairs from the roof top into a room with the elevator and then down the elevator to the first floor and walked outside. Agent Dale got out of the car looking really mad and furious then yelled at him, "Where have you been?!"

"Sorry it's a long story. Basically I saw one of the gang members from Texas, then I chased him and found out I had my abilities back, I took care of him and warped to Texas to visit Martin and Tara. When I was on my way back flying here, I got side tracked by a flying girl that led me to Cremo, Illinois. Oh, and then I flew back here."

"Oh brother, now Tom…I know there have been weird scenarios with you in the past, but that just sounds crazy. Still I guess it's possible."

"Are you going to tell the government I have my abilities back?"

"I don't know. Maybe next week you can tell them when we revisit them while we are on our way to Myles again. They won't like it if they think you lied to them and tried to hide your abilities from them. But I am sure some form of radar picked you up today."

"You're probably right. Maybe I will tell them next week."

"Come on; let's get you home before your parents worry." Agent Dale said gesturing for him to get in the car.

As he got in the car and buckled his seat belt, Tom responded, "Alright, but you do the explaining when we get there, since my story might make them think I really need therapy or a mental asylum." Dale smirked repressing a laugh as they drove back to the helicopter. Dale and Tom chuckled as they got into the car and went back to the hotel. Once they got there, Dale didn't have much to say about why they were gone so long.

Tom had his dinner and took some down to Todd telling him all about his adventurous day. Todd said, "See, I knew you didn't really lose your abilities. Sometimes all it takes is a little faith and things can go a long way."

"Yeah, well it is good to feel whole again...well partially whole. I still have that gaping hole feeling in my chest from Martin's death."

"Well, Tom, I bet you only noticed that when you said you feel whole again a second ago, am I right?"

"Actually you're right. How did you know?"

"Because you reminded yourself that you shouldn't feel whole again, and that sparked a memory of what happened with Martin and made you feel that way again."

"Wow, you're pretty smart for a serpent with limbs and wings."

Todd and Tom laughed then continued having a great time as they hung out a bunch in the pool that evening. Then Tom went back up to the room and laid there in bed wondering how things were going to change now that he had his abilities back and how the government might want him to do things for them. Then he thought about the super-fast flying mystery girl and who she was and how could she do what Tom did, and even faster? Why was she in Cremo and what was her purpose in flying at least half way across the country to somewhere so far? As he thought about all these different things he dozed off to sleep.

Hearing a knock at the door, Tom walked over to answer it only to find Agent Dale wanting to speak with his parents before they left. Walking in, he asked them if it was okay while they were in New York, if they could check out some schools that might be good for Tom to attend while they were living up there. He told them it would be better instead of doing the homeschooling work he had been doing in their apartment, that way he could have some socializing, they agreed it would be okay with them.

Tom was ready to go back to talk to Myles some more, but first he would have to deal with the Secretary of Defense. Agent Dale and Tom got in a car and headed over to the FBI building. As they went up the elevator, Dale was curious and decided to ask Tom a question. "So are you nervous about having to talk to them again?"

"Not too much. Not like I can't handle them if they try to pull any junk with me now."

"Be careful with your actions, Tom. The American government may have more power than you think."

They reached the floor where they were on before and they headed to the same room and sat down. Tom was being a little arrogant with his thoughts considering he had his abilities back now. He also realized he needed to be more cautious now that he had his abilities again because of what happened with Martin. The Secretary of Defense walked in then sat down asking him, "So, I hear you have something you wanted to discuss, Mr. Turner? Care to explain why you have called me up on such a beautiful day? I am a busy man you know and I hope it's worth my time."

Smirking Tom looked down at his hand and opened it to reveal his palm and said, "Oh, I think it will be well worth your time, Ignis."A ball of fire appeared in his hand as a flame.

The Secretary of Defense pushed back from the table a little shocked and spooked by what he had just seen. Then, he said mumbling at first, "Looks…like you have your abilities back, I take it?"

"Yes, I do now. Got them back last week after Agent Dale and I's visit to my therapist."

"Well well…who would think therapy could be that useful to give you such astounding capabilities." The Secretary said trying to suppress a chuckle.

Tom smiled saying kindly, "Guess therapy goes a long way. So what is it exactly that you guys want me to do or not do, I would assume more from our past conversation."

"Well, we have big ideas for you in the future, but right now, we sort of want to do what we consider a test run with you."

"A test run? Like a car or a product?"

"More like seeing how you can do on your own in a battle field like scenario."

"What exactly are you trying to get me to do, specifically?"

"Basically, we want you to try to clean up the crime in New York for a while without revealing who you are."

"So, in essence, you want me to be like a real super hero?" Tom said, dumbfounded by the idea. Tom started laughing at the thought of the idea.

"No, no…not like we are going to have you dress up in tights and say stupid catch lines. Just take care of criminals, as you clean up the crime rate in New York City without making yourself known, keep it secret who you're working for, and who you are. If it improves enough we will have bigger, more important missions for you."

"Okay, that sounds reasonable. It's not like you're asking me to murder anybody."

"Well, we hope you won't kill anybody. As well you better not do anything drastic, like hurt the earth's orbit again."

"Don't worry. I learn from my mistakes these days."

"Remember Turner, just cause you can do all these special things, don't you think for one second that puts you above the law."

"Depends which law you're talking about because some laws or at least physical ones don't have a hold on me." Tom said snidely feeling a little too confident.

The Secretary responded, "It's not funny Turner. It is a serious matter. I guess we will be seeing you again eventually when we see some progress or no progress." They both got up and shook hands as the Secretary left the room.

Agent Dale said in an odd semi sarcastic tone, "Well, that went well."

"I know, but I guess I shouldn't be so cocky and arrogant like I have been. It cost me my own brother and it might have gotten me in more trouble if I wasn't careful."

"No duh, you think?" Agent Dale responded rolling his eyes.

Walking to the chopper, Agent Dale asked, "So, you remember me asking your parents if it was okay to check out a school today?"

"Yeah, what about it?"

"Well, it was really just a cover for if you agreed to this whole crime clean-up thing."

"So I won't be going to school in New York?

"Nope. That will be the time you are cleaning up the city." Agent Dale said as they turned a corner of the final flight of stairs to the helipad.

"What about my grades and education?"

"We will have somebody doing it for you making sure you get the same average you have always maintained. A bus will come for you every morning, but you can either leave the hotel before or after it comes, as long as you're trying to clean up the city."

"Won't the bus driver notice I'm not getting on the bus?"

"The school gets extra funding for stopping by here. You don't have to get on it, but you can if you want. They know how we want this set up; they just don't know why we are doing it."

"I don't want to have to lie to my parents, though."

"Technically, we are the only ones lying; you just do what you need to."

"Still seems wrong, but alright." Tom said giving an annoyed duck face.

Getting in the chopper, they headed for New York to talk with Myles. Landing there they got in the same car as the time prior and headed over to Myles's office. Agent Dale dropped him off and Tom went inside and sat down.

Then Myles asked Tom, "So Tom, how has your week been?"

"Well, if getting useful old talents back is considered good, then it's been pretty great."

"Old talents, huh...such as the ones you mentioned last week?"

"Precisely."

"Care to demonstrate these talents in some fashion or manor?"

"Yeah, I think you could use something better than one of these dumb, typical therapy chairs. How about a nice gamer entertainment chair?"

Tom stood up and Myles responded, "I don't understand the point of why you just said what you did. I think my chair is pretty decent."

"Expello this therapy chair, and voco a gamer chair." The therapy chair vanished then a nice gamer chair appeared in its place.

A little surprised, Myles said, "Whoa, wait...what did you do with my chair?"

"Let's just say it's far away from here." Tom said with a chuckle and smirky look on his face.

"Well mmm....okay, guess I won't be getting it back?"

"Only, if you want it back."

"No. It's alright. I needed new scenery."

"So, believe in my abilities now?"

"I never said I didn't believe in them, and yeah, this uh how do I put it…totally confirms it."

"So, what else do you want to discuss?"

"Why don't we talk about how you got them back?" So, for quite a while Tom told Myles about the events that happened after his last session with him. Eventually, they talked about some other subjects then Myles decided to talk to Tom about Martin.

Myles said to him, "So Tom, now that you got your pride back, do you feel any better about losing Martin?"

"How could you ask such a thing? How could anybody feel better about losing their little brother at all?"

"I didn't mean it like that Tom. I just mean is the pain less than it was now."

"It kind of ended on its own a while back, but when people bring it up or bring up Martin, the feeling of emptiness comes back."

"I get what you mean."

"How could you know what I mean? It's not like you ever have had a little brother that died. Did you?"

"He may not be dead yet, but he is certainly going to die at a younger age."

"What exactly are you trying to say or imply?"

"Well, my little brother Dan once ran away from home then joined a cult in Cremo. So, I started to have that feeling of emptiness in my chest because he was ripped out of my life."

"Wow…that is sad. Sorry."

"Yeah, and from the cult Dan joined, he contracted a disease that will make him die very sooner in life. But, at least I know he is supporting himself and surviving on his own."

"So, you still get that empty feeling in your chest now days because of Dan?"

"Actually, eventually it does go away and you can talk about it without it affecting you. But everyone has different rates at which they get over things. Some might not get over something till they die. But then it doesn't matter anymore for them since they are dead."

"Maybe I will get over it soon. Who knows?"

"I am certain you will since you are already at the point where you only feel it, if you are reminded about it."

"Yeah, well it's copperonic I flew over Cremo the other day and your brother lives there."

"It was you mentioning that earlier, that reminded me of him, and made me want to talk to you about Martin."

"It sure is funny how coincidences like that happen in this world."

"Tom, in my opinion nothing happens by coincidence."

"Yeah, but who are we to say if things just happen randomly or if there truly is some purpose to them?"

"Well, I guess we won't know until we're dead and who knows if we even will find out then?"

Tom looked up at the clock and noticed it was a little after the time their session had ended last time. Tom thought this might be the normal time for the session to end and said, "This certainly has been an interesting session. It seems to have made me feel better about things."

Myles then said with a smile, "That's good. Guess that means I am doing my job right."

"I guess so. We'll see you next week, Myles."

"See you later Tom. Have a wonderful week." Tom walked out and headed down to Agent Dale and then they went back to the hotel.

The Near Future
Thursday, November 26th, 05:18 PM
The Turner's Hotel, Hoboken, New Jersey

Walking down the hallway towards Tom's apartment with his family, Agent Dale said, "Okay, Agent Myers, I will have some more free time to go on that mission since Tom starts school on Monday. Talk to you later bye."

"So you're traveling again soon?" Kathryne asked nonchalantly.

"Don't worry, honey, it will only be for two nights and one day probably. I should be home very quickly. For now, let's just enjoy this wonderful meal we have been invited to."

"You're right. We can talk about it later. But don't dread my reaction. Two days of your absence is better than a few months."

"Glad you're thinking that way." Agent Dale said kissing Kat on the cheek.

Walking up to the Turner's apartment, Agent Dale knocked on the door. Mrs. Turner opened it asking the Sizer's to come on in.

"Wow that smells amazing Mrs. Turner. What have you made?"

"Well Kathryne, I put in a lot of the usual assortments of Thanksgiving. There's Turkey with stuffing and two options of gravy for the mashed potatoes, sweet potatoes, green bean casserole, and many things. What I added that isn't typical, but our family loves, is tamales. Maybe that is what you smell."

"I think you're right. It smells very tasty. Sorry your other kids couldn't be here with us. Still, I am grateful you invited ours."

"It's alright; they have lives, like college and jobs."

For a while Tom talked with the kids as Agent Dale and his wife talked some with his parents. Then he along with everyone headed over to the table to enjoy their thanks-giving meal. Mr. Turner wanted everyone to take part in their normal family tradition of telling everyone what they were thankful for that year.

Mr. Turner was thankful that through all the craziness that had happened they still managed to live through it and remain a family. Mrs. Turner was thankful, that despite Martin's death, the rest of the family was safe and sound. Daniel was thankful he could spend more time with his father. Jackie didn't say anything since she was a toddler, and then Kathryne said how she was thankful that she was getting more time for her family to be a family. Agent Dale was thankful that he made it through his problems with the terrorists and managed to get a new family in the process all while maintaining his own family. Tom's parents, awed in happiness saying he was like a new son to them. Finally, Tom was thankful for all the trials he had overcome, and the fact he had the most wonderful girlfriend in the world and a family that cared for him.

Then they carved the turkey and had a wonderful meal together enjoying each other's company. Tom and Daniel pulled the turkey bone, but Tom got the longer piece. So he asked what Daniel wished for. Daniel responded, "If I had gotten the longer piece my wish would have been for us to stop moving all the time so mommy and daddy could be happier with each other."

Thinking how humble this kid was and wishing he could actually grant him the wish that he had made, Tom said, "Well who knows, it might come true, you are such a great kid with great parents and I'm sure they are happier just knowing that you want that for them and not just for yourself." Agent Dale and Kathryne smiled warmly at Daniel seeing that they agreed with what Tom said.

Agent Dale's family said goodbye and said how they were grateful for being invited to their great family event. A few minutes later after the Sizers left, Tom hung out for a while, and then his parents went to their room. Tom snuck Todd some of the lustrous meal down to him and swam with him a while. After having such a great time he went back up to his room to sleep.

Chapter 22
Blessings of Christmas

The Near Future
Monday, November 30th, 6:09 A.M.
Port La Cosa Nostra, Manhattan, New York

Descending down to an obscure place behind some giant crates wearing gloves to stay warm and hide his identity, Tom felt like the weather was getting a little too cold for his taste. While flying he noticed that the clouds were really gloomy and there was ice in the Hudson River. The ice was slowly floating down stream as bits of snowflakes were flurrying around everywhere making his view obscure. Enjoying it to some degree, he put out his tongue to catch one of the flakes as he stood there behind the crate after he landed.

Remembering the goal at hand, Tom peeked around a corner to not be seen. And then he thought about how this place might have so many people working in it that he probably didn't need to act suspicious. Walking around, he saw many people carrying crates of fish and other sea creatures to loading trucks, and to and fro boats. Then, he started asking different people if they had seen anybody that fit Justin or Sacra's description. Sadly, nobody really recognized who he was talking about.

For two hours, Tom ventured around trying to get some results. He quickly got bored since he wasn't getting anywhere. Thinking he would ask for descriptions, wasn't working so he asked one guy, "You have any idea where somebody might go if they wanted to catch a boat out of the country?"

The guy responded, "If somebody wants to catch a boat headed out of the country it would probably be best to sneak onto a cargo night ship that might be involved with crime. Partly because transporting people that were not part of the crews would be illegal, which usually doesn't happen during the day."

"Thanks for the info. I'm surprised I didn't think of that myself. Still I am more usually into science stuff than these kinds of topics. Again, thank you."

"You're welcome. I've got to get back to work. See ya kid."

Tom thought he would come back during the night time to find criminals by the docks since they wouldn't be hanging around there in the day light. Then he walked back to the obscure place behind the corner of crates and he flew away and landed on one of the skyscrapers deeper in the city. Landing there he looked around, trying to listen for sirens or anything that would indicate somebody needing help with something gone wrong.

The wind blew strong as Tom sat there. He loved the feeling of being up there high on the building where he could sit and relax while watching everywhere. He enjoyed not having to focus on watching where he was flying. He just soaked up the beauty of the scenery surrounding him, when all of sudden off in the distance he could hear a siren. He got up and looking closer from where the sound was coming from, he saw cops rushing down the streets driving fast towards the building where he was standing, and then he saw one of their turn signals come on.

Tom knew what he had to do. So he dove off the top of the building, falling at a fast speed down the side of the building then curving into a better flying position about three stories above the police cars, and followed them down the road. Whenever the policeman would turn, so would Tom, till they made a few turns coming to a halt on a corner surrounding another skyscraper. He just made sure he stayed high enough so they wouldn't see him.

Tom hovered there as he observed what was happening, but wondered how he could step in and help them. Below, in the bank, there were guys who had already got tons of cash into bags. They placed bombs all over the place. The robbers got behind the counter with all the hostages, but as soon as police started closing in on the bank doors the robber holding the trigger pulled it. Then, all the bombs exploded forcing the police off their feet falling backwards. This also, made the whole building rattle, causing the windows to explode as glass shattered. Fire and debris flew everywhere as the criminals ran with the money they had stolen. They went out a broken window and rushed to get into a car that was parked outside of the police circle speeding up to escape.

Tom heard screaming from above as he saw a man falling down the side of the building, which looked like a window cleaning person. Tom knew how physics worked. Trying to catch him at the rate he was falling in mid-air would make it probable that if they collided, one of them or both would be severely injured. So, Tom had to think fast. The first thing that came to his mind was a word he knew.

Tom quickly said "Cunctatio that window cleaner from falling so fast." The window cleaner slowed down as he was falling down, slow enough that he positioned himself to land on his feet.

Tom had already flown off, chasing the cops and the criminals by the time the guy safely landed. He was going pretty fast trying to catch up with them. Speeding through the city, the criminals kept looking out the side of the window trying to shoot the cops.

In hot pursuit on their tails, Tom caught up to the criminals. He quickly did a flip turn as he landed vertically on the hood of their car. The look on the criminal's faces was priceless. They were scared out of their minds when they saw this random teenage boy land on their car. Of course he just stood there smirking at them.

The bank robbers realized they must stop him, so they pulled out their guns and tried shooting. Luckily, they missed but shattered the glass in the process.

Tom looked at the guns they had and said, "Ventus the guns towards me." The guns flew out of their hands straight into his hands.

Tom bent over sideways on the side of the car shooting the tire below him. The robbers freaked out slamming on the breaks making them drive off the road, crashing into some trash cans. While that happened, Tom lost his grip with standing on the car and got flung off, spinning and dropping the guns he was holding. Then he stabled himself and landed on the ground.

The criminals hopped out of the car and came running up to attack Tom. The sirens in the distance were getting closer to them very quickly. A few of them threw punches at him, but he put his arms up in a guard position to keep them from attacking him. They came rushing again and then he round-house kicked one of them.

Tom shouted "Extollo!" Then the other one coming after him flew at a garbage can knocking it over.

The criminals stumbled on the ground but were trying to get back up to come attack Tom again. They were trying to run over to grab their guns when the police showed up.

The police officers yelled, "Freeze!" The bank robbers put their hands up in the air, but Tom quickly flew off so he wouldn't have to be identified.

Tom was amazed how he managed to do what he just did. He felt like he finally was using his abilities to do something good for the world and not just for himself. He decided to go into the park to avoid attention from the police once he landed in an alley nearby.

At first he was casually jogging into the park and then off in the distance he heard a woman yell, "Somebody stop that man. He stole my purse!"

Tom saw the agile thief running very quickly down the pathway in the green social hub. So he took off running. Then he flew off the ground going up a little above the tree lines. Pursuing the thief, he dove down in a curve, picking up the man who had stolen the woman's purse. Then he wittingly said while holding the thief,

"What's the matter; they don't let men like you buy purses at the store?"

The man screamed in terror as Tom held onto him, and then he dropped him on the pathway. The thief hit the ground dropping the purse. Tom said to the man pointing his finger down at him, "If you try to steal anything again from anybody again, I will personally be there to fly you to the cops. You got that?" He picked up the purse, then he walked back over to the lady it belonged to giving it back to her. The thief squirmed, getting up off the ground and ran off in terror at what had just happened.

Tom was getting a little tired from all his running around and he was getting really hungry. He noticed a restaurant outside the park that looked like a nice pizzeria. So he headed over there with what little energy he had left since most of it was drained from all the activity. As he was about to walk into the pizza place he saw a little girl past the restaurant standing there staring up the alley way. He wondered what she was staring at, so he walked a little further to see.

Once Tom arrived, he saw she was staring at a kitten on a ledge of a building at the end of the alley way. He said to the little girl, "Why you staring at that cat?"

"Because he is my little kitty cat, Flash"

"Flash, huh…funny name for a kitten that is just standing there."

"Flash got up there really fast. But once he realized how high he was, well he decided to stand there in fear of falling."

"I doubt he is scared. He probably just see's something he wants to reach but can't because he can only jump and climb so far. I used to have a cat like that who would just stare at something she couldn't reach and meow all the time."

"Well, can you please find a way to get him down; I don't want him to get hurt?"

"Yeah, sure I will help get Flash down, but you can't tell anybody how I did that okay?"

"Okay, thank you."

Tom flew off then went up to the ledge and brought Flash down back to the little girl.

She said to Tom, "Wow, thanks for getting Flash down. Someday I need to learn how to fly."

Tom chuckled while saying, "You're welcome. Just try to keep him from going places like that in the future so he is not ever stuck or hurt."

Tom walked away from the little girl into the restaurant sitting down and ordered himself a Stromboli for lunch. While he waited there for his food, he noticed the little girl walking in with Flash in her arms.

As she walked up to the chef, he said to her, "Rosita, how many times do I have to tell you not to bring Flash into the main way where all the customers can see him."

"Sorry daddy, I just wanted to tell you that boy over there helped me get Flash down off a ledge." She said pointing at Tom. As soon as he heard her say that he sort of cringed while swallowing some of his drink down the wrong pipe coughing some.

"He did, did he? Well, maybe I should go show my appreciation."

Rosita along with her father walked over to Tom, to talk to him as Tom got really nervous. The chef said, "Hello young man. Thank you for getting my daughter's kitten off that ledge for her."

"Oh, it was no big deal. Just helping out."

"Still, I am very grateful for your actions and my name is Angelo Leone."

"Nice to meet you. My name is Thomas."

"Well Thomas, if you ever need help with something, such as a job, I may have some room for more waiters, or even bus boys in here."

"Thank you, Angelo; if I need one I will remember your offer." Angelo went back to cooking while Rosita took Flash upstairs to their home.

Tom waited for his food and eventually Angelo brought it out to him. He ate it loving every bite since it tasted so magnifico. He was now feeling refreshed from lunch and decided to head back into the city to find crime to prevent. Working hard to help others he spent the rest of the day helping people in different kinds of ways, making a change in the world that day.

Landing in Russia near the Caucasus Mountains, Agent Dale was on a mission of his own to find out who was the puppet master behind Director Ford. Along with Agent Myers and Steven O'Brian to help him, the place they were heading was well hidden from the general public. They weren't taking any chances of getting themselves into too much trouble.

Getting in their CIA appointed car, the team headed out towards the coordinates they had pinpointed hoping to find some decent connections to Director Ford. It was pretty sunny there and yet somehow very cold from Steven's view. "Don't worry, we won't be here too long since Me and Agent Myers need to get back to America soon." Agent Dale responded.

"Well, how much further is this place from where we landed in Sukhumi?"

Agent Myers responded, "It should be about two hours to the nearest road according to our ELO coordinates."

"Did you just crunch those numbers onto your ELO PSI's?"

"Yeah, of course I did. Why?"

"Because I found some encrypted data mining software on the ELO mainframe database that take notes anytime somebody checks these coordinates. Lucky for the two of you though, I took it out of there so they wouldn't know anybody was searching for directions of where we are going."

"Man, these people really are uptight about this place. Do you really think the three of us will be enough if they have armed men guarding it?" Agent Dale asked concerned about the state of the situation.

Agent Myers responded, "I don't know Agent Sizer. This place seems so hidden that using data packets from another part of the world for their images and keeping such a tight lid on it, I would assume that they wouldn't put up much security to keep it from the public because that would attract way too much attention."

"You're probably right. Let's just hope you are. Anybody want to listen to some music?" Agent Dale concluded.

Driving together for the next two hours they listened to music and enjoyed the scenery, while they anticipated the situation to come. Reaching the spot on their coordinates, they stopped the car and got out for a minute, taking note of how there wasn't a public road to turn right on. There was just a dirt road without a name sign and hardly any tracks that led through the grass of the main road onto the dirt road. This implied nobody ever really traveled down this road. Seeing a yellow sign, Agent Myers asked, "Do you think we really should head down this road it shows a radioactive sign?"

Agent Dale, annoyed with this attempted setback, said, "No, we are going to keep pressing on. Obviously they want people to think this road leads to something dangerous, but look at my APpen with its Geiger counter feature; it shows nothing wrong with the area."

"You better be right. I don't have the salary to pay for cancer treatment like Director Ford did for Serzynkov's wife. Speaking of which, Nikolay is now with his wife in Tenerife and cured of his cancer because of the case we busted on Ford."

"That's good, but we should keep going and see if this road leads us to our destination. Agent Myer's you use your APpen to make sure we don't have any radioactivity as we head down this road." Agent Dale said getting back in the car driving off quickly down the road.

For the next ten miles it was nothing but lots of dirt and tree's on a flattened part of the lower parts of a giant mountain. The road was quite bumpy and enduring, possibly from rain in the summer time. This place, from all appearances, never saw the light of day to be modernized or built up to have decent roads to travel on. Coming out of a continuous trail of condensed trees, they found something that definitely wasn't natural.

On their right was an opening of tree lines that had been cut down, revealing down at the bottom of the mountain side the Gvandra River. To the left stood a weird flight of steps eight blocks wide or six wide, with two on each end and three high. Climbing up the giant blocks, they found that every block had one with a three block high on each end. So they pressed on further till they had climbed a totall of six blocks, reaching a giant hexagon shaped platform with six giant pillars aligned with the axis points of the hexagon.

Looking around in amazement, Steven said, "Who do you guys think built this place? Everything here is ginormous."

"I don't know, but I have a feeling they were pretty big. Some of these blocks are bigger than the ones of the pyramids and the craftsmanship of the pillars are astounding." Agent Dale said.

With intrigue in her voice, Agent Myers said, "Still come look over here guys. There is a giant door or some sort of rock slab."

Walking over the bits of grass popping up through the ancient blocks and avoiding vines, Agent Dale and Steven went behind the pillars to see the strange looking door or slab Agent Myers referenced. It was as wide as the whole platform on which they stood. In the center near the middle was a hexagon indented into the walls with six holes the size of an average man's hand at each of its open access points and a circle around it.

Very perplexed by the structure, Steven asked, "Is this place some kind of ancient temple or some kind of living facility?"

Agent Dale responded, "I don't know, but it might relate to the whole conspiracy we found out about involving giant bones. What do you think, Agent Myers?"

"I think it's pretty obvious it has to do with those bones. The only question that comes to my mind is how long ago did those giants live and did they originally build this place?" she said.

"I don't know, but we can come back with an archeology team that we personally hire to make sure we don't have some government alert concerning whoever was trying to hide this place." Agent Dale responded.

"I don't think you need to worry about that too much now that Director Ford is dead. Still precaution would be wise." Agent Myers said.

Mystified by the strangeness of this place, Agent Dale said, "Here guys, help me grab some big logs so we can see if we can turn the hexagon in the center. This might be the way to open it."

Together they put the big logs into three of the holes trying to turn it. Sadly and to no avail, they weren't able to get it to bulge one bit. Agent Dale was getting really annoyed they had come all this way just to be blocked by a giant stone door. "What mysteries lay beyond this thing?" He thought to himself.

Very angry by their shortcomings, Agent Dale said, "Come on guys, we need to get back to America, and we will figure this place out once we send an archeology crew to investigate it."

For the past couple of weeks Tom had endured many adventures. Saving the city and visiting Myles for therapy, but now Christmas had arrived. John was visiting Tom and his parents, with Jessica, Robbie and Joshua; they were all having a great time being able to spend time as a family after being separated for so long. That night their mom made them a wonderful roast beef with carrots, potatoes, and onions in her gator kettle.

Getting out of bed, Tom headed up to the roof top to meet up with Todd for a special event he had planned. To honor Martin's memory he planned on helping others be healed that were on their death beds in hospitals across New York City. Gliding over towards him, Todd asked, "Tom do you really think this is a wise idea to do considering some kids are naughty and some are good? There is no telling which is which since you don't know any of them."

"Todd, everybody in the world has moments when they are bad and everyone has moments when they are good. But any person could use a lift in spirits, especially during Christmas. I am not doing this just to give people blessings, but to save some lives from certain death."

"Well, if it's their time, then it's their time. Who are you to decide when others should live and when they should die?"

"Yeah true, but I have a gift and if it can help others. Who is to say I have not been given this gift to help others and be that miracle in their life to let them live longer?"

"Fine Tom, I get it. You want to help others out. What a nice cliché for Christmas time."

"Oh, come on Todd, don't mock me for trying to be a force for good to give others some hope."

"Sometimes forces of good present themselves one way and you don't know if you're messing with things you shouldn't. Sometimes they end up being a force for darkness in another way."

"How could healing those on the brink of death be a bad thing?"

"Think of it like this, maybe if you make them live when they were supposed to die they could end up dying of a worse fate then the one that was handed to them in the first place?"

Annoyed by his logic, Tom responded scoffing, "Whatever Todd. You might have a point there, but in the end we all die; so if they get longer to live then they may look at things differently in life since they were so close to dying and their illness was taken from them."

Debating these thoughts the whole way there, they flew from the roof top to an alley-way nearest the hospital where they were headed. Telling Todd to stay in the alley to wait for him, he headed in through the main doorway. Looking around for signs, he found the one that led to the room for terminally ill children. Coming out of the elevator on the seventh floor Tom tried opening the door to the room the kids were being kept in, but it was locked.

Then Tom said, "Allow me to Permeo these walls so that I may Sano the children in them." He put his hand up to the door knob and tried to grab it, but his hand went right through it. Knowing his words worked, he walked through the door into the room full of kids laying there on their death beds. He walked up to one of the bed sides noticing one was going to die from leukemia, another from cancer and then there was a boy who had lymphoma.

Tom walked up to each one with their issues saying, "Sano this child that they may live long and blessed."

Once they all looked better, Tom headed back out the door then down the hallway to the elevator, and headed up to the eleventh floor where the ICU was for people in severe accidents. To avoid the nurses and problems he ran through the walls from room to room where he healed the people in there from injuries they had gotten from tough accidents. One guy was in a car wreck; another couple was from the same accident, the couple was not injured as badly, but could use some healing. Then there was somebody who was in a fire who looked very deformed and needed healing emotionally as well physically. A bald guy got pushed out of a window and had a broken spine that needed healing, as well.

Tom understood that everyone needed the healing in this place. Then he went back down to the first floor after taking care of everyone in ICU. Noticing lots of people with common illnesses he then said under his breath, "Sano all these people of their ailments even if they are small ones."

All the people there seemed to start looking like they were feeling better. The coughing stopped, the runny noses stopped and everything that was sick about them seemed like it was getting better. Together, going all over the city, Tom and Todd went from place to place. Going to clinics and hospitals helping all kinds of people, Todd would wait for Tom to do his thing to help not attract too much attention.

Occasionally, Tom would have to stop a criminal or two from doing something. Even on Christmas crime didn't cease to exist in the big city. So he tried his best to help people during what some would consider a miserable time of year. His actions made quite a bit of those peoples Christmas holiday all the more special to them.

In one hospital, Tom healed a woman of breast cancer who then later decided not to get an abortion since she was going to live. Then there was a young man who had a disease that was bound to cause death to him. But once he found out that it was gone from him he swore to better his life and not cause himself any way of getting that disease again. He was certain he was responsible for getting it in the first place.

So, Tom was playing Mr. Healer for lots of people everywhere and eventually he had checked out every hospital he could find in the area. So it was time for his next part of his plan.

Tom went on top of a tall building and yelled with a shout "Amplifico my beo to everyone that they might have something vocoed to them that is not against any morals or evil in any way."

Tom didn't know yet if this had totally worked, but he was sure he would find out the next morning. Then he thought about how a week prior, he learned about the possibility that drug dealers and crime lords shipped their stuff out of a certain port at the dock on this night of the week.

So, now it was time for part three of his plan for the night, to find info on where Justin was headed through the crime lords at the docks. Tom and Todd flew over to the docks and now Todd's purpose in coming with Tom was clear. (He went with Tom to help him out if there was any trouble). Once they landed there he told Todd to watch from above while he tried to talk to them about info where their shipment was headed a few weeks prior. This may have been around the time Justin snagged a ride. As soon as he walked up to the dock number he had found out about the men were being really aggressive and were letting him know quickly this was not his place to be.

Tom held up his hands asking calmly and nicely, "Sorry to intrude on your business. But have any of you seen a tall bulgy dude that got a ride with a tall tanner-looking kid a couple weeks ago on one of your boats?"

A somewhat scrawny looking guy with a Brooklyn accent said, "What's it to you, kid?!"

"I just want to find him so I can resolve my issues with him."

"Well, we don't sell out our people that easily, boy."

Then one of the darker guys with a gun yelled, "Yo dog, you better scram before we have to dispose of your body!"

"Hey, I don't want trouble."

"Well kid, you sure have a funny way of not wanting trouble and coming directly into it."

Then the darker one pulled the trigger pointing it towards the ground trying to scare Tom. He could tell this was not going to be easy to get the info from them. He thought he was going to have to figure things out more elaborately. They threatened some more, so he ran off fast so he wasn't slaughtered right then and there. Flying back to the hotel, Tom and Todd discussed what a close call all of that was.

Once inside, Tom was really tired. He figured he should get some rest before the morning. He went to bed so he could wake up having a wonderful Christmas morning. Laying in bed, drifting off to sleep, he began to think about all the people he helped that night. He wondered how he could find a way to get that info from the crime lords at the docks.

The Near Future
Friday, December 25th, 7:36 A.M.
Agent Dale's temporary home, Hoboken, New Jersey

Hearing his son Daniel run down the stairs really fast, Agent Dale told himself it was time to get out of bed. Full of warmth from seeing his son so happy and from the fire, Agent Dale made some hot chocolate with marshmallows and whipped cream for himself, his wife, and his little boy. Walking into the kitchen with their morning snack, he admired seeing Kathryne holding their daughter, Jackie.

Tugging on his robe after he gave everyone their cup of cocoa, Daniel screamed with excitement, "Daddy! Daddy! When are we going to open presents?!"

"After we open our stockings." Agent Dale said, smiling at his son.

Rushing over to the fire place, his son grabbed the stockings and carried them over to everyone to look in, and see what they got. Agent Dale had quite a few nice things. He had a gift card for skylinking new music, some candy, and some nice shaving razors. His wife had some nice chocolates, roses, and a really nice surprise; a new diamond ring. Daniel, of course, had lots of candy, a few cheap toys, and a gift card to skylink him a new game for his Z-triad.

"So Danny, what would you rather do first? Go play in the snow outside or open presents?" Agent Dale asked his son.

"Are you kidding, open gifts, of course."

"Now hold on Daniel. Don't just go ripping them all open. Let's take turns opening them." Kathryne said, trying to not let the moment pass too quickly.

So for quite a while they sat there opening each their gifts to one another. "Who's this one from, Dale?" Kathryne said looking at one to Daniel with no tag on it. Handing the gift to him, Dale said, "I don't know. But we each got one with no name of who it was from?" Each of them opened their mystery gifts, Agent Dale got a new tie, Kathryne got some pink slippers to wear around the house and keep her feet cozy, and Daniel got a basketball.

"I wonder where those came from?" Agent Dale asked aloud and puzzled.

"I don't know, but why don't you show Danny his best gift we have been saving for last."

Excited, Daniel gasped wondering what he was about to get. Then Agent Dale walked in from the garage with a brand new crimson red bicycle. Boy was his son ecstatic with joy at the site of this. "Oh, thank you Daddy! Thank you, Mommy! This is the best Christmas ever!"

"Now son, you are going to need to wear your new helmet and pads when its iced over like this and even when it's not icy. You got that?"

"Yes Sir."

"Now, how about we go give that thing a test run and also play in the snow?"

"Definitely." Daniel replied.

After playing around for a while outside in the nice luxurious snow and watching his son ride his new bike, Agent Dale went back inside drained of energy, but really happy he was having such quality time with his son. Walking inside and very tired from all the fun, his wife walked up to him holding an envelope saying, "Hey honey, I forgot to tell you this came in the mail on Wednesday for you."

"Oh okay, thanks." Agent Dale said.

Opening it up didn't say much, yet it's message was very clear. It read saying, "If you want to know about the Ruins meet me in Prabhu, Nepal by the clock tower in the town center on January 8th at 9:00 PM. Travel here very discreetly to make things less complicated."

◇ ◇ △ ५ ⩚

Getting out of bed, somewhat excited, looking out the window at the snow outside the hotel, Tom ran into the living room. Seeing all the gifts under the tree was really making him energetic about it all. He ran over to John with enthusiasm waking him up, and then they had some breakfast with hot chocolate. Their parents woke up and then he went to get Jessica, Robbie and Joshua from the room they were staying in. Once they came over to the Turner's room they all exchanged gifts with each other. They loved what each of them had been blessed with.

Tom noticed on the TV while the news was playing that lots of people all over the world were calling in, surprised about receiving gifts in their family's that nobody had gotten for one another and they didn't say from Santa, either. So, where did all these random gifts come from? Once he saw and heard that info on the news, he smirked about it because he knew that his big plan he worked so hard on of bringing lots of happiness to people, actually got accomplished.

In each of their own ways, Tom had many blessings for Christmas, and Agent Dale himself had some unexpected blessings. So, even though their family had so much happen to them the past couple months, at least for one day it felt as though all the troubles in the world seemed to cease to bother them at all as they had a Merry Christmas. Tom still had a ways to go to find Justin and resolve his problems with him in an adult manor. At least he was one step closer. For the next couple of months things surely were going to change for him and the people in his life.

Chapter 23
What Memories May Come

The Near Future
Friday, January 01ˢᵗ, 12:01 A.M.
Time Square, New York, New York

Standing in the icy heart of New York City on one of the most crowded nights of all of the year, Tom looked down from the cold roof top of a building and watched all the people below him enjoying each other's company right after the ball dropped. Some were kissing; some were holding hands, and others talking friendly to random people. Even though they may have been strangers to one another, to them it was a night that didn't matter who you were; you could still be friends.

When Tom saw all these people that were filled with excitement making lots of noise and celebrating the beginning of a new year filled with lots of opportunities in life, he didn't quite feel that optimistic. Feeling responsible for alienating some of the people that mattered most to him, he thought he should start things anew instead of dwelling on the past so much. "This year I am going to be more responsible with my abilities and every aspect of my life to become a more independent man so that I might not make the same mistakes I have in the past. I will not let my past define me, but shall strive to make a better future for anybody I know or meet." He said to himself standing on the snow flurrying roof top.

The Near Future
Friday, January 08th, 12:11 P.M.
Angelo's Pizzeria, Manhattan, New York

Sitting down, Tom savored the Stromboli he always liked to eat when he came to this particular restaurant. He had other plans though as to why he was here today. Besides getting some food to feel full, he grabbed his glass of Orange Cayan soda and said to Angelo from a distance, "Hey Angelo, can you come here for a moment? I have something important I want to ask you."

"Sure, be right there." Walking up to Tom, Angelo asked, "What do you need?"

Speaking calmly Tom asked, "I was wondering if I could take you up on the offer you made when I met you."

"What did you have in mind, Thomas?"

"This year I want to be doing more responsible things. So I was wondering if I could possibly get an after school job here."

"Well, I am glad you finally came around."

"What?"

"When I told you that, it was my way of saying I wanted to hire you. I did mention we needed waiters and bus boys"

Tom chuckled saying, "Well, looks like you got what you wanted."

"Yes, I sure did. So, when can you start start?"

"I would like to start Monday after school."

"Good. Can't wait for it."

△ ㄴ > ▽ ◇ ㄴ ⨺

Sitting in front of the clock tower, Agent Dale looked around noticing all the guards in front of the holy palace. None of them looked like they were cold from the freezing weather like he was. Having left his hollowatch phone back home with Kathryne, he wondered if he had made the right decision coming alone using long bus rides all the way from Korea. Even with the cold damp winter air, it didn't stop him from smelling the unusual scent of tiger lilies everywhere in this city.

After having waited quite a while, the hour was upon him that he had traveled so long and so far for. Agent Dale definitely wasn't taking any risk coming alone, though. He kept his gun locked & loaded ready to defend himself if anybody should try to attack him. Out of the shadows of a nearby alleyway, a stubby Indian looking man immerged walking towards him.

Sitting down next to him the man said, "I presume you came alone?"

"Yes, you are right. Still, how did you even know I was looking into it?"

"I have my ways…as well your searches on the skylink for archeology teams are available for anybody's viewing if they have the resources and authoritative power."

"So, what is that place? Is it a temple of some kind or something?"

"Agent Sizer, let me tell you a little story of two temples. You see those guards over there not minding the cold like you obviously do?"

"Yeah, what about them?"

"Do you know how this palace or "temple" came to be?"

"Not really?"

"Well in the early twenty first century there was a man here from Nepal, his name was Prabesh. He didn't lead a very great life, but after getting saved by some Christian missionaries, he made it his life ambition to make Nepal a Christian nation. And eventually he did. When he finished, he had this palace built for God. It had become such a public spectacle everyone knew about it and it was all over the news, not a soul who liked to travel didn't know about this place. Of course this made many enemies. Like those of the kafir dunya brotherhood, which is why they have all these guards here protecting it."

"Okay, that's one temple. Now what about the one you know I'm more interested in?"

"The other temple…made long ago has its own purpose and honestly I don't know if my associates would appreciate me telling you the story behind it, or what it is meant for. Still, that temple was made long ago, only five others and I within this small community know its location. One of the men decided to tell his best friend about the location. He went there after stealing his key taking a bone from it to let the scientific community study the bones placed in the temple. The man who didn't protect the secret and the key, as you know him, is now dead. All from his own destruction of a bomb he put on his own chest."

"Wait…Sacra Asrar's father was part of your little group?"

"Yes, but that is beside the point. My point is one temple was built for the world to see and the temple you found wasn't meant to be known by many people. If it attracted too much attention then people would flock to it and be confused by what they found. As you can tell, we are willing to punish anybody who tries to reveal it to the world, even if it's one of our own members who might have accidentally revealed it."

"Why don't you just tell me then, what is so important about this place or tell me how to get in?"

"Because I don't have the authority to let you know what's so important about that place. It is a decision we have to make together to tell you. Still, I can give you a key to the temple."

"Alright, well let me see this place for myself."

"I must warn you though, once you open the door you can never turn back from what you will see and your destiny will be in place. You will no longer be able to choose what kind of life you want to live and you will live in service with dedication to our group's intentions. This is a very serious matter and I suggest you mediate on it for a long time before you make your decision. As well, you cannot take anybody with you if you decide to open the door." The Indian man said pulling a giant egg like cone-shaped crystal from a hand bag he had with him.

"What is that thing?" Agent Dale retorted.

"Agent Sizer, this is the key to the door, even if you had an archeological team try to open it, it wouldn't have mattered because you need one of these to open it. It's been claimed in the past that you need all six of them to open it, but as long as you have one and put it in the top center hole you will be good."

"Was this Director Ford's key?"

"No, he was nothing more than one of our many acolytes and he never had access to the inside of the temple except when we initiated him. This key belonged to Mr. Asrar, who couldn't even keep the place hidden from his own best friend as we already discussed before. Their village knew of the bones, but not the temple nearby that hid them."

"So who designed these keys, and why are they so odd?"

"That is info I am not permitted to tell you. Some answers may or may not be found in this life."

"Who are you guys?"

"We work in the shadows. Who we are is not of importance, only what we do and who we serve is what matters. The general public can never know what we do, for they would not understand it."

"If I am to open the door and be stuck, not able to live how I want to, is that supposed to mean I don't have any choice at all in the matter? How could you even control me, is the bigger question?

"Again these are things I cannot tell you. Just ponder your decision. If you want to open the door or not. Remember the importance of what you finally choose, for if you open it everything you know will change."

The stubby Indian man got up and walked off as he handed Agent Dale the strange key. Agent Dale sat there in the cold, wondering if he should or shouldn't open that door. He had come so far, but what memories might come for him if he committed to such a strange group that was willing to capture innocent people for some secret they themselves hid for many generations.

The Near Future
Monday, February 08th, 02:14 P.M.
Imperial Republic Bank, Sixth Avenue & 42nd street, Manhattan,
New York

Hoping this rescue would end quickly as Tom had to be at work no later than 4:09 just like on his first day working; Tom looked down and saw bank robbers hurrying out of the building, holding a gun to a woman's head and others carrying bags of money. As the robbers shoved the lady into their car, Tom thought about how this was going to be a much trickier scenario than that time he stopped a robbery because these guys had a female hostage. Zooming off fast and pursuing the robbers, he flew behind their car as the cops chased them, as well.

Catching up to the robbers, Tom flew by the window and noticed how the criminal still had a gun to her head. Landing gently on the roof of the car trying not to attract too much attention, he said, "Inflecto the woman in this car up here with me."

All of a sudden the lady in the car flashed before the robber's eyes as she vanished and emerged on the roof with Tom. Quickly, he grabbed her by the arm as she lost her balance, keeping her from falling off at high speeds. Then he said, "Please mam, put your feet on mine and grab my waist."

Looking confused and puzzled, she did as Tom said and grabbed his waist and stepped on his toes. Trying to get her to safety, Tom hovered away from the car over the highway landing on the side of the expressway by the side-walk. Then he flew off quickly doing an arch flip vertically down in front of the oncoming robber's car.

With a stern look on his face, Tom quickly yelled, "Consisto this car!" The car came to a screeching halt. Then as the robbers got out, he quickly said, "Ventus their guns to me."

The guns flew out of their hands and into Tom's hand, so he quickly threw them behind him. Two of the robbers came running at him as he put out his hand yelling, "Expello!"

They were flung into the car, but were in too much pain to get back up. Then, Tom noticed one of the three was the guy who requested his gang leader, Ricky, to get his memory back.

Tom said in a snarky manner, "So what happened to your pal Ricky. Die in a bank Robbery?"

"No he quit at being a gang leader after he got his memory back. Then he decided to go live what he called a "better life"."

"Good for him, looks like he learned his lesson. You, I am not so sure about."

"Dude, I've got to make a living somehow and nobody will hire me here."

"There are lots of ways to make money in this world and doing crime is the worst way to get money."

"Yeah, well, you don't know how hard it is."

"You're right. I don't know how hard it is for you, but you always have room for improvement, no matter who you are."

"Crap, the cops are almost here!"

"Well I need to know something. Do you know who ran the boat that that Justin guy you knew briefly got on?"

"Yeah. Are you kidding me! That smuggling cargo ship is run by Crazy Cokey or Crazy Cokehead and some people refer to him as Aaron Patel, the most powerful Crime Lord in New York City."

"What kind of Crazy names are those?"

"In the drug community, nobody goes by their real name, so they make up nicknames for each other so the cops will never know their real names."

"How did you know his real name was Aaron Patel, then?"

"Apparently, that Justin guy you were looking for, knows him by his real name and even referred to him as that a few times."

"Would you know how I can get on his good side to get info from him?"

"You could try to get on the inside with his business, but that may not work since most of the time he is uptight about letting new people in on his supply. And he is the one that normally brings people to his inner circle."

"Mmm…interesting. We shall see if that info is of any use to me."

"Please, don't let me be caught by the cops. I just want to go home to Texas."

"Fine, if that's how you want it, inflecto this man back to his home in Texas."

As the young man who had made plenty of bad decisions disappeared, Tom flew off and continued with his day and got ready for work. But contemplating over what use the info he got would be to him in finding Justin, so he continued taking care of crime as much as he could till it was time to get going to work.

The Near Future
Saturday, March 20th, 01:02 P.M.
The Turner's apartment, Hoboken, New Jersey

Winter had long passed for Tom's family and the people in his life. Many great things had happened for him over the transition of seasons. It was looking as though the skies were blue again as he took note of the beauty outside the hotel seeing flowers blossoming and gorgeous scenery as spring was in full motion near the end of March.

After reminiscing on all these things that had happened to him over the past few months, Tom flipped the eggs in the skillet and remembered he was cooking breakfast. Sitting down and turning the entertainment center on he began to enjoy his late breakfast of eggs, bacon, and toast as he watched the news. He loved eggs, even though John gagged at the smell of them cooking. Like any human, he had his own taste for certain foods. All humans are unique, having their own desires individually and sometimes being the same as others. Watching the news he saw something that he had been long awaiting. The head line read, "Who is New York City's Mystery Hero?"

Tom was amazed he was finally being noticed by the Media. He listened to the TV and heared what their view was about him. The reporter said, "Who is this Mysterious young man that has been helping people out in many different ways the past couple of months? Well we are about to get some insight into this strange hero helping the Big Apple. Here, we have a few witnesses who have met him personally."

Then the setting changed to a recorded video of interviews. The first one started saying, "So have you met the Mystery Hero of New York?"

"Yeah, I met him. He saved my daughter in a burning building and got her out."

Then another person appeared on screen. This time it was a guy wearing a snazzy business suit and the reporter asked, "So, what has the Mystery Hero done for you?"

"Well, a man with beat up crappie looking clothing ran off with my briefcase, while I was on my way to work, when a boy with brown hair and blue eyes came down from the sky and punched the thief off their feet, and grabbed my suit-case and then he flew back over to me bringing me back my suitcase."

"Hold it. Did you just say he came out of the sky and flew over to you? What is with all the emphasis on what the people in your story look like?"

"Yes, he was flying; you think I would make that up! As well the thief obviously had no taste in fashion and the boy had a very noticeable look to him."

Tom chuckled at the reporter's questioning about why he was so specific. For the next few minutes they showed different people expressing the deeds he had done for them. "Obviously, the criminals are not happy about this hero, but we are sure he will keep helping out those who need it." The Reporter said as the segment ended.

Then, Tom heard a knock on the door as he was learning what the big city thought of him. Walking over from the kitchen and opening the door he found Agent Dale ready to go and visit Myles for another therapy session. So, they headed out and did their routine for getting to Myles office. Once there Agent Dale left him alone with Myles as usual.

Sitting down, the two of them had an interesting discussion. They started off discussing Tom's heroics that were talked about on the news. After talking for a while, Myles asked, "So Tom, all in all, how would you say mentioning Martin affects you now?"

"Well, it's not as bad as it was months ago, that's for certain. Now his name doesn't even faze me, or somebody mentioning a dead relative doesn't make me get down thinking about him."

"Wow, Tom, this seems like a whole lot of progress in your development."

"Do you really think so?"

"You certainly have changed a lot mood-wise from when I first met you. I have noticed your confidence seems to have increased exponentially."

"I agree. I think it's because I finally see how I need to take care of myself and be responsible with the things I do if I don't want to hurt anybody in the process."

"That does sound like a very good idea."

"So, how does Dan like his new home?"

"Oh, he finds it to be totally different from how he used to live, that's for sure."

"So, what therapy discussions are we going to have now since I have gotten over Martin's death sort of?"

"Well, you seemed to have done so well the past three months I don't think you really need my therapy anymore. To be honest, it's because you seem to be able to handle anything emotional on your own now."

"So is this like "goodbye" or something?"

"Sort of. But who knows, how our roads will cross again?"

"So true…life does have a funny way of presenting random encounters with people you haven't seen in a while."

"Yeah, you are right. It's been great knowing you and seeing you progress into such a wonderful person, Tom, I guess this is goodbye for now."

"Goodbye Myles, thanks for being here for me."

"You're welcome."

Arriving at the car, Tom got in and told Agent Dale how he needed to take care of some crime now that his session was over. Agent Dale laughed, saying, "Man, Tom, don't you ever want a break from these criminals and all the crime you deal with?"

"Sorry, but crime doesn't sleep. I won't stop fighting till all the criminals in the city are scared of me." Tom said getting out of the car. Over the past month he had started devising and setting into motion a plan to get on Crazy Cokey aka Aaron Patel's good side.

So, after saying goodbye to Agent Dale, Tom got out of the car and started flying off to another part of the city to continue with his plan. Landing in the back alley where people would come for a supply of drugs that he would pretend to sell, he vocoed some of the stuff he needed for his scheme.

Tom reminisced on how he had been doing this gimmick in the back alley for a while. He remembered how he thought he should be clever and not give them any real drugs because he had been raised knowing that drugs were bad. He had been raised in an old fashioned life-style. He also knew the scientific effects they could have on him or anybody who used them. This was one of the prime reasons he never used them. Still, he was being ignorant of the repercussions and would voco in some crushed mint to give to any customers.

Clearly, Tom had not thought it through fully about what would happen if ever anybody noticed he wasn't giving them the real stuff. So, there were a few times he would have a customer go away angry getting mad as they sampled his stuff and noticing it wasn't what they were looking for.

Tom figured eventually, this would be a flaw. So he came up with a story about how he was smart and made a new drug that was hidden with the smell of mint so cops wouldn't catch on. Luckily, for him, some criminals and addicts were so desperate for a fix they were easy to fool and believed him. If they didn't believe him he even told them how to try out his stuff by sniffing the powdery mint which he referred to as mintified molly. From his knowledge, molly is what a drug dealer would refer to as pure ecstasy. The customers would sniff it or taste it, getting a tingle, so they fell for it and thought it might actually be real molly. But others, not so much because they expected more, so they would not buy it.

Tom thought he wasn't harming anybody by giving them mint, but boy did he not know the effects he was having on some people. Whether they were good effects or bad effects remained to be seen from those people individually.

Tom stood there as he thought about this. Then, some people came around the corner in a group. He said to them as they walked up in a gangster character like-voice. "Yo boys, you guys looking for goods?"

Then a big one responded, "Oh, I think we have found what we have been looking for."

"Oh, yeah? How would you even know I got what you're looking for?"

"Because we see your fake molly in a place noticeable to the public. And you fit the description of who we have been looking for."

Tom quickly changed his expression and attitude and had a horrible feeling in his gut as the big guy quickly punched him in the face knocking him out....

Who knew what memories may come when he awoke from his ignorant mistakes of thinking he could out trick drug addicts. Agent Dale certainly had interesting memories of his meeting, but what memories would come if he chose to open the door to the temple.

Chapter 24
Making His Way in the World These Days

The Near Future
Saturday, March 20ᵗʰ, 6:07 P.M.
Port La Cosa Nostra, Manhattan, New York

Waking up dazed and confused leaning against a wall, Tom wondered what had happened. Feeling very sore and drowsy as if he had been severely hurt, it had sucked all the energy from him. As his eye sight cleared and adjusted he saw five guys surrounding him. One of which was Crazy Cokey. Then he recognized where he was in the Cargo room at the docks. The very same place he met Crazy Cokey months prior.

Then Crazy Cokey was mad and yelled at him, "Finally, you're awake. I have got so many questions for you and all the crap you have put me through the past couple of months!"

"That's funny, because there are quite a few questions I have for you as well." said Tom.

"Listen here you little twerp, you are at my mercy now. Trapped and cornered by five different guys with guns ready to fire directly at you, if you so much as to try to be brave or bold and pull anything on us. We will shoot you dead, right here and right on my command."

Tom clearly got the picture responding, "Yeah, well still maybe we can make a deal for, say, an exchange of knowledge?"

Crazy Cokey chuckled, "Well, if that's what it takes to learn what's been going on within my city, then maybe I will tell you what you have wanted to know."

"That sounds reasonable. So what do you want to know?"

"First off, did you honestly think anybody would be dumb enough not to notice you were selling fake Molly instead of the real stuff?!"

Tom thought, "Honestly, I did think they were that dumb." But knowing it would yield bad results if he were bluntly honest with his view, he said, "Well, I figured it was a sophisticated enough plan, they might be fooled a little."

"Boy, you are a dumb teenager. These druggies crave this stuff every day when they are doing it. So they would never think it's what they were looking for and you don't know much about how drug dealing works. It's a shame you aren't ever going to know about how it all works or who runs things here."

Instantly, from those words, Tom knew his life was at big risk and said, "So, what else you want to know? Will you tell me what I want to know?"

"Well, for one, as you may have noticed, my crew is a little different now since our encounter in December." Tom had a puzzled but somewhat worried look on his face. Crazey Cokey yelled, "Yeah, I remember you from then. Do you think I would forget about you popping up on us during an important shipment?"

"Actually, I was hoping you did forget about me."

Then as he swung his pistol around, Crazy Cokey yelled, "Well, obviously you don't get it. I am the top crime lord in this city and you don't understand that everything is different in the mind of a drug dealer. Much different then how all you simple people live your lives."

"Listen, Aaron, I just want some simple info on somebody!"

"What did you just call me!? How do you know my real name?"

Tom quickly thought about it then realized how Justin must have known him or had a connection. Or, perhaps the gangster had a connection and remembered how Justin somehow made him look like a drug addict when he applied for that job. Then it dawned on him that Justin knew him personally before he had his Crazy Cokey nickname.

Tom said, "Well, obviously you know Justin real well."

"Oh brother, that idiot said as long as I provided him a ride I wouldn't have to be bothered with him anymore."

"Guess he had some extra baggage he forgot to mention."

"It doesn't matter now any-way at least not now that I got you where I want you."

"Well Aaron, where did Justin go when he got on one of your boats?"

"I only have one that actually goes out of country. And sorry, but you never should try to reason with somebody who has a hold on you with a gun. I am sure you're the boy who has been stopping crime in the city and because of you, from what I can tell, I have lost many good workers and they are in prison now!"

"Maybe they are there because of their own actions and arrogance; or maybe even ignorance which means lacking knowledge in case you didn't know."

"Wow, you are a brave idiot."

"Well, will you tell me where Justin went?"

"I only said maybe. And right now, since I know what I wanted, your time is up."

Crazy Cokey cocked his gun as he pointed it at Tom. Tom was concerned about what was about to happen to him. So he backed up a little against the wall more into a corner. As he backed into the corner he yelled, "Modus their guns to the floor!"

Instantly the guns all fell to the floor like they weighed too much for the criminals to hold. Each of them looked shocked as they tried to reach down to pick them up. But they couldn't disconnect the guns from the floor. Then one looked up as Tom was already in his face kicking him hard, and making him hit a cement pillar that knocked the criminal out.

All the others stopped trying to grab their guns so they could come after Tom to tackle him. Then, he round-house kicked one of them and swung a hook punch at the other one. Crazy Cokey came right at him, running fast as he could. But Tom grappled him, swinging him sideways and ramming him into the wall.

The fifth guy stood there, worried and rightfully thought he should get out of there as Tom gave him a really fearless glare. The fifth one ran off quickly so he wouldn't have to deal with Tom. Crazy Cokey and the two others got back up off the ground.

Crazy Cokey chuckled and said, "You think we are just going to give up on you that easily?"

"No, but, I can make sure that won't matter because now that I got you right where I want you." Tom said mocking and using Crazy Cokey's own words against him.

"Oh, what's a dumb teen like you going to do against three fully grown strong men!?" Tom smirked then said, "Modus these four men to the wall until the police arrive to arrest them."

Crazy Cokey and the three other guys bodies all jerked and flew quickly against the wall. Crazy Cokey had a confused but frightened look on his face. "Look who has a hold on you now, Aaron." Tom said with a firm confident tone.

Crazy Cokey then cringed as he said, "You saying my name doesn't make a difference and I will find out who you are."

"Good luck with that. Ventus Aaron Patel's hollowatch to dial 911." The cell hollowatch rang then a dispatcher reported, "What is your emergency?"

Tom looked over to the cargo ship and dock number and said, "We are here at dock 19A. There is a ship called the "Molly" and its crew is here sort of tied up and they have been importing and exporting drugs and other things. Please send some cops to arrest them all."

"Are you kidding me? Is this some kind of dumb prank call?"

"No, it's not. Just come see for yourself."

Crazy Cokey yelled, "Help us! This kid is nuts and he is holding us hostage!"

Tom smirked with a grin and walked off so he wouldn't have to deal with the police. He walked down the docks thinking how he could possibly get info now since Crazy Cokey wasn't willing to reveal to him where Justin was. Then it dawned on him that he would try to use a word he hadn't used in a while to find Justin's info so he said, "Ostendo to me a person who knows where the manifest for the Molly is."

Nothing happened. So he thought, "Great, guess I won't be able to find that info...I practically have tried everything."

Tom kept walking down the docks looking at the ground and bumped into an old looking dude with a grey outfit and he said to the Janitor, "Sorry. I didn't pay attention to where I was walking."

"It's okay. Are you alright?"

"Yeah, just down I can't figure out where to find the manifest for the Molly."

"Well you could check out records in the building at the end of the Dock. They have the schedules for all ships that import and export from the docks according to their number."

"Thanks so much for that info!" Tom said with excitement as he quickly ran to get to the end of the dock.

Once he saw the building he went inside and said, "Ventus me the records for the ships in November." That way he could see a report of all ships that had gone in and out within that month.

Tom looked up the Dock number and saw the Molly was headed for either Italy or England around the time he thought Justin was leaving in November. He was excited for this knowledge because now he could know where he might find Justin. Then he thought he should check out the ports where the Molly had landed in those countries.

Seeing his reflection, Tom knew his parents would question where he got those scars. As he headed out the door he said "thanks" and "goodbye" to the employee who helped him find the manifest info. Then he said, "Sano me of my wounds." Instantly he could feel his wounds get better.

Noticing the sun was setting he knew it must have been getting late. So quickly, Tom flew back to the hotel as fast as he could. Once he got home he sent Agent Dale a text telling him he was okay and that he was home now. When he walked in the door, his parents asked how his day was. "It wasn't too bad. At least nothing really bad happened to me. So, I guess it was good?" he replied. They noticed a certain area near their home town on the news.

They all looked at the TV in shock at what the headline said as it read on it, "Autumn Limb, Texas ravaged by a F7 Tornado"

They were all scared because of how close Autumn Limb was to their home in Smithsonian Valley.

The news anchor said, "It is an amazing story how today the small town of Autumn Limb, Texas was ravaged by the biggest tornado ever recorded. Many homes and restaurants were destroyed. But for some reason certain homes, buildings, businesses and even a small church that was in the eye of the twister were not harmed. It has baffled scientists how the force of the tornado had not ripped away certain buildings, but had gotten other ones." The TV showed many parts of the area that were destroyed and how the whole place looked like it was really torn apart.

Tom wondered if Tara, Benny and Matt were okay. His parents wondered if their house had been affected in any way by what had happened or if their restaurant or any of their employees had been hurt. They thought how they shouldn't let the news of the tornado affect them and that they should continue with what they were about to do, because they wanted to sit down to talk with Tom about certain things.

His dad said, "Tom, your mother and me are proud of how much you have grown up the past couple of months."

Then his mother added, "Yes Tom, you certainly have handled it well. We can't believe, even in all the trouble of losing Martin, you have gotten a job and have been more responsible."

"Well, you know what they say about hard times making people stronger." Tom responded incoherently.

His mom then said, "You certainly have been making your way in the world these days."

His dad said, "Yes son, we are so proud of you and want to let you know how much we love you."

"Thanks Mom. Thanks Dad…" Then they hugged each other saying goodnight.

Tom went down to talk to Todd and give some food, while he relaxed in the Jacuzzi. Todd asked how his day went and he told him about all the crazy stuff that had happened. Then he went back up to bed to relax and planned on going to sleep when he noticed on his hollowatch an instant message notification from Kevin.

It read, "Tom, we need you here as fast as possible. There is an emergency only you might be able to help us with!"

Tom was tired, but he needed to get to England fast from the sounds of it. So he said, "Inflecto me to Kevin's house, or where ever he is right now."

Vanishing, Tom set off on another big adventure that would be very thrilling. He thought he could kill two birds with one stone by helping Kevin with his scenario and possibly finding Justin to settle things once and for all.

> ⌐∭ ⅃

Lying in bed near midnight, with his wife Kathryne, Agent Dale had a very frustrated look on his face as he watched the same news report Tom had seen earlier. Kathryne asked, "What's eating you up so much?"

Nothing really…just that stuff about those ruins and that door I want to open, but I'm concerned about what that guy told me."

"Dale if that stuff bugs you so much you should just go and check it out. Besides, how could those people have control over you the rest of your life?"

"I don't know. Maybe they have some sort of mind control device or some way to force me to do their desires?"

"If they had a way to just control you, wouldn't they just keep you from investigating them? Maybe they are just scared of you figuring out their schemes, so they try to scare you with some wacky nonchalant claim about this door."

"Wow…that actually sounds really reasonable Kathryne. When I have some spare time I think I will go check out that door that I was given the key to. Would you be all right with that?"

"Sure, sounds like a great idea. Just make sure you are cautious when you get there."

"Oh, don't worry I will be. Trust me."

Chapter 25
In the Darkest of Places

The Near Future
Sunday, March 21ˢᵗ, 6:31 A.M.
105 Albert Road, Bexley Ledger, England

The sun was rising and it was a very sunny day in the small town of Bexley Ledger. Kevin was standing next to two friends of his while they waited for Tom to arrive. As they stood there in the park by their school, Kevin and his two friends, Joe and Alex, looked up to the sky expecting Tom to arrive by air.

Then there was a flash of light as Kevin heard a familiar voice he had not heard in a while say, "Why are you guys looking at the sky? You expecting me to fly all the way here from America when you made it sound so urgent?"

"Well, I didn't know there was any other way you could come here. How did you get here so fast?" Kevin said.

"It's called warping aka teleporting."

"They have a word in ancient latin for warp?"

"Apparently they do, it's called inflecto?"

Then one of the boys standing next to Kevin said, "So, how do you do these amazing things?"

"Well, like he mentioned ancient latin, basically I say something in that language and it makes it happen."

"What makes it happen?"

"I am not quite sure about that. I guess the universe makes it happen or, maybe somebody else hears what I request. I am not really sure how it works. Just that is does?"

"That is weird. But amazingly brilliant."

The second boy said, "That's sounds cool."

Then Kevin said, "Let's get back to the point of why I messaged you, Tom."

"Okay, so what is so urgent?"

"Basically it all started yesterday while me, Joe and Alex were boxing together at the gym. We saw the oddest thing."

Then Joe cut into the conversation saying, "Yeah, it was super odd. While Kevin and Alex were boxing with each other I saw Johnny Rodger walking right behind Ashley Harlequin. Billy Chamberlin and Louis Vogel were on both sides of her making sure she was heading a certain direction. Then I pointed it out to Kevin and he saw it."

"Yeah, it looked very unusual. Much like something wasn't right and she didn't look happy." Kevin said.

"Okay, is that all?" Tom said.

"No. Then this morning I got a very strange text from my friend Molly, and it said, "Kelly's friend, Ashley, has been kidnapped by Johnny. We need to find out where he is." That's when I sent you a text on your facespace messenger."

Tom was perplexed by this and wondered where Johnny was or why he had kidnapped Ashley.

Kevin quickly said, "Tom, don't just warp there. We all need to get together to find out where they went so we can go as a group to rescue her."

"You do have a good point. We can't just barge in otherwise they might do something irrational and kill her or try to kill us. Who knows what crazy things they might do? Trust me, I know the results of authority figures just barging in. That is part of how my little brother ended up dead."

"Oh, I am so sorry to hear that Tom." Joe said with sympathy.

Alex said, "Oh man, sorry. That must suck for you."

"It's okay. I have learned to deal with it. Thanks for the concern, though."

Then Kevin proposed an idea saying, "Let's gather together and ask Molly how she found out about this."

They started walking down the road, quite a bit, headed to Molly's house.

On their way, Joe said to Tom, "Sorry for not properly introducing myself earlier but my name is Joe Buscaglia."

"Buscaglia, isn't that Italian, though? Oh, yeah, my name is Thomas Turner, but everyone calls me Tom."

"Yes, it is Italian, but that's because my dad is Italian and my mom is English. Nice to meet you as well, Tom."

"Yeah, thanks! I figured you were Joe when I saw you. I hear you and Kevin have been boxing a lot lately?"

"Yeah, but you can thank Alex for that. Lately I had been going with Alex and our friend, Ross, to this youth group thing. Then one day he suggested we go to the boxing gym to do more cardio to get fit."

"So, that's where you met Kevin and started boxing with him while he was there?"

"Not exactly. We have been boxing there. But it was weird how we had not talked for years since I started going to another school. Then randomly we were reunited through a friend on the Triad Skylink all the way from America."

"That is odd. So, just some friend you met on there just happened to know both of you?"

"Right. I know it doesn't make much sense, does it?"

"Well sometimes these things just happen. For all we know, it's meant to be." Tom said curiously hinting at a deeper meaning.

"Yeah, who knows mate."

Then Alex said, "Yeah, nice to meet you, Tom. My name is Alex Hampson."

"Thanks Alex. You seem like a quiet, but nice guy."

"I am very quiet, but I love to play guitar a lot."

"My brother, John, likes to play guitar a lot as well. But I have never been into playing instruments really. If I was, it probably would be piano."

"Who knows, maybe someday you will learn how to play one of those."

Alex then said, "Still, Joe and I have been friends along time with Ross. I am just getting to know Kevin."

"Who knows, maybe Kevin will become your friend for a long time as well. I just met him during the summer." Tom responded.

"That's cool. It's always nice to make new friends no matter where they are from." Alex said.

"I like your outlook on things. It seems to be a nice way to look at it." Tom said.

"Optimism is better than pessimism as they say." Joe chuckled.

"Yep. It sure is."

They kept walking for a good while, but were really curious about what was going on with Ashley. Eventually, though, they got to Molly's house.

Once they were there they knocked on the door and Molly's mom answered it. They asked to talk to Molly. So her mom went to get her. Molly came running down stairs with Louie right behind her. She and Louie came out-side to talk to them about what had happened.

Kevin asked her, "Molly, what were you on about with that text message you sent me?"

She had a very pretty voice and said frantically, "This morning I got a very scary text message from Kelly about how Ashley was being held hostage and if Johnny's terms were not met then her death would be a result of all of our actions."

Tom then said, "Great. Looks like we will need Kelly to know what Johnny wants and why are you here, Louie?"

"Because Molly is my girlfriend. I stayed over last night."

"Does anybody know where Kelly is?" Joe asked.

Then Molly said, "She is at Charlie's with Jenny and Reece."

Kevin said, "Well Charlie lives not too far from here. Let's get moving so we know where to find Johnny and his blind followers."

They all headed down the road a few more blocks over to Charlie's house. Then one of them sent a text to Charlie that they were coming over. After quite a walk, they arrived at Charlie's house. When all of them were outside Tom tried to explain what was happening.

Tom asked Kelly, "What does the text say that Johnny gave you?"

"Who are you?"

"He is our friend, Tom, from America. You know the kid that flew away from a fight with Justin." Charlie said to Kelly.

"Oh, you're Tom! I have heard great things about you. Here, look at it. This really worries me." Kelly lifted her wrist so everyone could check out the message that was sent to her.

Tom looked at it and it read, "If you ever want to see your friend, Ashley, again get that Turner boy to come save her at the secret castle where the first Knight Templars of England resided. It may be almost impossible." Tom had read it out loud in case some weren't close enough to see it. So they all were shocked and wondered where that could be? He didn't have any clue and neither did anyone else.

Then Kevin had a great idea saying, "Why don't we use the skylink on our hollowatches to look up info on the old knights locations?"

Charlie then said, "That's a brilliant idea that way we can find Johnny and save Ashley."

"My dad has a nice computer at his gym, but this would be way quicker, saving us time." Kevin said.

Everyone thought this was a great idea, so they all started searching on their hollowatches, instead of traveling over to Paulo's gym. Each of them looked up info on where the first Templar knights resided in England. Some found useful info, others not so much, but all of it seemed so bland and obvious.

Then Tom said, "Maybe we should search for the first hidden castle. Johnny did say it was a secret one, so maybe we would be better off finding out what conspiracies there are and where they first began knowing Johnny liking hidden truths to the world in all."

So they looked for the same stuff, but used the words "secret" in their search and "hidden". They eventually came across an interesting site proposing an extraordinary theory.

It read, "Even though most sources claim that the knights Templar first arrived in England in 1118 AD, there is evidence that they had been a little hidden from the general public. Prior to Hughes de Payens arrival, there was a secret scout to check if England would be appropriate for gathering civilians for their beliefs and their cause forty nine years prior in the year 1069 AD. William de Warenne the 1st Earl of Surrey built the Lewes castle. But some are skeptical as to why it originally was called Bray castle which means the cry of a donkey. Some interpreted it to mean it stood for the cry of a donkey, or it represented a cry from the order of Templars to bring more followers to England. Some rumors even indicated that William did not choose to make this castle on his own, but was requested and paid by a rich looking Roman with lots of gold. Then there is the crazy mystery of the stone that has been placed at the base of the dungeon. There is a stone there with a symbol of a Lion, Lamb and a DONKEY. Obviously this symbol looks a lot like symbolism for the knights Templar since they liked Religious implications in their stuff. The stone has weird indentions seeming almost like there is Braille written there. But nobody has been able to figure out why these indentions are on the stone in the dungeon or what they mean. When the castle was originally built it was not made of stone, but of wood. And the dungeon stone is claimed to have been there since it was still made of wood. Not much is known of the origin of the stone, but it is believed to be from somewhere far from England originally, and much older than the castle itself."

After slowly scrolling down the page on their hollowatches reading all this, they seemed shocked at the mystery of the place and thought this definitely had to be the secret castle Johnny spoke of in his text.

Then Reece said, "Come on guys. If we hurry we might be able to catch the 12:19 train at Bexley Ledger station."

They all headed down the road passing Paulo's gym and ran across Woolwich Rd over to the school and cut across the campus.

They kept on walking till they came upon the Goals football centre. Then they walked around the football centre and decided to cut through the cemetery past a few houses on Banks Ln and take a right to head north on Church Rd, till they eventually reached Station Rd and then headed west until they got to the Bexley Ledger Station.

Once inside, all of them bought tickets to get on the train headed to London's Victoria Station, which then would have a train headed for Lewes station. Kevin bought Tom a ticket since Tom didn't have any pounds or pence with him.

Tom said to Kevin, "Thanks Kevin. Sorry I don't have any pounds to give you in return."

"It's okay, Tom. Most of the time we refer to it as quid in our area."

"Quid, what is quid?"

"Well, it's sort of the slang term for pounds here. Much like how you guys also call a dollar a buck."

"Oh, okay. Now I get it."

They both laughed about their conversation while they headed over to the waiting benches till the train arrived a few minutes later. Once it arrived they all got on and went to their seats and sat down.

Kevin had an anxious look on his face. Tom wondered what was going on with him. Jenny and Charlie held hands as they sat there talking about stuff. Louie was begging Molly to kiss him, but she didn't want to and had a look on her face like she was disgusted by the idea. Kelly and Reece were talking about how he and Jamie had been working on Lord Dribble mouth comics. Joe just sat there bored out of his mind as he read a magazine about boxing; then he started talking to Alex about youth group and theological things.

After a couple minutes of anxious looks, Kevin walked up to Tom and asked him if he wanted to come with over to the buffet car to check it out. Kevin looked like he was hinting at more than just wanting to show scenery, so Tom agreed and got up to head for the buffet car with him.

Once they got into it, Kevin bought some monster crunch crisps for Tom to try. He liked them. He had never had chips that tasted like roast beef before. They were quite tasty from his view as he licked his lip, savoring it's flavor.

Then Kevin said to Tom while he was eating the crisps he had given him, "As you could probably tell, I wanted to come back here to talk to you about something and not just buy you crisps."

"Yeah, what is it?"

"Well, I have been carrying around a secret lately. I want to tell her because it isn't fair that this is happening to her and she doesn't even know about it."

"Who is this "she" and why don't you just tell her whatever it is you have been hiding?"

"Well it's, Molly. Apparently Louie told me, but wanted me to keep it a secret. But lately he has been getting lots of action and snogging lots of girls. Especially Charlotte, who is one of my good friends. She also told me they were snogging." (Snogging meaning making out or kissing)

"Kevin, I don't want to get caught up in your rumors or have to keep secrets myself, so just leave me out of it. I can recommend you be careful how you respond to this because telling her could mean losing Louie as a friend and hiding it from her could have bad results if she finds out that you knew it in the first place and kept it from her."

"Man, Tom, what am I supposed to do?"

"Well, no matter what way you put it, it seems like you're in a no win scenario. I guess you will just have to be honest and tell her."

"Yeah, you're probably right. But I don't want to hurt her feelings; I care about her a lot as a friend."

"Well then, be careful how you tell her. Try to present your info in a way that is not very bad. You know what I mean?"

"I will try…well thanks for your opinion and advice, Tom."

"You're welcome, Kevin; I am always here for you as a friend."

"Awe cheers, mate."

So then Kevin and Tom walked back to the car where all the other kids from Bexley Ledger School were sitting down and talking till they arrived at the London Victoria station. Some places looked kind of trashy, while others looked decent or good looking going through the towns on their way to the station.

Once they were there, they all got off the train and sat down on the benches. Kevin asked Molly to come talk with him over away from the rest. Tom sat there watching Kevin and Molly walk off with a sympathetic look on his face. Kelly, though, had sat right next to

Tom and started talking to him. She asked how he was doing and what his opinion on Ashley's situation was.

Tom responded by saying, "Well, I think she will be fine once we find her and Johnny and those other guys they mentioned."

"Yeah, but you saw the text. It almost sounded like he is going to try to make it impossible to save her."

"Trust me Kelly I have total faith in what can be done to help her and she will be fine. I have dealt with way worse scenarios than just a kidnapping and a threat."

"I somewhat agree, but having faith in yourself doesn't always help. I admit I have faith that things can get better, but life always seems to knock you down and make you feel so pointless. Sometimes life has no meaning; like it's impossible to stop troubles."

"Well, Kelly, I think no matter what life must have some meaning to it. Otherwise why would we exist? I don't think it's just to be in each other's lives."

"True, I guess…but Ashley and I always had this in common. I would at least have some faith things could get better, but she never thinks they get better. We always look at the bad things in life and feel like we have no purpose or skills and we are worthless. But that is what makes us such great friends."

Tom was thinking, "What is wrong with these girls? They live in the thought that life is so dark and that somehow that makes a special bond for their friendship?"

Then Tom said cautiously, "Well, at least y'all have each other and your friendship."

"Yeah, at least we got each other. From what you said a second ago you can overcome troubles if you try hard enough"

Then a few moments later their trains arrived and the train was somewhat square and rounded at the same time. The front was Yellow like you would see on a stop sign. The side was green and white but it had tinted black windows. It was a real nice looking train. Once Tom and the others stepped inside, Tom thought about how it looked really nice. The seats were grey and sky blue, almost boarder line of looking somewhat teal. Tom grabbed onto the yellow handles making his way over to the seats to sit down and get ready for their trip that would take another hour to arrive in Lewes.

For quite a while Joe, Alex and Kevin discussed upcoming boxing events with Tom. Everyone was doing their own thing. Some would go to the toilet while some went to the Buffet Car for snacks. The scenery of the southern country side of England was majestic from Tom's point of view. It had grassy green fields and sights that would have made any person who saw them appreciate the beauty of nature with the things that grow in it. Tom occasionally would take a peek out the window at the countryside as the train would zoom forth to Lewes.

After quite a long trip they pulled up to Lewes Railway station. Once they got off the train they all talked about how they needed to figure out where the Castle might be. Joe walked over to the ticket booth and noticed that they had pamphlets for the Lewes castle along with a map of the town. So, he grabbed a few and took them over to everyone else and gave one to everyone. After looking at his pamphlet, Charlie told everyone to follow him.

They all followed, heading out of the station and cutting across Station Rd to Dorset Rd, then turning right onto Garden St and walking till they reached Southover Rd. Then they took another right walking for about a block till they saw Watergate Ln to their left. So then they headed north for two and a half blocks till they reached High St. On their left was a restaurant called Prezzo right next to the Sussex Guild shop and across from there the Castle gate road with the Lewes Castle&Barbican House Museum on the corner. They all scurried for the Castle road and then headed straight due north till they reached the Castle gate.

Once they went through the gate they headed down the walkway and went up the walkway escalating the zig zag path that led up the hill to the castle. Eventually, they all reached a rounded wall with two towers connected. It seemed to be the only part of the Lewes castle that was left from all the battles it had been through.

Tom said to them, "Why don't we split up so we can cover more ground and find Johnny. Alright?"

"Sure, that sounds like a great idea." Charlie said.

"Okay, but I am staying with you, Tom." Kevin said.

They split up as Tom went into the one tower on his left with Kevin, Alex and Molly but the rest of them went to the one on the right. Once inside, Tom noticed there was a stair-way that went down. He wondered if this was the stair-way to the mysterious dungeon with the old rock of mystery. All of them walked down the stairs following one another, curiously wondering if they would soon find Johnny.

They walked down a stony corridor, but at the end of it Tom saw the symbol of the Donkey along with the Lion and the Lamb. Slowly he approached it to get a better look, and then stared at it for a moment noticing something. There were indentions like the description had said, but there was spacing, as well, that made certain shapes like symbols that meant something.

Tom took note of this, too. So he looked at how many indentions there were for each little amount of space of a symbol. Eventually he started counting the number of indentions. He saw there were even greater spaces between some of the symbols themselves.

Then Tom said, "Voco me a textbook with writing paper and a pencil." Instantly some paper with a pencil flashed into his hands and he started to write down what he saw on the wall into a number sequence on his paper.

This is what he got off the numbers of indentions and the paper, it read: "11.7.6/ 10.6.6/ 6.10.5.7.9.9/ 10.7.5.8.8/ 6.5.10.10/ 12.7.6.9/ 11.7.6/ 10.5.5.10.6.6/ 10.6.11.6.9/ 10.7.10.6/"

Once he organized them, he wondered what all these random numbers could mean and even Kevin asked him, "Tom, what are all those numbers you have written about?"

Alex said, "Yeah man, what are those things about?"

Tom explained to them how he came up with them then told them he would check them out later. But right now they needed to find Johnny. So they headed back up the stairs and found another stair case that led up to the roof of this keep or tower. Once they climbed to the top and opened the wooden door, they found Johnny over by the edge, snoozing. But so were Ashley, Billy and Louis. Then, the wooden door made a loud creaking noise making Johnny open his eyes and accidently knocking Ashley in her side. Then Billy and Louis woke up pretty quickly.

Johnny then said, "Ahh, I see you finally figured out where I brought her…good."

"Yeah, it's kind of funny you would say that considering you were just snoring. I could of easily rescued her if that door didn't wake you up." Tom said with a smirk on his face.

Johnny said, "Well, it doesn't matter now, Tom, because I got her in my grip and two more boys by my side to stop you. There is nothing you can do to save her no matter how fast you can fly."

Luckily Johnny wasn't holding a knife to her throat like Justin did to Martin.

Tom said, "Well, first off, why do you want to hurt her and what purpose would it serve to hurt the poor lady?"

"What harm!? Getting rid of her would be doing the world a favor. I know all about how she has been cheating on me with that stupid Louie kid."

"That's no reason to kill a person. In fact I don't think any life is worth so little to get rid of."

"Tom, I have seen it with my own eyes. All girls are mental and make jumpy irrational decisions just like what Thomas said that one day."

"I'm surprised you even heard him say that. You know, considering you were beating up Jason for being a sensitive guy with good qualities."

"Well, I did and it got me thinking for months about Ashley and how she is always down. Besides, even if I don't end her life now, I would say by knowing by how she acts she will do it to herself, eventually."

"That still doesn't give you the right to do what you want with her and just kill her because of your own thoughts and views."

"It doesn't matter any way, Tom. All girls are crazy and loony, Maybe, even your own dumb girl will do something bad."

Tom wondered if this horrible case of misogyny came from what Thomas Mandarin said months prior or could it be some other issue he didn't know about. Then he said, "Man, Johnny, you got a lot to learn about the wonderfulness a girl can bring into your life."

"Well, so far none of them seem of any importance to me. Just more garbage to clean up. Well it's time for this one to go!"

Johnny quickly hurled her off the side of the castle as Tom yelled, "Cunctatio Ashley's fall that she may land safely on her feet."

Tom took off really fast, but as he flew, Billy and Louis grabbed him, trying to stop him from leaving their area. He pushed on as Louis let go and fell to the edge of the castle wall. But Billy clenched on tightly to Tom's leg, fearing he would fall to his death. This pressure surely didn't feel good on Tom's leg. Tom grabbed Billy throwing him down on the top of the castle with the others.

Then he did a U-turn and said, "Make a vermis Cavus from under Ashley that goes out the side of the wall by the wooden door on the roof of the Lewes castle." Ashley quickly came flying out of the side of the wall on the roof of the Castle and landed safely on her feet.

Tom flip landed vertically on the roof as Johnny said, "Bravo Tom! But don't underestimate what I will do in the future."

"Johnny, I am certain all of them will be telling your parents about this." Tom said with a stern look on his face.

"I don't live with my parents anymore. They could care less what I do."

Kevin said, "Yeah, but bet your nan would be mad."

"Listen Kevin; leave my personal life out of this!"

"If that is how you want it then you better not try anything like this again with anybody else. You got that? And learn to respect others even if you can't properly function around them." Tom said to Johnny.

"Tom you're more of a freak than me. So if anybody needs lessons on how to act around others it would be you! You stupid American!"

"Just because I come from a different culture doesn't mean I don't know how to act around people from my country. Nobody is perfect and for you to even expect that of others is an unrealistic concept."

"Besides you can't always be around to save the day. I could just get her whenever you're not around. You're never willing to do what needs to be done to take a life from a criminal. I have seen the reports on the skylink about New York's fine hero that always turns criminals into the police, but that hero never puts them out of business permanently. You the hero, I presume, just end their current action of crime. It just goes to show what a little halfwit you are, never willing to make the decisions that matter."

Tom, with a look of anger on his face, paced ahead and grabbed Johnny by the neck. He pushed him back against the edge of the wall of the castle making Johnny hang half way off of the edge.

Johnny then said with a froggy voice, "This is more like it. Come on Tom. End my reign of terror right now!"

"Don't push me, Johnny. I do know how to do things you could never achieve; like being a decent person!"

As Johnny looked up into Tom's eyes he chuckled as he said, "You truly do have some sense of misplaced self-righteousness or you are that special in your own mind that you wouldn't push me over the edge or let me go, would you? Well, how decent are you now, threatening to drop me over the edge of a roof top?"

Tom looked down at him with anger in his eyes as he grunted saying, "Ugh…you're right, I wouldn't kill you because I have morals and was raised to look for the good in everyone no matter bad they get."

"Come on, Tom! Kill me or I will make their lives Hell forever! You know you want to."

"No Johnny, you're not going to make me do anything as bad as taking another person's life!"

"So be it, Tom. If that's the way it is, I have one thing to say to you. Depression is like magnetivity all's it takes is a little push, to push somebody over the edge. Ashley will take her own life eventually, and then you will be miserable like the rest of us knowing you couldn't save her. You can't always be the hero Tom."

To make Tom blame himself for bringing him to the edge of the castle, Johnny punched Tom so he would let go of him and make him fall to his death. But even in being punched, Tom wouldn't falter, holding onto him with a very angry look and with blood running down his face. As Johnny stared into Tom's eyes, all of them noticed the Castle started to rumble. Some of them wondered if the castle was shaking from Tom's anger.

Tom pulled him back from the edge, then thrust Johnny onto the shaking castle ground saying, "Johnny, you really need to learn how to deal with people in a way that doesn't harm them or yourself in the process!"

Tom thought about the fact that the wormhole was going through the foundation of the Castle bending through certain parts and looping back into the wall. That thought made him wonder how the structure of the Castle was vastly different from the one of a cave being much smaller and fragile. But the cave was part of the whole planet and had its wormhole going to another planet in a dimension far away.

The rumbling got way more severe as Tom yelled, "Hurry! We have to get out of here. That wormhole is making this whole place unstable!"

They all started to run down the stairs that led out of the castle, but Billy was freaking out and fell off of the edge of the castle and into the wormhole. Then he went flying out of the wormhole inside the wall with lots of momentum and was flung over to the other tower. But he quickly grabbed onto the ledge and climbed onto the top of it and went down the stairs of that tower.

While running down the stairs, Tom, Kevin and Molly bumped into the others that had split up because they were coming up the stairs when they saw Tom on that tower from the top of the other one that Billy grabbed onto.

Tom quickly said, "Trust me, you guys don't want to go up onto this tower; it's collapsing, so let's get out of here quickly!"

Running for their lives, all them headed down the stairs outside to go over to some benches surrounding some giant trees. Hearing the rumbling behind them, they looked back seeing the Tower collapse in on its self since its foundations were shocked out of place by the wormhole. Then, Tom asked them if he could talk alone with Ashley. The others all walked off to another bench. Tom and Ashley sat there and had a small discussion for a moment.

Tom asked her, "Ashley, why is it everyone sees you as the kind of girl who would kill yourself and is always depressed?"

"Because, I always want to die. I am so tired of this pointless life. One day, I feel I am not going to be able to take it anymore and just end it all."

"Ashley, you're worth so much more than that though."

"No, I am not. I am not worth anything. I don't have any good skills. I can't get good grades. I don't have anybody there that cares for me. Life is just so worthless!"

"Ashley, even in the darkest of places, the light still shines bright out through the cracks. I know I care about you and I know for a fact that Kelly cares about you and you had seven others besides that that came here for you. That's nine people who care about you enough to come rescue you from a true nut case. You are only what you choose to make of yourself. Why don't you start thinking better of yourself and try to make your life worth something? I know it feels worthless at the moment, you know what I mean?"

"Yeah…I get what you mean. But you don't know how dark my life gets and how bad it is."

"Something tells me you don't have it as bad as I do. You probably don't know it, but a few months ago my little brother died."

"What…? That's horrible…"

"It totally made me upset and for quite a while I felt like it was my fault. But in the end, with patience and perseverance, I eventually got over it making myself a better person. You can do the same in your life if you choose to."

"You think I actually have a reason to live and am worth something?"

"I think all life is meaningful. Sure we don't all know why we are here, but just our existence must have some meaning otherwise we would be pointless and there would be no reason to live. So there must be some reason out there why we are here."

"Wow, Tom…that sounds very profound."

"Always know this Ashley; if you have a struggle you have me and all your friends here for you who care about you with all our hearts."

"Thanks, Tom. I will try to keep that in mind."

They hugged each other then walked off and caught up with the rest of them. Louie said he was hungry and so were the others, so they stopped at the Prezzo restaurant to eat a late lunch. Then they all headed back to Bexley Ledger on a long train ride to Tom's friends home town.

Molly was mad at Louie when she learned he had cheated with so many girls. So they broke up while on their way to the Train Station and Molly wouldn't talk to him either.

After they got on the train, they relaxed now that things were looking better. Charlie and Jenny kissed some when they were on the train and listened to music together while they held hands. Molly hung out with Kevin, Tom, Joe and Alex. Reece, Kelly and Ashley hung out with each other, talking about their wild adventure to find Ashley. Billy, Louis and Johnny sat in another car instead of the one with them, since they were mad with Johnny. Billy contemplated if Johnny was the right kind of guy to hang out with since he did such crazy things that almost cost him his life.

After a long trip with two train rides they got off at their station and headed for their neighborhood where most of them lived. As they were walking down the road out of the train station Kevin asked Tom something, that Tom never saw coming. "Tom would you like to come party with us tonight and get pissed? As well we can smoke some spliff?" (Pissed meaning get drunk and Spliff meaning weed or Marijuana)

Tom was shocked at the request and responded, "Sorry, I need to get home. Besides, where would you get that stuff anyway? Aren't you under age for alcohol?"

"We get our Spliff from Connell Sitten, and his mom also gives us beer."

"Well, I don't want to damage my liver or wake up with somebody I regret. So yeah, I will be going see you whenever you want to hang out. Goodbye Kevin, see y'all later."

"Later Tom, have a nice warp or fly home."

Tom chuckled nonchalantly as he flew off wondering if he should follow them to their little party just to see what would happen to them. He stayed high up in the air as he followed Kevin and his friends to a house; then heard loud music starting to play. He hovered over the house for a while to make sure they were okay, but didn't hear anything bad, really.

Then after a while the music was thumping very loudly with lots of bass. The front door swung open and a cute girl with brown hair and blue eyes just like Tom came running out and crying. He looked down on her concerned and came hovering, slowly landing on the side walk in front of the house. She sort of had seen part of him coming down out of the corner of her eye.

She looked up saying, "How did you do that?"

"Believe me, if I could fully explain it I would. Let's just say I have a knack for making things happen."

"Yeah, that is pretty amazing that you are able to do that."

"It is, but I was wondering why did you come out of there all upset? Are you okay?"

"Well, it's annoying watching how vile and disgusting they are in there."

"What do you mean?"

"One of my friends decided to get a free kiss off of one of the pissed guys in there and was using him."

"Yeah, I can see it's not great to have friends with no code of conduct. But people are people and I think they would only try to be better if they felt that they needed to. At least that is part of the reason I try to be a person with morals and integrity. I guess they just don't see the purpose."

"So true. Well, I just wish we lived in a better world. You know one that would be safer for my little sister, Holly; I don't want her to be influenced by all these kinds of people."

"Well...who knows, maybe one day they will see the mistakes they are making and things could be better for you and your sister."

"Yeah, well I sure hope so considering...." Then the door opened and a semi tall boy with brown hair walked out saying, "Are you alright, Chloe?"

"Yeah Craig, I am fine. Just having to deal with regular people is getting on my nerves."

"Okay, if you say so sweetie. Just don't want you to be unhappy."

"Sorry, I haven't properly introduced myself, my name is Chloe Manning and this is my boyfriend, Craig Shielding." Tom shook hands with both of them. While shaking Craig's hand said, "Nice to meet you. My name is Thomas Turner, but everyone calls me Tom."

"You seem like a decent guy by coming to my girlfriend's aid much sooner than I did." Craig said.

"Nah, just trying to be a good person. But I do try to be decent and I am sure you didn't notice her gone at first."

"You are right. I didn't, but I was concerned when I couldn't find her. Anyhow, Chloe, you want to go home since this party is annoying you?"

"Sure thing, Craig. Well it was nice meeting you, Tom. Have a nice evening."

"It was great meeting both of you, as well. Have a good evening yourselves." Tom walked off down the road in the direction opposite of the way they headed.

Tom then inflectoed himself back to the hotel pool and quickly said "hi" and "bye" to Todd as he headed back upstairs to his family's room. Then he remembered how he forgot to check out the docks in England for signs of Justin. So he figured he would take care of that sooner or later.

Tom was glad to have saved Ashley's life, but was disappointed at seeing his own good friends hurt themselves in a wild party with their hedonistic ways. Who knows where that could of lead or something happening. Only time would tell what happened after he left the party. He was concerned for them because of the way he was raised and what he knew scientifically what was bad about the things they were doing. He wasn't a bigot or self-opinionated, he was just concerned for their wellbeing. He spent the rest of his day trying to stay awake even though he was extremely tired, and eventually he went to sleep.

Even when things seemed dark for Ashley, Tom still stood as a beacon of light & hope in a weary world. In the darkest of times he wouldn't falter from trying to do his best for everyone that he could. Even if it meant others thinking poorly of him. No matter what, he would stand by them and be there for them. But in his eyes, he would never submit to their way of living.

Chapter 26
The Blood Moon

The Near Future
Saturday, April 17th, 8:11 P.M.
The Giant's temple, Caucasus Mountains, Russia

Climbing up the giant steps, Agent Dale pushed hard feeling a dark presence as the sun had just set over the horizon. It wasn't the most welcoming evening, but that might have also been from the decision he had already struggled with for months. The silence of the forest wasn't helping. Off in the distance he thought he could hear the river, but it wasn't that loud.

The Pillars looked so old; Agent Dale wondered how long these things existed. Still, if he wanted answers, opening this door was going to be the only way to get them. He thought to himself, "I don't really need to worry. Like Kathryne said, if they could control me they would of already. It's time to find out what's behind this door."

Walking up to the door with the six holes in it, Agent Dale reached into his pocket and pulled out the egg coned shaped crystal. It started glowing as he approached the door. Part of him wished he had brought somebody else along since this was starting to get really crazy. Still he remembered that he wasn't supposed to bring anybody with him if he did make this choice. Filled with wonder at finally figuring out the complex mystery, he had endured for the past year, he gave up the restraint that held him from moving on. He plunged the glowing key into the top hole.

Now, there wasn't going to be any turning back. The deed was done. Feeling the ground shake beneath his feet, Agent Dale exhaled as he fell backwards trying to catch himself. The giant stone door moved before his eyes descending into the ground as a gust of wind blew dust out the doorway.

Looking into the chamber, he could hardly see anything. So he turned on the illumination PSI on his hollowatch. Light filled the room revealing many things of an unusual nature. Walking in cautiously, he looked around, taking note how this place appeared on the ground as it had been built. But the walls and ceiling looked natural like a cave. It had an ominous creepy vibe to it, like one might find if they discovered an ancient mystery as old as time itself.

In the center of the chamber, Agent Dale found a stone slab alter with human remains on its edges. On the center of the alter was a dead jackal with its stomach punctured like something or someone had cut it open and there was a knife next to it. It looked as though it had been dead for more than thirty years. Creeped out by the dead animal remains, he walked off to check out other parts of the chamber.

Getting closer to the wall, Agent Dale's hollowatch gave it a better view with light showing what the wall was really made of. He didn't see this coming, but apparently the walls weren't made of rock and dirt like a cave. They were made of the bones of giant men. How they died though wasn't exactly written anywhere that he could see.

This whole place wasn't welcoming in the least, although out of his peripheral vision, Agent Dale did see something appealing to the eyes. At the back end of the chamber on the wall furthest from the door was a giant mural made of gems depicting some sort of situation. The more he looked at it though the more he had chills down his spine. The more he stared he felt like he wasn't alone. Then he heard a branch snap and he saw some orange light flickering off the reflection of the gems on the mural.

Turning around, Agent Dale saw four robed men approaching him from around the stone alter between them. Two of them had torches on each side of the outer edge of the group. Arriving right in front of him, each of them simultaneously took down the hood of their robes revealing themselves face to face with Agent Dale. The oldest looking one said, "Welcome to our temple, we see that you have made the decision to align yourself with us."

"Yes…I remember what your guy there on the left said about the result of me opening the door." He said pointing his finger at the man he met in Nepal. "I want to know what secrets are worth killing for? So, basically, I would just like some answers. Who are you people and what is so important about keeping these bones a secret?"

"Agent Sizer, to build a better future, one must first destroy any yoke of old hatred such as the history of any previous conflicts. If there are any ties to the times of old, then the great plan of our leaders won't come to fruition."

"Oh great. So you guys aren't the top of this hierarchy then. What is this great plan?"

"We have an apprentice who doesn't even know he is our apprentice yet. Someday, very soon, he is going to help our following usher in a golden age of peace. This is our leaders plan, to help the world become a better place. No more wars, no more suffering, everything you could imagine in a peaceful world."

"I don't know why you think that means we should kill innocent people? How could the knowledge of bones destroy this world peace? Is this new kingdom that fragile?"

The leader spoke, "I don't know how to put this lightly…our leaders who are bringing about this golden age do not have their bodies anymore. They are nothing more than a shadow of their former selves. To have the people agree to let them be whole again, they must first think they are something new. But they already are and they are to come again."

"What is my role in all of this? Are you guys going to want me to kill more innocent people?"

"No, not at all. We want you to do exactly what Ford did for us and look after things in the US. Help us with the minor details of getting things ready and sometimes you might not even realize you are doing things for us."

Agent Dale annoyed by this logic, said angrily, "So what, I am just supposed to take orders from whatever these things or people are and do as you guys want? Are you trying to say I won't have a choice in the matter about what I think? Or if it is right or wrong about what to do and what to say?"

Reaching out with his bony old hand, the man grabbed Agent Dale's right hand saying, "By opening the door, you already gave up those rights. Now you have no option except to serve us and those we serve." The three other men reached out placing their hands on Agent Dale's. "What's going on?!" Agent Dale yelled as a sharp pain shot through his hand.

Their eye's turned black as sackcloth reflecting the light of their torches as Agent Dale screamed in agony as a mark singed burning onto his wrist.

It had now been four weeks since Tom's family saw the news about the tornado that devastated Autumn Limb. The date was the seventeenth of April. Many people's lives had been tested through excruciating circumstances already, but none knew what was to come this dark hour of their lives.

Benny had been telling Tom how he had wished for him to be there for one of his football games. It was spring time and the season had started. Benny just wanted a good friend's opinion about him being a good player or a crappy one. So, he decided to take a surprise trip back down to Texas for the day since it was a big game for Benny.

Tom was in his own home kitchen for the first time in quite a while, eating breakfast when he noticed something on the news. The headline read, "FIRMA Bill passed in California"

Then Tom heard a reporter say, "Today is a big day for Californians on how the FIRMA bill might be passed and what may appear as a late Easter present to the public of their state."

"I would hardly call that Bill a late Easter present considering what it's all about." One of the other reporters commented as they changed topic.

Eating his breakfast, Tom didn't really care about it and decided to walk off. Remembering that California wasn't too far from Seattle, he recalled how his parents had told him the other day that

John would be working with David Walker himself in Seattle that weekend and would be staying at the Caspian Inn right by the Space Needle.

Todd begged Tom to come along to watch, as long as he promised to remain hidden from the audience. He was blowing fire balls at the fire place bored waiting to get ready for the game.

Thinking Benny might be up by now; Tom headed over to his house and knocked on the door. Benny came to the door and opened it. As soon as Benny noticed who it was, his face lit up with excitement to see Tom was there making a surprise visit on the day of one of his big games.

Benny yelled ecstatically, "Tom, I can't believe you came here for my big championship game! I didn't even expect you."

"Well, yeah. You think I would miss one of the most important games of your life?"

"No. I get it. But it just is odd for you to show up so randomly without telling me. But not odd in a bad way; if you get what I mean?"

"I totally get what you mean. But you know my family has been very busy trying to remain hidden from Justin far away from Texas."

"It's okay. I understand even though I do wish you could come over more often."

"Well, maybe I won't have to hide in the near future. Soon enough, we might be able to go back to how we used to do things."

"Yeah, that would be really nice. What exactly do you mean?"

"Let's just say that the authority's might have Justin soon because they think they have a lead on where he is. So, even though we sometimes talk on facespace, how have you been doing in life recently?"

"Well, that's good news. I have been good, but my parents are not doing so great since lately Dad has been going to church. Ever since the tornado a month ago destroyed most of Autumn Limb, Mom doesn't want to deal with all that church junk."

"I could see how different views would make things hard for their relationship."

"Yeah, but besides that, I guess everything is alright considering how things have been so hard lately. And in a month I will be graduating."

"That's good. So do you know where you might go to college?"

"I'm not quite sure about that to be honest. I don't even know what I want to do in life yet?"

"Who knows, eventually we either figure out what we want, or we are forced to live out our life however it all works out for us. You know what I mean?"

"Yeah, most definitely. It sure does seem that way most of the time."

"So, where is your game being held?"

"It's at Jumbo Smith Fields and I will have to go get ready for it soon. I have to be there to practice, so I guess I will see you there?"

"Well, could I ride with your mom when it's time to leave?"

"Where are your mom and dad?"

"They didn't come with me for this visit."

"Oh, okay. Well I will text you if she..." His mom interrupted saying, "It's alright Tom. Bee back within half an hour so we can leave."

"Okay, cool. Guess I will talk to you in a little while at the game?"

"Yeah, sure. See you later, Tom." Then Tom walked back over to his house as Benny went inside to get ready to go to practice. Todd asked what was going on with the game as he was getting impatient.

Tom responded, "Well you will need to follow me over to Benny's house. Then when I get in the car and we start pulling out of the driveway land on the car to come with us. Once we are there go and hide under the stands. Then try to get to me without being seen."

"Wow. That sounds like an interesting plan. Let's just hope it works out."

"It does get rather annoying always having to hide you. But it still makes for a fun challenge."

"Well, I know it's a challenge to come up with plans and stuff. But have you ever considered looking up in Alida's Book if there might be a word for transform or something along those lines? Then perhaps, I could be changed to look like a human."

"That's not a bad idea. Maybe I will check it out when we get back to the hotel room."

"That would make things so much easier for us."

"What about people at the hotel noticing a guy always going to and fro in the pool room? If we move home at some point and my parents wonder why there is some other guy sleeping in my room with me. Wouldn't that seem odd to them?"

"Yes, you're right. But I am sure we could figure it out and find a way for things to work out."

"Maybe. Who knows. Only time will tell."

While waiting for his shower to heat up, Tom sat there looking at the text conversation he had earlier with Agent Dale. From top to bottom it read, "Hey Tom is it alright if you come with me tomorrow to the FBI building. The Secretary of Defense wanted to speak with you again regarding the crime rate in New York City and how it has degraded rapidly?"

"Sure thing. I would appreciate that and I'm willing to check it out. I am visiting Benny here in Texas for a football game. Would you like to come join us? I could teleport you here."

"I know you could just teleport me from where ever you want, but I am going to be very busy today regarding an important matter. I can't come. Sorry. I will talk to you later."

"It's alright, see you later."

After getting his shower and getting ready, Tom got up off the couch and headed for Benny's house with Todd following behind him in the air.

Knocking on the door, Benny's father let him in. Benny's dad, Mike, said they would leave as soon as Benny's mom, Susan, grabbed her book and got her make up on upstairs. When she came down all of them headed out the door and got in their van. Driving off they headed for Jumbo Smith Fields taking in the scenery.

As they drove off heading for the championship match, Tom thought about how he had gone many places looking for Justin, for the past four weeks, but couldn't find him anywhere. There wasn't even a sign of him getting off of the cargo ships that came in from New York City. He looked all over the docks in England and even in Italy, but never once found a trace of him or a sign that he had been there. He even checked out the dock records, but couldn't find anything about Justin's name or Sacra, either. By that logic he assumed they were not officially on the boat and had just hitched a ride, unofficially.

While Tom was reminiscing about the past he noticed all the destroyed trees with debris everywhere. Some parts of highway 218 it's self, were damaged. The King Finnegan's Restaurant where he had eaten at months prior, was severely damaged. It was obvious the state it was in because it was being repaired.

Tom couldn't believe the damage an F7 tornado could do. It sure was a good thing that Autumn Limb was a small town; otherwise it would have been a worse death toll if it were a big city. Even some parts of Guadalupe River next to the King Finnegan's looked trampled and distorted by the power of the magnitude of the Tornado.

Tom wondered if he should help fix the place up. But then that might raise too much attention if all of its issues just disappeared. And that might bring either good or bad publicity to the area. So, he decided to leave things as were so he wouldn't do damage to the area and attract too many people allured by the miraculous recovery of the town. He wanted to help, but couldn't, due to the repercussions it might have. Still he was certain the people would recover in their own time.

Riding down the highway for a while Tom saw all the junk everywhere. Benny's parents, Susan and Mike, pulled into the Jumbo Smith Field with Tom in the back seat and parked the car. Tom got out of the car helping Mike, since he had suffered from severe arthritis. Sometimes it hurt for Mike to do things on his own strength, so people would help him. Tom was happy to be there to help him get up and out of the van.

Together they walked towards the other teens practicing their skills at football in the lush green field. Not too many cars were there yet. There would be later, when the other team arrived and once the game started. Benny's parents and Tom walked up to Benny. He was excited for them to be there.

Benny said to Tom, "So Tom, what you think of what's left of Autumn Limb?"

"Well, I do think they need to do a lot to get it looking good like how it used to be."

"Yeah. That's so true. Well I can't talk too long. I need to get back to practice."

Benny winked then ran back onto the field to practice some more. Tom wondered why Benny winked then looked over his shoulder at a pretty girl standing behind him. He had chuckled smirking at the thought of Benny trying to be a ladies man hitting on girls.

So, Tom decided to go take his seat. That way he would watch the game from a good view. So he headed up into the stands to find his place. Sitting there, he wondered what things might happen once he found Justin. He also, pondered how Tara was doing. Then after a while of sitting with more fans arriving, Tom called Tara just to check out what she had been up to since the last time they had spoken.

The hollowatch rang and she picked it up. Tom said to her, "Hello Tara. How is my wonderful girlfriend doing today?"

Tara blushed saying, "I am good. I'm just working on a school project while I've been thinking of going to the gym later to practice volley ball."

"Oh, yeah. Well I popped into town to see Benny's big game."

"That's cool. So you think he will do good?"

"More than likely. I think he will do an excellent job. You know how competitive he can get."

"True. He does have those tendencies."

"Anyhow, I was just wondering if you wanted to meet me here at his game?"

"Yeah. I would love to come to it. Let me go ask my parents."

Tara ran off with her hollowatch still held up asking her parents if they would drive her to the game. They of course said yes since they liked doing family like things. So Tara told him she would be there in a little while then they said their typical love you goodbyes to each other. Tom put on his wireless headphones getting out some music to listen to while he waited for Tara to arrive and the game to start.

Pretty soon the whole place was getting pretty crowded and there were lots of people all over the stands getting seated then the Macarthur Bulls showed up on their bus. They looked like they were very competitive; their confidence looked so high like somebody who would not lose this game very easily. As well, lots of other vehicles pulled in which were their big fan base and other fans of Smithsonian Valley.

The stands were then filling up with a countless multitude of people. All the stands that appeared empty to Tom less than twenty minutes prior were now very full then he walked down to buy some candy along with some water.

The game was now beginning with all the players going out onto the field then the Smithsonian Valley Wolves ended up with the ball rushing off trying to score. Benny himself was putting in lots of effort so they would win. One guy kept trying to block them a few times as the game was really heating up. Tom was cheering the wolves on putting his attention on them hardcore.

Then after a while Todd came flying up to the stands and came up from underneath near Tom's feet so nobody would notice him.

Todd then said to Tom, "So you think maybe if you find a word to somehow change me into a human people will like my personality?"

"Todd, I can't promise you anything because in this world there will always be people that like you for who you are or don't like you because of who you are or even for pointless reasons they won't like you or will."

"Well why don't I just make them like me or manipulate them to?"

"Because Todd, that just wouldn't be right plus you can't change people always. Most of the time it would be better if they changed their thoughts of you by their own will and not being forced or heavily manipulated."

"Yeah I guess you're right I just want to be accepted once I am human?"

"Accepted? Todd now you're just being silly, why wouldn't anybody like you half the time I think your charismatic maybe even too charismatic." Tom said giving a chuckle.

Then Todd said with a concerned voice, "Well long ago Dragons became hated creatures and were destroyed mostly…except a few dragons, they escaped the genocide and eventually I was made through my mother and father."

"Todd, if you become a human nobody will notice you're a dragon. Not to mention even if they did it wouldn't matter. At least not like people now days are going to want to murder you for what you are. Half the time, people in our world put odd things on pedestals. Even other people that become idols too, or even some people in certain categories get turned into living lifestyles, where people follow those by choice."

"Why would people do that? Isn't that just dumb to idolize other people and things to make it your whole life?"

"Not to some people. And who ever, really, could explain the complex philosophical question of why we do the things we do?"

"True...well, I guess, there is no reason to be afraid of what people think of me."

"You're right. There is no need to fear and besides, aren't you dragons supposed to be fearless?"

Todd and Tom chuckled watching the game together for a while. Tom noticed the score was getting interesting. The wolves were 3 and the Bulls had 1. But once Tom saw the score, he remembered talking to Tara and started to wonder where she was?

Well, obviously the next thing to happen was just as random as any other thing in life. Appearing coincidentally, as Tom got a text on his hollowatch that would definitely change the future for him and for many people in the world. His eyes widened when he read the text, "If you ever want to see your girlfriend in one piece, come to Mount Rainier by sunset or else you may never see her alive again."

Tom's heart filled with raging anger as soon as he read it. Then remembered he should not let his emotions affect him too much or else he might make things worse when having to confront about sending the text which, logically, had to have been Justin. He thought about how bad this could be. If he had only spoken to Tara not that long ago, it is obvious that Justin couldn't have gotten to Mt Rainier that fast to send him the text message.

So, Tom figured, with his great speed, he would be able to catch up with whatever form of air travel they must have been taking. But he thought he should first check out their house in case he hadn't taken her yet. And just to see if her parents were still there or if they were with Justin.

While everyone was watching the big game, Tom looked around to make sure nobody was watching him. He noticed the whole crowd had their eyes on the game. So he blasted off, vertically zooming about thirty feet above the stands as the players were being watched by the fans. He turned south on the field turning towards the goal.

Benny stumbled on the field because he thought he saw Tom flying up in the air. But he wasn't really sure that if what he saw really was Tom. Tom flew fast following highway 218 back to his neighborhood. Todd saw how he left without even saying goodbye and quickly followed him.

Once Tom was back in the neighborhood he landed in Tara's yard, and quickly ran into the busted front door. Then he saw that Tara's parents were badly hurt. Her father had an injury from a busted vase hitting his head. Her mother looked like she had been knocked unconscious. Their home looked very trashed. Tom started to stress and worry that things would not be all right because this time there clearly was a lot of damage. He wasn't sure if they were both either alive or dead, but he thought he'd better call for help.

Quickly he called Agent Dale, "Hurry, I need some help here with Tara's parents, I'm at their house!"

Feeling concerned not only for Tara and her family, but also for his own future, Agent Dale rubbed his sore hand with it's new mark and he said, "Wait. Hold on. Why are you there? What happened?"

"I am not sure what happened, but I think Justin has done this and he may have kidnapped Tara to take her to Mount Rainier!"

"Did he contact you or something?" He said not feeling well.

"Yeah, I got a text a few minutes ago from a random number I didn't recognize. So, I came here to see if she was okay and found her parents really hurt."

"Alright Tom. I will quickly be on my way by helicopter, once I get to SanAntonio by Jet. I just landed in America from a long journey to Europe. So I will try to get there as soon as I can. In the meantime, I am going to get some local police to check it out."

"Okay, I am going to try to stop Justin or whoever took her."

"I think it's a safe bet to say he took her. Who else would kidnap a girl close to you?"

Tom chuckled saying, "You would be surprised what guys I know that would kidnap girls."

"Okay? I don't get what that is about, but whatever you do Tom, be careful when you confront this kidnapper. You don't want to put the earth off orbit or do something too extreme to them when you get to the kidnapper."

"Don't worry Agent Dale, I have a plan." Tom hung up. Then Todd asked, "What's going on?"

Tom said with a stern voice, "I have got a great girlfriend to save. You head back to the hotel."

Todd nodded his head and flew off to the north east. Tom was fuelled with a powerful passion to save the girl he loved, so he blasted off heading north gaining altitude fast as he ascended into the beautiful, cloudy blue sky. Creating a powerful jet stream over Canyon Lake, he flew very fast, heading northwest chasing after the kidnappers.

Eventually, somewhere over the Rocky Mountains near Utah, Colorado and Wyoming Tom approached the only air vehicle he could find on that route; a helicopter. As he was getting close to it, he saw the side of the door open as a guy with a gatling gun was firing it up. He was getting it ready to fire rapid bullets at Tom.

Tom yelled, as the Gatling gun's chambers started to spin, "Exertus the bullets away from me towards the mountains below!"

The man clearly had a good aim as the bullets flew directly towards Tom at full speed. He banked over to the right like an airplane trying to avoid the bullets from hitting him, just incase what he had said was only limited to the first batch of bullets. The volley of the bullets was powerful.

Tom knew this because he could feel their strength as they created blast of air against the protection he had set up for himself. He figured he would have to follow the kidnappers from behind hidden if he wanted to retrieve Tara safely.

Tom remembered how he had rescued that one kidnapped victim in the car and thought, "Wait. I could just inflecto her to me." But then, he thought about physics and about that helicopter was going so fast to inflecto her at those speeds. To do that in the air or on ground she might move too fast and the momentum could kill her from flying into the ground. Or she could move too quickly for him to catch her. So he decided to hide out as he followed them more as they flew for a few more hours since the helicopter was slower.

Eventually, they reached Washington and were nearly to Mt. Rainier, when Tom approached from behind the helicopter. The door slid open. This time one of the guys hanging out the door pulled out an AT4-HS Rocket Launcher and aimed it towards Tom locking onto him. Seeing this, his eyes widened with fear, as he saw the launcher he quickly banked left and did a quick fly around to the front of the helicopter. As the Rocket was launched it propelled flying after him. He thought about how he should stop it from following him. He turned vertically and flew up higher. Then he did an upside down turn, flying back down heading past the helicopter then quickly he turned around and flew backwards.

As Tom flew backwards, he yelled at the Rocket, "Ignis!" Holding his hands aimed at the Rocket which was in between him and the Helicopter the Rocket exploded with a big explosion and damaged the tail rotor of the helicopter.

The Helicopter started to spin a little then it self-stabilized. It was letting off some smoke as it started to descend onto the top of Mount Rainier. Quickly, Tara, along with Justin, Sacra and some of the terrorists who still had a vendetta against Tom came out of the helicopter as it landed.

Tom landed very hard as he came down vertically to the ground. Justin grabbed Tara along with Sacra and they walked her over with them onto a higher rock.

Justin was holding Tara and saif with a semi sympathetic voice, "Tom, I didn't mean to kill your little brother. I am really sorry for what happened."

With an angry, sarcastic voice Tom said, "Judging by how you're holding my girlfriend right now, I don't think Martin's death affected you that much."

"Tom, it really did affect me in a big way. For months, I felt horrible about it. I couldn't sleep at night for weeks. But once we got to that place through that cave, everything I ever knew changed drastically and I learned how to deal with it."

Justin started remembering what had happened to him over the past many months. He remembered how he traveled over the ocean on the cargo ship and was affected to the point that he couldn't sleep at night because of that one moment of when he killed Martin. It kept playing in his head over and over again like a nightmare. Apparently, even with all Justin's cruelty, he still was emotional enough of a person to experience PTSD.

Eventually Justin along with Sacra and the terrorists arrived in England heading for the Knight's Cave. Sacra thought they should explore and set up a base there in this mysterious off the ELO world.

So they headed on through the wormhole into the strange land which they just thought of as the secret world. They wandered the land heading towards the mountains of the area that Tom had once seen past a valley forest. Out of the edge of the forest, the mountains were on the other side of a river, so they had to find a way across and not get swept away.

After being in there for a very long time they reached the lowest peak on the giant mountain which had a very odd architecture structure. It had some sort of monastery or domicile on a very lush green plateau. Justin remembered how they all entered the main hall of the odd structured building then looked around and soon some strange figures emerged.

These tall, anamorphic creatures were between seven and to eleven feet tall. They looked as though they were made of energy. As if their bodies were made of crystal, with giant auras surrounding them that looked like wings attached to their back sides. All the light they were made of scintillated off of them. What you saw with your own eyes was hard to tell if they had anything ocular going for them.

Justin, Sacra and the Terrorist were all afraid of these strange beings. Terrified at what the creatures looked like. The creatures saw their concern and transformed themselves into old looking human monks, much like the kind found in the Appalachians or Himalayan Mountains.

They stayed with these creatures for a while. These denizens of the mountain were very nice and caring toward them. Even though Justin, along with his retinue didn't seem to show signs of being grateful for their generosity. Eventually, Justin with the rest of them left to go back to Earth through the wormhole.

No time had passed on earth when they got back. For the next four months Justin plotted for this moment. They wanted to make sure their plan was flawless so they could achieve their devious goal.

"Basically, now I am a whole new kind of person, Tom." Justin said to Tom.

Tom had an absolute feeling of enmity that Justin's personality didn't change at all. So he then said jokingly, "Have you now?"

Then Justin said to Tom, "Doesn't matter now. I have got things that I need to take care of and you're in my way. It's time to end you once and for all, Turner."

Tara screamed, "Tom! Look out!!!"

Tom looked over his shoulder and out of the corner of his eye he saw the helicopter come flying towards him with its propellers spinning fast. He leaped up, doing a vertical back flip, and flew over the spinning propellers. Then the copter went under him as he came back down, avoiding the propellers.

Justin was furious with Tara and yelled, "Don't talk unless I tell you to, you stupid girl!" Then he slapped her in the face which sent her flying into the ground below the high rock they were standing on.

Tom then yelled to Justin on the rock, "I knew you didn't change at all. You will always be an amoral, belligerent, dastard!"

"What did you just call me?!"

"Oh, brother…it means somebody who fights all the time. Just like a malicious coward with no morals."

"I am no coward Turner. But you will be nothing once I am done with you."

Tom said, "You just never learn from your mistakes, do ya?"

"Neither do you, Turner."

Then Tom's face was stricken with horror as he noticed a giant rock flying at him. Tom had not realized the helicopter coming at him was done by Justin's will. Quickly he yelled, "Exertus!" The giant rock went flying back at Justin, as he ripped it apart into many pieces when it almost hit him.

Justin remembered when he was outside on the mountain top and the creatures were throwing big boulders as they moved their arms. When one of them moved their hand around, the boulder would move with their hand. He was amazed by this and showed interest in the strange beings. Then one of them walked up to him, holding out it's hand with a small river stone in it. It had picked it up from the local river by the structure up on the mountain.

In Justin's mind it was imperceptible how they were doing these majestic things. But he wondered if this is where Tom had gotten his ability. The strange creature smiled as Justin then moved its other hand up as the stone rose. Then it handed it to him. He had already felt peaceful and relaxed about Martin's death after being there for so long. But these creatures made him feel happy, constantly.

Justin got that happy feeling from what he saw. So he held out his hand making the river stone move up into the air. For quite a while, Justin kept practicing moving other things that were big in comparison to the River Stone.

Eventually, in-between their planning and raiding an American military ware house, Justin practiced his new found ability on big things. In his eyes, nothing could stop them now. He was ready to confront Tom as he had built up all his plans and all his wits for this one moment. As well he had his own plans for the future.

Justin said with a snide remark, "You see, Tom, you may be smart with science junk, but you miss out on the little things that any normal person could figure out. Such as, how can I just use my mind to make anything happen while you need to say things in ancient Latin? From my view, that makes you the weak one here!" Justin cackled manically as he swung his arm out sending Tom flying into the helicopter creating a dent in it.

Tom got back up and said with a snarky attitude, "Now…now Justin, don't let those delusions of grandeur make you think you're more powerful than you really are."

Angrily Justin flipped him and knocked him off his feet again. Once Tom had gotten back up, he paced towards Justin's rock with his chest held high as he said something with a very bold authoritive voice, "Justin, even if you do have that advantage of not having to talk to make things happen, at least I have one myself. And that would be my imagination and my capability of dealing with troubled beings just like you. There will always be people who oppose you and there will always be somebody to rise up against the evil in this world, I am here to do that now."

Justin was furious as he yelled, "Well Tom, just like you, I can do so much more now. Even beyond your capabilities. I will take this whole world down just to destroy you and every rotten creature with it! You can't save everyone in the world all at once!" Raising his arms as he yelled those chilling words, the whole ground beneath him began to shake chaotically as rumbling started going off everywhere. Then behind them, in the center of the volcano of Mount Rainier, it began exploding as it erupted powerfully with a massive earthquake.

Justin yelled, "This isn't the only one going off Tom. I am making every Volcano everywhere go off so that everyone burns in their own despair!" The terrorist along with Sacra got into the banged up helicopter and flew off as it was releasing smoke. They did this because they didn't want to get destroyed by the volcano erupting.

Tom saw the sun setting and the moon in the sky then thought of a way to try to stop the lava from killing everyone. He was thinking so frantically he didn't think of the consequences of his actions.

Quickly Tom yelled, "This one's for Martin! Make the moon Cruentus and amplifico a turbo ventus on every Volcano in the world!"

Combined with the darkness of all the ashes being spread everywhere from all the volcanos going off, the full moon turned blood red. It looked very super eerily creepy, as it turned blood red a great eerie trumpet sounded from the ends of the earth. Many people looked up as the fire rained down on them. They were scared of the blood moon, fearing the sounding trumpet loud in the sky.

Tom went running forward when he yelled his battle cry for Martin, throwing a left hook at Justin. As Tom was throwing the punch at Justin, a giant massive Tornado appeared and met with the volcano as it erupted making all the lava become sucked up into the vortex and dispersing everywhere. As that was happening from every volcano in the world, fire rained down on everyone everywhere. But, as soon as Tom and Justin heard the trumpet they both stopped fighting for moment wondering what that trumpet sound was.

Since Tom was distracted by the noise in the sky, Justin took advantage of the situation and power punched Tom backwards, making him fly at the ground he was standing on a moment prior.

Tom got up rubbing the dirt off of himself and reached his arm up into the air yelling, "Voco Lightning!" The lightning, very bright and powerful, descended from the sky as Tom swung his hand forward pointing at Justin. But as it was flying at Justin, it stopped and dispersed in midair as he had blocked it with his mind.

Tom reached both his arms back, like rewinding a clock, then shoved them forward as he flew forward at Justin, holding out his fist ready to punch him as he flew straight for him. But as he went flying towards Justin, Justin flew vertically up into the air. Then Tom turned, banking away to avoid the Tornado. Then flew back around into the air in front of Justin and went on full speed at him as he round house kicked him.

As they were both floating there in front of the fire twister, Justin grabbed Tom and tried to kick him. Then he threw him across the sky above the mountain's plateau. Tom stabilized himself in the air just as Justin reached out both of his hands oppressing him with extreme might with his mind. Then he made him crash into the ground really hard.

Tom was now a little banged up from all the damage being thrown at him. He looked up at Justin as he saw him reach his hand back then move them forward as lava came flowing out of the tornado in a massive river straight at Tom.

Things were looking bleak for Tom as he saw this. He tried to think of something to say, but was banged up from it so much that he couldn't think of anything to say as he saw the lava coming at him. The Lava was getting brighter and brighter till it flashed so big in his face he couldn't see anything or stop it…

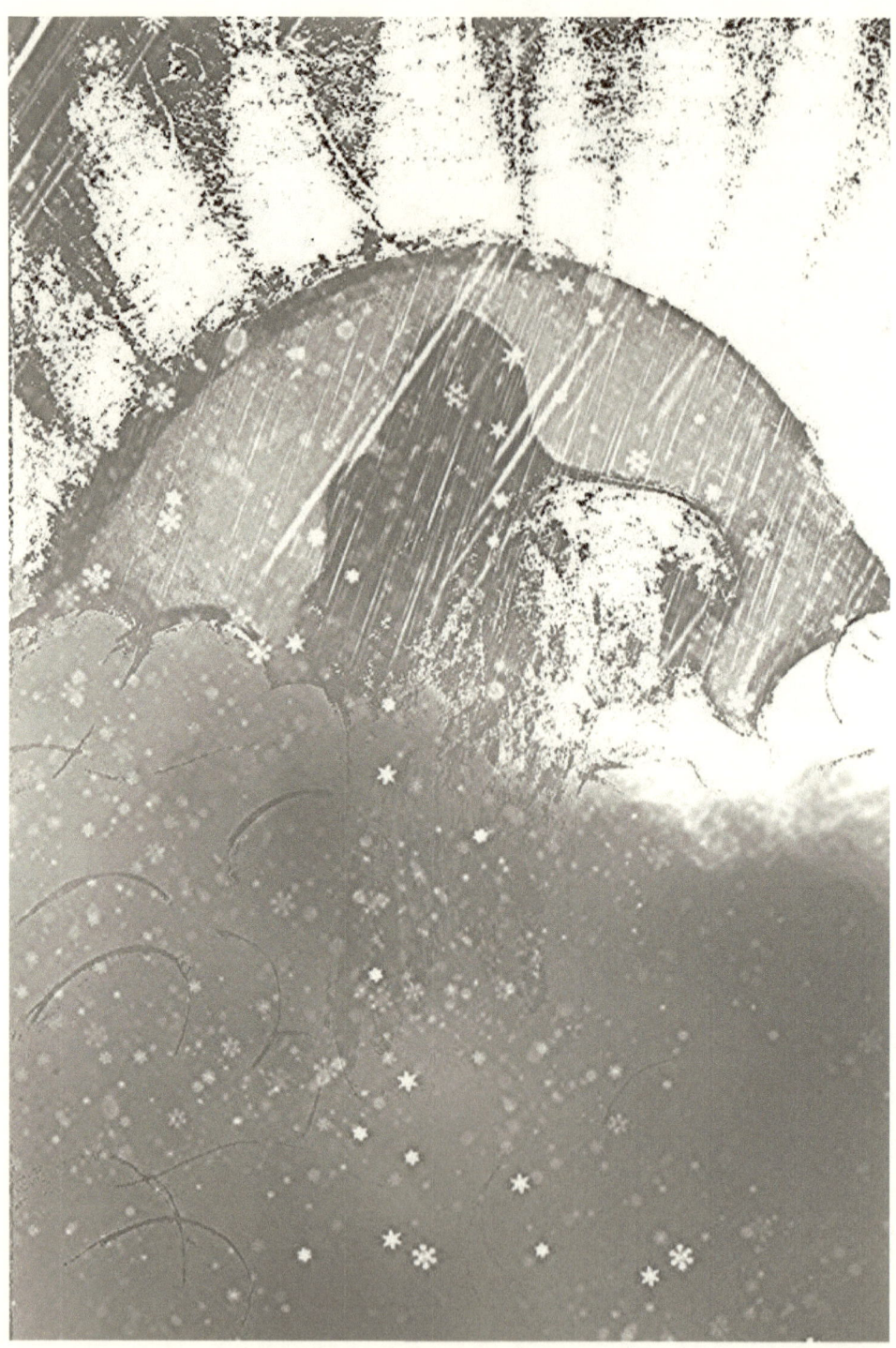

Chapter 27
Does He Live?

Very dazed and confused at what had just happened, Tom opened his eyes. Feeling dizzy, the last thing he remembered was fighting Justin. Then all that lava that had come flying right at him and how there was a bright flash before waking up here.

But then, Tom gave it some thought, "Where am I now?"

Looking around to see that it was really foggy and cloudy, he noticed how he was floating in the air. Then he wondered where the ground was? Realizing he felt naked, he looked down wondering if he was. When he looked at himself, there was a light piece of clothing surrounding his body that looked very unusual and semi futuristic. Then he thought to himself. "Where did this clothing come from and who clothed me?"

"Where are my glasses? Why are the clouds in front of me not blurry and my vision so extraordinary?" He thought to himself again.

Tom felt physically stronger like he was more developed, as well full of energy. The feeling was incomparable to anything he had felt before. He felt his arm and noticed his muscles were more toned and looked even more than when he was using his abilities to build up extra strength.

As he stood there feeling his new found muscles, he noticed he smelled everything in greater detail as well. Like the water vapor of the clouds surrounding him was crisp and clear.

Tom's head started to clear, and he looked around to see he wasn't the only one floating in the cloud or whatever this place was.

Over by his side and looking to his left, he saw his parents, and John, Jessica, Robbie, and Joshua. But nothing could prepare him emotionally for the next person he saw. As he looked down right next to him, tears began to swell up from within him. Not tears of sorrow, but massive tears of joy. It gave him happiness, but confusion and sorrow all combined into one. Standing there right with him was Martin, perfectly alive and well.

Martin looked up and grabbed Tom by the hand, as he said, "Are you alright?"

"I don't know how I feel right now, Martin? I thought you died?"

"Yes Tom…indeed I did."

"But then how are you here right now? Does this mean I died too, is this the end for me?" Tom asked as a tear rolled down his cheek.

Then a thunderous, ominous voice said, "No, you are all very much still alive. But now we must celebrate and rejoice, because your brother was dead and now he has come to life again. He was lost and has been found!"

Tom turned his head away from his family to see what looked like the sun rising. He saw in the center of the sun light, what looked something like a human figure, but he couldn't see fully because of the brightness of the sun.

Tom looked around some more at the people there and noticed there was a giant multitude of people beyond his ability to count. He noticed looking past Martin was what looked like younger versions of his grandparents. He recognized them from photos along with other relatives that were not in his immediate family. He looked some more and saw Tara's parents over in one direction, but the wounds to their bodies looked like they were gone. Christie was with them as well. Then he saw Benny's father, Mike, next to Tara's family jumping for joy that his pain and arthritis was gone.

Tom thought, "What is he jumping on if there is no ground here?"

Next to Benny's father was Mrs. Chaffin, She had her husband there with her, and next to her were lots of her children and grandchildren. Then in another row of people he saw Paulo with his wife and two boys. Tom presumed they were Kevin's half-brothers he had never met. "But where is Kevin?" Tom pondered in his mind.

Then he saw Rosita holding hands with her mom. Tom had occasionally seen her at the Pizzeria. Over in another row he saw Kelly with a man and a woman and a little girl. Then he saw Joe next to Kelly with his own family. On the other side of Kelly's group was Chloe Manning and her little sister, Holly, along with their parents and family. Past Chloe, he thought he saw Chloe's boyfriend, Craig Shielding, with his family. Past Craig was Jason Steward and his family. But surprisingly past on one side of Joe and his family, he saw Billy Chamberlin with people Tom presumed were his family.

In the row behind Joe, Tom could see Alex standing there. He was all alone with nobody there to hold his hand or greet him. But then he saw Joe and then they started talking. So, at least Alex had Joe there with him as a friend. To the side of Alex was a boy with dark, brown, curly hair Tom didn't recognize. It was Alex and Joe's friend Ross. He was touching his mouth like he was looking for his braces, then he looked over to his left and started to cry as he saw his mother. Tom recognized these tears as they were the same ones he had when he saw Martin.

On the other side of his father, Tom noticed Agent Dale's mysterious friend standing there. But he couldn't look past him to tell if Agent Dale was there or Agent Dale's friend's family because of the angle. On a different row, Tom noticed Matt and his family there with his brothers. But why wasn't Benny with his dad or maybe he was and just on a side Tom couldn't see? In one direction, he saw Ricky, the gang leader, with an older woman holding his hand. He had presumed that lady was Ricky's mother, but that really shocked him that he was there.

As Tom kept looking around he saw many local people from his home town and school as well as from other places. Some from the kids that would get out at the Bexley Ledger secondary school and many more that looked to be of different cultures and ethnicities throughout the multitude of people.

Tom wondered what was going on and why he and all these other people were there and if that ominous voice was honest? Seeing all these people from different places, some he thought were dead, it just didn't add up in his mind. It seemed very imperceptible or unbelievable. It was so illogical and irrational that all this could be happening. But then Tom thought a lot of things that had been going on his life didn't totally add up lately.

Then the great voice coming from the figure in the middle of the sun spoke ominously, "You are all here today because you have chosen me as your master and therefor shall follow me. Your lives may have been challenging, but for most it will only be easier now."

Tom thought to himself, "I didn't choose anybody to control me. What is this guy talking about? Then he said we chose him as our master, I wonder if this guy is the same master or related to the one from the Concero Regnum that Alida spoke of in her diary?"

Tom could see him fully because he was higher than everyone else around, but the light was scintillating off of his body very brightly. The Voice spoke more saying, "There will be no more sorrow, only joy for everybody where we are going. You will enjoy it every moment you are there. But when given an order, you will have to listen and act without hesitation."

Tom thought this place sounded like slavery to him and he wasn't ready to just give up his freedom. Then he remembered how he said there will only be joy there. "How could a person be joyful about being told what to do all the time?" Tom thought as he noticed this was all beyond his reasoning and logic.

Then Tom ascended a little higher and was on an equal line of sight with the one proclaiming to be their new master. Now, he was even brighter. But Tom could see that he was not totally human looking. What he could make out sort of looked like eyes made out of flames. He wore a white shiny, unusual piece of clothing like something the other people were wearing. Tom saw only his clothes were glowing with radiance and beauty beyond his comprehension. His clothes looked somewhat different than theirs. Somehow, though, what he wore seemed like it was still from the same branch of clothing line.

He was scintillating with lots of different colors radiating off of him. Even colors that Tom had never seen before and that amazed all his senses. He even thought that he smelled scents he had never even smelled before. They were magnificent making him feel like he did the first time he had flown. It gave him that feeling throughout his whole body that would make a man pause, as though he was paralyzed at its glory. The way it made him feel was unparalleled to any other feeling he had ever known.

The voice then acted as though it was speaking to Tom and a certain group of others all at once saying, "You all still have important destinies ahead of you. The seven of you will be known to me as the sacred seven. When the time is right, you will come together to help me in my time of need. May all of you be blessed and protect each other when needed."

Then Tom looked over to his left and saw the girl he had seen crash into the lake in Cremo. She was holding hands with someone he thought was Dan Hernandez. He had seen him in a photo on Myles's desk. Then, he looked down under the guy to see Myles look up at him and wave.

On the other side of Dan, he saw a girl wearing some futuristic looking clothing. A little different from the stuff the other people below had on. She clearly came from an oddly different culture than any culture, more odd than Tom could think of.

Then he turned to his right to see the guy next to him had weird shoes on and rings on his arms, wrist and legs. The rings glowed aqua blue with a strange outfit that one would swear looked like a superhero gimmick with a green cape along with some design on it he couldn't totally see. What kind of stuff was this guy into that he looked so oddly dressed?

To the right of that guy was a young teenager that looked Filipino. He was younger than Tom and was wearing an odd martial arts looking vest with no sleeves. The boy had a weird long stick with him and he was standing on a cloud. But the cloud was letting off all the smoke surrounding them or letting off more clouds around them all.

To the right of the martial arts kid was a guy with semi, long, dark brownish, black hair that looked like he had a dark personality. His hands were glowing purple and there was some purple light coming off his feet.

Tom pondered over who these sacred seven people could be and what all this was about as he was checking out all the differences in these people. Tom wondered why some people were there and why some were not.

Then the Voice spoke to Tom personally, "Tom, do not worry too much about why some are here and some are not. Tara, for instance, still has a role to play in this world and so do other people you are wondering about."

"How am I to know what you want us to do, though?"

"Don't worry, Tom, I will be with you always."

Then the Voice focused on the seven of them in a thunderous voice, "Now go forth and change the world!"

The others all started to ascend up into the heavens with the man in the sun, as Tom and the others of the sacred seven stayed below. As the ones below them ascended above, Tom focused and waved goodbye to his family.

Then with great reasons and purposes the seven of them headed west with great speed and persistence, chasing the night that was disappearing into day. The more they went forward it got brighter as the sun was coming up behind them and the darkness in front of them was quickly fading. As they were flying in their strange outfits, vibrations started coming off their feet and colliding with the other vibrations as they turned into colors much like a prism as they went forth creating what looked like a rainbow Jetstream.

They were going fast together and saw that fire was still raining down everywhere. In some places they saw tornados on mountains everywhere spewing fire balls in every direction. Together, they used their different abilities and technology to block balls of flaming lava and even just regular plasma like flames from flying at them.

Sometimes Tom would swerve out of the way to avoid an oncoming lava ball and other times he would exertus some of them away from him. The Asian boy was flying fast on his cloud, spinning his wooden staff that he had in his hand. It caused a horizontal cyclone to push fire balls and lava out of their way. The guy with the purple glowing hands and feet was holding out his hands blasting the fire balls apart with weird bursting flashes of energy from the center of the fire balls. It looked somewhat magical. The fire balls just seemed to randomly go in other directions when they got too close to Dan and the girl Tom had rescued in Cremo. It was as though they had some sort of shield around them. The super hero looking guy was blasting lava balls apart with these odd laser things on the sides of the lobe of his head, they looked like a circlet headband that was only covering half of his skull as he blasted the oncoming rocks with some bolts of energy he would blast had from the palm of his hands and finger tips of his suit. The girl at the end though, seemed like she had it the hardest, having to avoid everything coming at her.

They all kept going west till somewhere near Western Europe one of them split apart from them and left them there going their own way. It was the guy wearing the weird rings and super hero outfit, but as he left the others took turns and flight banks in different directions to get where they each wanted or needed to go. But Tom just kept heading west.

While he was getting closer to America, he wondered if Agent Dale was okay or if agent Dale had managed to get somewhere safe before the fire in the sky could have landed on him. Then Tom thought about how he needed to stop all the erupting from happening and thought of how he could do it. Crossing over most of America, he was keeping an eye out and watching everywhere for oncoming fire from the sky and he had to be careful not to get hit by it.

After a treacherous adventure across the distressed planet that everyone called home, Tom was finally approaching Mount Rainier again. Then, once he arrived he came down quickly landing on his feet with joy. He was happy to see Tara was okay and that she had gotten back up. Justin saw Tom, and was shocked, and then he started to get a little bit emotional. Tara was awake again and jumped for joy and excitement that Tom was there.

Tara said in a happy manner, "Oh Tom you're alive, I woke up and saw you right as Justin threw all that lava on you."

"Yeah, I am still here. Not quite fully sure how that took me to the other side of the world. But it did." Quickly putting his plan into action to stop Justin, Tom said, "Vinculum Justin to the rock slab behind him to where he can't become undone on his own."

Instantly, Justin became fettered to the slab of hard rock. "Tom, I'm so sorry for everything I have done. But I'm so grateful you aren't dead..." Justin said catching his breath from his emotional shock.

"How can you be remotely happy that I'm not dead? You tried to kill Tara and me so many times." Tom asked puzzled, yet rhetorically.

"Because, Tom, the world needs you. I killed your brother. I killed you. There is no room for me in this world. I'm a murderer. I'm a monster. I'm damaged goods...but you are everything a person should be. You were like a brother to me and cared for me. You forgave me when you shouldn't have. You are the only person who ever actually tried to be there for me and I ruined it...I have ruined the world."

Reaching out his hands, exasperated and emotional Tom exclaimed, "It doesn't have to be broken. Together we can fix it and help others like I have tried to help you. You can be a better person, Justin. It's not too late."

Chained up to the rock, Justin said, "That's exactly what I'm going to do...but this is the end for me." Justin turned his head towards the fire twister. "Justin, no!" Tom shouted, thinking Justin was going to commit suicide.

Debris started flying past all three of them going quickly toward the lake of magma with the tornado spinning upon it. "Justin what are you doing?" Tom shouted because of the loud rushing winds. "Saving the world from my chaos!" Justin yelled.

Sacrificing himself for the safety of mankind, Justin tethered to the rock slab went flying towards one of the many endless wormholes he had formed in the center of all the places he made erupt. Tara screamed as she got pulled towards it as well...

Watching Tara reaching out in fear with lava behind her, Tom quickly yelled, "Give Tara Lentus against lava and Tutela her from it and Praesidium her from anything hurting her!" Tara almost hit the lava being sucked into the endless wormhole when a bright blue light surrounded her as she went flying into the magma. Tom knew what he must do now.

Figuring how Justin was trying to save the world Tom immediately yelled, "Amplifico my words to all eruptions, Consisto all Tornados!" as he dived horizontally going into the endless wormhole of lava to try to save Tara and Justin.

The volcano started to implode as all of its lava & rocks was being sucked in by the endless wormhole Justin had made. Seeing Tara's body falling deeper inward, Tom quickly grabbed onto Justin's rock slab as he flew down into the black hole, taking Justin with him. Then they both kept falling and falling deeper. Clearly they were not on earth any more, but stuck in an endless vortex of raging chaos & destruction.

Picking up speed, Tom tried to help Justin out by saying, "Explico the chains Justin is bound to." Instantly, Justin was freed from the slab. "What is this, Justin?" Tom asked as they fell. Trying to keep rocks away, Justin responded, "I thought of something like a black hole from a documentary I saw that reminded me of you. But one that couldn't kill us."

"Okay, I know how to fix this. Adjungo all Vermus or Pullus Cavuses and Dismullio all exits and entrances to them never letting me or anybody else open them again." Tom said. Immediately every endless wormhole all over the earth Justin had made and the one worm hole connected to the mysterious world came together into a complex world wide web within the middle of the planet with no way out. The Wormhole in the cave by the sea & the black hole on top of Mount Rainier closed as they both sealed into weird energy bubble like walls. Quickly, Tom pressed against the rock slab's surface thrusting forward picking up speed to catch up with Tara.

Almost hitting a giant rock, Tom covered his eyes. Right as he flew into it he went right through it though. Somehow he phased through it. Lots of rocks were flying at Justin, but he ripped them to shreds with his mind so they wouldn't hurt him since he felt obligated to help save Tara. Justin would have just passed through the rocks, but he didn't know that like Tom had just found out. Tom kept looking for Tara when he eventually found her in some lava.

Then, Tom flew up to her saying, "Ventus Tara to me." The flames on the lava went away as the lava blew off of Tara as she drifted over to Tom's arms as they were falling with great speed.

Tom smiled as he said, "Don't worry, baby, everything is gonna be alright." Tara smiled back at Tom when he said this.

"Justin, are you ready to leave this place!?" Tom yelled from below.

Tara flew out of his arms as he spoke, going further down into the endless wormhole. Tom rushed forward, but was being propelled so fast that he went flying straight through Tara accidently phasing through her just like the rock. Tom turned himself around quickly then looked up at Tara.

Justin was building up his velocity to catch up with them. He was going so fast he didn't see Tara coming as he went flying right through her phasing just like Tom. Tom was concerned when he saw Justin's body almost hit her, but saw him phase through her safely.

As he continued to watch him coming down, Tom quickly moved out of the way. Then Justin flew right past him. Tom slowed down to catch Tara. He tried to match her speed and as he did they didn't phase through each other. Tom grabbed her by her backside holding her in his arms.

Then she said, "Thanks, Tom. I am so glad to have you as my boyfriend."

"I love you, Tara. I would never let you down." She blushed as they kept falling. Then Justin yelled up to him, "Tom, what have you done now? We are stuck in this thing."

"Don't worry. I have a way to teleport us out."

"No, Tom. I know you care about me, but I can't let you risk having me hurt the world again. I'm sorry for murdering your brother and trying to murder the both of you. But the world needs you still. That I am sure of. Make a better world than I did."

Tom saw Justin raising his hand to send them away so he could sacrifice himself in the complex wormhole tunnel and Tom yelled, "No!!! Voco lightning!"

As Tom held Tara with his left arm, he swung his right arm aiming his hand along with his middle and pointer finger at Justin. Then lightning went down fast. Justin made the lightning disperse as it continued pouring down toward him, continuously.

Trying to keep the lightning from shocking him so he couldn't be saved, Justin yelled up, "You can't save me, Tom. I made it where you won't be able to enter the black hole and neither will I be able to exit it by your choice or mine. Goodbye Tom. I will always be glad you were willing to be my friend!"

Tom tried to fly down to rescue him with lightning shooting at him as he screamed. "No, Justin, don't do this! You can still change to be good; I have seen the light in you!"

"Sorry, Tom, there isn't any hope for me now. Go away. You and everyone else are way better off without me." Justin said as he made Tom propel back up the endless wormhole farther from him. It instantly sent Tom and Tara away through a portal he opened only for moment.

Justin did this so he could sacrifice himself for the sake of the world in the endless hole of despair he was now trapped in.

As the two of them were falling with great speed though the portal, Tom and Tara seemed dumbfounded by the quick change of scenery. As both of them emerged falling towards the mountain, Tom was able to stabilize himself in the air and slowing down before the force of their falling had made them hit the mountain. Tara held onto him tightly as he descended landing on top of the mountain with her in his arms.

Setting her down on her feet, Tom ran quickly over to where the wormhole was. There was nothing there but a weird bubble of energy popping up from the caldera of the volcano. Tom ashamed and guilt ridden from the result of this final conflict with Justin yelled, "Inflecto me to Justin! Take me to him, please!" Nothing happened and it made Tom fall to his knees in despair. He slammed his fist down against the energy bubble, crying.

Tara walked up behind him and putts her hand on his shoulder saying, "It is okay Tom. He was a really tormented man. There was nothing you could do to save him. Only he had the choice to accept being saved. He won't have to suffer now and you did all you could."

Getting up, Tom hugged Tara in a loving embrace to feel comforted in this hard time.

Looking, around Tara said, "Wow, Tom, that sure was one crazy adventure. But look at all the forest surrounding us. It's sad they are all burning and will be ruined if you don't do something to fix them."

"You think that was crazy. You should of seen all the stuff that happened before I came back to you while I vanished from the top of the mountain."

"Yeah, I think you should put out those fires and what could have been more crazy than feeling lava, but not being hurt by it and getting sucked into a black hole?"

"You will understand when I explain everything later on. If that was a black hole and not just a wormhole without an end we wouldn't have survived it more than likely. Amplifico my words everywhere and Consisto all the forest fires in the world."

"Oh, okay. Guess you're right. That would have more force to it."

Tom saw the flames die down on every branch that was on fire from all that lava that had hit them and then turn into nothing more than a bunch of smoke.

Tom then said, "There, that should keep them all from burning."

"Yeah, but Tom, they all still kind of look dead?"

Tom looked around noticing Tara was right. He thought something needed to be done to fix them. "Can you heal them with any certain words?" Tara said concerned sounding.

"Yeah, hold on. Amplifico my words everywhere and sano all the trees and plants that have been harmed by the raging fire from the lava."

Like the beautiful time plants had grown by the beach, with Tom and Tara all the plants and trees started to bloom with a glow of the radiance of the soothing "hum" sound that came during a lot of the times Tom used his abilities.

After admiring the beauty of the mountains and plants Tara asked, "What do you think happened to Justin?"

"Well, he felt so bad about who he was as a person. I guess he decided to try to sacrifice himself so he couldn't hurt us or any other person ever again."

"Man, that is pretty sad. I think I understand why you just reacted the way you did when we landed."

"Yeah. He was finally willing to change, I think. It's a shame he couldn't deal with all the bad things of his past and just move on."

"Well, maybe we can help people who think there isn't any hope in life."

"Yeah, maybe. We shall see."

"So, what are we going to do now?"

Tom responded, "Well, I need to go check if my brother John is okay and make sure he is even at that hotel in Seattle. I am not fully sure how I went from being smothered in lava to the other side of the planet, but I need to figure out what all happened. We will need to travel and head due north-west to the Caspian Inn by the Space Needle Tower in Seattle."

"Okay, let's go check it out. But why not just warp there?"

"Because, in times like these, who knows if warping would be wise. Somebody could see us there and get the wrong idea. But, like I have thought, all that heat could possibly have affected the magnetic field of the earth."

"What does the magnetic field have to do with us warping?"

"Even though my abilities seem like Magic, I have always thought they worked in a complex science kind of way. Some people in pseudo-science (Which means not fully understood but still possible science) think the key to teleporting may have to do with manipulating the magnetic field of the planet and if all that heat affected it too much the magnetic field could be erratic, so we might warp into a wall or someplace far off course."

"Whatever Tom, let's just get going before it gets too dark. You're so cute and funny when you talk like such a genius."

Tom chuckled, "Thanks Tara. You're cute all the time. Well let's get going, baby." She blushed once more and nodded in agreement.

Tom, was very curious about all that was going to change now that Justin was out of the picture and Sacra had escaped with the other terrorists. It seemed very strange about the ordeal with the man in the sun.

But, for now all seemed better as Tom had just saved the world and things were at peace for the time being. He picked up Tara in his arms with his new found strength and she felt like she was as light as paper. Running with all his might and strength he lifted his legs leaping off of a cliff on top of Mount Rainier and took off. As he blasted into the sky, Tom held Tara in his arms as they flew off together into the sunset.

Timeline Bible Verse Index

1. Monday, March 09th at 4:07 PM Page 03
   1st John 4:07 Beloved, let us love one another: for love is of God; and every one that loveth is born of God, and knoweth God.

2. Saturday, April 17th 1221 A.D. at 8:38 PM Page 15
   Mark 8:38 For whoever is ashamed of me and my words in this adulterous and sinful generation, of him will the Son of Man also be ashamed when he comes in the glory of his Father with the holy angels.

3. Monday, March 09th at 4:13 PM Page 20
   Philippians 4:13 I can do all things through Christ which strengtheneth me.

4. Monday, March 09th at 4:48 PM Page 23
   John 4:48 So Jesus said to him, "Unless you see signs and wonders, you will not believe."

5. Wednesday, March 11th at 12:10 PM Page 29
   Romans 12:10 Love one another with brotherly affection. Outdo one another in showing honor.

6. Friday, March 13th at 6:10 PM Page 29
   Hebrews 6:10 For God is not unjust so as to overlook your work and the love that you have shown for his name in serving the saints, as you still do.

7. Sunday, March 22nd at 1:10 PM Page 42
   Galatians 1:10 For am I now seeing the approval of man, or of God? Or am I trying to please man? If I were still trying to please man, I would not be a servant of Christ.

8. Sunday, March 22nd at 4:12 PM Page 46
   1st Corinthians 4:12 and we labor, working with our own hands. When reviled, we bless; when persecuted we endure;

9. Monday, March 23rd at 6:14 PM Page 55
   2nd Corinthians 6:14 Do not be unequally yoked with unbelievers. For what partnership has righteousness with lawlessness? Or what fellowship has light with darkness?

10. Sunday, March 08th at 03:40 PM Page 65
    1st Corinthians 15:40 There are heavenly bodies and earthly bodies, but the glory of the heavenly is of one kind, and the glory of the earthly is of another.

11. Saturday, March 28th at 9:12 AM Page 69
    Matthew 9:12 But when he heard it, he said, "Those who are well have no need of a physician, but those who are sick."

12. Friday, April 17th at 4:02 PM Page 75
    Matthew 4:02 And after fasting forty days and forty nights, he was hungry.

13. Friday, April 10th at 1:17 PM Page 86
    James 1:17 Every good gift and every perfect gift is from above, coming down from the Father of lights with whom there is no variation or shadow due to change.

14. Friday, April 10th at 9:07 PM Page 89
    2nd Corinthians 9:07 Each one must give as he has decided in his heart, not reluctantly or under compulsion, for God loves a cheerful giver.

15. Sunday, May 31st 6:08 AM Page 97
Isaiah 6:08 And I heard the voice of the Lord saying, "Whom shall I send, and who will go for us? Then I said, "Here I am! Send me."

16. Monday, May 04th at 5:44 PM Page 99
Matthew 5:44 "But I say to you, Love your enemies and pray for those who persecute you,"

17. Sunday, May 31st 6:33 AM Page 101
Matthew 6:33 "But seek first the kingdom of God and his righteousness, and all these things will be added to you."

18. Sunday, May 31st 4:08 PM Page 116
James 4:08 Draw near to God, and he will draw near to you. Cleanse your hands, you sinners, and purify your hearts you double-minded.

19. Sunday, May 31st 5:05 PM Page 121
2nd Corinthians 5:05 He who has prepared us for this very thing is God, who has given us the Spirit as a gurantee.

20. Sunday, May 31st 12:47 PM Page 129
Luke 12:47 "And that servant who knew his master's will but did not get ready or act according to his will, will receive a severe beating."

21. Sunday, May 31st 6:12 PM Page 131
1st Kings 6:12-13 "Concerning this house that you are building, if you will walk in my statutes and obey my rules and keep all my commandments and walk in them, then I will establish my word with you, which I spoke to David your father. And I will dwell among the children of Israel and will not forsake my people Israel."

22. Monday, June 01st at 6:40 AM Page 135
Luke 6:40 "A disciple is not above his teacher but everyone when he is fully trained will be like his teacher."

23. Tuesday, June 02nd at 8:17 AM Page 148
Proverbs 8:17 I love those who love me, and those who seek me diligently find me."

24. Tuesday, June 02nd at 4:01 PM Page 151
Colossians 4:01 Masters, treat your bondservants justly and fairly, knowing that you also have a Master in heaven.

25. Wednesday, June 04th at 7:07 AM Page 161
Matthew 7:07 Ask, and it will be given to you; seek, and you will find; knock, and it will be opened to you.

26. Friday, June 05th at 7:18 AM Page 168
Micah 7:18 Who is a God like you, pardoning iniquity and passing over transgression for the remnant of his inheritance? He does not retain his anger forever, because he delights in steadfast love.

27. Sunday, June 07th 11:25 AM Page 179
Matthew 11:25 At that time Jesus declared, "I thank you, Father, Lord of Heaven and earth, that you have hidden these things from the wise and understanding and revealed them to little children;"

28. Tuesday, June 16th at 1:28 PM Page 197
Deuteronomy 1:28 Where are we going up? Our brothers have made our hearts melt, saying, "The people are greater and taller than we. The cities are great and fortified up to heaven. And besides, we have seen the sons of Anakim there."

29. Tuesday, June 16th at 9:33 PM Page 200
    Nehemiah 9:33 Yet you have been righteous in all that has come upon us, for you have dealt faithfully and we have acted wickedly.

30. Wednesday, June 17th at 1:16 AM Page 202
    Ezekiel 1:16 As for the appearance of the wheels and their construction: their appearance was like the gleaming of beryl. And the four had the same likeness, their appearance and construction being as it were a wheel within a wheel.

31. Friday, June 19th at 4:08 PM Page 205
    Ephesians 4:8 There it says, "When he ascended on high he led a host of captives, and he gave gifts to men."

32. Saturday, July 04th at 1:09 PM Page 209
    Acts 1:9 And when he had said these things, as they were looking on, he was lifted up, and a cloud took him out of their sight.

33. Saturday, July 04th at 1:37 PM Page 211
    Luke 1:37 For nothing will be impossible with God.

34. Saturday, July 04th at 9:09 AM Page 214
    Psalm 9:9 The Lord is a stronghold for the oppressed, a stronghold in times of trouble.

35. Monday, July 06th at 9:07 AM Page 219
    Acts 9:07 The men who were traveling with him stood speechless, hearing the voice but seeing no one.

36. Wednesday, July 08th at 8:09 AM Page 224
    Amos 8:09 "And on that day," declares the Lod God, "I will make the sun go down at noon and darken the earth in broad daylight.

36. Wednesday, July 08th at 1324 or 1:24 PM Page 228
    Mark 13:24 "But in those days, after that tribulation, the sun will be darkened, and the moon will not give its light,

37. Friday, July 10th at 8:17 AM Page 237
    Luke 8:17 For nothing is hidden that will not be made manifest, nor is anything secret that will not be known and come to light.

38. Sunday, July 12th at 12:31 PM Page 243
    Mark 12:31 The second is this: You shall love your neighbor as yourself.' There is no other commandment greater than these."

39. Monday, August 24th at 7:22 AM Page 247
    Mark 7:22-23 coveting, wickedness, deceit, sensuality, envy, slander, pride, foolishness. All these evil things come from within, and they defile a person."

40. Friday, August 28th at 4:13 PM Page 259
    Philippians 4:13 I can do all things through Christ who strengthens me.

41. Saturday, August 29th at 1510 or 3:10 PM Page 268
    2 Kings 15:10 Shallum the son of Jabesh conspired against him and struck him down at Ibleam and put him to death and reigned in his place.

42. Friday, September 11th at 4:01 PM Page 278
    James 4:01 What causes quarrels and what causes fights among you? Is it not this, that your passions are at war within you?

43. Friday, September 11th at at 5:38 PM Page 281
Matthew 5:38-39 You have heard that it was said, An eye for an eye and a tooth for a tooth.' But I say to you, Do not resist the one who is evil. But if anyone slaps you on the right cheek, turn to him the other also.

44. Saturday, September 12th at 11:05 AM Page 295
Hebrews 11:05 By faith Enoch was taken up so that he should not see death, and he was not found, because God had taken him. Now before he was taken he was commended as having pleased God.

45. Thursday, September 17th at 10:10 AM Page 299
John 10:10 The thief comes only to steal and kill and destroy. I came that they may have life and have it abundantly.

46. Friday, September 18th at 1307 or 1:07 PM Page 305
1st Corinthians 13:07 Love bears all things, believes all things, hopes all things, endures all things.

47. Saturday, September 19th at 10:12 AM Page 314
Proverbs 10:12 Hatred stirs up strife, but love covers all offenses.

48. Sunday, September 20th at 2:17 PM Page 331
Act's 2:17 "And in the last days it shall be, God declares, that I will pour out my Spirit on all flesh, and your sons and your daughters shall prophesy, and your young men shall see visions, and your old men shall dream dreams;

49. Sunday, September 20th at 2:01 PM Page 333
    2nd Peter 2:01 But false prophets also arose among the
    people, just as there will be false teachers among you,
    who will secretly bring in destructive heresies, even
    denying the Master who bought them, bringing upon
    themselves swift destruction.

50. Sunday, September 20th at 5:09 PM Page 338
    Ephesians 5:09 (for the fruit of light is found in all
    that is good and right and true),

51. Friday, October 30th at 6:12 PM Page 357
    Ephesians 6:12 For we do not wrestle against flesh
    and blood, but against the rulers, against the
    authorities, against the cosmic powers over this
    present darkness, against the spiritual forces of evil in
    the heavenly places.

52. Saturday, October 31st at 6:34 PM Page 364
    Matthew 6:34 Therefore do not be anxious about
    tomorrow, for tomorrow will be anxious for itself.
    Sufficient for the day is its own trouble.

53. Saturday, October 31st at 8:18 PM Page 377
    Romans 8:18 For I consider that the sufferings of this
    present time are not worth comparing with the glory
    that is to be revealed to us.

54. Saturday, October 31st at 10:09 PM Page 399
    Romans 10:09 Because, if you confess with your
    mouth that Jesus is Lord and believe in your heart that
    God raised him from the dead, you will be saved.

55. Saturday, October 31st at 10:14 PM Page 400
Mark 10:14-15 But when Jesus saw it, he was
indignant and said to them, "Let the children come to
me; do not hinder them, for to such belongs the
kingdom of God. Truly, I say to you, whoever does
not receive the kingdom of God like a child shall not
enter it."

56. Sunday, November 01st at 7:11 AM Page 404
Isaiah 7:11 Ask a sign of the Lord your God; let it be
deep as Sheol or high as Heaven."

57. Wednesday, November 04th at 11:32 AM Page 409
John 11:32 Now when Mary came to where Jesus was
and saw him, she fell at his feet, saying to him, "Lord,
if you had been here, my brother would not have
died."

58. Monday, November 09th at 09:11 AM Page 418
Jeremiah 09:11 I will make Jerusalem a heap of ruins,
a lair of Jackals, and I will make the cities of Judah a
desolation, without inhabitant."

59. Wednesday, November 11th at 6:02 AM Page 427
Galatians 6:02 Bear one another's burdens, and so
fulfill the law of Christ.

60. Wednesday, November 11th at 12:19 PM Pages 447
Romans 12:19 Beloved, never avenge yourselves, but
leave it to the wrath of God, for it is written,
"Vengeance is mine, I will repay, says the Lord."

61. Wednesday, November 18th at 10:23 AM Page 458
1st Corinthians 10:23 "All things are lawful," but not
all things are helpful. "All things are lawful," but not
all things build up.

62. Thursday, November 26th at 5:18 PM Page 466
1st Thessalonians 5:18 give thanks in all circumstances; for this is the will of God in Christ Jesus for you.

63. Monday, November 30th at 6:09 AM Page 471
Galatians 6:09 And let us not grow weary of doing good, for in due season we will reap, if we do not give up.

64. Friday, December 25th at 12:32 AM Page 484
Luke 12:32 "Fear not, little flock, for it is your Father's good pleasure to give you the kingdom.

65. Friday, December 25th at 7:36 AM Page 490
Luke 7:36 One of the Pharisees asked him to eat with him, and he went into the Pharisees's house and reclined at the table.

66. Friday, January 01st at 12:01 AM Page 495
Proverbs 12:01 Whoever loves discipline loves knowledge, but he who hates reproof is stupid.

67. Friday, January 08th at 12:11 PM Page 496
Proverbs 12:11 Whoever works his land will have plenty of bread, but he who follows worthless pursuits lacks sense.

68. Monday, February 08th at 1414 or 2:14 PM Page 502
Exodus 14:14 The Lord will fight for you, and you have only to be silent."

69. Saturday, March 20th at 1:02 PM Page 506
James 1:02 Count it all joy, my brothers, when you meet trials of various kinds,

70. Saturday, March 20th at 6:07 PM Page 513
Galatians 6:07 Do not be deceived: God is not mocked, for whatever one sows, that will he also reap.

71. Sunday, March 21st at 6:31 AM Page 525
    Luke 6:31 And as you wish that others would do to you, do so to them.

72. Saturday, April 17th at 8:11 PM Page 553
    1st Samuel 8:11 He said, "These will be the ways of the king who will reign over you: he will take your sons and appoint them to his chariots and to be his horsemen and to run before his chariots.

73. Saturday, April 17th at 12:40 PM Page 558
    Luke 12:40 You also must be ready, for the Son of Man   is coming at an hour you do not expect."

74. Saturday, April 17th at 7:17 PM or 5:17 AM Page 583
    2nd Corinthians 5:17 Therefore, if anyone is in Christ, he is a new creation. The old has passed away; behold, the new has come.

gotten ready for own wedding to Connor. She shook her head at the memory and remembered how happy she had been at that time.

"Mom," Eva said, gently, careful not to scare her. "Are you almost ready? The guests are waiting for you."

"Yes," Brynn said, smiling. As she turned around she was struck once more at the beautiful woman her daughter had become. Regret picked at Brynn, and not for the first time, at the many years that Brynn had missed from Eva's life. Her dream had always been to have a daughter, and when she finally arrived, she had missed the whole thing. Even though Brynn knew it wasn't her fault, she still felt guilty, the darkness overshadowing her beautiful moment without warning.

"Why do you look so sad, Mom?" Eva said, noticing the immediate transformation in Brynn's face.

"Oh, it's nothing, Eva," Brynn said, smiling.

Eva stared at her mother's face, so much like her own, and took a step closer to her. "Please Mom, talk to me. I'm not a little girl. I'm a grown woman and I'm here for you." Brynn's tears began to fall as Eva's words rung true in her ears.

"Yes! That's just it, Eva. You aren't a child any longer, you aren't a baby, and you *are* a beautiful, grown, adult, but I missed it. All of it! I missed your first steps and first words. I missed your first crush and your school dances. I missed the girl talks and braiding your hair and buying your first bra. I wasn't there when you needed me the most. I lay in that bed, helpless and pathetic and I missed everything and I hate it!" Tears streamed down Brynn's cheeks as she grabbed Eva and held her close. "All I wanted was to be a mother, your mother, but we were both robbed of that."

"Yes ... we were, but we have each other now, and for the first time with you, Nick, Noah, and Jack, we finally have the chance to be a family. A true family." Eva held her mom close, enjoying the sweetness of Brynn's perfume and treasuring the closeness of her arms. She had always dreamt of a moment like this with her mom, and now, as Brynn held Eva tight, she understood how lucky she was to have a second chance at such a beautiful life.

The knock on the door startled both of them.

"Are you ready, Brynn?" Jack's voice came from the

doorway. "Your groom is getting anxious down there."

"Mama," Noah's sweet voice came from Jack's arms, his little pudgy arms held out for Eva. "Mama, hold me."

Eva and Brynn smiled at the sight of Noah's face. His sweet, high voice was enough to remove the darkness from any day. He alone had saved Eva from falling into the abyss of her own sadness, and when she looked at him, she only saw love.

"Mama can't hold you Noah," Eva said, placing her hand on her swollen belly. "Mama has your sister in her tummy and you're too heavy, but I'll hold you on my lap in just a little bit."

"At the wedding?" Noah asked, anxiously.

"Yes, Baby. I will hold you at the wedding," Eva said, smiling at her sweet son.

"Not to rush you, but if we don't get moving, your groom is going to think that you got cold feet," Jack said, winking at Eva.

"Be patient, Husband, and let everyone know she'll be down shortly." Eva said, kissing him gently on the lips.

"Yuck," Noah said making a face.

"Mommy loves Daddy, Noah. It's not yuck," Eva said, planting a kiss on his cheek.

She watched the two people she loved so much as they left the room, her heart full. As she turned to look at Brynn, she caught a reflection of the two of them in the mirror and was struck by how lucky she was to finally have her mother.

Brynn had been the mother that Eva had always dreamt of, and she hoped that Brynn was proud of her too. There was nobody she had grown to love more than her Mom, and she wished that Adam had lived to see how much they loved one another. She imagined herself as the lonely little girl she had been and was struck by how different her life was now. She had a mother, a father, a husband, a child, and one child on the way, making her life far fuller than she ever imagined it would be.

For the first time in her entire life, the loneliness and fear had disappeared. Eva knew that the people she had ever loved the most had finally, saved her.

CHAPTER FORTY-FIVE

The Wedding

It's the day I've always dreamed of, only I'm not a young girl and this was never the dream of a young girl. As a young girl, I dreamt only of survival, not love.

But now I'm older. I've survived against all odds, and I have love that I never imagined possible.

As I watch Eva walk out of the room and I take one last look in the mirror, I realize for the first time in my life that I'm beautiful and I'm strong. I smile and I know that I should see an older woman, the scars still barely visible on my face, the lines etched in around my eyes and forehead where it was once smooth. Instead, I see the girl I once was with large brown eyes that reflect hope for the first time instead of sadness. I see strength that has been forged from years of endurance, created from the love of the people who surround me.

I am happy.

I open the door and I walk down the staircase of the home that was built for me by my grandfather into a grand ballroom and a sea of waiting faces, most of which I don't recognize. But there's only one face I'm looking for.

Nick.

I knew him the moment that he held me in his arms, and it's

unbelievable to me that he is here now. That he's always been here for me. I never imagined a connection so powerful and real; the kind that weaves its way into your soul and rests, waiting patiently for you to discover it.

I know that I should feel as though I'm betraying Adam, but he would want me to be happy. He would want me to live a full life because he loved me and I loved him. Even though our love was far from perfect, we chose one another, and I am so grateful that I had his love. I know that he would be happy for me and in a strange way, his love for me allows me to love again.

As I walk toward Nick, the beautiful bouquet of lilies in my hand, I can feel my palms sweating, but when I look into his eyes, all I see is the man who has loved me with his entire being for two decades. He has tears in his eyes and he looks as though he might never stop crying.

"Hi," he whispers.

"Hi," I'm struck with how handsome he is as he towers over me. He makes me feel safe and protected. When I'm in his arms I feel as though nothing can ever hurt me again and I want to shelter in them forever.

"We're here," he says, looking only at me.

"Finally," I reply, smiling as the tears fall down my cheeks.

The ceremony is short and sweet, as we requested, but Nick and I feel as though we are the only two in the room, our eyes locked, our hands touching, our hearts finally one.

"To have and to hold ..."

"In sickness and in health ..."

"Until death do us part ..."

I look down as he slips the band on my finger and I'm electrified by the warmth of his touch and know that with him I am finally complete. I slip the band on his finger and I grasp his hand, tightly. I don't know if I can ever let it go. I look into his eyes and I am beautifully lost.

"I'll never let you go, again, Brynn." He says.

"I'll never let you go, Nick."

He bends over and kisses me, not waiting for permission. Suddenly the entire world stops spinning and for the first time in my